West of Babylon

A novel

By Ted Heller

Acknowledgements

First and foremost I would like to thank Doug Stewart, Madeleine Clark, and Allison Devereux. Without them you would not be reading this book or this sentence.

And, in no particular order, I thank the following people: Michael Kates (on keyboards), Iris Johnson (she designed the cover and cooks my ziti), Matt Katz (on drums), John Moye, Sarah Irvin, Matt Moses, Ken Lipman, Ivy Heller (who I hope one day will crank "Whipping Post" and "Sweet Jane" up to 11), Van and Kathy Johnson, Leo Sacks (for getting me in to all those Clash and Joe Vitale's Mad Men concerts), James Spina (who actually saw Cat Mother & the All Night Newsboys live), Michael and Brooke Hainey, Rachel McFarland, Erica Heller (for her incredible record collection way back when), Joe Noce, David Kamp, David Trotta, and some of (but not all of) the people at Jack's Stir Brew Coffee. Thanks also to WNEW, WPIX, WOR, WABC (AM and FM), WPLJ (White Porter Lemon Juice), the WMCA Good Guys, WBAI, and to radio personalities, none of whom I've ever met, from Herb Oscar Anderson to Dan Ingram to Rosko to Steve Post to Jean Shepherd to Zacherle.

Also by Ted Heller

POCKET KINGS

"Ted Heller's brazen, often hilarious and always disturbing new novel, *Pocket Kings,* is a hybrid love letter and suicide note to 21st-century publishing. . . an illuminating and fully realized story about identity and reputation in the digital age." — *Washington Post Book World*

"A strange sensation crept into me while I was reading Ted Heller's new novel *Pocket Kings* and then I realized what it was: *enjoyment.*" — James Wolcott, *Vanity Fair*

"Heller's novel about a failed writer offers an unlikable protagonist, vivid writing and a comic depiction of our most disgraceful inner states." —*The New York Times Book Review* [an Editors' Choice selection]

"A satire with something for everyone. . . all wrapped up in smart literati humor and urban savvy." — *Washington Independent Review of Books*

"Laugh-out-loud funny . . . There is a certain Everyman quality to Frank, whose hopes gradually fade away but whose self-deprecating humor helps carry him through his midlife angst and denial of addiction; you want to wish him well." — *Booklist*

FUNNYMEN

"Heller's follow-up to his debut is a masterpiece of comic invention." — *The Guardian*

"An inspired send-up. . . a laugh-out-loud funny show-biz satire that'll knock you on your tuchis." — *Maxim*

"Heller's invention and comic versatility is dazzling. For sheer rib-pulverizing enjoyment, *Funnymen* is one of the most satisfying books I have read in years." — *The Times of London*

"Ted Heller creates not only an uncanny, gut-busting satire but a surprisingly heartfelt tragedy." — *Baltimore City Paper*

SLAB RAT

"Uncommonly smart. . . funny and dead on" — Jonathan Yardley, *The Washington Post* [One of the year's ten best.]

"Unkind and hilarious." — *New York Daily News*

"A brilliant social satirist. . . a delightful, smart, twisted, commentary on ambition, careerism, love, and modern life by the most likely newcomer since Nick Hornby to make you laugh out loud on a bus." — *Kirkus Reviews* [starred review]

A riotously scathing satire." — *The Hartford Courant*

Table of Contents

Part One
Road

One
Bass Drum

FURIOUS OVERALLS 8:00 2NITE 25$ AMDISSION GO SAWX!

"Overalls?" Danny says to himself, looking up through the evening drizzle at the old-fashioned marquee jutting out of The Granite Palace. *It's one thing to spell "admission" wrong, but for Christ's sake,* he thinks, *at least get the name of my band right.*

By no means is it the first time someone's gotten the name wrong. Some smartass in Newport News last year purposely put up "The Spurious Overspills" on the marquee.

It's another wind-battered, rain-swept seaside town, two days after the Swampscott gigs, this one on the New Hampshire coast. The Granite Palace's maximum capacity is 800, but it's a rainy Friday in September and there won't be anything close to 800 people. The Furious Overfalls will be lucky if they draw half that tonight.

Danny Ault, the band's founder, singer, and co-songwriter, summons over Howie Grey from the black SUV they've traveled up in. "Check it out," he says to Howie. "They either forgot to put the 'F' in Overfalls or they only have one 'F' and they used it for Furious."

"Or maybe," says Howie, the band's bassist, "they're just lazy."

Danny reaches into his damp blue-jean jacket and pulls out a pack of cigarettes. He allows himself one—and only one—cigarette a day and this seems like a good time for it, but he cannot light a match in the rain and puts back the pack.

"I hope Jules and Joey didn't get lost," Howie says.

The other two band members often flirt with being late but show up on time . . . usually. Somewhere out there on the road the two of them are rumbling toward the Palace in a rented U-Haul,

3

burping and calling each other dumbfuck, shit-for-brains, turdburger, and so on.

"I guess we should start unloading," Howie says. Of the four members of TFO, Howie is the smallest and baldest. Danny is almost a foot taller and has a bald spot the size of a quarter on his crown, but Howie is completely bald on top even though his graying hair on the sides makes it down to his narrow shoulders.

Howie goes over to the black Suburban—it's Danny Ault's family car—and starts pulling out a few guitars.

The Furious Overfalls don't use a real booking agency, don't have a manager, and haven't had one in over twenty years. Months ago when he booked his band into The Granite Palace for this tour, Danny was pretty sure they'd played the place about four years earlier. Or maybe last year.

"What time do you guys want to come in for a soundcheck?" Gary Tonelli, the Palace's manager, had asked him on the phone a week ago. "Usually bands come in at around four in the afternoon."

"Soundcheck?" Danny said. "We don't do that."

"Okay. You go on at eight. And when we say eight, we don't mean anything past eight-thirty. The natives here—they don't get restless, they just drink and leave."

Howie's wife does the bookkeeping, and dollars and cents, lodging and food have already been agreed upon. The band will get $1,050 a night; that extra fifty is for dinner for four. The thousand is split four ways. And they get paid *up front*. No dough, no show. (Three weeks ago in Syracuse the club didn't cough up the money—the band walked and had a welcome night off.) The four band members get two rooms at the Malibu Motel, immediately next door to the Palace and right on the beach.

"Here you go," Howie says to Danny. He hands him two guitars enclosed in black leather and Danny sets them down on the wet asphalt.

"Do you guys want a view of the ocean or the pool or the street?" Gary Tonelli had asked Danny on the phone.

"Whatever's cheaper for you is okay."

"The beach here is gorgeous. Our coastline is as fine as—"

"The TVs in the room get cable, I hope?" Danny asked.

"Where *are* they?" Howie asks now, looking at his watch. There are only a couple of seconds in a day when he doesn't worry himself to death over something, and this isn't one of those seconds.

"Wait out here," Danny says. "I'll go check in."

Danny picks up his guitars, slings them over his broad shoulders, and his aching lower back starts to ache him more. Groaning, he heads into The Granite Palace and, just as some tall skinny guy in a Patriots jersey opens the door for him, he hears wheels crunching over muddy gravel behind him. He doesn't even have to turn around: it's the U-Haul, and Jules and Joey and their gear have arrived on time.

"You're the band?" the Patriots guy who opened the door says to Danny.

Danny nods and is directed to the club manager's office. Straight down a dark hallway until you get to another dark hallway and make a right down a darker hallway.

Danny walks toward the manager's office. *This is it for me,* he thinks, each guitar getting five pounds heavier with every step. *I'm done. After the next tour, I am out of here.*

The other three have no idea. *When I tell them,* Danny thinks, *what is it going to do to them?* He has rehearsed the speech to them a million times in his head and can see their faces when he tells them he's calling it quits: Jules will be too stunned to believe it and won't say a word; Howie will have to keep himself from crying and will develop ulcers on the spot; and Joey Mazz won't be able to comprehend the import of it all. Together—somehow—the three of them are just going to have to survive without him.

But can they?

The Granite Palace has seen better days, but not that much better. In the 1930s, depraved days-long dance marathons were staged here, and later the place played host to entertainers such as the Dorsey Brothers bands, Frankie Avalon, Connie Francis, and Chubby Checker on their long way down. In the seventies the Palace was transformed into a disco with an only partially functioning strobe light and eventually became a venue that Time not only forgot but ravaged. In the summer, when working-class New England families descend by the thousands upon the small motels and shingled houses that line the beach, the Palace can occasionally draw capacity. The band Chicago played here two years ago and filled the place; so did REO Speedwagon the year before that. But those were July Fourth weekends, when the shoreline teems. The floor is sticky and splintery, there isn't much of a light show at all, but the piss the bathrooms stink of is vintage, salty and indelible.

After the Palace, there's a two-day break and then it's up to Maine. Lewiston, Bangor, Portland. And then down to Hartford and Providence, driving all the way. Then back home. After one more long tour in the winter, Danny Ault, who put this whole outfit together, is out. Finally. No more of the other three guys. No more Granite Palaces.

Outside, Jules and Joey get out of the U-Haul. The rain has eased up a bit but the sky is now fully dark, and when Joey opens a large black umbrella, four spokes break immediately upon contact with a raindrop. Jules Rose, TFO's lead guitarist, takes in the Palace through the billowy mist. He looks around . . . he can't see the Atlantic Ocean but can feel it out there somewhere. Howie tells him that they misspelled the band's name on the marquee, and they both know that Joey Mazz, the band's drummer, cannot spell too well anyway and wouldn't care about it if he could.

Joey, in jeans and a black T-shirt and black faux-leather jacket, starts pulling suitcases out of the Suburban's backseat, and Howie begins sliding gear down to Jules at the U-Haul. Then Joey comes over to help them stack the equipment. Nobody comes out of the Palace to assist them and they know why: the club manager probably volunteered some help but Danny turned him down.

TFO Rule #2: Never let anybody help you.

"Hey! Something's wrong," Howie says from inside the U-Haul, shining a flashlight around the van. "Joey . . . your bass drum? It's not here!"

Danny comes out of the club and joins them. He can tell right away that something is wrong and that none of the others want to tell him about it.

"What's going on?" Danny asks Howie, the only one of the three who wouldn't lie to him.

Howie tells him the bass drum is missing.

"Awww, fuck," Joey says, his crooked posture going even slacker than it normally is.

"You're pulling my chain," Jules says. His long, straight blond hair, halfway down his back, is already very wet. Under the parking lot's three foggy lights, his fake-baked skin takes on an alien orange cast.

Danny shoots Joey a look. The look that says: "You dumbass drummer." When he sees Joey's guilty reaction, though, he lets up. They all get on Joey's case enough as it is . . . how he takes it is a mystery. Like the prank they played a few years ago in Marblehead, Ohio, with the vending machine that dispensed live bait.

"I put it in there," Joey says. "I swear I did."

"Well, it's not there now," Danny says.

"I'm pretty sure I could swear I put it in."

Joey looks down at his worn-out black Frye boots. He can't remember putting the bass drum in the U-Haul . . . he can't remember not putting it in either. The more he thinks about it, the more he isn't sure. But he knows he needs that drum. A rock band without a bass drum is like a baseball team without bats.

7

Jules and Danny meet at the Suburban. Usually when they converse it's for emergencies such as this; other than that, the two of them, who've known each other almost forty years, barely speak. They know each other too well and, after all the shit they've been through together, what is there left to say?

"We have an hour tops to find a bass drum," Jules says.

"Okay, from now on," Danny says, "we should do a checklist when we pack. I've been saying that for a while, but we have to start doing it."

"Someone must have copped the thing in Massatwoshits."

Somewhere in Massachusetts, then, there is a drum with the red TFO logo on it.

"Maybe we can buy it back on eBay," Jules says. "With our band's name on it, it might be a lot cheaper than what it really costs."

"Jesus," Danny says, "I wonder how much someone'd get for that."

Joey walks over to the Jules and Danny. "I can't go on without a bass drum," Joey whines raspingly. A man in his fifties whining isn't an attractive sight to behold, but that's never stopped him.

"I know that," Danny tells him. Then he calls out to Howie: "Hey . . . go to the motel and check in for us, okay?"

While Danny, Jules, and Joey drag the instruments and amps inside, Howie takes their suitcases and checks in at the Malibu. The motel's facade is all dolphin blue but its neon light doesn't even bother to flash and its paint-sample-size pool is covered with tarp— tarp that's torn in places and getting pelted by rain.

"We've got a slight problem," Danny, his hands in his pockets, tells Gary Tonelli in the cramped office backstage. "We don't have a bass drum." In tight animal-print pants and a glossy gray leather jacket, Jules stands by his side, and Joey is just outside the office on a bench, starting to doze off. He can fall asleep at will anywhere, anytime, and can sleep for either ten seconds or, unchecked, ten years—it is sort of a talent.

Gary, sitting in an old wooden swivel chair behind his desk, is wearing a red-and-white rugby shirt and a blue Windbreaker, and all over the walls are photos of bands and artists who have played The Granite Palace, of Gary shaking hands with grizzled has-beens, wizened icons, and fallen idols with faraway eyes and fake smiles.

"So how big a problem is that?" he asks.

Danny and Jules glance at each other. Sometimes they can't believe the things people in this business say. They both have Gary figured out as a guy who got into the business because he liked music but now has become a guy who can't stand musicians.

"Huge," Danny says. "As in, seriously important huge."

"So?" Gary says. "You're not gonna go on? You don't go on, you don't get paid, plus you'll have to pay for your hotel rooms tonight."

Danny scratches an earlobe, takes a deep breath. Ten years ago he probably would have yelled at the guy; twenty years ago he would have lifted him up by the shirt collar and pressed him up against the wall, just to scare him; thirty years ago he would have had a roadie do it all for him. "Take care of business for me, Rev," he would've said. And Rev would have done just that. But if the Furious Overfalls had roadies today they'd also have their bass drum and wouldn't be in this jam to begin with. To defuse the tension, Jules asks Gary if he's related to the John Tonelli who played for the New York Islanders in the eighties, and Gary says no; Jules says, "You must get that all the time, huh?" and Gary says he's never once gotten it.

Danny draws in another deep breath and says: "Gary, we'd like you to help us find a drum. We're not really in the middle of nowhere and we have some time. I'm sure there's a school band around here, or that a few kids are in bands, or someone somewhere got a drum kit for Christmas or their birthday. So let's put our heads together and figure this thing out and everyone will be happy."

(Meanwhile, Danny clenches the keys in his pockets so tight that the metal starts to heat up.)

Gary looks up at the clock on the wall. It's seven-twenty, showtime is soon, and he starts making some calls.

*

Howie, with the band's wet suitcases and duffels by his side, stands in the lobby of the Malibu. It isn't much of a lobby. A front desk with one of those bells to summon someone from the back office even though there is no back office. Against the wall with the rack of things-to-do-in-the-area flyers (a water park, a whale-watch cruise, a narrow-gauge railroad a hundred miles away, not much else) are two foam chairs and a wobbly white stand bearing a Mr. Coffee machine, some stirrers, and nondairy creamer. The coffeemaker is what catches Howie's eye and won't let go. That and the spreading fingers of mold on the beige carpet where wall meets floor. The Mr. Coffee is white but there are faint streaks of old coffee all over it—when was the last time it was thoroughly cleaned? All the people coming in and out of here, hundreds of people over the course of a year. All putting their hands on that thing. At least they use Styrofoam cups here . . . those you use once and throw out.

A woman in her fifties behind the reception desk with dyed raspberry-red hair finally notices him.

"May I help you?" she asks.

"We have two rooms reserved for us," Howie says, trying not to look at the rug mold. The particleboard counter is five feet off the ground; Howie is only five foot four, and the woman is six feet tall. Her lipstick extends down to where her soul patch would be if

10

she had one. "The rooms should be under the names Ault and Rose. Already paid for by The Granite Palace?"

Howie rubs his hands and thinks he sees the mold crawling like a dozen snakes pouring out of a nest. Tonight he rooms with Jules, and Danny is stuck with Joey. Howie knows the score: Danny and Jules are the bandleaders; they write the songs and sing them. They never stay in the same room, and it's always a question with them of who gets stuck with Joey and who gets stuck with him, Howie.

In the old days everyone got their own room, but not anymore.

"Okay," the woman says, offering two sets of keys.

"You can put them down," Howie tells her. "I'll pick them up."

She hesitates, looks him in the eye, and sets down the keys on the counter. But not before Howie sees the Flicker—the flicker in people's eyes when they realize what they're dealing with. But who knows where this lady's hands have been? Howie counts to six before he picks up the keys. He prefers hotels with keycards. Not metal keys, which have passed through thousands of unwashed hands.

He drags the luggage past the pool—*thwop thwop thwop* goes the rain hitting the tarp covering it—then up the outdoor staircase, skipping, as he habitually does, both the second and second-to-last steps, and then to their rooms. He puts Danny's and Joey's suitcases in one room, then goes to the room that for the next two nights will be his and Jules's. Hopefully, Jules won't get lucky tonight (if you call some of the skanks Jules sleeps with getting lucky). Or hopefully he will and spend the night elsewhere, and Howie will have the night alone. The chances of that, though, are slim: Jules never sleeps with the women he sleeps with.

The rug in his room is moldier than the one in Reception. It's the sea air, the humidity—it's like syphilis raging through a

11

whorehouse. The toilet, Howie sees, has been sanitized for his protection. There's that strip of paper over the closed toilet seat telling him this. He stares at it for a minute. Then he goes into his duffel, takes out a fresh pair of plastic gloves from a box, puts them on, cuts the strip and throws it and the gloves—now both tainted— out into the trash can in the bathroom.

Howie looks at his watch. They're on in less than an hour. He should go help set up. Or should he call his wife and daughter just to see if they're okay? Freak tornadoes are not unheard of in Connecticut this time of year. At the door, he takes a look at the thermostat: it's one of the newer, high-tech ones—square, not round—and he knows that against Danny Ault's fist it doesn't stand a chance. (Danny does not like hotel thermostats, and they do not like him.)

He walks down the stairs. With so much exposure to the elements over the years, it's amazing the staircase doesn't tumble to the ground right now and send him to his death. Just when Howie reaches the next-to-last step, it occurs to him that maybe he didn't lock the door to Danny and Joey's room, so he turns around and heads back up to make sure. Yes, he did lock it. He walks back down, but when he makes it to the penultimate step, it occurs to him that maybe he didn't lock the door to his and Jules's room, so he turns around, goes back up, and double-checks. Yes, he'd locked that one, too. He heads back down the stairs—it's begun to drizzle again and the rain is cold on his scalp—but then, at the next-to-last step, he goes back upstairs to again make sure that both doors are locked.

Back in the lobby, Howie asks the woman at the front desk if the sheets are clean and she says of course they are. "When were they last cleaned?" he asks, and, flashing him the Flicker again, she tells him just that morning. He politely asks for three more towels for his room, and she says when she gets the chance she'll put some in there.

He takes a last look at Mr. Coffee and heads back to The Granite Palace.

*

Jules Rose, his golden hair almost dry now, sits with his legs spread all the way out and watches Gary Tonelli makes some calls while Danny hovers over Gary's desk. It takes Gary four minutes to find the phone numbers of the two school principals in the area: One principal he can't get in touch with—the phone rings and rings and not even voice mail or an answering machine picks up; the other principal picks up on the first ring but says there's no way he's going to drive to the school in the rain on a Friday night, open it up, unlock the music room, search for the bass drum, and lend it out to some band he barely remembers. "Not even for three hundred dollars in cash?" Gary offers, leaning back in his old swivel chair and winking to Danny and Jules. The principal says he'll be there in ten minutes but then remembers that the bass drum is, for the most part, broken, its skin patched together with tape. It's more tape than drum and is just no good.

Gary hangs up the phone, looks up at Danny, who is glowering, and Jules, and says, "Okay. Now what?"

"Local bands," Danny says. "Give us some phone numbers and addresses and we'll go."

Gary tells them to hold on a minute, then leaves them in the office. Jules looks at Danny and they both shake their heads. Worst-case scenario, they can't go on tonight; they'll get a drum somehow tomorrow and forfeit a night's pay but will salvage the journey here. Best-case scenario, Gary will come back with a few addresses and phone numbers.

Jules stands up and looks at the photos on the wall behind Gary's desk. Some are old Polaroids and five by sevens; others are from articles cut out of local newspapers and are turning yellow.

13

Gary with some band that looks like it might be 38 Special; Gary with five guys who might be the current incarnation of the Temptations; Gary drinking a beer backstage with a band that may or may not be Orleans, Kansas, or Boston; Gary with his arms around some wrinkled, grandmotherly men who might be the leftovers of the Moody Blues. *I guess our picture,* Jules thinks, *will be up there soon, too.*

"Okay!" Gary says, bounding back into his office. "I got two leads!"

A few minutes later Jules is at the wheel of the black Suburban, and Danny rides shotgun. Howie and Joey have been left behind. The rain is falling again, the wipers are on, they're heading inland. The first address is 58 Black Oak Street. Gary had scrawled sketchy directions for them on a yellow Post-it note: "Left up hill, left at third light, make another left, a right, 58 Black Oak." It's hard to see now, the traffic lights are blotches, and Jules, despite being a lead guitarist, is being careful and only going ten miles per hour. They're looking for the Cavanaugh house. The oldest boy, Gary told them, was the drummer in Rodent Population, a band that just broke up. His younger brother is one of the two teens setting up the equipment for the Furious Overfalls at The Granite Palace.

"Okay," Danny says, squinting and seeing the number fifty-eight in faded red on a *Union Leader* mailbox. "That's it."

Jules pulls into the driveway, avoiding the rain-beaded bikes and wagons, and they get out and ring the doorbell. He takes his hair and tucks it under the back of his leather jacket, and the door opens. It's a young girl, about ten.

"Is Caden at home? Caden Cavanaugh?" Danny asks.

Jules and Danny know how it works: Danny deals with kids and men and older women, Jules deals with the females age fifteen to fifty.

The next house, the next possible bass drum, is two miles away.

14

The girl's mom, a woman in her midthirties, shows up at the door.

"Hi, Kelly Cavanaugh," says Jules, taking his hair back out and whipping it one time, to Mrs. Cavanaugh, who's wearing bleached mommy jeans and a black sweatshirt cut off at the shoulders. No makeup, a slight double chin, one tiny mole under the corner of her lip. She's had three kids and is the worse for it, but Jules can tell right away what she looked like before all that—before the sleepless nights and breast pumps and driving to school and picking up from school and pounding weeklong headaches. Frizzy hair, long eyelashes, a nice C-cup. Probably a Duran Duran or Pat Benatar fan at some point. "Listen," he says, "I know this is straight out of the blue. Your son Sean, who's working at The Granite Palace right now, tells us that your other son, Caden, is a drummer?"

"Oh, he's a drummer all right," Kelly Cavanaugh says.

"I'm very sorry to hear that."

She smiles and asks who she's talking to.

"Well, darlin'," Jules says, flashing his killer smile, "I was getting to that. We're the band playing The Granite Palace tonight. And we don't have a bass drum. That's the big one on the floor that your neighbors probably do most of the complaining about. We'd love to borrow yours. And we'd also love to come in from the rain, and I promise you we won't kill you . . . unless you don't give us the drum. Gary Tonelli gave us your address. We're sorta desperate here, Kelly."

She lets them in and they go to the kitchen, and the daughter trots up the stairs. In another room downstairs, out of their view, Mr. Cavanaugh sits with a beer and watches the Boston Red Sox rain delay unfold.

"You want to borrow Caden's drum?" Kelly asks Jules. "Really?"

They both nod.

"And what's the name of your band?"

15

"The Furious Overfalls," Jules says. She's out of their demographic but certainly has heard their songs on classic-rock stations at one point. Everyone has. Just about.

Jules waits for the reaction. *If the husband weren't around,* he thinks, *this chick would probably drag me into the laundry room and we'd be doing it on her Maytag.*

"I've heard of you. My older sister had a few CDs of yours."

She smiles and leans against the refrigerator, which is covered with kiddy art and family photos; this new stance shows what curves she has underneath her coffee-sack mommy jeans.

"Oh!" Jules says. "Well, is she around? Does *she* have a bass drum?"

"Do you know the songs 'Borderline' and 'One More Time'?" Danny butts in. "Not the Madonna 'Borderline' or the Britney Spears 'One More Time,' but the rock songs?" He and Jules sing the chorus of "Borderline" and her face lights up.

"You did that? Oh my gosh."

Jules thinks she's melting. *So what,* he thinks, *if I've got twenty years on her?*

"And we still do," Jules says. "About three hundred times a year, darlin'. But we can't do it without a bass drum. And look, if you lend us the drum, I can get you and any members of your family into the show free and I'll even let you watch backstage if you want."

She puts her index finger to her lips, thinks for a second, and says, "Hold on. One minute, guys."

She goes into another room, and Jules and Danny, both in their late fifties and exactly six foot two, face each other. Danny is thinking, *Man, Jules is too damned smooth for his own good,* and Jules is thinking the same thing.

(That "darlin'" thing he whips out to charm women, though—it's been driving Danny up the wall for years. "Where the hell did you get your on/off Southern accent from?" he once asked

16

Jules. "Well," Jules said, "I *did* once own a house on the South Shore of Long Island.")

Kelly Cavanaugh dashes back in wearing a black down coat and some lipstick and mascara and says, "Okay, let's go. The drum is in the garage. And if I never get it back, you'll be doing me a favor."

*

Ten minutes later, Danny—he's going to have to pop three Tylenol to get his back through the show tonight—and Jules are back at The Granite Palace. There are many more cars in the parking lot and the rain has stopped. They walk down the narrow hallway leading to Gary Tonelli's office, Jules and Kelly carrying the bass drum. There is a deep rhythmic hum in the air, they can hear the crowd, everything's been set up and is ready to go. Showtime.

They arrive at Gary's office and set down the drum against the wall in the corridor. Joey is curled up and sleeping on the bench in a position too impossible for the average yoga instructor to even attempt, and the upper region of his ass crack shows above his studded belt (the one with the AC/DC buckle). Jules and Kelly look at each other and grin, then she looks down, ashamed of what she might do with him later on. Her sister was the one who bought the Overfalls CDs but *she's* the one who may hook up with one of them—how about *that?!* They'll finish their gig at about nine-thirty . . . Jules figures he'll drop half a Viagra at nine-thirty-five and be good and ready to rock her world by ten-fifteen.

Danny gently nudges Joey awake.

Joey Mazz sits up, runs his hand through his long, stringy salt-and-pepper hair, and slowly comes to, remembering where he is and why.

"We found you a drum," Danny tells him. "A Yamaha."

"Cool," Joey says groggily. "But fuck, man, I really don't feel too good right now."

Two
Gas

It was Alcoholics Anonymous that compelled Danny Ault to give up drinking and drugging. Not going to AA itself but the threat of having to go to AA, of having to attend smoke-filled sessions in dreary meeting halls with depressing, depressed people. Facing relentless pressure from Jessica, his wife, he went to two meetings and still believes that if he never had another drink in his entire life but was told he had to go to AA, he'd turn into an alcoholic overnight. So, during the second meeting (while some former Fortune 500–company VP recounted his journey from Shirley Temples to grain alcohol mixed with Kool-Aid powder), Danny decided that he wasn't going to drink anymore—not if listening to sagas such as this was going to be his daily fate.

And that was it. He's never had another drop again. Except for a drink every now and then. Anyone can quit drinking, that's easy—that's the way he sees it. The real test of one's mettle is not quitting but having it completely under control.

Sometimes—though not now, in the Malibu Motel, after the show—he is tempted to go on an all-out bender. When that happens, Danny will find out where the nearest AA meeting is. Once he knows when and where it is and how long it would take him to get there, the urge to numb his soul flees as quickly as it comes.

He looks out the window at the puffy evening sky over the New Hampshire coast. The rain has stopped, the postconcert cheeseburger and fries have turned to concrete in his stomach, the Furious Overfalls U-Haul is parked just outside. The black Suburban is not parked there—Jules is taking the borrowed bass drum back to its place of origin tonight. Well, that's the excuse . . . because not only is Jules taking the drum back to Black Oak Street, he's also taking Kelly Cavanaugh back home with it, and who knows what roundabout route they'll take to get there.

19

Joey is in the bed near the door, sitting up and listening to Humble Pie's live version of "I Don't Need No Doctor" on his yellow Sony Discman. (Of the four of them, only Howie has an iPod.) With a bag of Cheetos on the floor at his feet, he's playing air drums and intermittently singing aloud with the song that only he can hear in his headphones. This used to annoy Danny but he's used to it after all this time, and right now all Danny wants to know is whether he purposely played this song or not. Because, thanks to Gary Tonelli, a physician is on his way to the motel to take a look at Joey, who, even for Joey, looks like homemade shit right now.

The band played for an hour and a half, including the usual one encore. Typically, if there are no glitches, every show lasts one hour and twenty-three minutes. Tonight took a little longer because one of the pickups shorted out in Jules's 1970 Les Paul Goldtop and Howie had to perform brief emergency surgery to fix it. Two hundred and eighty people showed up, some men and women in their late forties and early fifties, some kids, too, obviously with nothing else to do tonight.

While Joey, who was once contractually forbidden from ever singing a syllable with the band, sings and air drums with his eyes closed, Danny looks at him and wonders, not for the first or the thousandth time: *How did I wind up with this dude?* The cruel joke behind Joey's back is that of the four members of the Furious Overfalls, Danny and Jules cannot read music, Howie *can* read music, and Joey can't read anything at all. (If Joey heard the joke, he wouldn't think it was cruel and would probably crack up.)

How different, Danny wonders, would things have been if Mickey Sanford, the band's original drummer, hadn't bolted in 1977? Mickey wasn't as solid a drummer as Joey Mazz and he was personally irresponsible (especially if you were a dope dealer). But, unlike Joey, he could take care of himself. On TFO's first European tour—which was Danny's first trip ever to Europe—when *Borderline,* their second album, was going Gold, the band was at

20

JFK Airport when Joey revealed he didn't have a passport, had never in fact gotten one. Howie's and Jules's jaws dropped, so did the jaws of the ten other people traveling with the band, and Danny grabbed Joey by the collar of his Deep Purple T-shirt and said, "What the *fuck?!* You don't have a *passport?!*" "I didn't think I needed one!" Joey pleaded as roadies Rev and Sweet Lou separated Danny from his drummer. "I mean, I'm just visiting there is all, right?"

The phone rings; Joey doesn't hear it and shovels a handful of Cheetos into his mouth, and Danny picks it up. It'll either be Jessica calling to say hello from Long Island, or . . .

"Hi, this is Rosemary, downstairs," the raspberry-haired motel receptionist says. "The doctor just called from his car. He should be here soon."

"Okay, Rosemary Downstairs," Danny says. "Thanks for keeping me informed." He looks over to Joey and the Day-Glo orange crumbs speckling his bristly chin.

Eyes still closed, Joey sings about getting prescribed a lotion that wouldn't do his emotion.

"Hey, Joey," Danny tells him. "Guess what? I'm leaving the band after the next tour. Okay? So you guys will be on your own. Sorry. Good luck out there without me."

Joey hasn't heard a word of it and keeps singing and drumming along with Humble Pie.

"Well," Danny says, "don't say I didn't warn you."

He sits down on his lumpy bed, hears the old springs quack and grind, and reaches into his bag to look at their itinerary and some maps. Looking at road maps is one of his favorite things to do on the road: there's something comforting about it, about the same old pale colors in each state, the strings of green dots, the blue veins and red capillaries of roads and highways leading everywhere and nowhere.

Tonight, as always, the band kept to the set list. TFO Rule # 1: *Never* go off the list. They always open with "Borderline," just to get it out of the way. You leave your best-known song for last, or even for the middle, and you're left with distressed voices begging for it. *Do "Borderline" or else I'm going to die!* People yell for a song and it sounds as though they're falling off a ship in the middle of the ocean. TFO plays their second-biggest hit, their last one, "Hurt," to finish their first set, and always ends their gigs with "One More Time," their third-biggest seller. The encore always begins with "Dog Water Girls." If there is an encore. There were three or four hard-core fans in the crowd tonight—some tall, silver-haired guy even requested "It's All Gone" from *Dead End Road*—but that was it. (Danny, Jules, and Howie shot one another looks when they heard him—*nobody*, not one single person, had ever requested that one before!) For twenty minutes after the show, Danny and Howie stood over a pile of *TFO 10* CDs, signed a few autographs and posed for some photos, and sold thirty discs. At ten dollars a disc, it all adds up.

Joey began flagging during the encore—Danny went over and asked if he was okay, if he could continue, and Joey said he was fine. But he wasn't fine and it was taking every ounce of strength he had just to lift up his sticks.

Looking at the map now, Danny sees the fastest way up to Portland is getting back onto 95 from Route 1 and taking that all the way. They're staying at a hotel there near a ballpark. He thinks about buying some plush lobster or moose dolls for his daughters but then remembers they're way too old for that shit now. Both of them have probably smoked weed or done worse—what do they need with big fluffy lobsters?

Soon, he knows, he will be spending a lot more time at home. He can keep an eye on his kids. He knows he will miss performing—he will even miss touring and crumbling motels like this one—but this is the way it has to be.

"It's really been a GAS. . ." Joey now announces with a lame British accent, talking along with Steve Marriott, to the imaginary audience at the Fillmore East. *He must have started the song all over again,* Danny thinks. How did Steve Marriott die? . . . Danny tries to remember. It was one of those unfortunate accidents, as with the lead singer of the Yardbirds, Keith Relf. Either Keith Relf was electrocuted by his guitar and Marriott died in a fire or it was the other way around. Not quite as lame as the Fairport Convention singer—Sandy Dennis? Sandi Patty? Sandy Denny?—dying with a fall down the stairs. It's terrible when that happens . . . you don't even live long enough to die young a better way, like Brian Jones or Jimi Hendrix. Whichever way it was for Steve Marriott, guitar or fire or stairs or pool, Joey Mazz telling the crowd in his headphones that it's really been a GAS is now starting to really annoy him.

"Joey! Shut up!" he says, thinking there's a fifty-fifty chance Joey will hear him.

He doesn't and Danny throws a pillow at him and looks back at the map.

Portsmouth. Saco. Biddeford. Biddeford sounds familiar. Minutes before they were supposed to go on there a few years ago, Danny approached the manager, a lanky woman who looked a lot like this road map, and told her they'd prefer not to play and that they'd gladly take no money at all, but the manager insisted. It was December and there were ten inches of snow outside and only fifty people showed up—fifty people who looked like they'd have been there whether a band was playing or not. But, with hardly anyone around, the Overfalls had fun for a change. They strayed off the set list and got the hits out of the way first thing. After a few more TFO tunes they segued into some Stones songs, then did "Melissa" by the Allman Brothers, then out of nowhere broke into "Summertime Blues" (the Who's version, not Blue Cheer's) and nailed it . . . Jules, with his reedy voice, even sang Cream's "World of Pain," and they ended the gig with a wicked fifteen-minute version of "Ventilator

Blues" that had the few people in the crowd bouncing off the floor. Although their popularity and prowess as songwriters had long since peaked, this was one tremendous gift they still had: the four of them knew each other so well that they could break into any song, without ever having rehearsed it or even discussed it, and nail it shut.

("We should do that more often," Joey said afterward as they were disconnecting from the club's wonky backline. "We'd go broke," Danny told him. "You want that? We're never doing that again.")

But maybe that wasn't Biddeford. That could've been some joint around San Antonio and maybe it was rain, not snow.

Danny folds up the map and goes into his leather toiletry bag and pulls out a can of Rogaine. It isn't helping the hair grow back but he hasn't lost that much for a few years so maybe he'll keep at it. Personally, he doesn't care about hair—he could lose every single one and not give a shit—but he's the band's front man and has to at least attempt to look the part. The long gypsy scarf that The Edge or what's-his-face for Bruce Springsteen wears is not for him. Little Steven? Miami Steve? Van Zandt. Little Stevie Van Zandt? Miami Ronnie Van Zandt? Little Townes Van Zandt? He stands up and is about to go to the bathroom when he hears a car door close. Danny looks out the window and sees a tall man in a black raincoat closing a black Audi sedan and carrying a medical briefcase. From this distance and in this light, he looks like Max von Sydow in *The Exorcist.*

Miami Steve, that's who it is. Whew. But who was the bald drummer for Spirit? Ed or Ted Cassidy? He certainly didn't wear a scarf. He was bald and proudly let it show, back in the good old days when nobody gave a damn.

Danny watches the doctor step into the reception room of the motel and quickly thinks of doctor songs. "Doctor My Eyes." "Doctor Jimmy and Mr. Jim." "Doctor Robert," of course. "Dear Doctor" by the Stones. There was some really dumb, catchy new wave song about doctors, too. "Doctor, Doctor" something. And, of course, "I Don't Need No Doctor," which Danny hopes Joey will turn off while the real doctor, who's been kind enough to make a house call on such a miserable night, examines him. *If he doesn't turn it off,* Danny thinks, *I'll just rip the Discman out of his hands and smash it against the thermostat and break the both of them.*

There's a light tapping at the door and Danny mutters, "Oh, the hell with this stuff," throws the Rogaine into the small metal trash can, and opens the door. Close up, the doctor looks even more like Max von Sydow, so much so that Danny almost thinks the whole thing is a prank. But the man is for real: he's a real doctor, just over six feet tall, with silvery blond hair and ice-cream-sandwich-thick glasses.

"Doctor Perryman," the man says warmly with a sturdy handshake. "Are you Joe?"

Another door opens in the hallway, and Danny sees Howie slowly padding down the corridor to make sure Joey's okay.

"No," Danny says to Doc Perryman. "That's your patient there."

Joey is still air drumming on his bed but he stops when he sees Dr. Perryman standing less than a foot away from him. Danny puts Doc Perryman's age at sixty-seven and assumes he was probably into the Four Seasons or Peter, Paul and Mary.

Joey takes off the headphones and shuts down the Sony.

"This is Doctor Perryman," Danny tells him. "You're still feeling bad, right?"

Joey nods and the doctor takes in the bag of Cheetos as though it were an unpromising CT scan.

Dr. Perryman and Joey begin talking to each other and Howie comes into the room. Danny sees that Howie is in his pajamas and antibacterial slippers, and he knows what Howie's room must look like: Howie won't walk on hotel room floors in bare

25

feet, so he lays down a path of clean towels from the bed to the doorway and from the bed to the bathroom. Even with slippers on.

"Jules hasn't come back yet?" Danny asks, just to make conversation.

Howie shakes his head.

"Hey, you'll know this. Who was the lead singer for Pentangle? The chick who died on the stairs."

"You mean Fairport Convention, don't you? That was Sandy Denny."

Why did it come out Pentangle, Danny wonders, when he meant to say Fairport Convention?

Dr. Perryman sits down on the bed with Joey and, after taking his temperature, he listens to his heart, looks into his eyes and ears, and starts asking him questions.

"Headaches?" Dr. Perryman asks.

"Yeah, I got three of 'em," Joey says. "A son and two daughters. But other than that, no."

"Trouble sleeping?"

Danny and Howie look at each other. *Joey?* Trouble sleeping?

"Hell no."

"Joint pain?"

"Nope. But I don't have a joint on me. Heh-heh."

"Shortness of breath?"

"Maybe some, yeah."

"Blood in the urine?"

"No!"

"Blood in the stool?"

Now there's the name of a band for you, Danny thinks. Blood In The Stool. Kind of like Blodwyn Pig. Danny's kid brother had a Blodwyn Pig album. Or was it Bloodrock? Or Pearls Before Swine?

"Cough?" Dr. Perryman asks.

26

"No."

"Diarrhea?"

"No."

"Any problems with erections?"

"Fuck no! What about *you*?"

Dr. Perryman clears his throat and resumes.

"Vomiting?"

"Nope."

"A drummer who doesn't vomit," Danny whispers to Howie. "There goes all his credibility."

Dr. Perryman lifts up the back of Joey's shirt and puts the stethoscope up between his shoulder blades and says: "Cough."

"I told you I got no cough."

"No. I *want* you to cough."

"But then I'll have a cough."

The doctor blinks a few times, and, finally, Joey coughs. The doctor puts the stethoscope over a few more places on Joey's slender tattooed back, and Joey coughs again, not really giving it his all. Joey also has ink on his forearms and legs, but the ink has all faded and what was once turquoise, scarlet, purple, yellow, and black is now all a very dull green.

"Stomach pain?"

"Yeah. A little."

"Most likely," the doctor concludes with a small-town grin, "it's just gas."

"It's really been a GAS," Joey says with a chuckle.

"When's the last time you had a checkup, Joe?"

"It's been a while. It may have been in tenth grade."

Joey pulls down his shirt and puts his headphones back on, and Dr. Perryman stands up and joins Danny and Howie at the door.

"Do I talk to you?" Doc Perryman asks Danny.

Joey is only two years younger than I am, Danny thinks, *and here I am, being his daddy again. What is he going to do when I'm not around anymore? They will be lost without me.*

"Sure."

"You're in a rock-and-roll band. So I'm going to have to ask you." He clears his throat. "Does he do drugs? Does he drink excessively?"

"Actually, no. Ages ago, yes. But not anymore. We're so clean it's embarrassing."

The doctor tells Danny that he took Joey's temperature and he had no fever. His chest sounded clear. Maybe he's coming down with the flu. But he should go to a doctor, get a full-scale checkup, have some blood work done, and take a stress test.

"I'll be frank with you," the doctor whispers. "He looks . . . terrible."

"A stress test?" Joey says. "I'm not stressed."

Another car pulls up outside and just from the sound of it Danny knows it's Jules coming back in the Suburban.

Joey puts his headphones back on and resumes singing to the appreciative Fillmore East audience in his head.

Dr. Perryman asks if Joey has health insurance. Danny says he isn't sure; he doesn't know if he has any through his wife, Angie, who manages a beauty salon a few days a week in Bay City, Long Island. He tells the doctor he can write a personal check, and the doctor asks him for $500. Danny rifles around his nylon backpack and finds his checkbook. While writing the check, he works it out: Tomorrow he'll tell Joey that he owes him $500. When they all get back home—Joey and Angie live only half an hour away—Joey can repay him. Joey made 250 bucks tonight playing with the band, but with this doctor's bill he is now in the hole 250. Tomorrow, if he's well enough, he'll make another 250 and break even. The doctor was here for less than ten minutes, poked around and played twenty questions, and just made half a grand. *(Maybe,* Danny thinks, *I should've become a dentist like my old man.)*

"Thank you very much," the doctor says when Danny hands over the check. "He really should undergo a thorough physical as soon as possible."

Dr. Perryman shakes Danny's hand and offers to shake Howie's, but Howie politely puts his hands in his pajama pockets instead.

Danny opens the door for the doctor to leave and sees Jules, stooping slightly more than he usually does and clutching his abdomen, slip his key into the lock of his door.

Three
Jar of Flies

Jules Rose dropped half a Viagra—the wonder drug he privately calls Blue Magic—between the first set and the encore, washing it down with half a can of seltzer. Not that he needs it. He can function reasonably well without it, but *with* one it's like he's thirty years old all over again (in his pants at least). If Danny or Joey ever knew about that, they'd really get on his case for it. Or nowadays, maybe they'd say nothing and just let it ride.

Kelly Cavanaugh danced backstage for the fast numbers, swayed languidly for the slow ones, her tousled hair going with the flow, her eyes more closed than open. In the encore they did, as always, "Babylon Boogie," and every few seconds Jules snuck a peek at her shaking her matronly hips to the infectious shuffle. "We'd like to dedicate this song to Kelly," Jules said into the mike before they started the song (which is not about the Babylon of Mesopotamia or the Babylon that reggae singers too often sing of, but about Babylon, Long Island, an uninteresting town where passengers often change trains to get to more interesting places).

That may have cinched it.

After the encore, the lights went up and the band unplugged and everyone but Jules wordlessly filed into the airless dressing room. The amps and drums would stay at The Granite Palace overnight for tomorrow's show, but Jules, Howie, and Danny would be bringing their guitars to the hotel for safekeeping. Jules didn't go into the dressing room, even though he was sweaty and boiling. Instead, he found Kelly and asked her if she liked the show.

"Yeah," she said, "you guys were great!"

He noticed then that the mole under her lower lip had grown from the size of a Skittle to the size of an M&M.

It was dark backstage and she was looking better to him, as he was looking better to her. His fifty-six-year-old skin was golden brown, just a shade lighter than his hair, thanks to the glow of

31

hundreds of F71-type tanning bulbs from Garden City to Manorville. He was still thin, unlike Danny, but wasn't scrawny and undernourished like Joey; he was much more sinewy and the python pants he squeezed into before the show really brought that out.

"You really dug it?" he asked her.

"Yep, I really dug it."

Howie came down the hallway, clumsily holding stacks of the new Furious Overfalls CD, which was two years old and that they'd had to produce, engineer, and press themselves. After Howie, who dropped the CDs, came Danny holding more.

"You gonna help us?" Danny asked Jules.

"I'll be right there," he said, knowing he wouldn't be and knowing that Danny knew he wouldn't be, too. Then he swiped a CD from the stack and offered it to Kelly.

"This is our latest," he told her. "I'd like to sign it for you. But not here."

She looked at him and said: "Okay. That would be nice. But where should we go?"

"Well, it's your town. You name the place and I'm buying."

They went out through the entrance, Jules abandoning the other three to selling *TFO 10,* and walked out to the Suburban.

Over the clamor of other car doors opening and slamming shut, he told Kelly: "You looked really nice dancing . . . you've obviously danced before."

"Aww, thanks!" she said with a smile. Jules could tell in a fraction of a second that her husband never complimented her, never could bring himself to say one nice thing about her, and that she was starving for it.

"Hey!" some guy called out from a gray Honda Civic. "I dug the show, Danny!"

"Thanks, guy," Jules called back. "But I'm not Danny, I'm Jules."

"Yo!" another fan, about to get into a pickup truck, called out to Jules. "Are you guys's songs available on iTunes?"

Jules shrugged and told the man he had no idea.

He asked Kelly where they were going. She tilted her head and thought for a second, and Jules looked at her thinking, *She's enjoying being young again. This is making her feel like she's seventeen and she's eating it up.*

"There's a bar about fifteen minutes away," she said. "The Jar of Flies it's called."

"Sounds posh. I hope your husband won't be there."

She giggled and got into the car and they drove off.

*

The Jar of Flies stands on a small pear-shaped pond at the edge of some woods. The tavern is basically a long, narrow cabin with a blue neon sign and an inclined dirt road for parking. You can get fried fish and hot dogs there if you so wish (few people do), and there's a jukebox with songs by Celine Dion, Josh Groban, Charlie Daniels, Taylor Swift, and Kenny Chesney. Nothing good, although somehow it has "Ferry Cross the Mersey" by Gerry & the Pacemakers. Probably an oversight.

Nobody seemed to recognize Kelly when she and Jules walked in, and they brought two beers to a booth in the back, near the one bathroom. The window at the booth overlooked the pond but at this time of night the glass could've been painted black. The only other people inside were a bartender who looked like Ed McMahon and two younger guys in down vests struggling to stay awake at the bar. A small TV hung over the whiskey bottles, and the Sox game was on.

Jules and Kelly made short work of the first round of beer and when she went up to get the second, he watched her. Twenty years ago, before the husband and kids, she may have been hot.

33

Maybe even a high school cheerleader, although she didn't seem like she'd ever possessed the requisite perkiness and insincerity. *She's a ten-minute chick now,* Jules thought, *but probably was an eight-minute chick in her prime. If she's thirty-seven,* Jules started to calculate, *that means she would've been eighteen in 1980 . . .* and he worked out the math. She probably liked Madonna, Duran Duran, the Human League, A Flock of Dipshits. All the bands that came along and wiped the Furious Overfalls off the map. If he makes it with her, he figures, he'd really be sticking it to the Human League. *Sweet revenge!*

When she came back Jules gently grabbed her wrist and it didn't take much work at all: she sat down on his side of the booth and nestled up to him. The mole under her lip, however, had grown from the size of an M&M to a penny, and Jules was worrying about it. If they wound up rolling around in the scratchy, wet woods outside, would it stare him right in the eye, get bigger and pulse and ruin the whole thing? It was a good thing there wasn't much moonlight tonight.

"You don't happen to know those two guys, do you?" Jules asked her, indicating the two lugs at the bar and getting a nice whiff of the Pert Plus on her frizzies when she turned her head.

"Oh yeah," she said. "They're my husband's brothers. *Just kiddin'!*"

They drank and he asked her if she always wound up snuggling next to whichever lead guitarist happened to be playing The Granite Palace, and she said, "No, this is really the first time and I don't wind up snuggling next to anyone." Jules could tell . . . he knew by the way she said the word "anyone" that it also included her husband.

He put his arm around her shoulder and kissed the sweet spot on her neck, then pulled his head away to gauge her reaction. Her lower lip was trembling. This was either going to be easier than he

34

thought, was not going to happen at all, or was going to happen and just not be worth the trouble.

He pinched her chin with his thumb and forefinger. The Viagra was starting to take effect, but then a Celine Dion song came on.

"So," he said, deferring either the ultimate Yes or No that was waiting for him in the Suburban or in the bushes outside, "do you want to tell me all about your life or do you want to hear about mine?"

They pecked for almost two seconds and then slowly backed off.

"Well," she said. "I already know about mine."

She moved closer to him in the booth, put her hand on his python pants, and everything got a lot warmer. The mole was where Florence Henderson's and Patty Hearst's were. *Maybe,* Jules thought, *I should've dropped a whole Blue Magic and not just a half.*

Damn, I forgot to take my Flomax, he remembered as his bladder began bothering him. This could be a rough night. It felt like a woodpecker poking at the neck of his bladder and he knew it was going to last until morning.

Did Kelly want to move outside and go at it right away? A few years ago, that's what Jules would've done. Inside the car, on the ground, on top of the car, in the pond, in the bathroom, wherever. That was fun, sure. But now he wanted to drag it out. The longer the amount of time leading up to it, the longer it'd be before he had to go back to the motel and spend time with Howie or Joey or Danny, not that anybody would talk or anything. But the motel looked terrible from the outside, just like the dump in Swampscott, and the rooms were probably small. Besides, *this,* in a way, was the best part. Will she or won't she? Will she make out with him but not fuck him? Will it only be a blow job? Will she take him half the way there so that he'll end up whacking off and getting the jizz on the

35

ground or on her nose or mole? Or maybe she won't even make out with him. Over the years, the game had become more fun than whatever the final score was. *If she puts her hand on my dick right now,* Jules thought, *I think I'd remove it, just to drag out the whole process.*

"You have really nice eyes," he told Kelly out of nowhere. When's the last time anyone told her that?

She thanked him. They kissed for half a minute, some serious deep tonguing, and when he pulled his face away slowly, the mole had doubled its diameter.

"Soooo," she said, putting her hands on his knee, "tell me the whole story! Tell me about how you guys met and what it's like being a rock star and everything."

"Whew . . . That's a freakin' epic and a half."

This might take some doing. Good—it could make the evening last. They drained their glasses, he went to take a leak and then got another round.

*

Green River, Long Island. Twenty miles east of JFK Airport. You can hear airplanes all day long, but if you grow up there, you don't notice them anymore, they're just up there droning the soundtrack of your life. In high school Jules got held back a year for the usual reasons. ("To put it as plainly as I can, Mrs. Rose," the principal told Jules's mom, "your son likes to screw off a lot.") Jules's father, who'd been in the navy in the South Pacific during World War II, sold Fords in nearby Hempstead; his mother was a housewife and she raised Jules and his younger brother and sister. Mom watched a lot of game shows and listened to AM radio, and sometimes engaged in muted conversation with whoever was on the air. ("You know, you're *right!*" Jules would often hear her say to Barry Farber, Barry Gray, and Long John Nebel.)

She had taken piano lessons growing up in Queens, and the Roses had a baby grand in their modest living room—the house's style was early Valley Stream: one story stacked upon another on half an acre, no porch, and an inflatable pool in the tiny backyard—and, growing up, Jules was interested in the piano. A lot more fascinated with the piano than with math, history, and current events. He would hear a song on the radio, such as "Pretty Woman," "Are You Lonesome Tonight?" "Leader of the Pack," or "Love Potion No. 9," and work out the notes and sometimes even the chords. He played "Spanish Harlem" by Ben E. King over and over again. His mom retained the services of a local piano teacher named Edith Grove who came over and gave lessons that didn't take. Jules didn't like Edith's teaching method or her mottled skin and lack of a chin, and he bristled whenever she told him what he was doing was wrong. Also, he didn't like the music she was teaching ("What good is 'Clair de Lune' ever going to do me?" he asked his mother in a rare fit of precociousness), and after ten months the twice-a-week torture sessions were through.

By this time, the Beatles, the Rolling Stones, the Animals, and the Kinks were all over the radio and had appeared on *Ed Sullivan, The Hollywood Palace, Shindig!, Hullabaloo, Lloyd Thaxton,* and *The Clay Cole Show.* Except for the Dave Clarke Five, the Zombies, and the Animals, hardly any good bands featured keyboards, and when they did have a piano, the piano player was usually some kind of geek. Pianos were for losers. Whoever played them had to sit down and was on the side of the stage, not in the middle like Keith Richards or George Harrison or Dave Davies. In terms of getting the girls, you had to figure it went in this order: Lead singers were tied with lead guitarists, then came, in order, rhythm guitarist, drummer, bassist, pianist. (And the chicks the pianists got . . . who knew what *they* looked like?)

When Jules was thirteen years old, a local band called the Missing Lynx played the school gym one balmy May evening. Jules was in the parking lot when they arrived. The guitarist got out of a station wagon with his gleaming cherry-color Rickenbacker strapped over his shoulder, and a deeply tanned girl with nice curves, blond hair, and stiletto heels came out of nowhere, put her arms around his neck, and started making out with him and thrusting her crotch into his. Jules was too skinny to have been popular with girls but when he saw this he knew just what to do.

He'd had a toy Emenee Elvis Presley guitar when he was a kid and loved the feeling of it—he just didn't like Elvis. (The Elvis that Jules was subjected to was the Elvis of *Viva Las Vegas* and *Spinout,* not the Elvis of Sun Studios.) Even when he'd watched the Beatles on *Ed Sullivan,* sitting on the floor in his living room, he didn't like them that much either. There was either something they had that he didn't like or something they didn't have that he did. He couldn't put his finger on it, but it may have been Paul's "Hey-look-at-me-I'm-cute" mugging.

But he knew he liked the guitar.

He wanted one, a real one, and, after a lot of pleading, one Christmas day he got it. A used, dented Fender Telecaster. He was fourteen.

This was pretty much the end of traditional education for him. He went (on most days) to school, loafing through it; he liked girls and girls were starting to like him; he hated gym and did as little as he could. He did poorly on the PSATs and the SATs but managed to get accepted to Long Island University anyway, where he was hoping to double major in music and cunnilingus. When he was seventeen he'd joined a band called Avalanche. The group consisted of two guitarists, a powerful drummer, a bassist, and a lead singer, and they rehearsed in the lead singer's basement, which was a shrine to Naugahyde, Drakes Cakes, Schaefer Beer, and RCA. They stayed together for two years. Jules got on well enough with the drummer, a tall, muscular dude named Mickey Sanford. Mickey had great drug connections and was high so often you couldn't tell

38

when he wasn't. A few times Avalanche, which churned out a loud, bubbling stew for eight-minute stretches, wound up opening for a band called the Tarnished Angels, which played a slightly grittier variety of rock . . . shorter and tighter songs; better, more cogent lyrics; bluesier and more mature sound. Jules wished that he was in that group and not Avalanche, a band he was fairly certain would not go far.

When *Revolver* and *Rubber Soul* were released, Jules had come to like the Beatles, but still, they were not his favorite band. He preferred the Animals and the Stones. He would teach himself Stones songs and, when he had them down, play them in the mirror, trying to hold his burgundy Telecaster just like Keith did. Whatever that thing was the Beatles had or didn't have that Jules found so troubling, the Stones and the Animals didn't have it or did. Would Paul ever sing a song about his slaving father dying and his hair turning gray? In songs like that, Jules knew, the sun really refused to shine. In Beatles songs the sun was shining even when it wasn't supposed to. It couldn't help itself.

One day he was reading the band classifieds in *Rolling Stone* and saw that a band in Westbury, Long Island, was looking for a new guitarist. The tersely worded ad said that the band did "lotsa Stones type stuff." At this time, Jules was taking an indefinite leave of absence from Avalanche and was playing with a band called Brittle Cringe . . . he didn't like the music they (and he) were playing: long, meandering psychedelic shit that put everyone—and there weren't too many of them—in the crowd to sleep. And it was for zero dollars. Jules got in contact with Paul Bianchi, the lead singer who'd placed the ad in *Rolling Stone,* and he drove his dad's red Mustang over to Westbury, auditioned, and got the job on the spot.

("I'm hiring you," Paul told him with his lip curled up at one end, "not 'cause you're any good but 'cause you're skinny. So just keep that in mind.")

It turned out that the band, called the Stoning Rolls, not only did "lotsa Stones type stuff," they *only* did Stones stuff. They were a cover band.

"One thing, man," Paul, who resembled Mick Jagger the way Mick Jagger in his prime resembled Butterfly McQueen in hers, instructed Jules. "Don't call me Paul. Ever. You got that? On or off the stage, I'm Mick to you. Even if you run into me in aisle three at the Bohack, I'm Mick."

(So being in a rock band, Jules surmised, was going to be a job like any other. There was you, there were the others down on your level, and then there was the person in charge, who more often than not was going to be an asshole.)

Jules nodded and espied the bassist rolling his eyes behind Paul's back.

Paul, who wore a corset under his shirt onstage, also told Jules to either dye his hair brown or wear a dark wig. Jules opted for the dye and quit both Brittle Cringe and Avalanche.

This was the first time that Jules ever got paid to play music and, as a result, he didn't make it to too many classes at LIU. Eventually, he stopped going altogether.

The Stoning Rolls played any and every town on the Island that they could, from Montauk to Great Neck, from Oyster Bay down to West Islip to Ocean Beach, Fire Island. They played some gigs on the Jersey Shore and in Westchester and southwestern Connecticut, where they often wound up playing with a very weird art rock band called anaesthesia. anaesthesia's lead singer, a large-jawed, overweight dude with huge eyeglasses who you could tell had grown up rich, would dedicate songs to people that Jules had never heard of. "This next song," he'd say, "is for Bertolt Brecht," or "I'm dedicating this next song to Antonin Artaud."

Jules moved out of his folks' house and moved in with the Stoning Rolls' pseudo–Brian Jones guitarist, whose name was Tim, in Sayville. They lived in a small brown-brick building above Sal's

Pizzeria, two blocks from the LIRR station. Tim disliked Paul Bianchi, hated the way he strutted his girdled frame and double chin à la Jagger all over the stage like a wounded stork, and was itching to leave the band. (Tim had been told to either dye his hair blond and grow bangs, like Brian Jones, or wear a wig: he'd opted for the wig.) Tim told Jules that Paul didn't even like the music and that he was just in it for the pussy. Jules came around to agree with that opinion but didn't mind the rejects he was getting.

The band's drummer, a kid named Joey Mazz, was fired because one night in Lindenhurst he'd called Paul "Paul" and not Mick . . . When Paul called him on it the drummer didn't back down. "You want me to call you 'Mick,' Paul?!" he said. "How's this sound—go to fuckin' hell, Mick. Was that good?"

They had a gig in three nights and needed to find someone fast, so Jules called Mickey Sanford from Avalanche and he joined the band. Playing the same old songs every night—somebody *else's* songs—wore thin, and Jules was always keeping his eye out to leave, but nothing that paid was popping up. Paul was always pitting one band member against the other: he'd tell Mickey that the bassist thought he played for shit, then he'd tell the bassist that Mickey thought he couldn't play to save his life. The real Keith Richards, Jules used to think in the diners they ate in, the studio they rehearsed in, the dressing rooms they dressed in, would not take this from the real Mick Jagger or from anyone else—he'd just slam his guitar on the dude's head and split. But Jules was making money as a musician and getting lots of girls and so he kept quiet.

One night backstage at a gig in Massapequa, Tim, Jules, and Mickey had to help Paul pull on his pants—the pants were that tight—this after Paul had smeared olive oil over both of his hairy legs to facilitate the process. Paul was still huffing and flushing all over when he took the stage and they opened, as they always did, with "Satisfaction." Four songs later they were doing "Midnight Rambler" and Jules was taking an extended bluesy solo. Paul did his

41

usual prancing and cavorting, hands on hips, his head pecking sparrowlike at imaginary food that was being dangled right in front of his beak. He strutted off the stage—he usually did this once or twice a show and then returned only seconds later—but didn't come back on. Ever. It turned out that was it for him: he'd gone backstage, gotten into his car, driven home, and given up on music. He was sick and tired of having to appear skinny.

This was the end of the Stoning Rolls as such.

The remainder of the band attempted to stay together, write some songs, and rehearse, but there was no true leader among them to give them direction. Tim tried to take command but he had neither command nor vision and it didn't work; Jules tried, too, and wrote some songs but no lyrics, and that didn't work either. Jules had a thin but passable falsetto and was always hesitant to use it (he wasn't shy about playing guitar but always held back when it came to singing), and Tim couldn't sing at all. (Was it possible that they really *were* Brian and Keith?) Two months after they disbanded as the Stoning Rolls, the band broke up once and for all, and Jules moved to Greenwich Village and dedicated himself to learning to play slide guitar.

One night Tim dropped in at Jules's Sullivan Street apartment and told him he'd tried out for a Long Island group that was looking to add a lead guitar, but he could tell from the bandleader's lack of enthusiasm that he wasn't going to get the job.

"What kind of stuff are they into?" Jules asked Tim.

"All sortsa stuff," Tim said . . . and then he rattled off the names of some groups that Jules had either heard of and listened to, heard of but never listened to, or had never heard of: Fairport Convention, Matthews' Southern Comfort, Pentangle, Lindisfarne, Stone the Crows. And yes, the Stones, too.

"To be honest," the guy had told Tim, "I'm looking for a sound that I don't have yet, and I'm not even sure what it is, which is why I'm looking for a guitarist." Jules asked Tim if it was okay if *he* tried out, and Tim said it was cool and gave him the address and phone number.

Jules bought a few Lindisfarne, Pentangle, and Fairport Convention albums and listened to them on his Pioneer stereo. He liked what he heard but worried that if this was what they were looking for, maybe he wasn't their guy.

It turned out that the band was the Tarnished Angels, which was at that moment in the process of disintegrating and becoming the Ventilators. By the time Jules showed up to audition, their singer/songwriter had already tried out ten other guitarists. After three auditions, however, Jules got the job. And then the Ventilators turned into the Furious Overfalls.

*

"Don't pull in all the way," Kelly asked Jules. "Just drop me off on the road outside."

"Okay."

It was almost eleven. After two more beers and four more trips to the bathroom, after Jules told Kelly some of his story and she told him just a bit of hers, they took a walk outside and lay down on the soggy leaves and wet soil beneath some dripping pines. What little light there was seemed to be shining right down on Kelly's mole and, despite the Viagra, Jules was having trouble concentrating. The mole was growing, glowing, crawling like a ladybug over her cheeks and forehead. After two minutes of dry humping he repositioned her—he'd tried to lift her up to do it but wasn't strong enough anymore—so that no light at all shone on her face and the mole. She kept invoking God's name for the three frantic minutes Jules was inside her: "Oh God." "Oh Jesus." "Oh God Jesus." "Oh Jesus God Lord!" When they were done, he stayed on top of her until he got his breath back, then rolled off and stood

43

up with a headful of foliage and took leak number six into a bush, the stream weak and going out at an odd angle for five nerve-racking seconds.

The car was slowly tooling down silent, dark Black Oak Street.

"Do I look like I just had sex?" she asked.

"You just did. You're a little smudgy, darlin'."

He pulled up along the road, wiped away her mascara smears and lipstick traces, and got the last remnants of nature out of her hair. Kelly looked out and could see that all the lights in her house were off.

"So did you have fun?" she asked him, demurely folding her hands in her lap.

"Oh, yeah. Lots of fun. You're really something, Kelly."

He was hoping that by the time he got back to the Malibu Motel, Howie and Danny and Joey would be asleep and that he could just creep in and hit the sack.

That is, if he could even find the place.

"I just want you to know that . . ." Kelly began. "This was the first time . . ."

Jules knew what she was going to say and, judging from his expression, Kelly knew that he knew, so she didn't finish.

They kissed for ten seconds, one final perfunctory exchange of disinterested tongues, and she got out of the Suburban, making sure not to shut the door too loudly. She took a few steps toward her house, smoothing out her black down coat and fixing her hair with each step, and then Jules called her back and asked her for directions to get back to the motel.

When they parted this time they didn't kiss.

Fifteen minutes later, his bladder bursting again, he was putting the key into his motel room door when the door to Danny's room opened. Howie and a tall silver-haired man holding a black doctor's bag came out.

Everybody was still awake.

Four
Psycho Mind-Rockin' Hot-Buttered Soul

Howie is taking a taxi to Re: Percussions, a drum and percussion store about fifteen miles north of Portland, and watching the shade-streaked New England countryside on Route 1 roll by. He knows how to drive, he has a driver's license—he just hates driving. He has recurring lurid nightmares about cars: cars plummeting over cliffs, cars crashing head-on into other cars at full speed, cars running over his daughter and decapitating his wife. Ever since his high school Drivers Ed instructor told him "Always expect the other driver to do the wrong thing," Howie assumed that he *was* the other driver.

The band wrangled bass drums in Lewiston and Bangor but they still need to get one for the rest of this mini-tour. Tonight and tomorrow they play the State Theater in Portland (neither show has come close to selling out—some U.K. band called Triple Facial is in town and hogging all the ticket action), and then it's down to Hartford. Melissa, Howie's wife, FedExed the stencil of the band's logo to the hotel; Howie has a can of spray paint in his jacket and knows to get Joey a Ludwig 26-inch drum. Joey was too out of it to go to the store today. Jules could have come along—Danny is going on a local radio show at noon to plug the gigs—but he picked up two sketchy chicks outside the State Theater this morning and they're hanging around Portland now. Howie just hopes that Jules and the two women won't be making lunch out of one another in his hotel bed.

The taxi driver has made minimal conversation so far, but here it comes . . .

"Where are you from? New York?"

"No. Connecticut."

"You don't drive?"

"I used to," Howie says, slouching in the back. "But . . ."

"But what?"

They go past a small hardware store, a shuttered shoe store that looks like a log cabin, an old stand that sells lobsters by the pound but is closed for the year.

"Something bad happened and I can't drive anymore. They won't let me."

That usually shuts them up. *They won't let me.* It's completely bogus but it's worked in the past.

They keep quiet for two minutes and then the driver asks: "What happened?"

"Let's just say I had my license taken away."

Howie looks at the rearview mirror and sees the driver's narrowing eyes check him out.

"Are we almost there?" Howie asks, thinking, *It'd be just my luck: I let other people do the driving and* they *kill me.* They pass a gas station and miss the post holding the Chevron sign by only a few inches. Had the taxi hit it, the sign could have fallen onto the taxi and killed them both. The driver turns onto a smaller road and there, up ahead and set back behind a small parking area, is Re: Percussions, which is surprisingly spacious for it being so out of the way.

It was after he and Melissa had Michelle that his problems really exploded—once he knew he couldn't die because he had to be there for other people and provide for them. That's when all the wiring in his brain started to frazzle.

One of these days, he vows, *I'm going to do something about it.*

Howie gets out of the car, looks toward the store, and sees he has to climb three steps to gain ingress. He'll go from the first step to the third and skip the second. The breeze blows his hair around and he zips up his nylon Furious Overfalls Borderline Tour jacket.

"So you'll wait?" he asks the driver. "I won't be too long, I promise."

The driver looks up at him. Does he think Howie once killed a person in a car? Or more than one person? Maybe Howie was stoned and drunk and mowed down ten people, even though Howie has never once gotten stoned in his life, other than off of contact highs.

"Sure," the driver says. "I'll turn the meter off, too."

Jules should be doing this—he should've driven the Suburban up here, maybe taken Joey with him, and gotten the drum. But he had to meet those homely bimbos, who are probably secreting millions of bacteria directly into Howie's pillowcase right this very second.

The driver gets out of the car and watches Howie walk toward the store and skip the penultimate step, the can of spray paint making a rhythmic *clacking* sound with each footfall.

*

Where is this place again? Up a hill, then you come to an observatory and make the next right.

Danny stops on the corner and takes out the map that the assistant stage manager from the theater had given him—the kid couldn't have been twenty-three years old and was a board-certified, card-carrying doofus. Danny gets his bearings, looks at the map, and reckons he's about five minutes away. "The hill is steep, dude," the kid had told him. "Sure you don't want a taxi?" Danny told the Doofus he liked Portland and wanted to walk around. You grow up in a flat suburban wasteland like Pleasant Valley, Long Island, a place like Portland is Heaven on Earth to you.

Danny's going on the air at noon to talk to some local DJ on a classic-rock station, maybe take a few phone calls—he has a copy of *TFO 10* in his coat pocket and hopefully the DJ will play a few cuts off it—then walk back to the hotel. Tonight he rooms with Joey again, and Jules gets Howie.

49

Up the hill he trudges, his back starting to ache, thinking of songs about hills. "The Fool on the Hill," "Solsbury Hill." Maybe he should've taken the car. The hotel has a fitness center, the usual three treadmills and a pool so small it resembles an American Express card. Later on, he'll do a half hour on a treadmill and swim a few laps. If his back recovers from this climb.

This morning, before the band checked in at the State Theater, he was slamming down a bran muffin and a black coffee in his room when the phone rang. There was no way that Howie, who'd dropped in, was going to pick it up, not unless he'd drenched the thing with Lysol first. So Danny answered and on the other end of the line was Jessica, his wife.

"Who's in the room with you?" she asked him after they said hello.

"Howie's here right now," he said. "What's up?"

"Maybe I should've called your cell so you could take this into the hallway."

They have two daughters, Emily and Lily, nineteen and fifteen years old. Emily is the pretty one, Lily the smart one. Emily has a wonderful singing voice but has never done much with it.

"Is everything okay?"

"Yes! We're okay. Emily . . . she's fine, she's okay. But guess what?"

The only thing that occurred to him was that Emily wants to drop out of Hofstra, where she's a sophomore majoring in some subject that offers zero job opportunities upon graduation. Media studies? Communications? ("Maybe she'll become a weather or traffic girl," Jessica has said. That wasn't a bad idea—she's pretty enough for it, but would she be able to handle barometric pressure or the concept of rubbernecking?)

Or maybe Emily and Peter, her boyfriend, broke up. That wouldn't be so bad.

"Let me guess. She and Peter broke up?"

50

"Who's Peter? Her boyfriend's name was Wyatt. And they broke up months ago!"

Right, right. Wyatt. Maybe Peter was the guy before him, the one with the blue Prius.

"Well," Jessica said, "you, uh, you are going to be a grandfather."

In a flash, before the truth fully sank in, sweat began to pour out of both armpits into his green plaid shirt.

"You're kidding me, right?"

"She vomited this morning," Jessica said. "And as a joke I said, 'What is it—morning sickness?' And she said, 'Yes, Mom, it is' and started crying."

"Holy fucking shit . . ."

"Everything okay?" Howie asked him, removing one iPod earbud.

Danny told Jessica to hold on and then, for no reason at all, covered the phone and said to Howie: "Hey, I need to talk here. Give me five minutes. Is the drum store open yet?"

Howie told him the store wouldn't open until eleven but then went down to the lobby.

Danny comes to a corner now and gets out the map again. Two more blocks straight up and then a right turn. The observatory, which looks as though it may have been built to celebrate the end of the War of Independence, is straight up ahead. "Muswell Hillbilly." "Running Up That Hill." The radio station interviewing him today is called The Rock. Radio stations don't even go by their real names anymore, like WOR, WABC, WNEW, WPLJ, WPLR, WBAB, or by their numbers, 102.7 or 99.1 or 102.3. They call themselves names like The Rock, The Buzz, The Beast, The AssWipe, or they have people's names like Jack, Sam, Phil, or Dave.

"Okay," he said to Jessica, "Howie's gone. So she's going to *have* this baby? And Peter broke up with her? That little goddamn punk . . ."

Danny liked the idea of grandfatherhood. Most of the rock stars he worshipped growing up are grandfathers now—the ones who didn't die young. Jimi Hendrix and Jim Morrison would surely be grandfathers had they lived. John Mayall might even be a great-great-grandfather! Danny looked forward to it; to again holding a baby who was his own flesh and blood . . . but he found the notion that his oldest daughter was having sex, and had gotten knocked up and abandoned, repellant.

"It's not Peter, Danny. There is no Peter! Where are you getting that name from?"

"Oh, he's somebody else who was on my mind."

Peter is the name of the DJ who's going to interview him today—that's where he was getting it from.

"When they broke up," Jessica said, "Emily had no idea she was pregnant. Also, I asked her if she'd told Wyatt and she said nothing. Then I asked her, I said, 'Emily, is this Wyatt's baby?' and her face went even blanker than it was, which is to say very blank since she was in the middle of barfing."

Emily. Pregnant. Emily pregnant. Emilypregnant. Those two words shouldn't be said within two breaths of each other. There ought to be a ten-minute intermission between the uttering of the two words. "See Emily Play"—Danny and Jessica named Emily "Emily" after an early Pink Floyd song. And now look at her. Emily was playing all right.

"You know," Danny said, carrying the phone to the window and looking out at the dull morning sun hanging over the ballpark half a mile away, "this thing can be nipped in the bud."

"You don't think I suggested that? For Christ sake, there's a Planned Parenthood five minutes away."

Well, Danny thought, it's too damn bad Emily and Wyatt or whoever the hell is the father didn't stop there on the way *before* having sex, rather than afterward.

"So she wants to have the baby?"

"Yes. YES!"

That loud "YES!"—not only was there shock in it, there was some glee, too. It was like a cocktail: four ounces of shock, three ounces of glee, and a jigger of what-the-fuck.

"She's only nineteen," Danny says. Nineteen years and a few months ago he was at Saint Vincent's Hospital, and Jessica, herself nineteen at the time, came up with Emily, all seven pounds of her. You were supposed to think that it seemed like only yesterday, the whole "Sunrise, Sunset" and "Father and Son" deal, but in truth it seemed like a hundred years ago.

After a few seconds of silence, Jessica asked him if he wanted to pass along anything to Emily—she was upstairs in her room now, sleeping—some words of understanding and encouragement, and he said to her, "You think of something, okay? Make it nice. I don't want to scare her or anything."

Okay, Danny wonders as he turns right at the observatory, *who do I tell? Or should I not tell anyone?* Anything could happen. Maybe she'll come to her senses and decide to not have it. Why would anyone want to be a mom at nineteen? Why flush the best years of your life down the toilet?

He's almost out of breath. *I've known Jules the longest,* he thinks, *I could tell him. But he's Jules Rose and he'll say something like, "Well, at least she's gettin' some."* Joey would be all smiles. He loves kids, has three of his own, and would slap Danny on the back and offer to get him a cigar. But Joey is Joey and wouldn't understand the gravity of the situation, not if it hit him on the head from twenty flights up. *Howie?* He could tell Howie but that might begin a three-hour conversation, and that's the last thing he wants. A five-minute conversation with Howie seems like three hours—what the hell would a three-hour conversation be like?

Danny walks past a pizzeria and a butcher shop. He won't tell any of them. Howie didn't tell him right away when Melissa got pregnant; Danny didn't tell them when Jessica was pregnant, both

53

times. Jules didn't call up Danny in the middle of the night when either one of his parents died, and vice versa. That's just the way it is. They're in the same band . . . it doesn't mean they're brothers.

He works out the timing: By the time Emily gives birth, TFO will be no more. He will have left the band. So he'll be home for all of it. "Shit," he says aloud to nobody.

"Over the Hills and Far Away." "One Tree Hill."

There it is. The radio station. It's in a green, three-story Victorian on the corner of the road. Five cars are parked haphazardly outside, and there's a metal sign rising out of the grassless lawn with the frequency number written in white lettering: 89.7 FM. That's pretty low on the dial . . . it's barely where the college stations usually are. Beneath the numbers is the name of the station in small white lettering: THE IT.

But, he thinks, *I thought they were sending me to The Rock. Or was it The Sound?*

Recovering his breath, Danny rings the bell outside, finds the door open, and walks in.

*

"Someone from my band called before," Howie says to the tall balding man at the counter, avoiding eye contact as always. "And we have a gig tonight and are desperate for a bass drum." The counter is smudged with dozens of fingerprints.

"You probably talked to Brendan. Where are you playing?"

"The State Theater in Portland . . . we're looking for a—"

"Oh!" the man says, his posture straightening, impressed. "What band are you in?"

He's in his mid- to late forties, so there's a chance. He's right on the cusp.

"The Furious Overfalls?"

54

There are hundreds and hundreds of drums here. Cymbals, congas, snares, high hats, timpani, bongos, tabla. There are tambourines, maracas, and cowbells, and every make of drumstick the world has. If you can bang it, tap it, beat it, or shake, rattle, and roll it, they've got it. There are posters of Keith Moon, John Bonham, Neil Peart, Ginger Baker, Tommy Lee, and Charlie Watts, none of whom has ever set foot inside this store. There are dozens and dozens of hooks on the ceilings, and hanging precariously from these hooks are immense congas, and . . . and . . . if one of them were to fall, it would easily pulverize someone's spine.

"Yeah, I remember you guys," the man behind the counter says. He offers to shake Howie's hand, but Howie, leaving his thrice-Purelled hands in his tour-jacket pockets, demurs.

Howie explains that they lost their bass drum and that their drummer isn't feeling well. He's looking for a twenty-six-inch Ludwig just to get them through the next few weeks.

"Hey! Brendan!" the balding man yells. "Hey, Boom-Boom!"

A young and skinny pale kid in his early twenties, with dirty-blonde hair and wearing a sleeveless Kiss T-shirt, emerges from the back, and the balding man tells him to take care of Howie.

"This guy's the drummer for the Furious Overfalls," he says. "They're playing the State tonight. This is Brendan—but we call him Boom-Boom."

"Oh yeah," Brendan says to Howie. "I spoke to you on the phone. My dad—"

"You spoke to Danny, our singer," Howie says. "I'm the bassist, not the drummer."

"My dad is a huge fan, man. After I spoke to you I called him and he told me to tell you that 'Borderline' and 'One More Time' are like two of his all-time favorite tunes."

Howie forces a smile. Of course, those would be his two favorite TFO songs. Those are two of the three that still get played.

55

(They never play anything from *Dead End Road,* which Howie still insists is their best effort, even if it is the album that brought upon them the crushing end.) If Howie were ever to die in a plane crash or a car crash or of *E. coli* or in a terrorist event, his two-paragraph obituary in the paper would read: ". . . bassist for the gritty blues-rock band the Furious Overfalls, whose hits included 'Borderline,' 'One More Time,' and 'Hurt'. . ." They're also the two TFO songs that Howie likes the least.

"You guys didn't do that 'Layla,' too, did you?" Brendan asks.

"No, Eric Clapton got to that before we did."

"So let me take you to the Ludwigs, dude. And hey, maybe you could hook my dad up with a few tix for the show?"

"Okay," Howie says. "I could do that." But he doesn't want to move. Well, he does want to move, but his feet do not. The path that Brendan is about to tread goes directly beneath the dangling congas, steel drums, and a passel of vibraphones clustered together so closely it looks like something out of a planetarium. He's afraid that, merely by the vibrations of his beige desert boots on the linoleum floor, a 500-pound steel drum will fall on Brendan and tear off his shaggy head. He decides to stay right here, on these two floor tiles, for a count of exactly thirty seconds, until Brendan is safely among the Ludwigs, before he will join him.

"You go back there," Howie says, taking his cell phone out of his pocket. "I'll be with you in a minute. I have to take this call."

Brendan heads back and Howie flips open his cell—which isn't even on—and begins counting to thirty.

*

"Hey," Danny says to the first person he sees inside the house, a woman about twenty-five years old in jeans and an unfortunately tight Decemberists T-shirt. "I'm here to be interviewed at noon."

56

"You *are*?" says the woman, a rumpled pale blonde. She's the radio station's receptionist and works in a small, cluttered office only five yards in from the front door. Music—whatever obscure band The It is broadcasting right now—plays throughout the building, and Danny sees several posters on the walls of groups he's never heard of. The National. Animal Collective. Foxygen. Beachwood Sparks. MGMT. Tame Impala. In addition to these bands, Danny's never heard of the Decemberists either.

"This is The It, right?" he asks her. "Wyatt, the assistant manager from the State Theater, sent me here. Here's our new CD."

"You mean Chris, don't you?"

"Right. Chris." The Doofus.

She stands up and takes a copy of *TFO 10* but is looking at Danny as though she'd sent out for sushi and instead they'd delivered her a jar of dog stool.

"*You're* Ian from Triple Facial?" she asks him, barely looking at the CD in her hand. Her nails are painted a loud silver with cranberry tips. "Peter is—"

"I'm Danny Ault from the Furious Overfalls and my band is playing the State Theater tonight and tomorrow. I was told to come here."

She puts her hand over her mouth and gasps, and the music fades from one very slow droning song that Danny's never heard into a much faster one. When Danny does radio interviews the stations crank out the usual classic-rock suspects—Beatles, Stones, Kinks, Dylan, Allman Brothers, Queen, Bowie, Springsteen, Rush, etc.

Danny hears footsteps shuffling down the stairs. A man peeks his head in the reception area: he's short, is also quite rumpled, and has a five-o'clock shadow. He's wearing a torn Dinosaur Jr. T-shirt and has brown bangs and heavy black glasses.

"I'm Peter Green," he says. "The DJ. *You* are . . . ?"

It's eleven-fifty-five and quickly Danny, Peter, and the receptionist work things out: Chris, the assistant doofus at the theater, had completely screwed up ("And not for the first time," Peter throws in). Danny Ault of TFO was supposed to go to The Rock, on the other side of town, and Ian Farrell of the Manchester-based (England, not New Hampshire) punk-house-dance-trip-hop trio called Triple Facial was supposed to come here, to The It. Danny's first thought is to punch out Peter Green, shove the receptionist into the clutter on her desk, and storm out, but he doesn't pull shit like that anymore. His second thought is to go find Chris and throttle him, but that's out of the question, too. So instead he shakes his head and starts to head out, but Peter Green stops him after two steps.

"Look . . . Danny, we can still do the show. I'm on in a few minutes. Come upstairs. It'll be— We'll work it out."

Danny looks at Peter, then looks at the receptionist; the receptionist and Peter look at each other, and she hands Peter the *TFO 10* CD. Danny, feeling like a useless old fart, follows Peter up the stairs to the studio. More climbing. *Okay,* Danny thinks, *maybe I won't do the treadmill later.*

"Hey, you know," Danny says, his nose only a few inches away from Peter's teal boarding shoes, "you've got the same name as sort of a hero of mine."

"Who?" Peter asks. A song ends and a commercial for an auto dealership comes on.

"You've never heard of Peter Green? From the original lineup of Fleetwood Mac?" They come to the second-floor landing and head toward one of the two studios.

"Oh?" Peter says. "I didn't know that. 'Landslide,' right? Like, with Stevie Nicks?"

Peter opens the door to one of the studios and they step inside.

58

"No," Danny tells him. "This was before Stevie Nicks and whatever the other girl's name was." He cannot remember right now if the other woman in the band was named Christine or Lindsay. "This was the original lineup, when they were still really good."

"Uh-huh. Okay, we're on soon. Take a seat, put these on."

Peter hands him a set of bulky headphones, and Danny sits down in a swivel chair and nods to the engineer and the producer on the other side of the soundproof glass. The engineer looks a lot like Peter Green, the young Maine DJ (not the-guitarist-from-Fleetwood-Mac-who-went-nuts Peter Green), and could be his brother. The producer is a friendly looking woman with magenta hair and brown roots and orange-tinted glasses.

"We'll breeze through this," Peter tells Danny as the commercial ends.

How, Peter Green, could you possibly not have heard of the other Peter Green? Danny wants to ask him. "The Green Manalishi," "Oh Well (Parts 1 and 2)," "Albatross." The original "Black Magic Woman." *Danny Kirwan and Jeremy Spencer. Where do you get off calling yourself a rock DJ?!*

I could do this! he wants to yell into his microphone. *I could get a show, play some great old tunes, and just coast for the rest of my days.*

"Okay, we are back," Peter Green says into his mike, "and we've got a huge surprise here at The It. Ian Farrell of Triple Facial was *supposed* to join us, but—well, nobody's perfect—and thanks to some serendipitous, stupendous screwup we have Danny Ault of the group the Furious Overfalls with us today. We have no idea where Ian is but . . ."

He continues, and Danny sees that the DJ, while he addresses the five or ten people who may be listening at this downtown ghetto end of the dial, is also on Wikipedia, scrolling down and learning everything about TFO as quickly as he possibly can.

59

". . . tonight and tomorrow, is it?" Peter asks Danny.

"Yes. Both shows are at eight-thirty sharp. At our ages, we've all got to be in bed by eleven. Doctor's orders."

"And how do you like our little city so far?"

On Wikipedia, Peter is up to *Borderline,* their second album, going Platinum.

"I love Portland. And I'm not just saying that. We've been everywhere, all over the world, and this is a great town. You should see some of the places we've played."

"Uh-huh? Such as? Do tell."

Peter wants Danny, who usually is too reticent to talk lest he reveal too much, to open up, so that he, Peter, can keep reading Wikipedia. Danny complies as best he can and starts talking about playing a firetrap in Hull in England five years ago, and how all the toilets in the club exploded at once. In the back of his mind, though, he's worrying what Peter might be reading on Wikipedia . . . What if he's reading about "The Incident," the momentous catastrophe at the hotel outside San Francisco, and what happened to one Alan Wilbur Murdock during the Dead End Road Tour? What if Peter brings that up? Danny rolls his hands into fists and keeps them on his lap. Nobody ever talks about that . . . Jessica doesn't talk about it, the band never brings it up. It simply is not mentioned. Ever. And, if Danny has his way, it never will be.

While Danny talks about Hull toilets exploding, Peter tells the engineer to download three or four of the Furious Overfalls' biggest hits, ASAP.

"Wow, that is one funny story, Danny," he says, neither smiling nor laughing. "Hey, have you ever heard Triple Facial?"

"To be honest, I'm really not too familiar with them. But when I get home I'll definitely give them a spin."

"On your, uh, record player?"

"Huh?"

I'm not familiar, Danny thinks, *with Triple Facial any more than you are familiar with vintage Fleetwood Mac, before Stevie and either Christine or Lindsay, and before they started selling millions of records. Those sellouts.*

"Hey, we're going to play . . ." Peter says, and then the engineer flips them a thumbs-up from his side of the glass, ". . .'Borderline' now, and when we come back we'll talk about it. Danny, you must have some serious stones to name a song after one of Madonna's biggest—"

Danny, feeling the headphones getting tighter on his ears, says: "No . . . no. Our song was years before Madon—"

"Just kiddin', my brother. Okay, let's give it a listen."

The intro of "Borderline" comes on and Peter and Danny, both knowing they're off the air for at least three and a half minutes, breathe deeply and lean back. It's at this second that Danny remembers: Emily, Jessica, Emily, pregnant, baby, no father.

"Hey, check this out," the receptionist, dipping her head into the studio, tells Peter. "It's hilarious! Ian Farrell is on The Rock and they don't know what to do with him either!"

Danny feels himself blush and sees that Peter is discomfited, too. The receptionist leaves and the first chorus of "Borderline" peals throughout the studio.

"This was nice of you," Danny whispers to Peter. "I appreciate it."

"You know, I *have* heard this song before," Peter says. "Many times."

"Our biggest hit. I bought a house and a few cars with this."

"When we come back, I'll ask you some bio shit about the band, okay? We'll fill this hour, everything'll be chill. Is there anything I *shouldn't* ask?"

Danny draws in a deep breath, moves in closer, looks the DJ straight in the eye, and says: "If you bring up *anything* about what went down outside San Francisco in the eighties, which I saw you just read about, I'm afraid I'll have to make your life extremely uncomfortable for the next few weeks. And don't think for one second I wouldn't and couldn't do that. Other than that, please feel free to fire away."

Peter blinks his eyes and gulps, holds his hands up, and says, "Okay, got it. As for the rest of the band, like, everyone's all alive and everything?"

"Oh, yeah. We're all still here and pretty much in one piece."

*

Danny could take you to the house and point you to the exact spot where he was sitting on the living-room floor when the Beatles first appeared on *The Ed Sullivan Show*. (Actually, not anymore, as the house and most of the street are long gone now.) One reason he remembers it so well is because he really wasn't taken with them, and almost everybody else he knew was. He'd heard their songs on the radio, and the buzz throughout his school was about the Beatles and nothing else, but when he saw them live on TV he felt disappointed. (His younger sister shrieking in his ear that night did not help any.)

The main thing he didn't like about the Beatles was that they were all wearing the same thing, from collar to boot, and all had the same haircut.

The long hair was cool, though. He recognized that at once. It was new and different and they sure wore it well. But here were four talented guys in their twenties and they were trying to look and sound exactly the same. Even to his preteen, pre-rebellious, pre-testosterone soul, that seemed wrong.

Danny immediately began to grow his hair longer and recoiled whenever his mother suggested a haircut. He asked his parents for a guitar and got one for his tenth birthday. It was a brown and tomato red Sears Silvertone, a little too cowboy-looking for his taste but still okay, and for the first few days he was afraid to go near the thing. When he first learned how to tune the guitar, Danny would un-tune it over and over again just so he could retune it. He kept it under his bed at night and finally began taking lessons from a bony man with a slight limp who'd played with the Louisiana Hayride in the fifties. (He'd met Elvis when he was just a skinny little thing with bad skin, he told Danny.) His teacher had long, weathered fingers and could make the guitar ring and rip. Danny learned the chords to some basic songs ("Red Sails in the Sunset," "Blue Moon of Kentucky," "Deep in the Heart of Texas") and practiced every second he could. He grew into a big, broad-shouldered kid and played tight end and outside linebacker at Pleasant Valley High, and he possibly could have been All-County but he quit football in his senior year after dislocating two fingers. He hated the regimentation, the following of orders, and, despite the mangled-finger mastery of Django Reinhardt and Jerry Garcia, he needed his fingers intact to pick, pluck, and strum.

His father was a dentist with a successful practice and he urged his son to follow him into the profession, but there were a thousand jobs Danny would have taken on before becoming a dentist. He played in a few bands in high school, bands that covered rhythm-and-blues and rock 'n' roll tunes, never even dreaming of doing any original songs, and they played in school gyms and auditoriums and on boardwalks in neighboring Long Island towns. Danny didn't like taking orders from anyone and formed his own band in his freshman year at Adelphi University. Peach Pudding was the name of the group and it had the classic lineup: two guitars, bass, and drums. They played hard rock; their songs usually had a thirty-second guitar intro, four lines of gibberish verse followed by a chorus, another verse, the chorus, and then five minutes of an anxious Fender Strat solo, heavy on the whammy bar. Danny wrote the songs but never played lead guitar. Peach Pudding lasted almost two years and their lead-guitarist slot was a veritable Bum of the

Month Club: they went through ten of them. Gradually, though, Danny grew more confident as a singer and began to trust his voice and feel comfortable with it.

He listened to whatever he could get his hands on, which was a lot since he worked part time at a record store in Hicksville. He listened to the Yardbirds, Cream, John Mayall, Blind Faith, Fleetwood Mac, McGuinness Flint, Jeff Beck, Led Zeppelin (whom he didn't like that much), Derek and the Dominos, the Allman Brothers, Delaney & Bonnie; he listened to the Kinks, Fairport Convention, Pentangle, Lindisfarne, Small Faces. (Except for the Band, he thought at the time, the Brits did American music better than Americans did.) He went back in time and gave Howlin' Wolf, Robert Johnson, B. B. King, Lightnin' Hopkins, and Muddy Waters a shot. He liked it, it was great, he *got* it . . . it just didn't move him or make him sway. (For him, the original "Crossroads" by Robert Johnson had nothing on the Cream version—it was like comparing a glass of brandy to four lines of great coke.)

But the band he liked the most, without question, was the Rolling Stones. He scratched and wore the grooves off their records, playing them over and over again on his Marantz stereo until the songs were just skips and cackles. He went through six copies apiece of *Beggars Banquet* and *Let It Bleed.* The second he'd seen them on television for the first time—it was on *The Hollywood Palace* in 1964—he somehow knew that this was the direction he wanted to go. You could not get further away from dentistry than this! Sure, the Stones had worn suits like the Beatles had . . . but at least beneath those suits they had on different shirts. And their hair wasn't nearly as uniform either. "Eww," his younger sister had commented, "they're *dirrrty.*" That was it! She was right . . . they *were* dirty! And it was good. The guitarist behind the lead singer, the way he held his guitar—you could tell right away that wherever he'd go, and no matter who he was with, he'd always be the coolest person around. "A Day in the Life" was supposed to be the greatest rock song ever written, but where was the pain, the feeling, the blood? Danny thought there was more passion in five seconds of "Wild Horses" than in all of *Sgt. Pepper* combined.

He lasted two years at Adelphi, then dropped out and broke his dad's heart. He spent all day writing and rewriting songs, talking to other musicians, absorbing everything he could, and playing guitar. He smoked cigarettes and drank bourbon, which made his voice sound rawer and bluesier; he smoked a lot of pot and hash, took acid and mescaline a few times, drank more bourbon, ate poorly, and wrote hundreds of songs and threw out all but five. There was a gritty sound he was looking for but could not get close to. Was it possible, he wondered, that he was listening to too much music and had lost his way?

Refusing to join anybody else's band, he kept forming his own, picking up the detritus of shattered groups in Long Island and Queens. From the Stunning Little Darlings out of West Hempstead he'd pluck a drummer; from Yellowcake in Lindenhurst he'd snag a bass player; from the Moonstones in Oyster Bay he'd filch a lead guitarist. And so on. They would play gigs, rehearse, argue, fume, break up, get drunk and high, and re-form. No manager wanted to represent them; no booking agency would take them on.

Guitarists came and went through the revolving door. One thing Danny, even at that age, could not abide was lateness. If he said practice was at two o'clock sharp, he did not mean two-thirty or two-ten or even one minute after two: he meant two o'clock. A guitarist showed up an hour late for a gig one night in Levittown and Danny fired him on the spot and punched him out, and the band went on without him. Danny was bigger than most of the musicians he played with; he was more muscular and was able to radiate authority, and he knew he had to make his bandmates afraid of him. Still, rarely did anyone ever show up at the appointed time. Musicians, he found out, were not high-school footballers. Some of them were just too out of it to be scared.

He wasn't making it, nothing he did was working, he was no nearer to the sound he wanted than when he started, and he realized that, for a little while at least, he'd have to join someone else's band.

*

This might be a tough one. And would it be worth it?

Jules had spent most of the morning stumbling around Portland with Lauren and Amber, the girls he'd met outside the State Theater earlier in the day, going all the way west and then back east. He assumed either that he was going to get them back into his and Howie's hotel room, or that they were going to drive him to a house five miles outside of town, which Lauren, the plumper of the two girls, shared with her trucker boyfriend (who was at work and wouldn't be home), Amber, and Amber's sister.

Neither Lauren nor Amber was pretty. They just were.

But Amber, the skinnier, more emaciated of the pair, had the Silver.

She had that look about her . . . There was something in her eyes, a silvery gleam, that told Jules she would be great in bed—that she'd know what to do with her hands and her mouth and the rest of her body, that she'd make great noises and talk filthy. Eight times out of ten when Jules sensed the Silver, he was right. The other two times, it was just heartbreaking.

Besides, there were two of them. And though neither one was attractive, they sort of complemented each other. One was too wide, the other too narrow; one had dark hair, the other had blond; one had flabby breasts, the other had none. Lauren and Amber had no moles, beauty marks, or freckles (that he could see), but aside from that, they didn't have much else going for them. Jules pegged Lauren as a seventeen-minute girl and Amber as maybe a fourteen-minute girl. Out of the two of them, he'd get one good-looking girl out of it.

66

He knew that at some point he had to go back to the hotel and pop half a Viagra. Or maybe, since this could turn into a threesome, a whole tab. After walking to the west side of town and gazing out over the Fore River, he asked the two of them if they wanted to go to his room. Amber said nothing, but Lauren giggled shyly and said, "Not yet," and they kept walking.

The three of them went to a dark, woody bar near a gas station and talked and drank, Jules buying the beer. He made out with Amber for five minutes in the women's bathroom and then, half an hour later, he made out with Lauren in the men's. At one point Jules was telling them how he was on *Guitar World Magazine*'s 100 Greatest Guitarists of All Time list (though he didn't mention that the next time they did the list he'd been replaced by some guy named Billy Zoom and was out of the rankings entirely) when his cell phone rang. He looked at it, saw that it was Joey calling, and let the call go to voice mail. (He took a guess as to why Joey was calling: *Yo, Jules, bring me back a cheeseburger and fries, okay?*)

"Hey, I have to go back to my hotel room," Jules said. It was twelve-thirty in the afternoon, and he'd had a lot of beer by this point and was getting sleepy. He didn't want to get Lauren and Amber into bed anymore, either separately or together. He just wanted a nap. Also, if they came up to the room, he'd have to explain why there were towels on the floor—that Howie, his bassist, did this so that the bottoms of his feet would never touch dirty carpet or tile.

"Why?" Lauren asked.

"I just do." And then, just for the hell of it, just to see what they'd say, he said: "Why don't you two come up?"

Amber looked at Lauren and then at Jules. Lauren looked at Jules and then at Amber.

"Why would we do that?" Amber asked.

67

Jules felt relieved, although his bladder was really being pushed now. Still, he also felt a little disappointed.

He estimated that, looks-wise, both of the chicks would be in the lower tenth percentile of all the women he'd had sex with. (As far as he was concerned, the best-looking chick he'd ever been with was Rhonda Wentworth. It wasn't that Rhonda was so gorgeous— she wasn't—it was the fact the he was so head-over-heels crazy about her.) Maybe he should've gone to the radio station with Danny, or to the drum store with Howie, or just hung out with Joey and goofed off. Of the four Overfalls, Jules was the only one who'd never gotten married and had kids, and he felt he was by far the luckiest.

"Look," he said to Lauren and Amber, no longer aware of which one of them once possessed the Silver, "I'm going back. I need to do something there. If you wanna say good-bye here, then, well, I had a great time and thanks for showing me around town."

The two girls looked at each other again. Amber was chewing her gum like a maniac.

"I'll go back to the room with you," Amber said between gum pops. Then she looked at Lauren and asked her if she'd come up, too. Lauren said she would. Is this a case, Jules wondered, of one chick accompanying another to make sure she wouldn't do something stupid, or of one chick accompanying another to make sure that she would?

"Great!" Jules said.

But inside his heart was sinking.

*

Peter Green played "Hurt" (the studio version, not the blistering eight-minute version from *Live in 'Lanta*) and told Danny he was going to open the phones. Then they went to a few commercials.

"How are you holding up?" Peter asks him now.

"Everything's cool. Believe me, I've done radio before."

Peter had asked him on the air a few minutes ago what new music he liked, what groups he was listening to, and what was on the Recently Played list on his iTunes, and Danny had to fudge his answers. He didn't like new music, really. (He loathed rap, which his two daughters were into; he wasn't that familiar with any new groups; he didn't own an iPod. To him, the names of pop stars today sound like medication for prostate enlargement or osteoporosis: Ciara, Shakira, Cialis, Cymbalta, Rihanna, Boniva, Beyoncé, Chantix.) "You know, I like a lot of things," he'd said to Peter, who realized what was going on and then dropped it.

"You really have never heard of Peter Green?" Danny asks him. "The first lineup of Fleetwood Mac was tremendous. You should check them out."

A commercial for Burger King comes to a close. They're back on the air.

"Okay," Peter tells his audience, "this first call is from Kevin from South Portland. Kevin, you're on The It."

"Hey, Peter," Kevin from South Portland says, sounding as though he woke up only ten seconds ago. "I thought Ian Farrell was supposed to be on."

"There was a mix-up. Do you have any questions for Danny Ault?"

"Nope. Not really."

"You're on The It," Peter tells his next caller, Brian from Falmouth.

"Yeah, I've gawt two questions," Brian from Falmouth says, his accent as thick as lobster bisque. "How'd it feel when your brawther Duane died on his motahbike and was he really run over by a trawk deliverin' peaches?"

Danny shifts around in his swivel chair and feels the temperature in the studio shoot up 15 degrees.

69

"It's Ault, not Allman," Danny says. "And it was not a peach truck."

He looks over to Peter, who has no idea what's going on. Peter is thirty at most, Danny assumes, and wasn't even born when Duane Allman died.

"Okay," Peter says, "let's listen to your song 'Hurt.' So you had a super-huge hit covering a Madonna song and so what did you do? . . . You went and covered a Christina Aguilera song, too. Shame on you, dude."

"Hurt" comes on, and while Danny tries to remember which one Christina Aguilera is, he feels his cell phone, which is on mute, start to vibrate.

"So you guys are originally from . . . *Long Island*?" Peter asks when the song ends, pronouncing "Long Island" as though it were an enemy planet. "Is that really true?"

"Three of us are," Danny concedes, bracing for what he knows is coming next. "And, hey, Long Island's not so bad. Lou Reed was from Freeport." He leaves out Vanilla Fudge and the Vagrants but mentions Lou Reed because he correctly assumes Lou Reed is someone Peter would approve of.

"Yeah, Danny, but Long Island also gave us . . . *Billy Joel*."

They've heard that one many times before, and Danny resorts to using the standard TFO reply: "Well, there was nothing anyone could do to prevent that."

He looks up at the clock on the studio wall. He's got thirty more minutes of this on-air waterboarding.

They take a few more calls, and Peter Green plays "Waiting and Wilting" and steps out of the studio. Danny feels his cell phone vibrate again. He sees it's the Clarion Hotel calling, assumes it's probably nothing, and ignores it.

Peter comes back into the studio just as "Waiting and Wilting" ends and he asks Danny how he got started in the music business and how the Furious Overfalls came to be.

70

When he was twenty-one Danny joined Jakey Gee and the Aerosouls as their rhythm guitarist. He was to do no songwriting unless asked by Jakey or his father (he never was asked), make no suggestions as to the direction of the band and the music, and never raise his voice or complain. He was merely a piece in a puzzle; a quiet, smoothly running cog in the Aerosoul machine; an ant on the march.

Jakey Gee's real name was Josh Garfein. His father was the dapper Sy Garfein, who ran Conglomerated Shippers, a heavily Mafia-connected trucking outfit in New York's Garment District. Josh wanted to be the next Tommy James or Gary Puckett, which, in retrospect, does not seem that ambitious. He had a serviceably soulful voice for a white boy, and his reddish-orange afro rose a foot off his scalp. He shaved his chest and back and wore mauve jumpsuits, gaudy bracelets and necklaces, and large aviator sunglasses indoors. (His solid-gold, diamond-encrusted Chai necklace cost more than four grand.) Had Jakey ever been asked to leave his ego at the door, the door it hung on and the walls around it would have collapsed.

There was no way he was going to make it with the name Josh Garfein. There was a brief window in the history of rock music when you could get away with the name Chad or Jeremy or Peter or Gordon or Arthur, but Josh Garfein, or even Josh Gee or Joshie Gee, was out of the question. If you were born with a handle like Manfred Lubowitz, you had to change it to Manfred Mann. So Josh Garfein became Jakey Gee.

The act was managed by De Facto Entertainment in Manhattan, which also had ties to organized crime, but everyone assumed that all the decisions were made by Jakey and his old man, both of whom were tyrants and could chew a yard off your ass at any second. Had Danny not been half Jewish, he might have joined a local chapter of the American Nazi Party (if there was a local chapter on Long Island, which most likely there wasn't).

It was the largest band Danny had ever played in. The Aerosouls consisted of two guitarists, a bass player, two keyboardists, a drummer, a four-man horn section, and the Moist Towelettes, a trio of amply curved black backup singers. The songs were simple, there was a lot of wah-wah and fuzz, and Danny just had to stand in the background and play while Jakey Gee sang, growled, wailed, hammed it up, mumbled, shimmied, and perspired.

The music was a combination of soul, rhythm and blues, and psychedelic—"Crystal Blue Persuasion" crossed with Wilson Pickett's version of "Hey Jude" crossed with Screamin' Jay Hawkins's "Constipation Blues." Jakey sang songs like "(Blow) My Mind" (a song with cryptic cocaine references), "(Oh Yeah) Dig This, Little Girl" (a song loaded with cryptic intimations about sex with a minor), and "Big (Fat) Jimmy, Part One," (a not at all cryptic song about his own penis: "Big Fat Jimmy, two nuts and a knob / Big Fat Jimmy, he always do the job.") Not only did Jakey sweat more than Elvis Presley in a sauna and often lose up to ten pounds a night in water weight, but his accent sometimes sounded more Tupelo than Elvis's, and sometimes more Welsh than Tom Jones's, depending on what he was saying or singing.

He always made sure when introducing the members of the band one by one to the crowd to screw up every single name. "And on rhythm guitar . . . *Mister* Danny Osmond!"

Everyone in the band, except for Jakey himself, had to have their hair the exact same length and wear a uniform. No beards or mustaches were allowed. They all wore lilac blue velvet suits (with loud purple stitching) and bell-bottom pants and ruffled pink shirts, and the Moist Towelettes wore skintight lacy white jumpsuits and gold lamé stilettos. The outfits were designed by Jakey's sister Naomi, who was an assistant designer for a low-budget clothing manufacturer called Talking Togs. Unbeknownst to Jakey and Sy, Naomi Garfein, whose banana of a nose defied the best that plastic surgeons from Manhattan to L.A. could throw at her, had slept with five members of the Aerosouls (including Danny), some two at a time.

The best thing about being in the band, other than the steady paycheck, was that it was integrated. Danny got exposed to music he otherwise never would have heard, or might have ignored. The Meters, Huey Smith and the Clowns, Lee Dorsey, Rufus Thomas, the Bar-Kays, etc. Also, the black guys in the band always knew where the best food was in each town.

Danny hated Jakey and said horrible things about him behind his back. Everyone else who had to suffer Jakey Gee on a daily basis hated him, too, including the Moist Towelettes, one of whom, Viola Williams, confided to Danny that she hoped "Imo be fucked up enough in the head one night to slice his tiny little mouse balls off in his sleep."

They did play legitimate gigs, though, and had a few minor hits: "(Let My) People (Blow)" made it to number twelve on the *Billboard* chart, despite its suggestive lyrics, which few listeners could decipher amidst the honking and spasmodic braying. They played New York and Philly and Chicago and Miami and New Orleans and L.A. They opened for Bad Company, Bob Marley, Little Feat, and Joe Vitale's Madmen. (Neil Young took one long look at Jakey Gee backstage one night in Kansas City, shook his head with disbelief, and never looked in his direction again.) Jakey billed himself as "The Mighty Moses of Psycho Mind-Rockin' Hot-Buttered Soul," and the band appeared on a few TV shows. Before each of these appearances Jakey would warn Danny and the others: "After the song when the host interviews me, nobody but me makes a peep. Even if Merv sticks the mike in your pants and asks your asshole what its name is, make sure your asshole doesn't answer." After the band's one appearance on *Don Kirshner's Rock Concert*, it was reported that Jakey had sweat so much that viewers were cleaning their television screens with Windex afterward.

"I really think," LeVon, the bassist, told Danny one night in their dressing room after a gig, "I'm gonna quit the band soon and shoot Jakey point-blank in the forehead."

This became the chief diversion of the band, to plot all the gory, painful ways they would do in Jakey Gee. Chester the drummer wanted to slowly bash his head in with a drum mallet; Jerry, one of the keyboardists, wanted to garrote him with piano wire; Delores, another one of the Moist Towelettes, wanted to stick her ten-inch heels into his eyes.

But it was hard to take men wearing lilac velvet suits with bell-bottom pants and ruffled pink shirts seriously.

Jakey made sure that everyone was aware of his father's notorious connections. The more scared everyone was of him and his father, the better. When they played shows in New Jersey or Philadelphia, members of the extended "Family" got all the good seats. Playing onstage, Danny could barely see the audience for all the pinkie rings, pompadours, and chinchilla coats. After the shows were over, Paulie, Vinnie, and Louie and their wives and girlfriends would come backstage to hug and kiss Jakey and tell him how wonderful he was.

The money was good, the drugs and the girls were often very good, and Danny was seeing the sights beyond the Elmhurst Gas Tanks in Queens. Also, he could now tell people, including his parents, he was a professional musician.

But he didn't want it to last.

*

Brendan and Howie carry the new bass drum to the taxi in the parking lot. The driver is still there, leaning against his car and soaking up the uninspiring light of the elusive Maine sun. It's just

74

about one in the afternoon and there are five cars in the parking lot now.

"It was nice meeting you," Brendan says as the trunk pops open.

"I'll put your dad's name on the list at the theater," Howie says. "I'll put you down for four tickets. How's that?"

"You can just make it two. My dad and my mom."

Brendan puts out his hand to shake, but Howie, with a nod, indicates his hands are full with the drum.

Howie and the driver load the drum into the trunk; it fits, but only barely.

"Back into town?" the driver asks.

"Yeah," Howie tells him. "Back to the hotel."

If Jules brought the two girls back to the room, Howie thinks as they start rolling back to Portland, *they'd be gone by now.* He knows Jules's "3F" M.O.: Find 'em, Fuck 'em, then Find a way to get rid of 'em. At least Jules wears a condom . . . but even with the strict use of prophylactics, Howie sometimes, in the middle of the night, imagines the millions of bacteria rising up off of Jules's body, floating like butterflies over to Howie's bed, and descending on him and making their way into his skin, mouth, ears, etc. Howie has asked Jules to always please throw the condom out—not just out into the trash but out of the room—and usually Jules complies, but there have been instances when Howie, while tossing something into a trash can, has espied a used ribbed-for-her-pleasure rubber squiggled up in a coffee cup.

The taxi gets back onto Route 1 and Howie turns his cell phone back on. They pass a diner and a hair salon, and he sees that he has missed a call from the Clarion Hotel but that nobody had left a message. *It's probably nothing,* he thinks. It's probably just Danny calling to tell him about what went down at the radio station, or Jules calling to tell him that the coast is clear, or Joey calling just to say, "Yo, could you bring me a cheeseburger and fries?"

So Howie turns his cell back off. The less radiation coming out of that thing, the better.

*

They had just played a show in Memphis and Danny was in bed in his room at the Commodore Hotel. It was four in the morning and he was sharing a room with Chester, the drummer, and Bobby Joe, one of the two keyboardists. After the gig, the three of them had walked around Memphis, eaten ten pounds of barbecue, gone to the hotel bar, and then crashed. *Vanilla Thunder,* the third Jakey Gee and the Aerosouls LP, had been out for two months and was getting no airplay anywhere. The thing was dead. Record stores couldn't give copies away, and not even Paulie, Vinnie, and Louie were listening to it or coming to see Jakey perform. The band's days were numbered—no one in the band had gotten a check for a month—and soon, everyone in the group knew, Jakey would move back to Long Island and probably, after a hiatus of a year or so, be either working for his father in the trucking business or transforming himself into an entirely different type of showbiz entity. They'd all be looking for jobs soon.

Danny was fast asleep and dreaming about houses on fire, about guitars slowly burning up and shriveling to ashes, when he woke up with a heart-pounding start. Sirens were wailing outside, people were running down the hotel hallways, doors were being banged and kicked.

A fire, Danny thought, even though there were no alarms going off inside the hotel.

He woke up his two roommates and they quickly put on their clothes. Danny grabbed his guitars, took the stairs, and hustled to the lobby.

There were no fire engines outside. Only police cars.

Within twenty minutes the rumors were flying: Someone had been murdered, three people had been murdered, nobody had been murdered but someone had been kidnapped, a bomb had been found inside a linen closet. It was a sultry August Tennessee evening, and the Aerosouls, Moist Towelettes, and many other guests and hotel workers hung around outside and watched the hotel drowsily empty out.

By seven in the morning, everyone knew the truth: Jakey Gee had been found dead in his bed, the sheets dripping with blood, his scrotum and his throat slit ear to ear.

Danny and the rest of the band had to stay around for a few more days for questioning, but nobody was ever arrested. The crime was never solved. On the flight back home, he avoided eye contact with Viola Williams, who kept to herself and didn't say a word to anyone.

*

The hour is winding down, and Danny feels as though he's just undergone a brutal cross-examination on the witness stand.

"Well, I'd like to thank you for dropping by," Peter tells Danny over the air, "albeit accidentally. And good luck tonight and tomorrow. I'm sure the shows'll be kickin'."

"Thanks for having me, Peter," Danny says, amazed at himself for making it sound so convincing. Insincerity was not a gift of his, and it wasn't one he ever wanted.

A commercial comes on. The producer comes into the room and Peter stands up; she hands him some paperwork, he signs it, and they don't say a word. Danny stands up and takes a few steps toward the door before realizing his headphones are still on . . . They snap out of the jack, the cord goes flying, and Peter and the producer look at him for a split second. Then he takes off the headphones and sets them down on the chair.

"I'll see you downstairs and out," the producer says to him.

Danny thinks of recommending a few tunes to Peter, but just as he is about to, Peter hands him *TFO 10* and says, "Here, dude, you can keep this."

"You know how to get back?" the producer asks Danny downstairs as she opens the front door. The day has darkened and chilled, clouds are rapidly lowering overhead, and the old observatory looks as though someone has painted it a much darker brown.

"Yes," Danny says, knowing he's going to have to look at the map that the doofus assistant manager had handed him.

He heads toward the observatory. They have a show tonight. He'll grab lunch at the hotel, eat dinner at about six tonight, check in with Jessica before the show, and maybe get a chance to talk to his pregnant daughter. His pregnant daughter, his pregnant daughter.

Hey, Em, he'll say, *I hear congratulations are in order!*

But who really talks like that? He doesn't.

He comes to the observatory, takes out the map, and sees that he has to make a left and walk downhill.

When he makes the turn he takes his cell out of his jacket. There's a voice mail waiting for him and he plays it.

"Mr. Ault," a flat, polite, but nervous female voice says, "it's just after twelve-thirty, and this is Heather calling from the Clarion. I'm very sorry to tell you that Joe Mazz, a member of your party staying in room ten-oh-nine, has been taken to the hospital. He called down to us and said he was having chest pains. We sent a doctor up to his room right away. He's at the medical center now . . . he had a very bad heart attack but is resting. He'd like you to visit him."

Part Two
Home

Five
The Bigger the Bumps

OUR NO-NONSENSE GUARANTEE: 100,000 ROLLS OF TOILET PAPER OR ELSE WE WILL GIVE YOU A LIFETIME SUPPLY!

That's what a big sign hanging over Aisle 4 promises. Aisle 4, like all the other aisles at the Gentle Giant megastore, is long enough and nearly wide enough for a small airplane to land. *It seems like a good deal,* Danny thinks as he slowly pushes a cart down the aisle, Joey Mazz ambling by his side (in—what else?—black jeans, black boots, and a black leather jacket), but is someone really going to take the time out to count all the rolls?

It's the day before Thanksgiving, a few weeks after Joey's heart attack, and while Jessica and the girls are preparing for tomorrow's dinner, Danny has been given the task of, in Jessica's words, "getting some stuff for Emily's pregnancy." Those were her exact instructions—there is no shopping list. Danny leapt at the assignment as it got him out of the estrogen-infested house, and after he buys whatever it is he's suppose to buy, he's taking Joey to Hicksville Cardio & Pulmonary for a stress test, about ten miles away.

For the better part of both of Jessica's pregnancies, Danny was on the road with the band, though he was able to make it home for both births (and he wasn't exactly hurrying either). He never had to endure the whole nine months of bellyaching, worrying, and house-girding, and so he has little idea of what he needs to buy. A jumbo pack of paper towels is in the cart, and now Joey helps him pile in a twenty-pack of toilet paper. So Gentle Giant is now down to 999,980 rolls, and somewhere out there is a lucky sonuvabitch who feels like counting.

"Any idea of what else?" Danny asks him.

Joey doesn't seem too nervous about his upcoming appointment. For him, it's just another thing to do, like going out to get a carton of milk.

"Beats me, bro. I don't remember. I could call Angie."

But Angie's busy, too, prepping for tomorrow. (The Mazzes, with their foosball-table-size lasagna, take their Thanksgivings seriously.) That's why Danny is taking her husband to see a Dr. Ford at Hicksville Cardio & Pulmonary, to be scanned, probed, measured, and pricked, and whatever else they'll do there. But the real reason is that Angie is terrified of hospitals. "A beauty parlor," she told Danny over the phone a few weeks ago, "is as close to a hospital as I ever wanna get." Angie has been saying weird shit like that for decades—she did marry Joey after all.

When they come to the end of Aisle 4 and turn up Aisle 5, a Muzaklike version of "Our House" (the Crosby, Stills, Nash & Young song, not the Madness song) comes on and wafts throughout the store. Danny has been in stores and heard watered-down versions of "Borderline" and "Hurt" and always wondered: *Are we getting any money for this? And if so, where is it?*

Aisle 5 might be the mother lode, the main vein, the prenatal El Dorado he's looking for. There are enough Huggies, Pampers, and nursery accoutrement on display here to keep Lichtenstein's next two generations diapered and stain free for a year.

"You could get diapers now," Joey advises, "but the kid ain't even born yet. But it'd be nice to get some so that way when it is, they'd be there."

Danny nods and Joey asks him if he knows if it's going to be a boy or a girl. Danny says he just hopes it's a human being, and Joey says: "Well, boy or girl, it don't matter. The diaper won't care either way."

Danny looks at his watch. Joey's appointment is in an hour. Afterward, if they're still up for it, they'll go to the Ikea in Hicksville to buy some . . . some . . . something. Once again,

Jessica's instructions were vague to the point of useless. Should Danny buy a crib, a bassinet, a rocking chair? Joey said something about a Diaper Genie on the way to Gentle Giant, and it took Danny a few minutes to remember what that meant. Just as it came back to him, Joey said, "If you was a diaper genie and could get three wishes granted, what do you think they'd be?"

Joey grabs a sliding ladder and glides it over to the columns of Pampers. There are about ten other people in the aisle right now. Danny doesn't have his glasses on and cannot even see the far end of the aisle, where there might be two pregnant women or two stacks of boxes—it's all lost in the megastore mist.

"Danny," Joey whispers, still up on the ladder. "Check out those jugs."

A woman with a wriggling two-month-old boy strapped in her cart passes by them obliviously.

"Huge, huh?" Joey says.

"She's breast-feeding, Joey," Danny snaps. "That's why they're big."

"Yeah, I know. That's, like, cheatin'. But that is one lucky kid. Here, bro."

His ass crack showing for the millionth time, Joey throws down a pack of Pampers Stage 1's to Danny, who puts them in the cart.

What am I doing here? Danny asks himself. *We used to travel with a road crew and an entourage in the dozens. The best hotels, strangers licking my boots and catering to my every whim, Seconals bobbling around in my pockets like M&M's. Now look.*

"You okay up there?" Danny asks, but Joey doesn't answer.

In the history of coronary disease, has anyone endured a heart attack so unflappably as Joseph Mazz? When Danny walked into his hospital room in Portland, Joey was flat on his back, a dozen wires and tubes going in and coming out of his body . . . it looked like he was wired to a plate of capellini. For an instant Danny had to fight back a flood of tears. For over thirty years Joey had been his drummer . . . and even that wasn't really supposed to have happened; it was only because their original drummer skipped town, that idiot. And here he was, barely conscious, with every hiccup, thump, murmur, twitch, and brain wave being measured. (The machine keeping track of his vital signs sounded like a combination metronome and theremin.)

This was the guy who'd pounded out the rhythm and fills for all the songs they ever recorded, including the dozens that were dropped from albums because they weren't good enough, and for all the songs they ever played all around the world. Only once did Joey ever ask if he could do a prolonged Ginger Baker– or John Bonham–esque solo ("Like, you know, something like 'Toad' or 'Moby Dick' or something?"), and when Danny, Jules, and Howie explained, No, that's not really what we're about, Joey never brought it up again. Once they were no longer signed to any label, Joey asked if the Overfalls could cover Mountain's "Nantucket Sleighride" or "Theme for an Imaginary Western," or Jeff Beck's "Beck's Bolero," and, again, that suggestion was roundly voted down. (Every once in a while, though, Joey still brings it up.)

Why Danny had to fight back the tears he couldn't figure out, and it kept him frozen for almost three minutes, listening to the ticks and beeps and to Joey's unsteady breathing. He knew he didn't love Joey, he wasn't sure if he even liked him. Was it because Joey had once—perhaps—saved his life, years ago in St. Louis? But the way Danny sees it, Joey didn't save his life . . . He would've cleaned up his act eventually anyway. Had Joey not been his drummer, Danny probably would never have had anything to do with him. There were roadies and hangers-on who he had more in common with—guys like Sweet Lou, Rev, a few guitar techs, and Chunky Scrofa, their engineer. Danny thought and thought about it, and it worked: he was no longer fighting the tears. *He's just my drummer,* Danny said to himself. "My drummer." Supposedly, Mick Jagger once called Charlie Watts "my drummer" over the phone in a hotel, and then

Watts, God bless him, met him in the hotel hallway, punched him out for it, and said, "Don't ever call me your drummer again. You're my singer."

But Joey would never have done anything of the sort.

Danny wheeled a little chair over to Joey's bed, sat down, and examined all the tubes and wires, thinking of some of the weird devices that Howie had tried to foist on the band throughout the years. Clavinets, mellotrons, harpsichords . . . clumsy coffinlike devices that looked like telephone switchboards from the 1930s. Joey's skin had lost all its olive luster, Danny saw. Above his dented Idaho potato of a schnoz, his eyes were almost open. Danny looked at Joey's arms and hands, at his veins and faded tattoos. In perfect 6/8 time, the heart monitor he was hooked up to went *BLIP-blip-blip-BLIP, BLIP-blip-blip-BLIP*. It reminded Danny of the infectious drumbeat intro to Fleetwood Mac's "Hypnotized."

Joey stirred, swallowed, moved his knees under the sheets. He turned his head, saw Danny, and blinked. It may have taken a few seconds before he realized who was sitting right next to him. With a voice as dry as salt, he groaned five words: "Huh? What . . . the . . . fuck, man?"

Now, Joey starts coming back down the ladder, and Danny grabs it with two hands to keep it steady. Joey has his color back and has even gained some weight—the cardiologist in Maine told Danny, Jules, and Howie that Joey needed to gain weight, not lose it. You didn't hear that too often following a heart attack. But in Joey's case the doctor was right.

"Wipes," Joey says.

"Huh?"

"You'll be needing some wipes, Gramps. Tons of 'em. For the kid's butt, for his face, for the carpets, for your hands. And also—I don't remember what you call 'em—but you'll need these condom-type things for the milk bottles. To keep 'em sterile and whatnot.

85

They look like rubbers but they go inside and they ain't ribbed. You know, they're like insert things."

"I think they're just called inserts. We can wait on those. I've got six whole months." Six months . . . and then: Grandpa. Gramps. He's gone from drinking Old Grand-Dad to being one.

"Hey! Joey-*boy!*" Joey yells out.

For a second, Danny doesn't understand why the hell Joey would be calling out to himself, but then suddenly, popping into view, directly beneath the Pampers Stage 4's, is Joey's son, Joey Junior. The kid is twenty-two years old and two inches shorter than his dad but equally as scrawny. Joey Junior has bumpy white skin, a slender nose, shoulder-length light brown hair, and blue eyes. He graduated high school by the skin of his teeth, has had a few minor scrapes with the law, and still lives at home with his folks.

"Hey, Joey," Danny says to the kid.

"What the fuck are you doing at Gentle Giant?" Joey Senior asks his son.

Even though he's heard Joey talk to his kids like this before, Danny still can't believe it. Never once did he drop the F-bomb on his daughters. He always kept it clean.

(But a lot of good it did.)

"I dunno," Little Joey tells his dad. "I was just around, you know."

Joey Junior probably had no more desire to spend Thanksgiving Eve Day in his house than Danny or Joey or millions of other men did. Had Danny not been told to go to Gentle Giant, he knows what he'd be doing right now: He'd be in his room above the attached garage with either his Martin or his beloved Guild 12-string, or at the piano. Almost sixty years old and still practicing. Do bankers and brokers ever have to practice? "You can just leave, Daddy," Lily had said to him as she printed out new stuffing recipes from her iPhone. "You're not wanted here."

"You can help us shop for Danny's daughter then," Big Joey says to his son.

"Yeah," Little Joey says to Danny. "I heard about Lily. Congratulations."

"Thanks," Danny says. "But it's Emily, not Lily. Unless you know something I don't."

Emily is nineteen and was in college, but is now pregnant, unmarried, and not in college. She still isn't telling anyone who the father is and will only concede that it isn't her ex-boyfriend Wyatt, or Peter, or whatever his name is. Lily, his younger daughter, is smart but is a social misfit, always overwhelmed in groups of more than three people.

Joey's oldest kid is a loser: Little Joey would probably still be living at home when he's forty and would never set foot inside a college, unless he were the guy mopping the floors at night. Danny tried to remember what he had gotten in trouble for . . . it was small-time, slap-on-the-wrist stuff. One time, when he was sixteen, he'd gotten busted for stealing a six-pack of Old Milwaukee. Danny was there when Joey went to the police station in Commack: Joey Senior grabbed his son by the hair, yanked it, and said, "What the hell are you doing stealing Old Milwaukee? If you're gonna steal beer, take the fuckin' Heineken!"

Of the three band members with kids, Howie, miraculously, probably had the sanest, most-together kid. And even she—from the little that Danny knew of her—was just slightly off. This is what happens, Danny knew, when you are rarely home and you phone in your parenthood from Marriotts and Hilton Garden Inns.

Joey Junior plays drums, too: he is talented and has played for a few metal groups, but that's it. Like Danny's kids, Joey's kids and Howie's daughter were not into the Overfalls . . . They never listened to the old tunes or the new ones. They found the Stones, Derek and the Dominos, and the Allman Brothers unlistenable (for heaven's sake, how can you possibly not love "Sway," "Little

Wing," and "Dreams"?!), and they could only abide a few Beatles songs (and one of them was "Yesterday"). It was devastating. *TFO 10*—Danny didn't even bother giving copies to his kids. He didn't want to give them the chance to not listen to it.

"Maybe one day," Joey Senior says to his boy, putting his hand on his shoulder, "you'll make me a grandpa, too."

"Yeah, maybe," Junior says, slumping his shoulders. "I dunno."

"Hey, after this, Danny's takin' me to a clinic to get checked out. You wanna hop along? Or you just wanna go back home and hang with your mom and sisters?"

Danny wheels his Smart car–size cart up Aisle 5 with a Joey Mazz on each side of him. They go by the wipes, bottles, inserts, and sanitizers, and a megastore version of the Stones' "Dandelion" is being piped in now. It sounds as if it were produced on a toy cell phone: Were there actually human beings involved in the process of manufacturing this song?

"Nah," Little Joey says, "I got some stuff I gotta do. I'm hookin' up with some friends later on."

"Joey," Danny says to the elder Mazz, "it's not like it's going to be fun."

Big Joey stops in his tracks and points out what's on the shelf immediately to his right.

"Whoa! Check it out. Nipple lotion!"

*

In the small dining room of his house, in front of his wife and daughter, Howie slowly slips the turkey out of the grocery store shopping bag until it slides onto the dinner table.

"Here it is," he says, forcing an unconvincing smile. "Fifteen pounds."

It was a good, plump bird, perfect for four to seven people for two or three days. Howie's mom and Melissa's mother and sister were coming over for the meal tomorrow, but after that, it would just be Howie, Melissa, and Michelle, his daughter. The house they lived in was about thirty-five miles, as the crow flies, from the Gentle Giant in Hicksville.

"Looks like a good one," Melissa says. "Is anything wrong?"

"No. Why?"

"It only took you an hour and a half, daddy," Michelle says. They're sitting at the counter that divides the kitchen from the dining room, and Howie is still at the table.

"It was really crowded there," Howie says. Already the bird is starting to look jaundiced.

The grocery store was, naturally, crowded on the day before Thanksgiving, but not terribly crowded. After ten minutes of poking and pinching around the necropolis of turkeys, Howie had picked out a bird, walked up Aisle 2, and briefly touched a jar of applesauce. He brought the turkey to the express lane and waited in line until he was the next customer to be rung up. Then, after much deliberation, he changed his mind. He went back to the poultry section, put the turkey exactly where he'd found it, then prodded and weighed a few others with his hands and picked out another one. He walked back to the registers via Aisle 2, touching the same jar of applesauce on the way, but by the time he returned, there was nothing express about the express lane anymore, so he shifted to the next line over. He couldn't stop looking at the bird: its bumps were the size of boils. Just as it became his turn to plop the turkey onto the conveyor belt, he said to the cashier, "Uh . . . hold on . . . I forgot something" and went back to the poultry section.

The bigger the bumps, Howie figured, the greater the chance for bacteria to nestle and thrive. So he looked at every turkey, examining the bumps and all the other nooks and crannies. He thought of calling Melissa and telling her to drive to the store with Michelle so that they could pick one out together and he could recuse himself from the matter, but then he found one he truly believed in. It was, he realized, the original turkey, the one he'd brought up to the express lane first. He carried it back to the express lane, making sure to touch the same jar of applesauce, and waited in line—then went back and got a different turkey. But on the way back to the registers, he saw that his jar of applesauce was gone— *someone had bought the damned thing!*—and he stood in front of its gaping absence for a full five minutes before one of the supermarket's green grocers came along and asked, "Everything okay, sir?" Howie, embarrassed, was able to pull himself away. He shuffled back to the cash registers and purchased the turkey he's staring at right now, which seems, despite having been decapitated, to be looking back at him.

Has the turkey changed color in the six-minute drive from the grocery store to the house? It sure looks that way. It was gold when he put it in the car . . . now it looks gray.

"It's a good one, Howie," Melissa assures him. "You picked a winner."

Sweet Melissa. Howie knows he could not have married any other woman, and that probably no other woman would have married him. Despite the fleeting rock star status.

"I think I may go upstairs and practice. I'll be back down soon."

"Stay down here for a while," Michelle says. She's sixteen, only five foot one, and nerdy cute. She has her quirks and sullen moments but she's a good kid, especially for one who, in Howie's imagination, has been kidnapped and run over a thousand times.

"I really should practice."

He lifts up the turkey, which is encased in plastic so tightly that it's as if the plastic were the bird's second skin. Surely no germs could survive in such an airless environment. Or maybe they could . . . maybe that's just the sort of thing they need to multiply by the thousands.

A few minutes later he's upstairs in what he calls his "studio." It's a good-size room at one end of the top floor; Michelle's bedroom is the next room over, then comes the bathroom and the master bedroom. The house is so Southern New England suburban that any bassist worth his E string would find it sickening, but it's just the sort of home that Howie always wanted. The son of a college professor and a high-school teacher, he grew up only twenty miles away.

Howie reaches into a tight, orderly stack of CDs and pulls out one labeled "BP #5." Bass Practice #5. He slips it into his CD player and presses the Play button. He goes to the door and makes sure it's locked, then pulls the blinds down on the lone window and sits down in a black leather chair and turns on his desktop computer. He picks up his 3-Tone Sunburst Fender Bass VI and plugs it into a small amp but doesn't play . . . he just rests it on his lap. On the stereo, the bass starts playing and runs through some scales and riffs. The volume goes up and down . . . the bass is heard being tuned, then retuned. Downstairs, if they're listening, his wife and daughter will believe he's actually practicing. BP #5 is one of a hundred different discs that he's recorded so that anyone within earshot—whether they be upstairs, downstairs, or out in the small backyard—will think he is practicing. (He also has CDs for guitar, keyboard, sax, accordion, violin, and the myriad other instruments he knows how to play. He even has discs that go from tuning and playing guitar to tuning and playing cello and then back again. A few of them even incorporate feedback and long pauses with no sound at all.)

He goes onto the Internet to a website called connecticuttraffic.net.

Should I bring the turkey back to the store? He could tell them it just wasn't big enough, or that it was too big, or that it changed color or was twitching. *I could take it back with Melissa and she could pick one out.*

The phone rings. Howie jumps up and pauses the disc so that it sounds as if he's stopped practicing. It could be news about Joey's stress test.

He opens the door and shouts downstairs. "Is that for me?"

"No! Just Taiyo calling!" Melissa calls up. Taiyo being Taiyo
Perlmutter, a friend of Michelle's. He may be her boyfriend.
Nobody knows. Michelle and Taiyo aren't even sure.

Howie locks the door, starts the CD again, and scrolls through
connecticuttraffic.net.

A few days ago he warned his family that, because of Joey's
heart attack and the gigs they had to cancel, it might not be such a
merry Christmas this year. Joey spent four days in the hospital in
Portland . . . The band canceled the first State Theater gig but then,
as a trio, played the next night, with Danny and Jules alternating
between guitar and bass, Howie on drums. After thousands of nights
as a quartet, it was like appearing in someone else's dream. For
decades Howie had stood on Danny's right while Jules stood on
Danny's left and Joey sat at his kit behind the three of them. Howie
has witnessed thousands of his band's shows out of the corner of his
left eye. Sitting behind Danny and Jules was a whole new
experience and it was disconcerting. They'd had to rework their
songs—most of Jules's guitar solos were now out, a lot of the songs
were shorter—but for the most part it worked. Still, they had to
cancel the remaining gigs and were out thousands of dollars. He and
Melissa were planning to buy Michelle a used car for Christmas, her
first. But no more. When Danny called the club in Hartford to break
the bad news to the manager, the manager told him, "Thanks for the
heads-up, Danny, and don't sweat it . . . we weren't expecting much
of a gate anyways."

"Everything okay, sir?" the green grocer had asked him in Aisle
2.

For years he's been telling himself he's going to get help. As
every year winds down to an end, he tells himself that one of his
New Year's resolutions will be to finally see someone, maybe even
check into a hospital. But when New Year's Day comes around, he
doesn't even make the resolution: that way he doesn't break it.

The thrumming of BP #5 vibrates the floor underneath his bare feet. Downstairs, Michelle is probably still on the phone with Taiyo, and Melissa is probably still dicing celery. Or perhaps she's pouring over the TFO books.

Howie lives close to New Haven and not far from Boston and New York City. He's right in the epicenter of the Psychoanalysis Triangle. Maybe there's no cure but surely there's help.

It's been more than twenty years since he's gotten more than five hours of sleep in a night.

Howie thinks there's a chance that, driving to the grocery store to get the turkey, he may have run over someone a few minutes after he got off Route 1. He didn't see anyone, he didn't hear or feel anything, but he thinks there's a chance. He also thinks there's a chance he may have hit someone a minute or so before he got back on Route 1 on his way back home. Now, on connecticuttraffic.net, he clicks on TODAY'S ACCIDENTS, but he sees no reports of a hit-and-run. Or maybe he did hit someone but it just hasn't shown up yet on the site. He logs off and listens to BP #5 for a minute and then logs back on to the site to see if any newer accidents have shown up. But, of course, they haven't.

What would therapy be like? He has run through the scenario hundreds of times: He finds the name of an expert in the field, someone with a few published papers and books under his belt. He makes an appointment. A consultation, they'll call it. Would he tell Melissa . . . or would he just say he's driving into New York City to go to Sam Ash to suss out new equipment, something he does frequently. It's a lie she would believe. (But what if she says, as she's done in the past: "Hey, can I hop along? I could go to a museum and we'll meet up for lunch.") And, if he starts seeing a shrink regularly, wouldn't she notice that he always disappears from the house at the exact same time on the exact same day every week? And what if this expert doctor wants to see him three times a week? Then surely Melissa would notice the pattern.

93

Or he could just tell her the truth. "I'm finally going to get some help." It would turn into one of those sappy scenes that Jules has spent his whole life avoiding. (Except for the time Jules cried for four days straight when he and Rhonda Wentworth broke up.)

I'm so proud of you, Melissa would say.

He calls, he makes the appointment, he takes the 8:50 A.M. train to Manhattan, and he walks into the office and sits and waits. He waits, the minutes pass, he gets more anxious. Other patients in the waiting room, while they wait for their appointments with other doctors, look at him as though he's crazier than they are (which he might be). A door opens, a doctor comes out and says, *Howard Grey?* Howie tries to stand up but cannot. He cannot rise off the couch.

Or he does stand up and shakes hands with the doctor, and then the doctor sees Howie wipe off his hand on his own pants—or else Howie doesn't shake hands with the doctor at all.

Lie down, the doctor says in his office, waving his hand to the couch.

Howie lies down and the doctor will say: *Okay, Howard, so let's begin. Tell me a little about yourself. Where are you from, tell me about growing up, when did you first start to realize you had a problem, you gettin' any lately, what do you do and what do you think about, are you married, any children, you're a musician so how much drugs have you done, how unmanageable is the problem, and how rotten is your existence? We have forty-five minutes.*

*

Howie's Austrian-born father, Professor Grunfeld, had a Ph.D. in chemistry and was tenured at Yale, where he was the assistant dean of the chemistry department. His mother taught music at the local public school, but when they scaled down the music program she switched to teaching English. Music was a huge part of Howie's youth . . . he cannot remember a time when there wasn't music playing. Opera on Sundays, Handel and Mozart and Mahler and Stravinsky the rest of the week. Sometimes Howie's mom would put on Sinatra or Billie Holiday or Artie Shaw. At first, Professor Grunfeld had only a majestic, brown-shelled Grundig radio, its dusty grille the color of English mustard, and when he was very young Howie thought that the tubes lighting up inside the thing were actually people talking and playing music. The old man got better equipment through the years, eventually moving up to a McIntosh, which at that time was like driving a Rolls-Royce. He kept all his LPs squeaky clean and in perfect order—they were often stored still in their original wrapping. He had a Tandberg reel-to-reel tape deck and had hundreds of tapes. He had six different versions of the Brandenburg Concertos alone. Only his father was allowed to remove and put back a tape . . . he alone understood the Köchel and BWV numbers and his own unique filing system. One time Howie's younger sister, just to be a pain in the ass and thinking it would take her father a year to notice, moved the *Jupiter* symphony (K.551) to where the *Piano Trio in* C for piano, violin, and cello (K.548) was stored. It took only two days, but the Professor spotted the aberration and wasn't amused.

Howie had the violin forced on him at the perilous age of five years old and was the best young pupil his teacher had ever had. The instructor swore the kid had perfect pitch. After only three lessons, the usual hair-raising, tympanum-shattering screeches ceased, and after seven lessons, his teacher and parents thought they had the next Yehudi Menuhin on their hands. He studied violin for five years, but by this time Howie had seen the Beatles, Stones, Kinks, Animals, and Zombies on TV and had heard Bob Dylan, "Eve of Destruction," Smokey Robinson, Curtis Mayfield, and Dusty Springfield on the radio. When he told his parents he didn't want to study violin anymore, they were crushed but understood . . . and immediately switched him to cello.

The same thing happened. As much as an entirely disinterested kid was capable of mastering an instrument in less than a year, Howie mastered the cello and then gave it up. His teacher nearly cried: she thought she was dealing somehow with the long-lost love child of Pablo Casals and Mstislav Rostropovich. After the cello came the oboe, but by this time Howie was listening to radio stations out of New York City and Boston, and to Rahsaan Roland Kirk, Edgard Varèse, Charles Ives, and James Brown. Because of his odd taste and meticulous manner, he didn't fit in with any existing clique in high school. He didn't want to hang with the kids who did drugs, but he did want to hang around the kids who listened to cool music—though this often tended to cancel each other out. He wound up spending a lot of time alone, listening to music nobody else would, and teaching himself how to play all the instruments he could. When nobody was in the house he would play songs of his own invention into the microphone connected to his father's tape deck. Ten-minute arrhythmic dirges and ecstatic fantasias for flute, guitar, mandolin, glockenspiel, and buzzing egg timer, with echo and feedback effects and the ambient sound of running bathtub water and birds chirping outside. When he was in his mid-teens, using scraps he'd bought from Heathkit, Dynakit, and stores that sold used hi-fi equipment, he built a four-track recording console and was able to accompany himself and overdub different parts of his songs.

In his junior year, Howie heard that four guys at a different high school were looking for a bassist. The name of their band was Common Decency: they played breezy three-minute pop tunes and produced a kind of jaunty, cosmic, bubblegum sound. The audition was set for a Sunday at noon at the keyboard player's house, and Howie only slept for one unpleasant hour the night before, rehearsing in his mind through the whole evening all the things that could go wrong. (He hadn't slept much the night before that either.) He worried that he'd forget to bring his bass, that he'd forget—if he remembered to bring it—how to tune it, that he'd forget how to play it, that he'd get lost and be three hours late, that he'd drive into another car and be five hours late, or that he'd plug in his bass and electrocute the guitarist.

In the end, Howie did show up on time, didn't kill anyone en route, remembered to bring the bass and how to tune and play it, and got the job on the spot. He knew he could play guitar and keyboard better than any of the others, but he also knew to keep this information to himself. He didn't want to make waves—he just wanted to be in a band and make music.

After nine months of occasional gigs and stabs at recording songs, the rest of Common Decency caught on to the fact that Howie knew a lot more than they did—he could not keep it hidden—and they began to resent him for it. Knowing the boot was coming, he did the right thing and quit first. After leaving Common Decency he latched on to a Hawkwindlike band called ProtoSpasm in his senior year, and the music was so simplistic and repetitive he found himself able to play bass and worry himself sick at the same time. He worried that the people he was playing for were all going to go deaf as a result of his bass lines, that he was going to hit a note a certain way and radiate ProtoSpasm's singer and kill him (which might not have been such a bad thing), that the other guys in the band were going to spike his Sprite with acid (they never did . . . they didn't want to waste any of it). It turned out he needn't have tortured himself about telling the others he was quitting—he was going to Yale the following year anyway, and nobody in ProtoSpasm could even spell Yale—because they let him go one day over the phone. "We need somebody with a harder edge and more vicious mentality," they told him, and Howie wished them good luck.

At Yale, after playing in a party band called the Jolly Poles based out of Quinnipiac University (which is how and where he met Melissa), he heard of a fine arts major named Drew Howell who was

97

putting together a progressive-rock band called the Dementia Peacocks. Drew was a big dude, six foot six and almost 300 pounds, and not much of it muscle; he wore thick black glasses and had shoulder-length black hair, and had a jaw as vast as his forehead. He was given to wearing expensive foppish suits, which was easy for him to do since his father was a senior partner at a very successful Boston law firm. Drew had not only inherited his father's Brahmin accent, he'd warped it to perfection.

"What we want to do," Drew told Howie in the former's dorm room (all decked out with framed Godard, Resnais, and Bergman movie posters) the first time they met, "is wed the sensibility of, say, a Darius Milhaud with the groove of, say, a Chuck Berry, to the total orgiastic debauchery of the Velvet Underground's 'Sister Ray,' to the otherworldliness of, say, a Roy Orbison, to the anarchic savagery of the Stooges."

"Okay," Howie said, taking notes on the small memo he'd brought with him. "Got it."

"And we could throw some dying humpback whale in there, too."

Drew Howell was the singer/songwriter of the group, even though he could only play as many—or as few—chords on the guitar as Elvis Presley. There was another guitarist, a drummer, and two keyboardists (one of them played piano and electric piano, the other played a Hammond organ; in those days, synthesizers were not so easy to get: they were unwieldy, complicated, expensive, and broke a lot—for professionals only). Howie told Drew that he, too, was into prog rock, but for every band's name that he threw out there (King Crimson, Soft Machine, Van der Graaf Generator) to show he knew what he was talking about, Drew responded with a much more obscure one (Premiata Forneria Marconi, Henry Cow, Gong). Even the Dementia Peacocks' drummer, Drew told Howie, was into bands so esoteric you could not find them in your local record store, bands like Magma and Curved Air. "If you hear it on the radio," Drew said, "we won't like it. Unless maybe if it's a jingle for SpaghettiOs or Roto-Rooter."

For that first meeting, it was just Drew and Howie, the latter clad in jeans and a blue polo shirt, the former wearing a fuchsia Thomas Pink shirt, a purple pinstripe suit with comically wide lapels, and bespoke boots made on Jermyn Street in London. Drew chain-smoked Gauloises and Howie did his best to pretend he didn't mind the black Turkish cloud engulfing him. Drew played a cassette of a song the Dementia Peacocks had recorded: the song was called "Green" and it was, for the most part, e. e. cummings's poem "All in green went my love riding" set to music . . . or something approaching music. The song was over eighteen minutes long.

"For our very first effort," Drew said, "we're going to record an album-side-length song for every color of the rainbow. We're thinking of calling it *In a Rainbow* or, better yet, *Roy G. Biv's Blues,* and it's going to make *Atom Heart Mother* look like . . ." He couldn't think of anything, so he lit a new cigarette with what was left of the dying old one and resumed. "'Green' is the first tune we've worked on."

"And, uh, all the songs are going to be eighteen minutes?"

"Do you have a problem with that?"

Howie shook his head but wasn't sure Drew could even see it behind the smoke, which was so thick it was as if they were sitting in two separate rooms. This wasn't necessarily a bad thing, for all during the "interview," Drew was fondling his crotch with his non-cigarette-bearing hand. (Howie eventually realized, with great relief, that Drew was sneaking glances at Anna Karina and Brigitte Bardot in the movie posters directly over Howie's head.)

Howie quickly worked it out: seven colors of the rainbow . . . eighteen minutes each . . . that's a first album—a *triple* album no less—lasting a 126 minutes! And then he realized that it would be a *quadruple* album with one completely empty side. It would be like Johnny Winter's infamous three-side album but times two. Or three.

99

"'Indigo,'" Drew answered when Howie brought this problem to his attention, "would be two sides long. It's 'Indigo, Parts One and Two.'"

Howie jotted that down in his memo pad, too.

He had brought along his own cassette that night. On the tape were examples of his work with the bands he'd played with (Drew had heard of Common Decency and had even seen them play in Wallingford once) and some of his own compositions, the pulsing, seven-minute, deeply textured songs he'd recorded alone in his parents' home. Howie watched Drew while he listened and couldn't tell whether he approved or not, and the butterflies in his stomach soon turned into hornets. What little beat there was, Drew wasn't even keeping with his feet.

After the tape ended, Drew leaned back in his chair, took a fatal drag off a Gauloise, and, still caressing himself, said: "Well, this is all fine, dandy, peachy, and keen, but what we're looking for is not just a bassist but someone who can play a mélange, a pastiche if you will, of instruments. Strings, woodwinds, horns, keyboards. Someone with a vast knowledge and appreciation of all forms of music, who can read music and fill in our gaps, which it pains me to confess are not inconsiderable. You can play bass . . . *fine*. So can twenty people in this dorm. So can my hamster. But can you also play violin? Contrabassoon? Can you play the viola da gamba and the vibraphone and trombone and, if need be, the hurdy-gurdy? That's what we're looking for. You know, King Crimson has this chap Ian McDonald who can play about a zillion instruments, and Frank Zappa has this cat Ian Underwood who plays piano and sax and any woodwind you were to shove in his mouth. We're looking for our own Ian, too—that's what we want."

That was when Howie knew he had the job. He was just the Ian they were looking for.

*

100

On green plastic chairs, Danny and Joey Junior sit a seat apart in the waiting room of Hicksville Cardio & Pulmonary, struggling to make conversation. Danny leans forward with his hands clasped, and Little Joey, who decided to tag along after all, slumps back in his chair as though he'd been born with a latex spine. In front of them, medical personnel and receptionists loaf in and out of the two hallways leading into the clinic. Hicksville Cardio & Pulmonary, managed by Doctors Ford and Fitzroy and located at the northern end of Cypress Avenue, takes up half of the third floor of a building solely devoted to the medical arts. Podiatry and Urology are on the first floor; Gynecology, Renal, and Gastrointestinal are on the second; Ear, Nose, and Throat and Neurology are one floor up at the top.

Somewhere back there, beyond the doors and hallways, in the guts of the building beyond the view of Danny and Joey Junior, Joey Mazz the Elder is undergoing a stress test.

"So what happened to you hooking up with your buddies?" Danny asks in a whisper. There are eight other people sitting around them, most of them reading glossy brochures about healthy hearts and lungs.

"What buddies?" Little Joey says.

"The guys you said you were going to hook up with?"

"Oh, yeah. I'll just hang out with 'em later."

So maybe there were no guys, Danny thinks. *Maybe Little Joey purposely showed up at Gentle Giant and then tagged along to keep an eye on his pops.*

"So what do they do back there?" the kid asks Danny.

Danny wants to say something like "The hell if I know!" but he assumes he might be dealing with a worried son so he says, "They're just going to check him every which way they can to make sure he gets healthy."

101

Joey Junior nods and leans back. Danny sees he has a few tats, too; some tribal designs in black on his wrists and a gothic cross on the left side of his neck. And probably other junk all over his arms and legs.

Has Joey written a will? Danny wonders. It probably never dawned on him to do such a thing since it probably never dawned on him that one day he might die. John Bonham, Keith Moon . . . neither of them made it to thirty-three. Maybe Danny should yank his drummer by the hair, the same way Joey once yanked his son's, and say: *What the fuck makes you think you're immortal? You're already on thirty years' borrowed time!* But Angie . . . maybe she brought up the matter of a will, and maybe he took care of it. Three kids, a small, decaying house, a wife, two cars, dozens of drums . . . and several records that never got close to Gold or even Bronze. *If he hasn't written a will,* Danny thinks, *I'll talk to Angie and recommend Jessica's cradle-to-grave lawyer-cousin Ernie in Great Neck.*

Or maybe he shouldn't bring it up with her. Curly-black-haired, taut, and only about five foot three, Angie is as volatile as Joey is mellow. If Danny were to ask her if Joey has made his will, she'd yell: "WHY?! WHO SAYS HE'S GONNA FUCKIN' DIE?!" The cross she's worn around her neck every day for the last twenty years looks like four razor blades conjoined and ready to slice. It had fallen upon him, of course, to call her from Portland and tell her that Joey had had a heart attack. He was expecting (and hoping for) shocked silence on her end, or maybe a phone dropping to the kitchen floor, but instead she yelled so loud he had to pull the phone away from his ear. "FUUUUUUUUUUUCK!" she screeched. And then she screeched it three more times.

"So when's the last time *you* had a checkup?" Danny asks Joey Junior.

"I can't even remember."

"Maybe you should take care of that."

"Why? You wouldn't have a doctor tell you something's wrong with you unless you go to a doctor. Like, I never had one cavity until a dentist told me I had six of 'em."

Danny stands up, paces around the waiting room, picks up a three-page brochure about congestive heart disease, and sits back down. The elevator doors open and an elderly couple inches out, the man needing both a walker and his wife's elbow to move half a mile per hour. The old gent looks as though he's already had ten heart attacks and is coming here to have his eleventh.

Danny sits back down and Joey Junior asks him if he's excited about Lily having a baby, and for the second time Danny has to tell him it's not Lily, it's Emily.

"Lily is the oldest, right?" Junior asks.

"No, Emily is!" It's difficult not to snap at this kid. "Lily is only fifteen, Joey."

"Nah. Lily is the oldest. She's nineteen."

Is he possibly right? Danny had screwed up the directions getting here and they were ten minutes late, although it didn't matter: like any good doctors' office, they still made Joey wait half an hour. Danny was sure he was going to 3010 Crescent Avenue, but after finding there was no such place, he remembered it was 1030 Cypress Avenue. But no, Emily is the oldest, the pregnant one, and Lily is the youngest and is hopefully not pregnant.

Little Joey takes out a pack of Marlboros and starts to light one up with a Zippo Mötley Crüe lighter.

Danny grabs his arm before he can light up and says: "Hey! You can't do that here!"

The kid says, "Oh, yeah," and tells Danny he's going outside to smoke and will be back up in ten minutes.

Forty minutes ago Danny felt his heart sink when Dr. Ford came out, introduced himself, shook Joey Senior's hand, and took him back inside the clinic.

"You wanna come, bro?" Joey asked him before he went in.

Danny looked at Dr. Ford, then back at Joey, and said, "You're on your own now, pal."

(The last time he'd felt something close to this, Danny was standing with Jessica and watching Emily walk inside the school building for her very first day of kindergarten. Fourteen years ago. It was a unique combination of apprehension, pride, guilt, and rottenness.)

Joey brought with him a hodgepodge of workout gear today: Angie's purple Juicy Couture sweat socks and headband that she used for Pilates, Joey Junior's short gray sweatpants from Bay City High School, a clunky pair of old red Air Jordans, and a black-and-purple Neil Peart/Rush T-shirt. *(Does Neil Peart,* Danny asked himself, *wear a Joey Mazz/Furious Overfalls T to* his *stress test?)* Was Joey on a treadmill now, huffing and puffing and sweating while some machine was accurately counting all the Twinkies he'd ever eaten? Danny, leaning back and wishing he were outside smoking his One Daily Cigarette, wonders why he has to be here today. The old question, going back to Genesis: *Why me? Why am I stuck being my bro's keeper?* Joey Junior could have taken his old man in, or Angie should have sucked it up and brought him. *Why am I the one who has to call and cancel all the gigs and speak to all those schlemiels personally? Jules could do it. Or Jules could do some of it, Howie could do some of it, and I could do some of it. But it's always me.* It all, he knows, comes down to this: *It's because I started the band.* The Furious Overfalls was his creation. And because he writes the lyrics and cowrites the music. It's that simple. But why—just because he can put together a few lyrics, does that make him the band's daddy? It makes no sense. *Just because I can rhyme dirt and flirt and hurt and skirt and then sing it . . . why does that make me any better at arranging our schedule than Howie or Jules?* Why does that mean he has to make sure Jules doesn't knock up any more women than he already has; why does that mean he's the one—and not Jules or Howie or Joey's wife or kids or brother or

104

sister—who has to bring Joey into this place to have his circulatory system Martinized, or whatever they're doing to him back there? You put together a few words and chords and so that makes you responsible for everyone in your orbit? It doesn't make any sense.

A year from now, he thinks, *they'll all be on their own.* If Joey dies of a heart attack, if Jules dies of drug-resistant clap, if Howie manages to run himself over in a car . . . Danny will read about it in the papers or find out about it on the news.

When do I tell them? he thinks. Before *the next tour or after it?* Or should he just drop it on them backstage one night, or in a hotel coffee shop?

Jules, he'll begin, *there's something I have to tell you. This isn't easy for me to do, but it's been a long time coming . . .*

He goes over to the waiting room's window, which looks out over the parking lot, and stands close to the elderly couple, now seated, who just came in. The old man is completely bald and liver spots tar the whole dome of his head. Danny looks out and sees Joey Junior on his cell phone, snuffing out one cigarette with his boot and lighting another.

Danny knows that it will wind up being him to whom Dr. Ford tells the results. Angie wouldn't want to hear it from the doctor, and neither would Joey Senior. *He has six months to live,* he'll have to tell Angie, or else, *He's going to be fine—all he has to do his change his diet.* Maybe Dr. Ford or Dr. Fitzroy will have to open him up and remove a Cheeto from the aorta, and everything will be hunky-dory. Danny hopes so. As dumb as he is, it's tough to imagine the band without Joey. *Maybe, just maybe,* Danny thinks, *after this whole ordeal is over, we'll let him take a drum solo. Two minutes, tops. Or you know what? We'll finally cover "Theme for an Imaginary Western."* Or, better yet, they'll cover it and Joey can do a drum solo within the song. Kill two birds with one stone.

He sits back down.

Best case scenario, he figures, TFO will only be out of commission for a few months and then can get back on the road in February. He, Jules, and Howie will just have to make sure that Joey sticks to whatever ruthless regimen Ford and Fitzroy impose on him. No Cheetos, no Oreos topped with Reddi-wip, no Snickers or chili fries. *You want your drum solo, Joey? Well, no solo until you finish your vegetables!*

The elevator doors open and so does one of the doors leading back into the clinic.

Joey Junior comes in, his cheeks flushed by the November cold, and Joey Senior comes out, looking haggard but alive and happy.

"Whew, that was rough," he says to his front man and son as he buttons up his leather jacket. "If that didn't kill me, nothin' will. So let's go get a burger or something, okay?"

*

The Dementia Peacocks' "mission," even though Drew Howell and the others never used that word (they referred to their plan as a "manifesto," which they issued via mimeograph machines and tacked onto bulletin boards), was to lull listeners into a mild comatose state, but make them have vivid, horrible nightmares while they were out. "Our Anti-Muzik," the manifesto stated, "is The Four A's: Atonality, Anti-Rhythm, and Absolute Amorality."

The band met four times a week at Yale's Albert Sprague Memorial Hall to talk, jam, fine-tune, rework, and argue incessantly. Their studio space was a bare, windowless room, the uncarpeted floor was splintery and dull, and the acoustics were nonexistent. In the first months, Howie did as he was told and went along with whoever happened to be the loudest or whiniest that day. Sometimes he sat in a corner, his bass, violin, or alto sax on his lap, and waited for the storm to blow over. The arguments were over ridiculous things and usually strayed from the matter at hand: music. A four-note lick that Steve, the lead guitarist, would introduce twelve minutes into "Indigo, Part 1" would lead to Drew stopping the song on a dime and to a heated discussion about how that riff was "totally purloined" from an Amon Düül II tune ("I mean, are we going to have to send our royalties to *Germany* now, Stevie?" Drew asked him). That, in turn, would lead to a discussion about Tangerine Dream, which would lead to an argument over Arnold Schoenberg, which would lead to a tussle about degenerate art and the Bauhaus, and three minutes later Drew was yelling something about Brion Gysin to Steve, who was yelling something about André Breton to the drummer, who was yelling something about Vorticism to Drew and Stevie, while Howie just waited for everyone to calm down.

They'd break for fifteen minutes, huff and puff, smoke their Gauloises and Gitanes and Sobranies, and then pick up the song from where they'd left it, only to stop ten minutes later and hurl around the names Big Sid Catlett, Faron Young, Alban Berg, Arthur Rimbaud, Wassily Kandinsky, and Spike Jones.

"The Band Who Knew Too Much": This is what Howie, chagrined and exhausted after every rehearsal, called the Dementia Peacocks when he recapped each day's events to his new girlfriend, Melissa.

They changed the band's name to anaesthesia and all graduated the same year. Howie and Melissa moved into a two-story house together, along with five other people their age, on the woodsy outskirts of Fairview, ten minutes from New Haven. The band stayed together; at first, the infighting got more intense (and sometimes shockingly personal, Steve having stolen Drew's girlfriend and then Drew having won her back), and then it settled down. They played gigs as far north as Williamsport, Massachusetts, and as far south as Raleigh, North Carolina (where someone threw an unhusked ear of corn into Howie's chin). Howie did freelance proofreading for Yale in his spare time to make ends meet while his bandmates, to do the same, just took their parents' money.

107

Nobody in the band and nobody in the Fairview house, including Melissa, knew what was beginning to form inside Howie's mind. He kept it hidden too well. He'd leave the house and not take three steps before he realized he'd left a burner on the stove turned on, then go back into the house to check the stove (where he realized that he hadn't left a burner on). Then he'd go back out and be absolutely sure that when he'd checked to see if he'd left a burner on he had turned a burner on. So he'd go back in and check it again.

Or he'd clean the house's two toilets and tubs three times a day.

Everyone else in the house was too grateful to have clean toilets and baths to realize what was happening.

Using his father's tenuous entertainment connections, Drew Howell was able to send demo tapes to Atlantic, Columbia, Elektra, A&M, and other record companies and get them into the right hands. This was when Howie, fearing the inevitable, spoke his peace for the first time.

"I'm not so sure," he suggested, "we should send this to them. Our songs are good but they're too long and . . . ambitious. Why don't we work on some shorter, crisper songs just to get them interested?"

Drew looked at Steve and they both rolled their eyes, then Drew looked back at Howie and said: "I wasn't aware that anybody had asked you."

The record companies sent back the demos without even a form letter. Nobody was interested.

Howie did not say, "I told you so."

anaesthesia was hamstrung, they all felt, because they didn't have access to a mellotron or sophisticated synthesizer, something that could emulate other instruments and the sounds of the distant galaxies. That is what they need, Drew and Steve were dead certain, to make it.

On a windy autumn day, Howie drove to practice at Drew's apartment in New Haven in a rented U-Haul. Out of the back he dragged a homemade synthesizer, and after that a homemade mellotron, both made up of bits and pieces of discarded scrap that he'd bought, found, or bargained for. When Drew saw them amidst the eddying autumn leaves, he shook his large square head with disbelief, and Howie could tell that from that point on, nobody in the band was going to take him for granted anymore.

anaesthesia stuck together for another year and a half. They developed a cult following in a few pockets in the Northeast, but not one person in that cult worked for a record company that wanted to sign them. They made more demos and sent them out to record companies, this time scaling down their ambition, aspirations, and song lengths. They even performed and recorded some songs that people who couldn't dance could sort of dance to. But it was to no avail. They were too much prog and not enough rock. Drew sent the demos to record companies in West Germany, England, and Iceland but never heard from anyone (which was ironic since one of the songs on the demo was called "Nary a Peep.") The drummer quit the band and went to law school, one of the two keyboardists stole Steve and Drew's girlfriend and absconded with her to a dream home in New Zealand, and then the bickering finally tore the remnants of the band apart. There was never any official breakup, and one day Howie found himself waiting alone in a rented New Haven studio for everybody else to come and rehearse. He waited for six hours. No one ever showed up, no one called, and that was it: anaesthesia was no more.

Music was in Howie's blood, and playing in front of an audience was the greatest thrill of his life, so he was anxious to join another band—any band at all. One day this guitarist who'd played in the Stoning Rolls, and had appeared on a few eclectic bills with anaesthesia in New Jersey and Westchester, called him up and told him he'd just hooked up with a new band and that they needed a bassist. The singer/songwriter lived in Pleasant Valley, Long Island, and was from the Tarnished Angels; the drummer, Mickey Sanford, had played in a lot of bands, including Avalanche and the Mud Lushes. They didn't have a name yet and were only charting out their direction but were aiming for something earthy, gutsy, and gritty.

"You wanna grab your ax and try out?" he asked Howie.

Howie, barely able to contain his enthusiasm, said yes, he definitely did want to. The guitarist told him where to go and when, and Howie, already worrying he'd forget his bass and ram two school buses off the Throgs Neck Bridge on the way out, said he'd be there.

"And one thing, Howie," Jules Rose said. "Leave your mellotron at home. We're not into that artsy shit, okay?"

Six
Here for the Music

His silver, black, and white imitation python pants tucked into his magenta ray-skin boots, Jules hands his round-trip ticket to the conductor. The conductor checks him out with one raised white eyebrow, punches his ticket, and places the stub into the slot on the seat in front of him. There aren't too many passengers tonight on the LIRR: it's coming on seven o'clock on the evening before Thanksgiving.

Jules has treated himself to a day of beauty and now it's time for a night of booty. In addition to the new boots and pants, he's got on a black brocade shirt with faux-pearl snaps and a belted burgundy leather coat that he bought in Germany during Stuttgart Rock und BluesFest 2010. Earlier today at a clinic in Valley Stream, Jules endured six hits of Botox: one shot each right over his eyebrows, two to the upper forehead, and, just for the hell of it, since he was already there anyway, one around both corners of his mouth. After that he drove to Hempstead and lay in a tanning box for an hour. He practically had the Hempstead Tannery all to himself . . . it was just him and Olga, the husky Russian woman in charge. Olga was about six foot two and fifteen pounds overweight, all her overflowing girth stuffed into a white dress and white pantyhose as if she were a real nurse and not a mere tannerizer. Jules flirted with her and hoped that she wouldn't fall for it. In addition to her chintzy bottle-blond hair and runaway black roots, she had the kinds of moles, on her neck and cheeks, with hairs coming out. Jules does a fake bake around ten times a year; it turns his normally buttery skin a lush golden brown, and though he does not glow in the dark, if you saw him in the daylight you'd assume he would.

After that he drove to Baldwin and got a Brazilian boykini wax, then drove home to his house on Love Street in Kingstown, cracked open a box of Revlon and dyed his hair "very light ash blonde" to match his skin, played guitar for a few hours with the TV on, and napped.

"Deer Park!" the train's PA system announces. "Deer Park! Wyandanch is next!"

Jules hasn't spent any quality time in the city in over a year. Tonight he's going downtown.

Jimi Hendrix's "Third Stone from the Sun" still echoing in his ears from an earlier listen today, Jules reflects on all the stops on this line of the LIRR, and all the women he's known along the way. The train originated in Greenport out on the North Fork. Jules got laid in Greenport about twenty years ago. He was heading back out to the Island one afternoon, having just bought a new Telecaster at Manny's on Forty-eighth Street, when he struck up a conversation with a MILFy brunette in her late forties who'd heard of the Furious Overfalls and seen them play a few times. ("Wow," she told Jules, "I really used to like you guys." "Hey," he said to her, "I *still* like us.") He wound up staying on the train past his stop and going out to Greenport, where she lived. She became known as the Purple Fishnet Chick because every time he saw her afterward she always made sure to wear purple fishnet pantyhose. (She still does—Jules spent a sweaty hour with her only five weeks ago.)

The stop after Greenport is Southold. The Chipmunk Pillow Girl. Over twenty years ago he bumped a woman in Southold . . . She had chipmunk cheeks and lived with her mother in a small ranch house. She and Jules had to be very quiet, she advised him, and then she proceeded to muffle her roof-raising shrieks with a pillow. After Southold comes Mattituck. Mattifuck? Check. *Two* different girls in Mattituck, as a matter of fact. Riverhead? Check. A few times, once in the bushes near a pond in the middle of the afternoon. One time, just when TFO was really getting going, he even did it in the train station bathroom there. He and the girl were both zonked on Quaaludes and, to be honest, he wasn't entirely sure he'd ever really stuck it all the way in. (He called her Seven-

Fourteen, because of the number on the 'Ludes, and because, after they were done, he put her on the 7:14 train back home.) And there was another one, the Chocolate Chip Girl. She either had one bipartite black mole that looked just like a Chips Ahoy! chocolate chip under her left tit, or it was two different chocolate chips separated only by a pore. Once he saw that—or those—he almost couldn't go through with it.

The train pulls out of the Wyandanch Station. Nobody gets off, nobody gets on. Except for some jowly guy in a rumpled suit reading the *Daily News* in the rear of his car, Jules is alone now. Next stop: Pinelawn.

Pinelawn? Check. The Islander Goal Chick lived in Pinelawn.

From Riverhead to Penn Station, he reflects, he had slept with a woman at every stop. Farmingdale? Check. Bethpage? Check. (The one in Bethpage was even named Beth . . . beat that! That was almost as good as doing someone from Roslyn named Roslyn.) Hicksville? Definitely. Dicksville. Westbury and Carle Place and all the way into Manhattan. Ronkonkoma? Check. Wait . . . maybe not. He tucks his pants further into his boots and thinks about it. He cannot remember ever getting laid in Ronkonkoma. Is that possible? The train pulls into, and then pulls out of, Pinelawn, and nothing comes to him. Ronkonkoma is the one notch in his belt that he hasn't yet punched, the missing jewel in the LIRR crown.

It's dark and chilly and Jules can barely see any houses, trees, or streetlights, but that's mainly due to the webbing of grime scrawled across the window—it looks as though he's going through a tunnel. Jules thinks of other LIRR stops on other lines. Copiague. Check. Wantagh. Maybe not. Babylon. Definitely. Babe-lon. (After TFO released "Babylon Boogie" it was like an E-ZPass right into any Babylon woman's crotch that he wanted, and there were a lot of those.) Assapequa Park. Balledwin. Fuckville Centre. Check, check, check. Lindenhurst? Yes, definitely Lindenhurst . . . but who was that? Was there a Lynne or a Linda in Lindenhurst? He tries to think back but he cannot picture a face or a body or hear a voice. And then, just as the train pulls into Farmingdale, he realizes: *Oh yeah! It was Angela Dukakis!* Joey's wife! (Before she was his wife.) *How could I forget?* Angie was great, too, and she actually knew what she was doing; knew what worked on men and loved to give it to them—she even walked around with a cock ring in her crowded Fiorucci handbag. Nice tight little body, nice tight everything, just like a clamp. Lucky Joey. Although after three kids . . .

Joey's test was supposed to be soon, Jules knows. *Was it last week? Or is it next week?*

What if, he wonders, *Joey has another heart attack the next time we take to the road? And dies?* It could happen onstage or in a hotel or at a diner . . . what if he buys the farm? Would Jules tell Danny, *Hey, we can always get Mickey Sanford back.* That would be the obvious move, but who knew where Mickey was? There was a good chance he was dead, too, killed decades ago by the drug dealers he'd crossed. But Jules knows he's still out there. Danny, Howie, and Joey feel the same way: rarely did a show go off, no matter where it was, that one or more of them didn't *swear* they could see Mickey somewhere out there in the crowd.

And there was this: If Joey died, would Danny leave the band and retire? And if that happened, Jules wonders, *then what?* Then it would just be him and Howie. That's not a band, that's a conversation.

No way, he thinks, *Danny'd ever do that to us.*

Jules undoes his belt and unsnaps his python pants. Easier to breathe that way. When they pull into the city, he'll just have to remember to snap everything back. He only weighs ten pounds more than he did thirty years ago but he's just not as tight as he used to be. Cottage-cheesy love handles in the back, a slightly poochy tummy. But he's still in good shape. Look at Danny . . . he has to go to a gym and sweat and eat healthy food to keep trim. These python

114

pants are a size thirty-four . . . but maybe he should get another pair, size thirty-six. It might be time.

The conductor, yawning, more asleep than awake, shuffles through the train.

"Is there a bathroom on this car?" Jules asks him. His bladder is starting to burst and he realized a moment ago he forgot to take his nightly Flomax.

"Yeah," the conductor says. "But use the one on the next car. This one's a federal disaster area. And there's no smoking."

Jules puts out his cigarette, goes to the bathroom in the next car, returns to his seat, and takes out his wallet. He's got one hit of Blue Magic and three ribbed, disease-proof, baby-proof, death-proof condoms. The Viagra might be a bit sketchy, though; too embarrassed to keep getting it from his doctor and local CVS, he ordered this batch online. It's a lot cheaper that way, too. It only took two weeks to arrive, but when it did, Jules saw that it had been sent from Mumbai, India. And it wasn't really Viagra, despite what the site had claimed. It was some generic form he'd never heard of, and it wasn't the same color blue. Viagrex or Viagrola or Vinaigrette—something like that.

At the next stop the rumpled suit with the *Daily News* gets off the train, and Jules has the car to himself the rest of the way into Manhattan.

*

Instead of telling the taxi driver to take him directly to Vagrants on the corner of Bleecker Street and West Broadway, Jules told him to drop him off outside Matt Umanov Guitars on Bleecker and Morton. It was at Umanov's where he bought his first National guitar. (That beautiful hunk of reverberating steel was what sealed the deal between him and Danny Ault, and Jules still has it. When he played the slide part of the Stones' "No Expectations"—that was when

115

Danny realized Jules could play lights out.) Jules gets out of the cab and buttons up his leather coat to the top button. He needs to pee again even though he went at Penn Station. Umanov's is still open but some dude with spiky white hair is pulling the gate down.

"You're closing now?" Jules asks the guy.

The guy turns around for a second and says, "Yeah. I gotta get my ass home."

Spiky White Hair is in his forties and is too young to have been working here when Jules began coming to Umanov's regularly, which was only a few weeks after he moved to Manhattan from Green River. He was working at Big Bertie's Stereo Outlet on Canal Street, on the border of Chinatown. He was a pretty good salesman. "Whatever isn't moving at all, you gotta move!"—those were Bertie's instructions to him, and Jules could've sold a pair of speakers missing their woofers, tweeters, and midranges to a deaf person, he was so convincing. The more he sold, the higher the commission, and the more he made at Big Bertie's, the more guitars, amps, and accessories he could buy. He lived in a large studio on Sullivan Street then, between West Third Street and Bleecker, above Googie's Bar, his favorite pickup and burger spot. He could walk to work; he could walk to Vagrants, Kenny's Castaways, The Bitter End, and to the Academy of Music on Fourteenth Street; he could walk to all his el cheapo food spots on MacDougal Street; and, on a good day, he could walk up to Forty-eighth Street to Manny's, Sam Ash, Terminal Music, and all the other shops. When the first (and then the second) Furious Overfalls album came out, Jules, still living downtown, couldn't walk past Umanov's without a sales guy rushing out and offering him strings, picks and capos. Or they'd come out and say something like, "Jules, you gotta check out the Rickenbacker that just came in." It was sweet, it was a sign that he'd arrived, but it got so tiring that sometimes he walked on the other side of the street or avoided that section of Bleecker entirely.

Jules looks in the unlit window as Spiky White Hair locks the gate. There are two Fenders hanging in the window, as well as an old cherry sunburst Gibson B-45 12-string with a trapeze tailpiece. Danny would love this . . . and Christmas is only a few weeks away. It could cost anywhere from a grand and a half to three thousand, the way Jules figures it.

"Wow!" he says, pointing to the 12-string. "How much would that Gibson set me back?"

There's no reply, and Jules looks around to see that Spiky White Hair has already taken off for the holidays.

Jules, Danny, Howie, and Joey never exchange presents anyway.

The Furious Overfalls played their first gigs at Vagrants, and you could've gotten in to see them for a dollar. Mickey Sanford was still the drummer then. At Vagrants they give you an hour: you can play one song that lasts sixty minutes or sixty songs that are a minute each—if you're still playing after sixty minutes, it doesn't matter if you're Vladimir Horowitz, Louis Armstrong, or Joe Blow, whoever happens to be the sound guy that evening pulls the plug. It was at Vagrants where Velcro Pravda (née Lenny Sussbaum), their first manager, discovered them, and it was at Vagrants where Joey Mazz played for the first time with the band.

Jules walks toward Vagrants, but purposely takes a roundabout way and thinks about his finest Vagrants memory, the night right after "One More Time" made it to number one on the *Billboard* chart (it fell to number four the following week and never looked back), when he found himself talking to and playing with Keith Richards (not that Jules understood much of what he was saying) and Ian Stewart at three in the morning. They did eight songs together, and after the first two, Jules wasn't even bothering to wipe the grin off his face. Already wobbly to begin with, between songs he chugged off the same small bottle of Jack Daniel's that Keith did. (He would've gladly ingested whatever combination of drugs that

Keith had that night, but he didn't need to, he was so buzzed.) Jules took a great four-minute lead on Chuck Berry's "Carol" and he could tell Keef appreciated it. They were wailing on a jacked-up, funked-out version of Robert Johnson's "32-20 Blues" when, sure enough, the sound guy pulled the plug. They had gone over sixty minutes.

That was actually the second of three times Jules got to see Keith close-up, and on the wall above the grand old brass cash register at the Vagrants bar, amidst all the other photos, is the old photo of Jules, Keith, and Stu jamming (Howie had tagged along with Jules that night and played bass), the eerie mercury-like ring of silver light behind Jules's hair and his sublime smile making him look as though he'd been canonized earlier that day.

On Sullivan Street, Jules walks past his old apartment building and where Googie's Bar once stood. It's a prefab Irish pub now, and the record store that was next to it is a taco joint. Vagrants is only a few blocks away. There will be chicks at the bar tonight, he knows, and chicks out on the holidays are out for one reason and one reason only.

If Rhonda, he thinks, *and I had ever gotten married, I'd probably be home right now. With her. And some kids.* How boring is that?

One evening, around two weeks after *Come and Git It* came out, Jules was out going bar to bar—it might have been a Thanksgiving Eve or Christmas Eve then, too—and he was just about to give up when he met a slinky, long-necked, short-haired blonde at the bar at Googie's. She lived on East Seventh Street, not far from McSorely's bar, and, after dry-humping for ten minutes on a stoop outside, they went to her place at around one in the morning. He left an hour and a half later and, even though he was plum fuckered, he decided to go back to Googie's for a self-congratulatory nightcap. But he met another blonde, this one not slinky at all but with a bigger chest and thicker lips, and he wound

118

up at her place at about three-thirty. Unlike the previous woman, this one had the Silver: he knew at once from the sparkle in her eyes that she'd be great in the sack. (He was right.) It turned out she lived immediately next-door to the first blonde, the slinky, long-necked, short-haired one, and when Jules was sneaking out at six the next morning, Slinky opened her door and caught him holding his boots, shirt, and coat.

"Ya got me," he said to her, putting his hands up.

He made it with chicks in the bathroom at Googie's, too, which was no mean feat considering how small it was. He couldn't even remember all the women he'd done in there. At first, there was Googie's Bathroom Chick 1, then Googie's Bathroom Chick 2, but after seven or eight he lost track. Number 5 made for the best story: her pudgy, bald stockbroker boyfriend, who was buying Jules drinks that night and treating him to a lot of good coke, had no idea what had just gone down.

Jules lights a cigarette, turns on to Bleecker Street, and sees the neon red lights of Vagrants flickering on the corner. This part of Bleecker is more crowded and alive than Sullivan Street, but it's still pretty quiet. The last few years, he had spent Thanksgiving with the remnants of his family, who never left Green River. His younger brother was married and had two kids; his younger sister was divorced with three. He usually alternated holidays with their two families, though sometimes he was able to shuttle between them on the same night. But tonight he wanted a break from that. Holidays and family, he'd often thought, are for suckers.

Danny was probably home with his wife and kids, one of whom was going to have a baby. *Danny, a grandfather—ha!* Howie was with Drippy Melissa, his boring wife with the birthmark near her ear, and their nerdy kid, and Joey was with his family. (And since when do rockers have nerdy kids? They were supposed to look like Liv Tyler and Jade Jagger, or become juvenile delinquents. Howie and Melissa's kid looks like Bill Gates if he'd been born a she.) It

119

just didn't sound like fun. Although Jules does like Joey's oldest kid, even if he is a handful of trouble. (Joey Junior is Jules's pot connection.) And who knows what Rhonda Wentworth would look like now, twenty years after the fact and with a kid or two. Tonight Jules is going to either score some NP (New Pussy) or scare up some OP (Old Pussy, such as Islander Goal Chick or the More Parks Sausages Mom girl or Jennifer Jupiter or the B. B. King With Tits chick or . . .) or maybe ring up an old buddy, like Ike Kates, who once almost played keyboards and sang vocals in a band Jules was going to start up, or Sweet Lou, or Big Bob, and then score some NP or OP with them. Sweet Lou still lives in the West Village, on Grove Street; even though he'd gotten married and had kids and quit the music business, he still lives in the same second-floor, two-bedroom apartment that he lived in thirty years ago.

Jules walks past a pizza place that's open but empty, a poster store that's closing, then a dark sushi joint that may or may not be open. A few of these places were here decades ago, but so many of the places from back then are now long gone.

"Excuse me?" an extremely blond Scandinavian man says to Jules now, holding a map of New York City in one hand and his wife's hand in the other. "Can you help us?"

"Sure," Jules says.

"Can you tell me where is Gween Witch Willidge?"

Gween Witch Willidge. Greenwich Village.

"Uh, this is it," Jules says.

The man and the woman look at each other, then at the map, then back up at Jules.

"Here?" the man says, a five-pound Nikon dangling from his neck. He and his tall, equally blond wife are both dressed in teal from hat to shoe.

"Yep. You're looking at it."

Jules shrugs apologetically and walks on, leaving the teal Euro couple dumbfounded.

An overweight black guy, about thirty years old with a shaved head, sits on a stool outside Vagrants with a Styrofoam cup of coffee in his hand. He's wearing Timberland boots, blue jeans, and a cheap leather jacket, and doesn't look too happy about having to work tonight. The front door behind him is two inches ajar, and there's a sign indicating what groups are playing tonight and at what time. Some band called Banal Fissures is coming on in fifteen minutes.

"Hey," Jules says to the guy.

"Good evening." Leaden eyelids and a voice like Barry White on Valium. "Ten dollars."

Just to see if he can save his ten bucks, Jules tosses out a name. "Does Billy C. still work the bar? If he's on, tell him Jules Rose is out here."

"I'm not familiar with anybody by the name of Billy C. at this time."

"Stan Heyman still owns the place—I'm a buddy of his going way back."

With his eyes mostly closed, the bouncer tells Jules, "Stanley Heyman is indeed the proprietor of this esteemed establishment but is, concurrently with your question, vacationing on the sunny island of Anguilla, where I wish my overworked ass was, too."

Jules relents, forks over two fives, and gets his hand stamped. He puts out his cigarette as per the bouncer's instructions and goes in.

The place hasn't changed at all, not since the last time Jules set foot inside, which was four years ago, and not since the first time either. The same beer-and-pine smell, the same reek of cigarette smoke—even without any cigarette smoke—and everything cluttered, brown and black. The bar is up front and fifteen yards long, and the area around the bar is narrow and the floor is sticky. Past the bar the space opens up into a square room with black walls and wooden tables and chairs. This is where the bands play. There's

121

no stage and the acoustics have always been lousy. If the room is packed, eighty perspiring people can sit and watch.

Jules goes to the deserted near-end of the bar and orders a beer from a tall bartender with a Southern accent. There are about six other souls at the bar. The walls are covered with photos, most of them black and white, of bands and performers and famous people just dropping in to check out the scene. Here's Norman Mailer with his arm around Phil Spector's shoulders. Here's Walt Frazier yukking it up with Jerry Lee Lewis and Bill Clinton. A young and alive Joey Ramone with his arm around an alive John Gotti, who has his arm around a questionably awake Loulou de la Falaise.

At the far end of the bar two women in their twenties are talking to another bartender. Jules orders another beer and asks his bartender, "So Stan's away now, huh? Lucky stiff."

The bartender nods.

Two men and two women, all bearing instruments and gear, walk down the narrow passageway to get to the back. This is the next band up. Banal Fissures.

"My band played its very first gig here," Jules says, finishing his second beer, which is as flat as they always were here.

"A lot of bands have," the bartender says.

"You heard of the Furious Overfalls?"

"Hell, yeah. You were in them?!"

"I still am, guy."

"Yeah, I heard y'alls started here. That's cool."

Jules asks for another beer and this one's on the house. But the next one isn't. His bartender goes to the other end of the bar to talk to the other bartender, who's still with the two women. The four of them all turn to look at Jules and then return to their conversation, and Jules knows that he's telling them that one of the guys in TFO is here tonight. A minute later, the band begins warming up and a few more people come in and head toward the back.

"Hey, everybody," a woman says into the mike. There's a yelp of feedback but then it dies. "We're Banal Fissures and we'd like to thank you for coming here tonight."

Jules slowly walks to the back to check them out. They don't start just yet, there's some technical problem . . . the female lead singer is talking away from the mike to the bass player and lead guitarist. Jules feels the urge in his bladder again, and his contact lenses are so dry they feel like another pair of eyes glued to his own. He checks out the two chicks at the bar and sees one of them, the shorter one, looking at him. She's wearing jeans and a fuzzy yellow sweater; she's about five foot one and has reddish brown hair and bad skin. The other is two inches taller and four inches plumper.

Jules walks up to them.

"You here for the music?" he asks them. The classic line.

They look at each other and the smaller one says that they know somebody who knows somebody who knows the Fissures drummer, but neither of those somebodies has bothered to show up yet. Jules offers to buy their next round but only the plumper one, the one he's not interested in, takes him up on it, which is maybe how she got plump in the first place. The one he is interested in, he sees, has crooked teeth, but other than the acne, there are no visible freckles or moles or beauty marks. *A fourteen-minute girl,* Jules thinks.

"Okay," the lead singer says. "Now we're ready. Thanks."

The drummer counts down the song and then they begin. It's a loud but not deafening whoosh of thrashing monotony with a Robert Fripp–like lead guitar skirling through it. After a minute of intro, the singer starts. Whatever she's singing, the words don't rhyme, and she's profoundly anguished about something. *Some guy,* Jules thinks, *didn't just break this chick's heart—he took a blowtorch to her vocal cords, too.*

He heads to the bathroom, which is more graffiti than porcelain, and while taking a stammering on-again/off-again leak he looks in his coat pockets and realizes he didn't bring any drops for his

123

contact lenses. When he comes back out to the bar he sees, to his surprise, that the plumper girl has left and it's just him and Short Bad Skin. Banal Fissures go from one song to another, though sometimes the brief applause is the only indicator that a song has ended, and Jules is trying to make time. They have more drinks and she laughs at his jokes, but he's pretty sure he's not getting anywhere. She lives in Queens with four other people, is from Tucson, and babysits for a living. She doesn't have the Silver but she has sexy jewelry on, including an ankle bracelet, and raspberry-color nail polish with black tips. And hoop earrings, which are always promising: Chicks who care enough to put on hoop earrings will always go the extra yard for you. That's just a fact. They make sexier faces, too . . . the B. B King With Tits chick wore large hoops, and nobody made sexier faces than she did (when she was doing it, she sort of looked like B. B. King bending a note, hence the nickname).

Short Bad Skin asks him, "Is something wrong with your eyes?" and, blinking, he tells her there isn't. A few more people come in and, after another beer and another pee, Jules drops the Stones bomb on Short Bad Skin.

He nearly has to yell to be heard above the Banal Fissures racket.

"Yeah, so one time I was hanging around here and guess who walked in? Keith Richards! Nicest dude you've ever want to meet! Seriously . . . he could not have been nicer. A total mensch from the word go. And fifteen minutes later—it's about three in the morning—all of us plug in and do a set for an hour! We burned this place to the ground! We did 'Carol,' did 'Factory Girl,' and some old blues tunes, and we even did 'Midnight Rambler.' When it was done, he hugged me and told me he'd had a blast!"

(Jules doesn't mention that Keith's exact words were: "I had an absolute blast, James.")

"Really?!" she says, having to yell, too. "Wow!"

"Yeah! I couldn't believe it! I had been digging Keith since I was a kid and here I am with the number one record in the country and I'm jamming with my idol! I'll never forget—right before he left, we hug and I say to him: 'Keith, it didn't work out with Brian, it didn't work out with Mick Taylor . . . Hey, if it doesn't work out with Woody, you know where to find me.'"

Jules sees the bartender and signals him over, and asks him to bring the photo of him and Keith on the wall over the register. The guy says he'll go get it, and Jules continues. "I'm telling you, it was the high point of my life! Other people, it's them having babies or getting married, but this was it for me. Ah! Here we go!"

The bartender shows Jules and Short Bad Skin an old black-and-white photo in an aluminum frame. There's Keith, dressed to the nines, with his head cocked, his mouth open, and his eyes somehow zonked but riveted at the same time—his claret jacket alone must have cost two grand; there's Howie behind Keith, plucking his Fender in his usual workmanlike style, but, as always, standing perfectly still onstage; there's the drummer's blurry right hand banging the high hat that seems embedded in Howie's left shoulder.

But where's Jules? This is the photo—this is *the* photo—but there's no sign of Jules!

"Hey," Jules says, shaking his head. "What happened?" He sounds as though he's talking to a high-priced lawyer who'd guaranteed him he would not be found guilty but was.

"Stanley," the bartender explains, "had a lot of the photos cropped about two years ago. On this one, I think he wanted to get closer in on Keith, you know? Great pic though, dude."

"To be honest," Short Bad Skin says, "I'm not sure I even know who Keith Roberts *is*!"

*

125

Three minutes later, blinking his dry eyes crazily, Jules is walking down Bleecker, which is emptier, darker, and colder now, heading for Mamoun's on MacDougal Street for a falafel. He takes out his cell phone, sees that his battery power is low, and looks up Big Bob's number and calls. Big Bob was Rev's best friend and right-hand man and could raise hell with the best of them. He was a major-league pussy bandit: not once did he ever turn down any of Jules's rejects, no matter how skanky, psycho, or possibly diseased. Danny and Howie never approved of him, though, and, after a lot of discussion, he was let go from the road crew. That was after *Dead End Road* and "The Incident" near San Francisco, when the records weren't selling anymore and nobody was coming out to see them. The vote was split, two to two, but since Danny was one of the two wanting all the changes, that side won. Danny always wins anyway. It's as if his one vote counts for four.

"Hey, it's me," Bob's voice mail greeting begins. *"We're out of town right now but will be back on December first, so please leave a message."*

Jules is about to leave a message telling Big Bob that he's in town but sees the teal Norse couple again on the corner of Bleecker and Sullivan. The woman is looking up at a street sign and the man is still examining his map, trying to get their bearings. Both of them look as if they've flown to the wrong hemisphere.

Jules hangs up without leaving a message and exchanges brief, confused eye contact with the man with the map. A moment later he makes a right on MacDougal and, the cell's battery light flashing red now, he calls Sweet Lou.

"Yo, Sweet Lou!"

"Jules? Jules Rose? Dude! Long time, no conversate."

He sounds like he may have just woken up.

"I'm solo and on your turf. About to get a falafel and a baklava," Jules says.

"Mamoun's?"

"Damn straight. Come out and join me. You're still on Grove?"

"Fucking-A yeah. They'll probably bury me here. I hope not soon, though."

"So you wanna come out and play or what?"

Jules can see the striped brown-and-white awning of Mamoun's and its fogged up windows. They're open, but a lot of the other places on the block have already shut their doors.

"I'd love to," Lou whispers as though he were plotting the president's assassination. "Hey, let me call you back when the ball and chain falls asleep. I got three kids here, too, tonight. I think I could sneak out then, okay?"

"Definitely. Hope it's soon . . . my cell's running out of juice."

He turns off his cell and goes in and orders a falafel, a Sprite, and a baklava. There are no other customers and he takes his dinner to a table. After their upcoming tour, the band is going to Europe, Germany included. Jules likes the German girls the best . . . big Bavarian titties, no guilt or pressure, wham-bang-thank-you-fräulein, one-and-done, and the way some of them urge you on by saying, *"Shpritz! Shpritz!"* He giggles into his pita, squirts some red sauce into it, and wonders if this could be his thousandth meal here . . . or maybe his five thousandth. Danny, Howie, Mickey Sanford, and then Joey . . . they'd never heard of this place before, or of the ten other lesser establishments on the block. In the early days of TFO, when they were just making their bones, this was their go-to joint, before playing at Vagrants, after playing at Vagrants, and during breaks when they were recording at Electric Lady Studios five minutes uptown.

The ball and chain, huh? You got that right, Sweet Lou.

Those were the best days of his life. Right around the time the band was making its first album. Playing guitar alone in his apartment; practicing with the band and playing their first gigs in the Village, Long Island, and Jersey; eating Middle Eastern junk on MacDougal and getting coffee at cafés Le Figaro, Borgia, or

Reggio; and staying up until four in the morning talking about music. (One night he and Danny spoke for an hour about the cop on Thirty-fourth and Vine in "Love Potion No. 9"; why did he break the little bottle? Shouldn't he have kept the bottle as evidence? Should he have pocketed it for himself?) And chasing skirt all over town, from the East Village up to Inwood, from Belmar out to Montauk, and from SoHo down to Brighton Beach. Making out and getting his fingers wet on the rooftops and fire escapes along MacDougal, Sullivan, and Thompson Streets and Saint Mark's Place, and sometimes waking up with a girl and he couldn't remember her name, and she couldn't remember his, and nobody cared.

Outside Mamoun's he takes out his contact lenses and tosses them into a trash can. He feels around his coat for a pair of glasses. But all he's got on him are his prescription Ray Charles shades, which he puts on. The better to see the cold evening.

*

Jules was on edge driving to audition for Danny Ault the first time. Seldom did he ever get nervous but he was nervous that day. They'd crossed paths a few times before, and he knew about Jakey Gee and the Aerosouls and the Tarnished Angels; he had even seen the Angels perform at Rumbottoms a few times. He knew Danny could write decent tunes and had a better than average voice—he sounded like a cross between Delaney Bramlett, Bobby Whitlock, and, in his better moments, Steve Winwood—but he just wasn't sure if they'd hit it off. Jules brought three guitars with him that day: two electric, which he put in the backseat of his celery green Ford Torino, and his Ovation, which he lovingly stowed in the trunk.

He got out of the car at Danny's house in Pleasant Valley, and Danny helped him unload the guitars, asked him about the drive, and made small talk. They spoke for an hour about the bands they'd played in, about the bands they'd seen and liked and didn't like, about the cities, towns, and clubs they'd played, and about the musicians they'd met. All the time, they were drinking Schlitz and eating Ruffles and onion dip. There was a carton of Marlboros on the coffee table, and on the TV *Superman, The Three Stooges,* and the Yankees played with the sound turned off. Danny had a guitar on his lap, and Jules had a guitar on his. They tuned up and started to fiddle around for a bit, then Danny broke it off. He explained to Jules that he was going to dissolve the Tarnished Angels . . . he didn't like the direction they were going and confessed that it was his own fault: He'd found himself writing and playing songs he wouldn't ever listen to.

"I've got a bunch of songs written that I think are okay," he confessed with a trace of embarrassment, "but could probably be a lot better if someone else maybe tore them all up and put them back together."

"Well," Jules said, mindlessly plucking the wicked intro of "Stray Cat Blues," "who knows? Maybe that's my specialty."

A few beers later, Danny was taking Jules through a few of his songs. Jules didn't venture an opinion about them, though. He thought there was something a little soft about them and wanted to tell Danny that, but even though Danny was seeking out opinions, he didn't want to offend him. Not at their first meeting.

They ran through five songs, Jules taking a few solos and then singing harmony, and took a break. When they resumed, just to get in the right mood, they screwed around on "My Son Calls Another Man Daddy," and before they knew it, it was coming on nine at night. Jules had a date with a girl from Virginia later, the girl he called Sweet Virginia—they were supposed to meet at Googie's at eleven—and Danny said he was tired anyway. Danny walked Jules back to the celery Torino and, his hands in the pockets of his jeans, asked, "So when can you come back out again? That is, if you still want to." Jules had a day off from Big Bertie's that Tuesday and said he could be out at ten in the morning.

The next meeting didn't go so well. The night before, Danny and Allison, his girlfriend at the time, had called it quits, and she was beginning the process of moving out just when Jules arrived. For three hours as she collected her stuff, Allison huffed, snorted, and cursed under her breath, but not so far under it that Jules and Danny couldn't hear.

("I can't tell you how glad I am that she's finally out of my life," Danny told Jules.)

Jules left at seven that night and this time he flexed his muscles on guitar, soloing for as long as seven minutes on a song. While he played he looked at Danny's face and couldn't tell what the dude was thinking. But after a while he recognized that Danny was not into guitar histrionics, that this was the last thing he was looking for.

Again Danny walked Jules to his Torino. By then, Allison had moved out, but had managed to leave one box of high-heel shoes so that she could storm back in, huff, snort, curse, and storm out some other day.

"I could come back Saturday at around nine or ten," Jules said to Danny when he got into the Torino. "If you're still interested."

Danny thought about it for a moment and said: "All right. Saturday, but make it noon, okay?"

That Saturday it was Jules who was in a bad mood. Sweet Virginia had told him she didn't want to see him anymore ("Our relationship isn't really going anywhere," she'd said, to which he'd replied, "So who ever said it had to be anyplace?"), and he wasn't sure where his next really good piece of ass was coming from. Still, he was relieved to see that Allison had picked up the box of high heels.

"You got a National?" Danny said, helping Jules and his gear into the house.

"Yeah. That okay?"

130

"Sure. How are you with the slide?"

Jules took out an empty vial of Coricidin and said, "I'm no Duane or Ry Cooder, but I'm all right."

When they sat down around the cheap coffee table, Danny said, "Okay, I'm still not too sure about a few things. If I put together a new outfit, I don't want it to sound like America or Crosby, Stills and Nash, but I also don't want it to sound like Grand Funk or West, Bruce and Laing either. I can't stand that heavy stuff."

"I got it."

"So just tell me, Jules . . . It's a Friday or Saturday night and you're in your apartment. You've drunk a bottle of Tango, you've smoked a J all by yourself, you're all alone, and you know you're not gonna get laid tonight. Or tomorrow. It's around 3 A.M. and there's no one around. What album do you put on? What would you listen to?"

Was there a right or wrong answer here? Jules felt as though he was being asked who was the twenty-fourth president of the United States. He wanted to answer, *I'd probably play "Gimme Shelter" or something from* Sticky Fingers. *Maybe "Wild Horses."* But what if that wasn't what Danny wanted to hear? So he didn't say anything.

"Well?" Danny said. "Just tell me, man."

Jules sighed and confessed the truth.

"Yeah," Danny said, looking relieved. "'Wild Horses.' Good choice. Anything else?"

"Or I'd maybe put on 'Dead Flowers.' Or 'Sway.' You know, yesterday I played all of *Exile on Main Street* . . . the whole album. And then I played it again. After that I put on *Let It Bleed* and played that about three times. It's got a few scratches but that didn't stop me."

"What song on *Exile* really blows your skirt up? What floats your boat on that album?"

The conversation was heating up. Danny was leaning in and talking louder and drinking beer faster. The floor was littered with crunched-up cans.

Jules said, still fearing he'd be wrong, "Well, I'd maybe say it was 'Ventilator Blues'? That kicks some serious ass. Or I like 'Sweet Virginia,' too. It's country, it's bluesy, it rocks, it's kinda . . . *dirty,* you know? I like the dirt. Plus, this chick from Virginia dumped me the other day. But if that's not—"

"Hey, don't worry about being wrong here, " Danny said. "I just wanna know where we're at." He kept quiet for a minute and then said: "Okay, Jules, go ahead. Start up the ventilator. Heat it up, man."

"You want me to—"

"Yep. And let's get real, real gone . . ."

Jules said, "All right, you asked for it," and began playing the opening riff of "Ventilator Blues."

There were no drums, there was no bass; Bobby Keys, Jim Price, Charlie Watts, and Nicky Hopkins were nowhere to be seen. It was just the two of them in Danny's shabby living room, but this was the first time since they'd met that playing together was outright *fun*, where they'd forgotten what they were trying to do and gotten lost in the music. Jules took out the Coricidin vial and wailed on the song's outro . . . which Danny and Jules stretched out to five minutes.

When it was over, Danny said, "Okay . . . okay. Progress. Hey! Grab the National! You think we could do 'No Expectations'? I wanna try something a little slower and less brutal."

Two minutes and one Schlitz later, Jules had the National on his lap and they were doing "No Expectations."

They went to a local bar that night and talked about music, about being kids and seeing the Beatles and the Rolling Stones on TV for the first time, and about a lot of other things. Jules picked up an eighteen-year-old blonde who was going to college in

132

Southampton, and Danny went to a phone booth, made the call, and hooked up with Allison, the girl who'd just left him. "After this," he told Jules, "that's it, I'm never seeing her again. We're done." (A year and a half later she became his first wife.) But before they parted, Danny asked Jules when they could get together and talk again. Jules told him he was coming out to the Island on Thursday evening to spend Labor Day with his family in Green River.

"So how about I come over Sunday morning?" Jules asked.

"How about Friday afternoon?" Danny said, wagering that Jules probably wasn't too eager to spend so much time with his family.

"You got it," Jules said, greatly relieved.

*

After the falafel, Jules turned on his cell and saw that Sweet Lou hadn't called him back, so he got in a taxi and went all the way up to 111th and Riverside Drive. Many years ago he had an Upper West Side squeeze he called Patchouli Julie. Far from pretty, she had red hair, clear skin, no marks in sight, and slim legs, and she wasn't one of those women who just lay there and took it.

Uptown, he turns on his cell—the battery light is still flashing—looks up Patchouli Julie's number, and calls her. He hasn't spoken to her for about four years, but the last time he did it was only a matter of minutes before she said, "Hey, you wanna come up and visit?" That's what Jules would love to hear her say now. He'd go upstairs, take a leak, drop the Blue Magic, talk and make out for a while, then do the deed and head back home on the train.

He has a perfect exit strategy, too: He'd taken a few pictures of Tank, a white lab who lives directly across his house on Love Street, before he left the Island today. *I gotta get back to walk Tank,* he'll tell Patchouli. If she says, *You have a dog?!* he'll just show her the pictures on his cell.

133

"Hey, it's me," Patchouli Julie's voice says in her greeting. *"Leave a message and I'll get back to you when I can. Thanks!"*

The beep sounds and it take Jules an eternal five seconds to decide whether or not to leave a message. There's a lot to think about in such a short time: he's about to take a cab to Midtown to see if he can score with Toilet Teeth (there was nothing at all wrong with her teeth; she earned that moniker by being one of the best, loudest, and most disgusting dirty-talkers he's ever known) . . . but what if he calls Toilet Teeth, whom he hasn't seen in five years, and she tells him to come right up, but then Patchouli Julie calls him and says, *Hey, you wanna come up and visit?* or *Let's meet somewhere!*? He'd rather do Patchouli Julie than Toilet Teeth, who was good in bed but wasn't pretty and who always insisted—never once successfully—on Jules staying the night . . . But what if Patchouli Julie *doesn't* call back? Then where would he be? So Jules decides to leave a message with Patchouli Julie, gives her his cell number and tells her he's buzzing around her neighborhood, and then hangs up and turns off his cell.

Wondering if Toilet Teeth will fall for the gotta-leave-to-walk-the-dog strategy, he walks to Riverside Drive and, while taking a staccato whiz on the dirty stone wall lining Riverside Park, turns his cell back on to make sure he still has her phone number, then zips up, gets a taxi, and tells the driver to take him to Fifty-third Street and Eighth Avenue, the whereabouts of Toilet's crib. While the taxi whisks him back downtown, he lies down in the backseat, his sunglasses still on. If Toilet Teeth isn't home and if Patchouli doesn't call him back, there's always the Max's Kansas City Waitress, whose first name may or may not have been Candy. Thirty years ago she had a truly magnificent pair of all-American, size-thirty-six double-D melons, and the only person who liked to play with them more than Jules did was her. She's got a face, though, like Albert Pujols, but with the lights out, who cares? Jules doesn't even

134

know if he's got the Max's Kansas City Waitress's number stored on his cell.

At the corner of Fifty-third and Eighth, the taxi driver nudges Jules back to the living. Jules pays him and gets out, shakes his head of the cobwebs, and gets his bearings. He turns his cell back on and sees that neither Sweet Lou nor Patchouli Julie has called him. A phone number from years and years ago now begins to buzz in his head. *212-555-something. 212-555-3841, was it?* But whose number was it? He can picture himself dialing it many times in the East Village in the wee, small hours of the night. Was it the Belgian Waffle Girl? Was it Jennifer Jupiter, who was fairly slim but who had the biggest ass in the solar system? It's not Islander Goal Chick . . . she never lived in the East Village. It had to be someone around there. There was this one girl who had an A-plus, close-to-perfect, tight, round ass but had a big brown birthmark the shape of a fried egg on her left butt cheek. Was *she* 555-3841?

As Toilet Teeth's phone rings, he realizes that the Clapton Page Beck Chick used to live on Forty-ninth Street between Ninth and Tenth Avenues, not so far away. He nailed her right around the time *Wasted and Tasted,* TFO's third album, came out. An A-and-R guy from AaZ (pronounced "Oz") Records hooked them up, and the guy told Jules, "Hey, this bitch slept with Eric Clapton, Jimmy Page, *and* Jeff Beck, so you know she must be seriously top-notch." Maybe she still lives there. He's got her number programmed, too, but resolves to call Toilet Teeth first. Besides, he's already got the call in to Patchouli.

"Hello?" a man's voice at Toilet Teeth's number says.

Momentarily flummoxed, Jules doesn't know what to do and, after four seconds, hangs up. He checks his Dialed Calls and sees that, yes, he had just called Toilet Teeth. *But who was that dude who picked up?* Sure, she could have gotten married or maybe some guy moved in with her. Or maybe it was just a gay roommate. The wind picks up and Jules buttons his leather coat to the top button and wishes he'd worn a sweater. He sees that one leg of his python pants has come out of his boot but the other one is still safely tucked in.

He has to find out about Toilet Teeth so he calls again.

"Hello!" the same man says again, knowing that whoever is calling him now is the same pest who called a minute ago.

"Hey, uh," Jules begins, struggling to remember Toilet Teeth's real name. "Uh, is"—it comes to him, out of nowhere, just in the nick of time—"can I speak to Gina?"

"*Gina?* You want to speak to Gina?"

"Yeah. Is she there? This is Jules Rose . . . I'm an old friend."

"Gina died! Gina is dead!"

"She's dead?"

"Yes! Whoever you are, you obviously weren't a close friend."

"No, I just . . ."

"We got married three years ago, then she got diagnosed with cancer and six months later she was gone."

Toilet Teeth is dead. Jules cannot believe it . . . but believes it. She used to curse so much while getting eaten out, banged, and fingered that it was almost embarrassing. No more.

"I'm really sorry," Jules tells Mr. Toilet Teeth.

555-3841 is still pealing in his mind and he can't turn it off or down. *Who was it, where was she?*

"So who were you anyway, Jules?" The man sounds angry, and Jules feels like telling him, *Hey, pal, I didn't kill her, it was the cancer.*

"I was just some guy she used to know, that's all."

"Sure. Some guy."

There's fifteen seconds of silence and then Jules ends the call. Shaking his head, he erases Toilet Teeth from his cell's directory and turns off the phone. Now she's really gone.

Five minutes later, after getting a beer and taking a leak at a dingy, mostly empty subterranean bar on a side street, he's walking on Forty-Eighth Street between Seventh Avenue and Sixth Avenue.

136

Sam Ash is no longer on this block, he remembers now. They moved a while ago, and where new guitars once sparkled in its windows there now stands a grimy pizza joint with a bad grade from the city's Health Department. Was this whole street once *all* musical instrument stores or did it just seem that way? You could get anything here. Mandolins, banjolinas, sitars, balalaikas, didgeridoos, piccolo and contrabass saxes, guitars from every corner of the world. Manny's was the most famous place and Jules loved going in there—it was like walking into the Taj Mahal—but there was also Terminal, Stuyvesant, Alex, Silver & Horland, We Buy, and other places whose names Jules can't recall. He could and would spend hours on the street, going in and out of stores and testing new gear, sometimes with Howie and sometimes not, and when TFO were at their prime, he was treated like the prince of a small country. It was inside Terminal where he encountered Keith Richards for the first of three times, a year or so before the Overfalls were formed. Jules wanted to walk up and introduce himself, but he didn't have the guts to do it, and besides, Keef looked as though he didn't want to be bothered that day.

Jules leans against the window of the pizza joint, red-and-blue lights swirling around him, and the faces, names, and phone numbers of women float in and float away. He takes off his sunglasses and looks at the gray nebula his breathing makes and unmakes on the glass.

*

It can be said of the Furious Overfalls that Joey Mazz gave the band its backbone and its beat, Howie Grey its brains and ambience, Danny Ault its heart and soul, and Jules Rose its balls and its dirt. But that's just what the band needed. Balls, sex, sweat. Filth, muck, and outright nastiness.

137

Danny had gone over five songs with Jules. Neither of them could read music, but Jules could remember the chords, the choruses, and some of the lyrics. After the third meeting, when he got home to Sullivan Street, Jules picked up his Ovation and worked on the songs from the bottom up. He gutted them wholesale . . . changed them all to an open D tuning, sped up the two slow ones, and slowed down the three fasts one. He went over and over them for days, alone in his apartment. The lyrics were fine . . . he wasn't going to fuck around with that. One thing he kept in mind was that he wanted to be in a band he would pay to see, a band whose records he would rush out to buy.

If Danny Ault didn't like what he'd done, then the hell with him and whatever his band would be.

He put the songs through the wringer . . . They now sounded, to his ears, as though they'd been *Beggars Banquet*ed, *Let It Bleed*ed, *Sticky Finger*ed, and *Exile*d. They were grungy, country fried, funked up, and extremely mean. As he worked, Jules imagined the bass and drums and piano and backup singers, even the horns and the overall production. They would be gritty and not pretty, naughty and not nice, and it was as if someone had given him a pristine slab of alabaster and he'd worked on it with a jackhammer and a bucket of sludge. Danny's songs had existed somewhere between Earth and the clouds, but Jules took them down into the stained bedsheets and gutter where they should have been all along. "10 Day Load," a song about not having had an orgasm for almost two weeks, would never have existed as such without Jules's input.

A few days later at Danny's house, Jules sat in the living room and played.

"You might not like what I did," he warned Danny, "and if you don't, then, well, don't worry. My feelings won't be hurt."

Three bars into the first song, Danny started to play along, but Jules told him not to.

138

After he finished, Jules waited. He was sitting on a beaten-up cloth couch, probably from Seaman's or Levitz, and Danny was in a bulky cloth chair that was falling apart. Cigarette burns and zipperlike rips and brown stains all over. Danny leaned back in his chair, rubbed his chin, and didn't say a word, and the music hung in the air along with the cigarette smoke.

Then he leaned back in and said: "Okay. Now show me how you completely fucked up the other four."

Jules was in.

*

Almost a year later, the band—whose original name was the Ventilators, but Danny changed it to the Furious Overfalls (the name came from Howie having overheard a discussion about a geography test between two high-school kids one day)—had just signed a record deal, Velcro Pravda was their manager, and things were looking good. They were going to make an album! Mickey Sanford was gone and Joey Mazz was in, and three hours ago, following four punk bands in a row, they'd just played Vagrants for the twentieth or so time. It was coming on three in the morning; some guy was playing piano and a woman was singing a slow song, and Danny and Jules were at the bar. There were only about twenty people in the house. Jules was leaning over and facing the bartender and the bottles, and Danny was standing straight and facing the other way, his elbows on the bar's edge. They'd just smoked a doobie outside on the street and were both smoking cigarettes and drinking beer. In two days they were going to start recording at Electric Lady.

"She can sing," Jules said about the singer, who was presently singing "I Wanna Be Around."

"Yeah. Pretty good pipes. But nobody listens to this torch shit anymore. She's doomed."

Danny took a long swig. He had a lot on his mind. Jules and he had fifteen songs, but there was no way they were going to record all fifteen. Some had to go, some would stay. But which ones? (One new song of theirs, "Waiting and Wilting," about a guy who encouraged his woman to flirt with other men he believed were his betters, was so wretched it made "Sister Morphine" sound like "Stars and Stripes Forever.")

"What about us?" Jules said. "I mean, we're not exactly . . ."

He didn't finish the sentence, and Danny signaled for another beer.

"I don't know," Danny said.

"What about this disco crap? Have you heard this tune 'Get Down Tonight'?"

Jules sang it and as soon as he made it to "little dance," Danny told him, "Yeah, I've heard that. I don't know where, but I've heard it." Then Jules brought up two Bee Gee's songs, "Jive Talkin'" and "Nights on Broadway," and Danny said he'd heard those, too, though again he couldn't remember where exactly. He'd just heard them, that's all. All over the place he'd heard them.

"I'm not worried about it," Danny said. The songstress was now singing "The Man that Got Away" and she sounded like a wounded nightingale on smack. "The people who listen to that and dance to it—they aren't going to buy our stuff anyway. Totally different crowd."

Jules stood up straight and turned around so that both he and Danny were facing the same way and could see the songbird. She was in the back room and was dressed in a black gown, but her skin was luminous and white, and the lights in there were low and blue.

A girl about eighteen years old, wearing too much perfume, in a tight blue-jean miniskirt with spiked heels, an ankle bracelet, and scruffy red hair, walked in from the street, smiled at Jules, and went to the back. (She eventually went on to become Patchouli Julie.)

140

Jules had seen her in the audience a few hours before and at other recent shows.

"Have you heard the Ramones?" he asked Danny.

"Yeah. Good stuff. You sound worried."

"Nah. I like us. I like what we do. We're good."

They didn't say anything for a while, then Jules got the next round and brought up the Sex Pistols and Bruce Springsteen, and Danny told him not to worry, that they (the Furious Overfalls) were who they were and couldn't change that. It was in their blood and was a done deal. Disco is disco, the Ramones are the Ramones, Springsteen is Springsteen, and we are who we are. Just like the Beatles were the Beatles and Dylan was Dylan and the Stones were the Stones. That could not change. If you tried to be something else, Danny said, you were a fraud and you were fucked, and Jules thought of the Stones trying to sound like Dylan in "Jigsaw Puzzle." He also thought of *Their Satanic Majesties Request,* not their finest hour.

The scruffy redhead came out from the back room, sat one stool away from Jules, and crossed her legs. They glanced at each other again and she smiled.

"Whatever happens," Jules said to Danny, "I just hope that . . . I never wanna live on Long Island again. Seriously, Queens? . . . That's my boundary. I never want to go east of Queens again. Unless it's to see my folks, and even then I'm not so sure. I've fuckin' had it with Long Island . . . that scene is dead for me."

"Yep," Danny, who'd just moved to the East Village, said. "I hear that."

They raised their bottles of Bud and clanked them together, toasting the fact that soon they would put Long Island a very long way behind them.

*

141

Twenty minutes later Jules is back outside Vagrants on a much darker Bleecker Street. He'd called the Clapton Page Beck Chick but there was no answer—no answering machine or voice mail or human being. Nothing.

The same bouncer is sitting on the stool with either the same Styrofoam cup of coffee in his hand or a new one.

"I'm back," Jules says to him.

"Evi*dent*ly."

"Is Billy C. working here tonight?"

"You had asked me that in the hitherto and I answered in the negative. I do so again."

Jules raises his hand but he and the bouncer see that the stamp has vanished. They look at each other.

"You're really going to make me pay again?"

The bouncer, whose body may be half awake on Bleecker Street but whose soul is sound asleep someplace else, opens the door and lets him in.

A semi-hard-core rap-punk band called the Young Hegelians is playing in the back and the place is as empty as it was before. The singer is from Rego Park but is affecting a heavy cockney accent, so maybe he's from Rego Park's East End.

"Couldn't stay away?" the Southern bartender says when he plunks down Jules's beer.

"Nope. I'm a slave to rock and roll. So when's Stan coming back again?"

"Hey, I'm afraid I'm going to have to ask you to put the cigarette out."

Jules snuffs the Marlboro, and the bartender tells him he doesn't know when Stan's coming back, but it looks as if he does know and just isn't sure the information is safe in Jules's hands. Jules looks over the action at the bar and sees that Short Bad Skin is still there, and that some guy who looks familiar is talking to her. Jules stumbles over and intrudes.

142

"Hey, again," she says with a smile. "Um, sunglasses? In here?"

Jules puts his beer on the bar between her drink and the guy chatting her up.

"This is . . ." she begins to tell her friend.

"Jules Rose," he says to the guy. "And you are?"

The guy tells Jules he's the drummer from Banal Fissures, and Short Bad Skin tells the drummer that Jules was in a band called . . .

"The Furious Overfalls," Jules says.

"Oh yeah?" the drummer says. "Hey, I think—did you guys once do a thing on *Sesame Street*? With, like, Big Bird?"

"Yeah, that was us. Long time ago. I was pretty wasted on reds. Big Bird was startin' to look sexy to me."

"You guys were all from Billy Joel Land, right?"

Jules feels himself blush and says: "Hey, I had nothing to do with that. I never met the man."

"You were on *Sesame Street*?" Short Bad Skin says, unable to contain her glee.

Can you imagine, Jules thinks, that *getting me laid tonight? Thirty years after the fact?!*

"Hey, guy," Jules, apropos of nothing, slurs to the drummer, "I was once on *Guitar World Magazine*'s list of the top hundred guitarists of all time. Yeah, I was on that list."

The drummer and Short Bad Skin look at each other.

"Uh-huh?" the drummer says.

"Yeah. But I won't tell you what number I was."

"What number?"

"I just told you I wouldn't tell you."

"Oh, come on," Short Bad Skin says, flirtatiously grabbing the lapel of Jules's leather coat. "Just tell us. What number were you?"

Jules feels his mouth getting very dry and his face getting warm.

"I was number seventy-eight. Leslie West was seventy-seven, Alvin Lee was seventy-nine. That ain't bad company."

143

The drummer and Short Bad Skin look at each other and giggle, and the drummer mutters to her: "Yeah, whoever *they* are."

Number seventy-eight and the next time they did the list, I wasn't even on it. Goddamn motherfuckers. Replaced by Billy Goddamn Zoom!

"Are you all right, Jules?" someone, maybe the Southern bartender, asks him.

Jules goes to the bathroom, leans against the wall, and aims toward the putrid, black-streaked toilet bowl. He hits the seat for a few seconds, then the floor, then one of his boots for two seconds, then gets it into the bowl. When he comes out, the Fissures drummer has his tongue down Short Bad Skin's throat and his hands down the back of her jeans.

Back out on Bleecker, the wind slashing in all directions, Jules takes out his cell and turns it back on. It's blinking red again . . . it's losing all the juice. He calls Sweet Lou. Maybe they can hang out, or he can crash on Lou's living-room couch and split in the morning.

"Jules?" Lou answers in a whisper.

"Yeah. You coming out tonight or what? 'Cause my last train—"

"I can't. I'm asleep."

"Huh? Why not?"

"Maybe on Sunday? Call me Sunday morning."

"You really can't come out now? I'm still on Bleecker, just a few blocks away."

"Call me Sunday." Still whispering.

"What is it? Your kids?"

There's a pause, then Sweet Lou says: "My *kids?* Jules, it's the *grand*kids. I gotta go."

Jules takes a taxi to Avenue A and Fifth Street and walks around, stops into a few bars, sees that hardly anyone is out tonight, and leaves. He finds a pay phone on the corner of A and Third and dials the number 212-555-3841. *Who was it?* As the pay phone rings, he pulls out his cell and sees that someone has left a message for him.

"Hello," a sleepy woman answers.

"Uh," Jules says, his head flush against the glass. "Who is this?"

"I think I'm supposed to ask you that."

"Who were you?"

"It's late, whoever you are!"

The voice isn't ringing any bells. There was a woman who lived way downtown who he used to bang about fifteen years ago. The only handle he could ever come up with for her was Eveready because she lived near Battery Park and liked to use a vibrator while he was doing her, but other than that there was nothing special. *Was this her?*

"Battery Park?" he asks.

"Who is this?!"

"Did you ever get down with the guitarist from the Furious Overfalls?"

Five seconds of silence and then she slams down the phone. Then he remembers whose phone number 212-555-3841 was. It was his own. When he lived on Sullivan Street above Googie's Bar.

Jules tries to listen to his message but it takes a while to get to it. Fumbling with his phone, he accidentally looks at three pictures of Tank, his supposed dog.

"Hey! It's me!" Patchouli Julie's message says, her voice sounding much huskier since they'd last spoken. *"You're in the neighborhood?! Great. Do you want to meet for a drink or maybe come on up? Call me back!"*

Jules gathers his breath . . . then he goes into a small bodega across the street, buys a bottle of Poland Spring water, and drops the Blue Magic—the one from Mumbai.

"Aww, shit," he groans aloud as soon as it slides past his uvula.

Usually he only takes a half. He didn't mean to take the whole hit.

Thirty minutes later a taxi driver wakes him up in the backseat, back on 111th and Riverside Drive. Jules comes to with not only a raging hard-on but the worst case of heartburn he's ever suffered. It feels as though gallons of acid are seeping out from his inner organs and singeing his bones, skin, and shirt. He cannot even stand up all the way. The driver asks if he's okay and Jules adjusts his shades and says he is. (Fortunately, the driver doesn't notice the puddle that Jules has peed onto the taxi floor.)

Jules looks at his watch. The last train back to Long Island is in an hour. Can he pull this off? It's going to have to be a real hit-and-run job.

There's nobody and nothing where he is on Riverside Drive. It's midnight. Across the river, behind the bare trees and gray light, is the indigo smudge that is New Jersey. Jules takes out his cell to call Patchouli Julie. But it doesn't turn on. The battery is dead. He walks to the east side of the avenue and tries a pay phone but he can't get a dial tone. He staggers two streets south but the next two phones are broken, too.

"Broadway," he mumbles to himself.

Now his heartburn is so bad that he doubles over and groans. Dozens of lit match heads are crawling inside his ribs. He comes to a pay phone on 108th and Broadway that works. The quarter is down the slot, there's a dial tone, his finger is about to push a button . . . but then he realizes he doesn't know Patchouli's number—has no idea what it is. He tries again to turn his cell phone on, but it still won't work: it's dead for the night. Her first name isn't even really Julie, it's . . . it's . . . Janie. Or is it Janet? Or maybe it *is* Julie. It doesn't matter. He has no idea what her last name is. It's hopeless.

She's just going to be up in her apartment waiting for him to call her back, and he's not going to call. Because he can't.

146

While the sky whirls, he presses his head against the cold metal of the pay phone and says, almost in a whimper: "Rhonda. Oh, Rhonda."

He walks back to Riverside Drive, sits on a bench, smokes his second-to-last cigarette, and waits for his hard-on to die. The heartburn sears his innards, subsides for a few seconds, then sears again. Jules wonders if the workers in Mumbai are all terrorists and spiked his Viagrola with some kind of secret vindaloo powder.

Fifteen minutes later he's back at the pay phone that works. One number he knows by heart is Islander Goal Chick's—it's etched into the Little Black Book of his soul. She is a dental hygienist and moved from Pinelawn to Farmingdale. Dark blond hair, mark-free skin, could lose twenty pounds, dumpy thighs. He first started up with her during the dynasty of the New York Islanders in the early eighties. He was a huge fan of the club but IGC was off the deep end . . . she'd even had sex with two of the team's equipment men and a Zamboni driver. Never missed a game. Every time Jules did her and finished and pulled out, she'd expertly imitate the Islander PA announcer and say, "Islander goal scored by number twenty-eight, Jules Rose!" (Jules was number twenty-eight because he was the twenty-eighth guy she'd slept with. He never asked her what she was going to do when she hit triple digits.)

He dials her number and recites her name while the phone rings. Mindy, Mindy, Mindy.

"Hello," Mindy answers the phone. She's awake and the TV is on in the background.

"Mindy! Hey! It's your favorite guitarist."

"Jules?"

"Yeah! Number twenty-eight, Jules Rose! What's goin' on, darlin'?"

"Nothing! Just hanging around, honey. The Islanders are in Vancouver, the game is on."

"Score?"

"Vancouver two, Islanders one right now, but it's between periods. Where are you?"

"I'm in the city. You have any plans tonight? Are *you* between periods?"

"Ha-ha. I'm just watching the game. You wanna hop on a train?"

"Yeah . . . but I have a dog to walk now."

"Huh?"

"I'll explain later. All right. I'll go to Penn Station, get the train out to Farmingdale."

"Farmingdale? I moved over a year ago, honey."

Jules is leaning on the phone for support. The match heads are flaming and have multiplied to the thousands, parading from his navel to his throat.

"So where are you now? Tell me and I'm there as fast as I can."

"I'm all the way out in Ronkonkoma now . . ."

Seven
Taking Care of Business

In his black Suburban, Danny drives through the blustery December air to make his secret meeting. It's a Sunday afternoon and he's on his way to a strip mall somewhere in the bleak no-man's-land between Bay City and Pleasant Valley. Danny knows the area will be pretty empty: the meeting is set for four-fifteen, which is when the Jets kick off.

He pulls up to a Curves gym and stays in the car. On one side of the Curves is a TD Bank and a closed Mail Boxes Etc.; on the other is a nail salon and empty storefront for rent. Danny wonders if this salon is one of the places Jules goes to for his mani-pedi's, but there are hundreds of places for that on Long Island alone.

He feels around his jacket for his cigarettes. His One Daily Cigarette. He had half a pack but emptied them all out but for one before he left, just to make sure he keeps to the plan.

To his left, cars rumble by on the road leading to the strip mall, and beyond that is the drone of the Sunrise Highway. A tall woman with a periwinkle scarf over her head leaves the TD Bank after a visit to an ATM. Christmas is in a few weeks and already today Danny's done some shopping. Lily wants a new bicycle and an iPad . . . they're in the back of the SUV. Emily isn't being so demanding: with a baby on the way, her days of asking for presents and getting them are over. Welcome to the club, kid. She wanted a gender-neutral stroller and so, beneath Lily's bike, is a gray unisex Bugaboo. Danny won't even bother wrapping the thing; when he gets home he'll just stash it in the attic behind a few old amps where he can't see it or think about it.

The Suburban creaks with a sudden gust of wind and then a blue Chevy Malibu pulls up alongside it, and Danny feels his hands get cold in a flash.

He gets out of his car and Angie Mazz gets out of hers. They look around the parking area to make sure the coast is clear, then

149

make eye contact. She's about a foot shorter than he is. She keeps her curly hair metallic black and weighs the same now as when she and Joey first started dating (if you can call banging each other, doing lines, and hanging around "dating"). She and Joey met at a postconcert party in New Jersey and married soon thereafter; less than a year after that, Little Joey came into the world. Angie has thick dark lips and bright gray eyes. Right now she's wearing a black leather coat that reaches down to her knees. Of all the TFO wives, Angie is, without doubt, made of the toughest stuff.

They kiss on the cheek. Right now, her cheeks are much warmer than his lips. That could be from the heat she naturally generates or because she's just come from her Sunday spinal-decompression session.

"*Your* car," she orders. He opens the door for her, then goes around to the driver's seat and gets in. Out of habit, he grabs the steering wheel. He always has to be touching something—a chair, a guitar or a pick, a cell phone, the lining or contents of his pockets, or his own hand.

"You want to smoke in here," Angie says, "go ahead."

"No, I'm going to wait."

"So? Tell me."

"It's not so good. It's not terrible, but it's not—"

"Just fuckin' tell me, please, all right?"

Dr. Ford from Hicksville Cardio called two days earlier. As Joey had asked him to, Dr. Ford called Danny. Not Joey, the patient himself; not Angie, his wife; not Joey's primary-care physician (since he doesn't have one), but Danny. The Leader of the Band. Daddy.

"He needs open-heart surgery. There's a lot of blockage. It'd probably be a triple bypass. There's nothing to be afraid of and it's pretty simple so—"

"Oh, so *you're* gonna do it? Or maybe Joey should just do it on himself?!"

150

Her lower lip is trembling and her eyes are blazing.

"Yes, Angie," he says, "Doctor Ford says that Joey should do the surgery on himself. In the bathroom with a dirty drumstick and some Brut aftershave to sterilize everything."

She looks at him for a few seconds. She wants to scream but knows it would do no good, plus she knows that the angriest person in the car right now is not her. Danny is the angriest person she's ever met . . . he just never shows it.

"Oh, just smoke your cigarette already," she says. "It's killing me to look at you."

He rolls down the window and then takes out the pack and lights up. Even though she's short and thin and possesses few curves, Angie has always struck Danny as incredibly sexy, as a panther stuffed into a kitten's body. She always wears black, never any other color. Skintight black everything. He'd always suspected that she was great in bed, and Jules confirmed that for him a long time ago. (Joey would never have divulged such a thing.) She was flirty twenty-two years ago, when she was still single, and marriage hasn't changed that.

"So when would this surgery happen?" she asks. She nimbly twists around to face Danny, who sits facing Curves, which is open but empty.

"As soon as possible. As in, this week."

She nods, moves her veiny wrist and thin hand to Danny's hand, and takes the cigarette, inhales, hands it back. She has a few tats, on her calves and forearms and who knows where else, but none of them are TFO-related, which always bothered him. It's one thing for your kids not to listen to your music—as a parent you have to expect such a thing—but for the wives to sport ink for other bands? That's inexcusable.

"Jesus Christ," she says. "I can't believe this."

He fidgets around, adjusts his ass in the seat. Over the last few years there hasn't been much contact among the Overfalls wives,

151

girlfriends, and kids. It just never worked out. Danny can converse with Melissa, Howie's wife, but only for so long: he has to touch base with her at least once a week as she does all the accounting and bookkeeping for the band. After two minutes on the phone with her, however, he just puts himself on automatic pilot and starts saying, "Yeah, " "Uh-huh," "Anything you say," and "Sounds good to me." Jules, though, goes to great lengths to avoid her, and Jessica, Danny's wife, has said that she'd rather go to the dentist than spend more than an hour with Melissa. Jules and Jessica never hit it off either. Jules looks at her and shakes his head, never fathoming the reason why any rocker—or any man—would ever settle down; she looks at him and sees a preening male slut. "I swear," she's told Danny a few times, "he uses coital fluids for an aftershave." She knows that Jules would love to sleep with her but she can barely stand to politely kiss him on the check. Angie is too rough, unpolished, and emotional for Jessica, and Jessica is too smooth, polished, and unemotional for Angie. Jessica is afraid of her, but so sometimes is Danny. The times Jessica and Angie have found themselves in conversation, it always drifts to benign subjects such as the kids and the weather. If Fate in the guise of the Furious Overfalls hadn't brought them together, these women would have nothing to do with each other.

And then there are the kids. That never went too well either. Many years ago Danny, Howie, and Joey took a stab at maintaining a band/family alliance. One Christmas evening, Danny and Jessica drove to the Mazz house with the kids, and Howie and Melissa dragged Michelle from Connecticut. But the kids didn't hit it off, nobody was saying much, and Little Joey, all five years of him, clobbered Emily over the head with a Wiffle bat for no reason other than that she was there. The next year, Danny and Jessica held a small New Years Day party. Jules said he couldn't make it, but the Mazzes and the Greys came, and again there was zero chemistry, although this time Emily returned the favor and bonked Joey Junior with a plastic pork chop from her brand new toy kitchen. The following year it was Howie and Melissa's turn, and had one of the kids belted another it would've come as a welcome relief, because nothing happened and the kids wouldn't play with one another or stay in the same room. And that was it: a forced get-together under the same roof was never tried again.

"You know what the doctor told me?" Danny says now to Angie. "That it was amazing Joey had made it so long without a heart attack. He said that Joey was a lion."

"*Joey?*" she gasps. "A *lion?* Are you sure he checked out the right guy?"

She straightens herself out so that they're both facing forward, looking at the gym.

"Doctor Ford would do the surgery," Danny says, making sure to exhale out the window. "He's good. It turns out he did my Uncle John's heart surgery and Uncle John lived another fifteen years, not that anyone wanted him to. So listen, if you want me to bring Joey in—"

"No, I can do it."

She's not weeping but her eyes are tearing up and she wipes them with her left fist. Her bangles clang throughout the vehicle.

"He'll be okay," Danny says.

"And how do you know that?"

"I don't. You're right."

Angie takes the last hit off the Marlboro and he flicks it out of the car.

"So Emily's pregnant, huh? You're going to be a grandpa, Danny."

"Thanks for just ruining the last ten minutes of my life because I'd forgotten all about that in that time."

"Like the last ten minutes were so great? Well, anyway, congratulations."

"You don't really mean that, do you?"

153

"Of course I do! Don't be such a piece of shit. It's a good thing. Babies rock."

He shrugs and asks: "If you were me, what would you get Emily for Christmas? I want to get her something not baby-related."

She wipes away another stream of tears and says, "She'll be showing soon. And it'll be winter. She'll need a good coat with some room in it. There's a Burlington Coat Factory in Massapequa. There's one in Hicksville, too. Get her something nice."

Thinking he might drive there now, he looks at his watch, but she says, "No, don't you pick it out . . . You're gonna end up getting her a coffee sack. You know what? When I bring Joey in I can go shop for her. It'd probably do me some good. And you can pay me back."

Danny nods and takes in Angie's zigzag-patterned hose and slender calf, showing beneath the hem of her long black leather coat, and her shiny black patent-leather pumps. Would it kill her to wear a speck of some other color, just for a second? (She is still what Jules would call "a five-minute chick": it would easily take her less than five minutes to pick up a man in a bar.)

"All right," he says, "there's something sort of unpleasant to bring up. Has Joey made out a will? Does he have any life insurance? I'm sure everything's going to be okay, but . . . we're not kids anymore, obviously. If he hasn't, it should be done before you bring him in."

She says nothing, stares out at the vacated mall, and another set of tears starts to flow out of each eye. This time she's biting her lip to prevent herself from sobbing. Danny places his right hand on her bony left hand and can feel her veins and the warmth within. She intertwines her fingers with his and, just as it gets a little bit too intimate and arousing, he slowly pulls his hand away.

"I don't know. I'll ask him. But you know Joey . . . he may have a will and not even know it."

"If he doesn't, I know someone." He waits a beat and says: "Do you want me to call Doctor Ford and arrange things and then give you a call?"

She nods and wipes away the tears again. It's amazing the racket her jewelry makes.

She looks at her watch and says she should be getting back home, and Danny wonders if Joey will fully understand the import of what Angie is going to tell him today. Open-heart surgery. Triple bypass. Taking a vein from your leg or wherever. It's like cutting and pasting text on a computer except it's your body. Nothing has ever fazed Joey. Even when AaZ Records, their label, dropped TFO after *Dead End Road* . . . all Joey did was smile and say, "Well, we just gotta keep on truckin' then." It's not that information goes over his head . . . it's more like it never really makes it there in the first place.

Angie opens the door to leave, puts a leg out, then comes backs in and shuts the door.

"Tell me," she says, waving a threatening black index fingernail, her eyes searing his, "you're not already thinking of having to replace him in the band! You better fuckin' promise me you haven't already thought of that!"

"I promise you," he says, "that has not even crossed my mind!"

*

I'll have Angie get Emily the coat, Danny thinks, back on the road and heading vaguely in the direction of home. *It'll get her mind off Joey and the operation.*

Did she really believe him when he lied to her? When he said the thought of having to replace Joey had not crossed his mind? Usually Angie is less gullible than that . . . but maybe in her present desperate state she's willing to believe anything.

155

Not knowing or caring where he is, Danny makes a right turn and gets off whatever road he's on. The radio is on and the Jets are already down six points. On this cold Sunday afternoon, Jessica will be in the living room with the girls right about now. Or maybe Lily will be in her room texting, and Jessica will be talking baby stuff with Emily in the kitchen. He could go upstairs and watch the game and catch a snooze, or he could go into the garage with a guitar and while away the time until dinner. It doesn't get more serene for him than that.

What if Joey dies?

One quarter of the band would then be gone. Just like a man losing a leg.

But the band is going to be gone soon anyway. So, in a way, it won't matter.

Brian Jones died, and not only did the Rolling Stones not die with him, they got better. A *lot* better. Keith Moon died and the Who went on (though they were never the same). Jim Morrison died and that was the end of the Doors, even though they did put out another record that nobody remembers but which wasn't so bad. Duane Allman and Berry Oakley died and their band played on, and it was the same with Canned Heat, which had more band members die than were ever in the band to begin with. Lowell George, the heart and soul and voice of Little Feat, died and the band still soldiers on, though not anything like it once was.

And Joey is just a drummer.

What do you call people who hang around with musicians? Drummers. What did the drummer get on his IQ test? Drool.

He cruises past grassless lawns and flat oyster-shell-color houses, past tire stores, pizza parlors, and satellite dishes, and he thinks of what the Overfalls would be like without Joey if he died before the upcoming tour. *Would* they be at all? Would the tour be canceled and the band undone sooner than Danny planned? There were millions of drummers out there, and Joey was a drummer who,

156

Danny was almost certain, didn't even like his own band's music that much. Joey was a temp who'd been called in one day and ended up never leaving the office.

But one Friday afternoon, twenty years ago, Danny woke up in his St. Louis Hampton Inn hotel room, poured himself half a foot of Jack Daniel's, snorted eight lines of coke off the Gideons Bible, and lay in bed, drank, and watched TV. He closed his eyes and when he opened them again it was three o'clock the following afternoon and he was in a different Hampton Inn hotel room in a different city, in bed with a skinny woman he didn't know who *may* have been eighteen and who had a complexion like a Krispy Kreme glazed donut. He rushed to the bathroom and fell to the toilet, where he vomited everything he'd eaten the past twenty-four hours—it could not have been too healthy—into the bowl. A few minutes later, someone was knocking on the bathroom door and asking him if he was all right. It was the woman. Or the girl. Whatever and whoever she was, she sounded like she'd been anesthetized. He retched again into the bowl and thought he might see some of his inner organs come out.

"You all right in there?" a male voice asked ten minutes later. It took a full minute before Danny realized who it was. Danny, wracked with chills all over, lay prostrate on the floor. "Cancha hear me knockin', bro?" the man asked. Danny crawled to the door, propelling himself by his fingers and toes. He gazed upward, saw the bottles of unopened Neutrogena shampoos and conditioners on the sink, and raised his arm, not without a struggle, to undo the lock. There, in black jeans, a leather jacket, a Deep Purple *Machine Head* T-shirt, and black boots, stood Joey Mazz.

"Jesus, bro, you look like fuckin' Death itself." Somehow, someway, Joey had found him. Joey lifted Danny up, wrapped him in towels and then in his own leather jacket—the woman/girl sat on the edge of the bed biting her nails and covering her little-boy body with the bed linens—and filled him with glass after glass of water.

157

After the chills subsided, Joey said, "We got a gig in a few hours . . . you gonna be able to make it?"

"Yeah," Danny groaned. "I'll make it."

That was the end for Danny . . . After that day, after Joey carried him outside of that hotel room, into the elevator, through the lobby, and into their rented U-Haul, Danny quit smoking, except for one cigarette a day, quit drinking, except for a beer every now and then, and quit drugs, except for the occasional hit off a joint. That was it.

He comes to a red light at an empty four-way intersection. He's surrounded by houses bunched so closely together that it's a wonder they don't all have the same address. For a second he's sure he's been on this street before, then he realizes he hasn't . . . it's just that there are a thousand streets exactly like this from Valley Stream to Riverhead. Inside one two-story house, a man and a woman are raising their voices at each other and two or three kids are crying. The light changes and, though nobody is in his way, he pounds his fist on the horn and yells, "YOU BETTER NOT FUCKING DIE, YOU FUCKING IDIOT! YOU DUMB MORON!" so loudly it hurts his own ears.

But is Joey Mazz possibly too stupid to die? In no hurry to get home, Danny makes a right turn and heads down a street that looks like an old washed-out picture post card. GREETINGS FROM LAWN GUYLAND! WISH I WERE NOT HERE! Does Joey's brain even know to send the message to his heart to stop? Maybe there's nothing to worry about.

And if he does die? They could cut him open and he could die right in the operating room, or maybe he'd get an infection after they sewed him back up. So many Cheetos and Yodels, so much Reddi-wip and Mountain Dew. Truckloads of Mountain Dew. In hotels and motels and backstages all over the world. He regularly orders slices of lemon-meringue pie in hotel coffee shops and pours three packets of Splenda over them. Who knew you could get a jumbo bag of Fritos Corn Chips in Osaka? . . . but you could.

"Breakfast of champions," Joey has said to him many times when caught chomping on a Butterfinger bar at ten in the morning. "Peanuts, bro . . . chockfull of protein."

Danny makes a right turn, then another, and keeps going, driving deeper and deeper into whichever South Shore town he's at the farthest or nearest edge of, and then comes to a caged baseball field the world seems to have forgotten. The bases and the pitching rubber on the diamond are long gone, the mound is lower than home plate, and the outfield looks like charred pizza crust. Danny pulls up alongside the fence behind home plate and gets out of the Suburban, walks onto the field, and sits on the splintery green bench along the third base side.

At the top of his lungs he yells: "GOD DAMN IT! GOD DAMN IT!!"

Where do rockers go when they don't die? Where is the bassist from Crabby Appleton now? Selling furniture or sweeping floors or tending bar? What's the pianist from Stone the Crows or the guitarist from Frijid Pink doing to put food on his plate? Or the drummer from McGuinness Flint or Pentangle? *GODDAMN SON OF A BITCH!* Do they drive forklifts in factories or teach music to local kids for ten bucks an hour? The mandolin player from Lindisfarne, whose name Danny knows but is now slipping his mind—does he make sandwiches at a café in an aquarium? When Danny was seventeen, he and two buddies journeyed up to the Powder Ridge Rock Festival in Connecticut only to find it had been called off. Among bands such as Ten Years After, the Allman Brothers, and Savoy Brown, a band called J. F. Murphy and Free Flowing Salt was supposed to play. Forget J. F. Murphy . . . what the hell was Salt doing for a living now?

A tree branch blows across the base paths and looks like a spastic kid trying to steal a base.

159

Danny stands up, puts his hands in his coat pockets, and sees, where the fence meets the stubbly ground behind third base, bottles and cans of beer, soda, and juice all gathered together.

When he was very young, not yet in his teens, Danny was a bully. He liked to punch out other boys and wrestle them and make them cry uncle. He thought this was a way of making friends but came to realize that all the kids he'd impressed didn't want to be his friend any more than the ones he'd beaten up. So he stopped. He had dozens of plastic toy World War II soldiers and he used to imagine them slaughtering Krauts and Japs, bayoneting them through and spraying them with lead just like in *Sgt. Fury and his Howling Commandoes.* It never stopped, the desire to yell at people, shake them up, smash a head into a wall. Football helped for a while but that was too controlled: you *had* to knock this guy's head off and you had to do it a particular way, right here, at this certain point.

On the Dead End Road Tour, when the bottom was falling out from under the band, they were just outside San Francisco about to board the bus and head up to Eugene, Oregon, to play to yet another half-empty house. Tickets there and in many other cities were being given away, and *Rolling Stone,* which Danny had hoped would give the album five stars, hadn't even bothered reviewing it. In the parking lot of their hotel, some twenty-four-year-old creep with a purple Mohawk in a torn army jacket and black jackboots began taunting them. That's why the prick had shown up there, just to be a wiseass.

"You guys fuckin' suck!" he yelled at Danny, the band, and the entourage. "Your fuckin' band sucks donkey dongs in Hell! I fuck your mother!"

Danny ran toward the guy, followed by Rev and Big Bob. It was midnight, nobody else was around. Purple Mohawk spat a wad of Juicy Fruit into Danny's nose, then poked him in the forehead (and drew blood) with a sharp fingernail, and Danny swung at the guy's jaw and knocked him down, then jumped on him on the ground and started flailing away. Purple Mohawk head-butted him hard and Danny staggered backward. The next thing he knew, Purple Mohawk was spitting on him. Purple Mohawk, whose name turned out to be Alan Wilbur Murdock, kicked Danny square in the nuts. Rev then grabbed him by the throat, Bob had him by the Mohawk, and Danny came at him like a bull.

"What the fuck do we do with this creep, boss?" Rev, a former tackle at Oklahoma State, asked.

Danny was flailing away at the guy. "We'll just take care of business," Danny spat out, gasping and punching, Mohawk biting him when he could. *We'll just take care of business*—that was all he said.

The next thing he knew, Sweet Lou, a guitar tech, and Jules were trying to rip him and the roadies away from the Mohawk. By the time Rev was pulled off, Alan Wilbur Murdock, the kind of professional pest who travels to international summit meetings on his parents' dime just to throw cans of piss at the police, wasn't moving anymore, and the ground was soaked with his blood. Nobody was sure who had done what. An ambulance showed up ten minutes later, and two days after that it was certain that, though he would live, Alan Wilbur Murdock would never run, walk, go to the bathroom, eat like an adult, or fuck again.

Danny picks up an empty twelve-ounce bottle of Budweiser and cracks it against the bench, and chunks and beads of glass fly all around, going past his eyes like sparks. "FUCK! FUCK YOU!" he yells.

He lifts up a bottle of Miller and flings it as hard as he can . . . it lands in center field. *ASSHOLE! ASSHOLE!* He thinks about Emily with a baby in the house—his house—and knots of rage rise up his throat. Not only does he have two kids living in the house . . . he's going to have *three*. One ex-wife, one wife, two kids, one grandkid, three band members who are incapable of taking care of themselves, and *TFO 6, TFO 7, TFO 8,* and so on. *FUCK FUCK FUCK!!!*

161

Albums that don't get bought, songs that don't get heard; going everywhere and playing for a hundred people at a time, all that hard work and for what? For being a Blast From The Past? The "Blast" part of it rocked, sure, but it was that "Past" part which was excruciating.

Danny thinks about Allison, his first wife. She married another guy and was just about to leave him and file for divorce when he got diagnosed with terminal something-or-other. So she just waited it out and in a year all her problems were solved. *If Joey dies,* Danny thinks, *then I'll just use it as the excuse to break up the band.*

"FUCK ME!" he yells three times. He grabs a forty-ounce bottle of King Cobra malt liquor and swings it down as hard as he can against the bench, and when it cracks, it sends glass onto his coat, pants, and shoes. He's out of breath, from screaming and cracking and hating, and holds up what's left of the bottle to his eyes until its jagged edges catch the oncoming twilight.

*

Mickey Sanford, at six foot four, was taller than Danny and a year older. If you were a musician on the Island, the chances are you knew him or knew of him. By the time he was twenty-four he'd already played in ten bands. Hard rock, blues-rock, heavy metal, dance bands—he didn't care. He was a good drummer, a bit of a showboat who insisted on at least one meandering solo per show that would put half the house to sleep, but he had great connections: he could get you the best pot, hash, and mescaline around, as well as straight-out-the-jar Seconals, Tuinals, Dilaudids, Valiums, Nembutals, Quaaludes, and Demerols. "Where do you get this stuff?" Danny and Jules and many others had asked him, and the only reply they ever got was "Hey, I know people." He sure did, and it seemed as though these people were never too far from wherever he happened to be standing. One night, just three months into the existence of the Furious Overfalls, the band was sitting in a booth at Mamoun's about to play Vagrants when Danny said he could use some coke.

"Be right back," Mickey said, the baba ghanoush trickling down his chin.

Five minutes later he was back with two grams.

He never played a gig straight, probably never ate a meal or slept with a woman straight either. Howie tolerated him but stayed safely away; Jules viewed him as a rival for girls (they were, however, able to bury the hatchet and bang a few of the same chicks, sometimes at the same time); Danny kept him around for the sake of consistency and for the drugs. And because the band was new and nobody was really sure what was going to happen, Danny put up with Mickey's excesses and occasional tardiness. Jules was always angling to get rid of him, was always telling Danny he knew this guy Johnny from Valley Stream, or some guy named Ronnie from Carle Place, or Vinnie from Mattituck who'd played in Mauve Protrusion and had sat in with the Blues Magoos once. Danny told Jules to wait, to give Mickey a chance. "This Carl Palmer thing can't last," Jules kept saying, alluding to a drummer given to taking long, nap-inducing solos. The worst crime for Jules by far was that Mickey liked—was the *only* person alive who ever admitted to having liked—Grand Funk Railroad. Mickey had all their albums, and he didn't like them in some ironic, amusing way . . . *he genuinely liked them!*

One day Danny and Mickey met for lunch at Googie's, and Danny laid down the law. "You have to start showing up on time, for gigs and for practice. I'm not screwing around here. You can't take downers or 'Ludes for a show. Coke is okay, but nothing that puts you to sleep, please. And no more drum solos, we're cutting those out as of now . . . this isn't what the band is about. We're about *songs,* not playing songs." Mickey nodded, said, "Yes, boss"

163

and "Got it, chief" and promised him, scout's honor, he'd clean up his act.

By this time, Velcro Pravda was their manager and they were making a name for themselves around New Jersey and New York. The *Village Voice* had called them "probably the best new band on the scene that isn't named the Ramones or Television," and they were playing venues like Tramps, Ungano's, and the Hotel Diplomat. A record contract, they knew, was imminent.

"See you tonight," Mickey said as they were leaving. He even slapped down the ten bucks for the lunch. "And it'll be the New and Improved Mickey Sanford, you have my word. Check this out . . ."

To Danny's horror, Mickey whipped out a virgin gram of blow and emptied the bindle out onto the floor, then smudged it into the sticky tiles with the heel of his boot.

That night neither the New and Improved Mickey Sanford nor the much more reliable Old Mickey Sanford showed up for the gig.

The Overfalls were supposed to go on at ten at Tramps and open for a U.K. band called the Ska Tologists, and by nine-thirty Danny was ready to hit the ceiling. He took a taxi over to Saint Mark's Place, where Mickey shared a railroad flat with a dreadlocked bass player named Wendell. Wendell, despite being stoned off his rocker, was able to buzz him in upstairs, and when Danny asked him, "Where the hell is Mickey?!" Wendell answered, *"Say, what?!* Mickey packed his shit two days ago and told me he was movin' in wich *you!"* Danny asked Wendell if he could use the phone and then dialed about thirty numbers—friends of Mickey, girlfriends of Mickey, boyfriends of girlfriends of Mickey—but nobody had any idea where he was.

Because he wasn't anywhere. Danny couldn't find him, Wendell couldn't find him, no friends and girlfriends could find him, and neither could the coke dealers in Howard Beach who he'd ripped off for two grand. Or maybe the guys in Howard Beach were able to find him and had made damn sure nobody else ever would again.

Danny cabbed it back to Tramps—en route, he kicked in the bulletproof partition separating him from his terrified driver—and Howie played drums that night. "I am never doing that again!" Howie declared after their uncharacteristically abbreviated set.

The next day, only a few days before Thanksgiving, the remaining three Overfalls and Velcro Pravda met for breakfast at noon in a coffee shop on Bleecker Street. Over the loudspeakers, "More, More, More" by the Andrea True Connection played softly.

"Well, boys?" Velcro said, stroking the Yorkshire terrier, also named Velcro, on his lap. Velcro always wore oversize dark sunglasses, even inside and at nighttime, and purple velvet jackets.

"So, Jules," Danny asked, sleepily pouring syrup over his pancakes, "what drummers do you know again and how reliable are they?"

Jules had one hand around a steaming cup of coffee and the other around a steaming thin redhead in a white faux-fur vest who reeked of patchouli. One of her false eyelashes fell into her oatmeal, and Jules leaned forward and said: "Well, there's this one pretty competent cat I know from Bay City named Joey . . ."

*

Lindenhurst, Babylon, West Islip, Bay Shore, Islip, East Islip, Central Islip . . . and on and on.

At the baseball field, Danny had gone into his car, pulled the stroller out from under the bike, and dragged it onto the field. With all his might he brought it down against the green bench, again and again, yelling, "MOTHER*FUCKER!*" each time. Metal was bending, parts were breaking, nuts and bolts flew all over. After a while, there wasn't much to break anymore and he dropped what was left of the thing to the ground and got back in his car.

165

Alan Wilbur Murdock. Parking-lot heckler, nuisance of the first degree, calamity on legs, Moody's Grade AAA–rated asshole. The Stones had their Armageddon with the whole world watching . . . they were at the peak of their fame and power and there were movie cameras rolling and hundreds of thousands of fans to see it. But this was the best the Overfalls could do for an Altamont. The Eugene gig had to be canceled, Rev and Danny were arrested. Eventually the band was out two million dollars. The guy at Altamont at least had a gun on him; all Alan Wilbur Murdock had was his fingernails, his forehead, some gum, and the line about sucking donkey dongs in Hell. Three weeks later AaZ Records dropped TFO, the tour manager quit, and they were on their own.

North Bay Shore, Deer Park, Brentwood. What was it that Jules had said to him at the bar at Vagrants so many years ago? *I never wanna live on Long Island again. Seriously, Queens? . . . That's my boundary. I never want to go east of Queens again.*

Look how far we've come.

Danny takes an exit and follows it, then makes a right. It's dark out and menorah and Christmas-tree lights and flat-screen TVs twinkle from within quiet houses.

Tomorrow he'll call Jules and tell him the news, then he'll call Howie.

Jules, he'll say, *Joey needs to have open-heart surgery. Right away.*

No way! Jules will say.

Howie, he'll say, *Joey needs to have open-heart surgery. Right away.*

I was afraid that would be the case, Howie will say.

If I were going to die, Danny thinks as he drives past a small brick grocery store and a plumbing-supplies store, *I'd want to know it . . .* but would Joey? And what would Joey Mazz's Heaven be like? Congas, cowbells, crash cymbals, and timpani pounding, a toga-wearing, feather-winged, gold-haloed Keith Moon, high on

166

coke and cognac, signing Joey in at the Pearly Gates? (In Hell, it would surely be Buddy Rich signing you in.) Would Joey's drum Valhalla be him taking a solo on "Moby Dick" that shakes the Milky Way and never ever ends?

He turns the Suburban down a quiet, curving lane and, one by one, the houses roll by.

Where am I? Danny asks himself. Shady Lane, the street where he lives, should be right here. But it isn't.

It takes him a minute to realize he went the wrong way and drove to the opposite side of town, and to realize where he has to go.

Ten minutes later, he pulls up in his driveway. Jessica and Emily are putting ornaments on the tree, he sees, and Lily is upstairs studying in her room.

Carefully, he takes out Lily's new bike from the car and wheels it up to the door.

When he opens the door, Jessica comes up to him and says, "So? How'd it go with Angie?"

"Eh . . . it went," he says. "We need to hide this."

Jessica tells him she'll go up to Lily's room to keep Lily occupied, and that Danny should stash the bike up in the attic.

Emily goes to the bathroom off the kitchen, something she's been doing a lot of lately.

"So? The stroller?" Jessica whispers. "Did you get one?"

"Couldn't find a good one," he whispers back. "I'll look again tomorrow."

Eight
Come and Git It

"No," Michelle Grey says, sitting in the backseat with her nylon Mumford & Sons backpack on her lap, "you can just pull up and let me off here." On the seat to her left is a violin case that is so battered it's being held together by duct tape, Elmer's Glue, and a prayer.

Melissa is driving, and Howie sits on her right.

"Why don't we just take you all the way to school?" Melissa asks. "Are you embarrassed of us?"

Melissa pulls up across the street. It's 8:30 A.M. and the four-story, brown-brick high school is already buzzing with bleary-eyed kids and rushing, caffeinated parents. It's the week before the Christmas break and the morning air in Connecticut is bright but cold.

Michelle gets out and hoists her backpack, which is bigger than her head, onto her back—the weight of it nearly sending her down to the sidewalk. (Howie turns around to make sure she hadn't accidentally sat on the violin case . . . it's the tenth time since he left the house that he's checked.) She was always a clumsy kid but is smart in the nerdy subjects; sometimes she tries to get B's or B-plusses instead of all A's but even then can't pull it off.

Howie looks at the school and shudders. So many kids, hundreds of them. Kids who go to the bathroom and don't wash their hands and then touch one another all day long in school—it's like an 800-person relay race with a beaker of bacteria as the baton.

He gets out of the car, doesn't even close the door. He's worried that Michelle, while sticking her head through the driver's-side window to kiss her mom good-bye, will get clipped by a passing car. He sees that no cars are coming down Schoolhouse Lane, a very broad, tree-lined, child-safe avenue.

"I'll be okay, Daddy," Michelle says, trotting off.

Howie gets back in the car and closes the door.

169

"That backpack is going to permanently damage her spine," he says. "She should use rolling luggage instead. I hope she doesn't turn into a hunchback."

He keeps an eye on Michelle, who climbs the stairs into the school, nearly loses her balance on the second step, but then gets in safely.

"She'll be fine," Melissa says. "We better get going. Train time."

The train to New York City leaves in fifteen minutes. Melissa has some TFO accounting to do and will have to send a few files to Danny—files which, as usual, he won't be able to open. Howie, Melissa believes, is going into New York to take in his beloved cobalt blue, six-string Violectra, one of his three electric violins, to be fixed. But that's just a cover story, and all night long in their bed, Howie tossed and turned and hoped that he wouldn't forget to bring the violin, which today is nothing more than a prop.

"When will you be back?" she asks.

The Metro-North train station, a John Cheever paragraph come to life, is directly up ahead, and Howie can see briefcase-toting men and women, most of them interchangeable with one another, getting out of cars and climbing the stairs to the platform.

"Should be around four or so. I'll call."

"If I hear anything about Joey, I'll call, okay?"

They pass under a small bridge—Route 1 is directly overhead—and Howie suppresses a cringe. Over the years, thousands of tons of traffic have gone back and forth over that bridge, and he knows one day it's going to collapse, hopefully not on him, his wife, or his daughter.

Melissa pulls up their white Volvo sedan parallel with the train station.

"Is everything okay?" she asks him.

"Yeah. Fine. I just don't go to New York so much anymore."

"You're not worried about terrorism, are you?"

170

"No. That hadn't crossed my mind yet."

He gets out of the car, feels one pants pocket to make sure his wallet hasn't fallen out, feels a coat pocket to make sure his cell phone is still there, feels another pants pocket to make sure he has his keys, feels another coat pocket for his travel-size bottle of Purell. Everything is in its right place, and he hears the train to Grand Central cruising into the station. There isn't a car on that train, he knows, that won't be overflowing with mold.

He starts for the platform and Melissa says: "Aren't you forgetting something?"

"Oh yeah . . ."

The train comes to a stop, and Howie opens the rear car door and pulls out the violin.

*

An hour and twenty minutes later, Howie is strolling in Midtown Manhattan with his violin case in one hand and with a lot of time to kill. His appointment isn't until 2 P.M. But he was so worried about being late, about something going wrong with the trains (another train could derail and screw up every other train that day, or his own train could derail, or there could be a fire in the wooden piles beneath the railroad bridge in Harlem, or a blackout, or . . .), that he purposely got into New York City early. Too early, as it turns out.

One thing he wants to do is make sure that if anyone were to run into him by chance, he gets seen around Forty-Eighth Street, where he *would* be taking his electric violin to be fixed. His appointment is on Central Park West and Seventieth Street, and he's going to take a taxi right to the building and rush from the cab straight into the lobby so that nobody will see him around that neighborhood. He hates lying to Melissa and, a week ago, when he told her he was going into New York to get his violin fixed, he thought that she could see right through him. (He made sure to

171

"break" its pickup just in case she asked him to prove it was broken, which is something she would never do.) *What if somebody sees me around Central Park West,* he wonders now as he walks down bustling Lexington Avenue, *and then tells Melissa?* Will she think he's having an affair? Howie Grey, the one guy in the Overfalls, the one musician in any rock band, perhaps the one man in the world, who wouldn't ever have an affair.

A few minutes later, he sees some shoddy-looking scaffolding on the east side of Sixth Avenue and crosses over to the west side. One false move, one tiny misstep, and the scaffolding topples down over him and everyone else below it.

After weeks of Googling doctors who specialize in his problem—and of erasing his browsing history to make sure nobody would see it—Howie settled on a psychiatrist with the off-putting name of Dr. Robert Love. Harvard. Johns Hopkins medical school. Ten years at the Anxiety Disorders Center at the Institute of Living in Hartford. Affiliated with NewYork–Presbyterian Hospital for fifteen years. Howie waited until the house was empty one day and he made the call on his cell. The receptionist told him Dr. Love could see him as early as next week. They settled on a day and time, and then she told him the address. "And we're in suite number ten-D," she added.

"You're, uh," he said, feeing himself go pale, "you're on the tenth floor?"

"Yes," she said. "Is that okay?" He told her it was and then immediately erased the call from the Dialed Calls list on his cell.

Dr. Love's office was only a block away from the small studio he and Michelle moved to in the early days of the band, when the Overfalls were gigging all over town and recording *Come and Git It,* their first album, at Electric Lady. If anyone sees him up there and tells Melissa, he'll just say he was taking a nostalgic visit up to their old neighborhood.

She would believe that.

Ten floors up. Howie hates elevators. Not only does he hate the fact that the box he has to stand in, borne aloft by a flimsy cable that probably has not been inspected in ten years, is carrying him up to suicidal altitudes, he also hates the fact that other people are in that box with him, pressing against him, breathing all over him.

Could Dr. Love's receptionist sense that in his voice? Could she tell? On the other hand, this is what Dr. Love does for a living. *I will not be,* Howie has told himself a hundred times in the last few days, *the craziest guy this man has seen.*

Or will I?

Violin case in hand, he comes to a massive office building on Forty-Eighth Street and Sixth Avenue, in front of which a mammoth silver Christmas tree twinkles in the daylight, and makes a right.

There's a man who works down the street who could fix the violin's broken pickup. But Howie could fix it too, easily. He walks west slowly and wonders if he should actually bring it in to be fixed anyway. Just so Melissa will never know what he's really doing today.

*

A wicked jolt of pain shooting up from his heels to the base of his neck, Danny nearly drops the Christmas tree onto his living room floor. It feels as if a box cutter were slicing him up and down. Maybe he should have had someone help him. Maybe he should lose ten pounds come January. Lily, home from school today with a mild cold, could have come and helped him and even picked a better tree.

"Are you okay?" she calls out from her room.

He wasn't even aware he'd made a noise.

"Yeah!" he calls back. "For the most part!"

This five-foot Fraser is not that heavy, it's just a good, serviceable tree. But Danny's back is not so serviceable anymore,

173

and the cold air doesn't help. Years and years of loading and unloading gear, thousands of nights of standing on a stage . . . it's taken its toll.

Jessica and Emily are at Emily's ob-gyn—they'll be home any minute—so right now it's just Lily and him in the house. As soon as he gets the tree into the stand, he's going to the garage to play some piano and guitar and hope that Angie calls with good news. If she does, he'll call Jules and Howie. If she calls with bad news, he doesn't know what he'll do.

"Lily!" he says. "Get off your butt and help me with this tree!"

Even though the tree is presently wrapped in plastic twine, he cannot get it properly into the stand to then tighten the screws. He should've gotten a smaller one. But then his wife and two kids would've asked him: "Why so small?"

No answer.

"Lily! Can you come down and help?!"

She must have her iPod on. Danny can't stand the thing. Howie got him one for his birthday a few years ago—of the four Overfalls, only Howie ever remembers birthdays—and he told Howie he liked it, of course, but after a few times with the thing he shoved it into a drawer. The sound was great . . . Danny just didn't like the lack of controls, or of control. The Shuffle mode was terrible, it was way too random, and you couldn't control the bass or treble or balance between the two earphones or earbuds or whatever they're called.

He drags the tree across the carpet, fragrant pine needles (which will still be around in eight months) tumbling to the floor, and rests it against a wall, then bends over to recapture his breath . . . but bending over makes his back hurt even more. He trundles up the stairs, comes to Lily's room—the door is open—and sure enough, there she is, on her bed with a copy of *Allure,* the TV on with the sound off, and her iPod blasting into her ears. Some supposedly sexy chick who can't sing is singing; maybe it's that Katy Perry or Lady Gaga, or one of those types whose voices have to be filtered a thousand times before they become palatable, and who all end up sounding like Stephen Hawking's computer. Lily, too busy gazing at ten different genres of makeup on the page, doesn't see her old man, and he pinches her toes to get her attention. It's a good thing all she was doing was reading a magazine.

"I need some help with the tree," he says.

"I have a cold."

Oh yeah? I have a bad back and creaky knees and a never-ending sinus headache.

"I know," he says. "But you don't sound so bad. Help me out."

"Are Mom and Em back yet? Mom said she'd take me to the . . ."

She goes on and Danny stops listening. She doesn't even pull the buds out of her ears . . . all she does is lower the volume. Another reason Danny doesn't like iPods: he's used to knobs you can *feel* when you turn them and that are dedicated to doing only one thing. Bass, treble, balance, volume, mode. *Control!* And earbuds . . . they're built for sissies. What's so wrong with the old black Koss headphones, the ones that looked like bowling balls sawed in half? Those were the days, my friend.

"Not yet. They should be home soon. Hey, you don't happen to know who the father of Emily's baby is, do you?"

"Huh?"

He makes a hand gesture to her to pull out her earbuds, and she does.

"What did you say?" she asks with a sniffle.

"Nothing."

The phone rings, and Danny dashes to the next room and sees from the caller ID that it's an 800 number (and not Angie), just some robo-telemarketer who's going to hang up on the answering

175

machine. He walks back down the stairs to take another stab at the tree when the front door opens and in walk Jessica and Emily.

"Well?" he says weakly.

"A boy!" Jessica says, beaming. "A penis and everything!"

Emily, tall, radiant, and close to model-gorgeous, isn't beaming, however.

A son, Danny thinks as he starts singing the Who's "It's a Boy" inside his head. *Holy shit.*

"That's great news," he says, looking into Emily's eyes from his place above her on the stairs. "A boy, huh?"

Plates breaking, windows smashing, furniture burning, guitars blown up. Firecrackers, crystal meth, cheap wine, stealing cars, and knocking up fifteen-year-old girls.

His heart sinks. He was hoping for a girl. They're so much easier to deal with. If he can't insert a fucking five-foot Christmas tree into a stand then how the hell is he going to deal with a boy running around the house destroying things?

"Great tree!" Jessica says, throwing her keys and resting her handbag on the kitchen counter. "Although kind of on the small side, don't you think?"

"I'm going into the garage for a while," he says.

*

He couldn't lie to Melissa any more than he already had, so he took the cobalt blue Violectra to the man who could fix it. The man fixed it—for eighty dollars (it took less than ten minutes)—and now Howie can tell his wife that he did indeed get the Violectra repaired in Manhattan and he would not be lying.

"You could've done this," the man said to Howie when he handed back the instrument.

Howie then walked west to Eighth Avenue, got a taxi, and told the driver to take him to Seventieth and Central Park West. He's

176

in the car now, belted in securely, and he tells the driver, "Hey, could you let me off at Seventy-first and Columbus Avenue instead?"

Out of the car now, he checks his cell phone to see if anyone has called—Melissa making sure he's really in Manhattan getting the violin fixed, Danny calling with news about Joey, Michelle's school calling with news about a massacre—but nobody has. *Joey will be okay,* he thinks as he walks past rows of homey three- and four-story brownstones, some of which, under the bright sun, take on the color of chestnuts.

He puts his cell back in his pocket and makes sure that he has his wallet, his keys, his Purell, and, just for safe measure, his cell.

He's closing in on the house he and Melissa once lived in. They had one room and shared a bathroom with three other people on the fourth floor. It was an old-fashioned rooming house on the Upper West Side and cost less than $500 a month. Dr. Love's office is around the corner and down a block. He's very early for the appointment. But being two hours early is better than being two hours late.

Here it is, right in the middle of the street, virtually indistinguishable from the brownstones on either side. It looks exactly the same, of course, except the building is radiant and somehow looks sturdier than it used to be. It was quite an array of people living here back then: actors and actresses and waiters and waitresses, a junkie or two, a woman who told everyone she was a clothing designer but was a dominatrix, a defrocked French priest, and a cross-dressing short-order cook (a she passing herself off as a he). And Howie and Melissa, two short, quiet people who went about their business and kept to themselves. She got a job with a large accounting firm in Midtown and worked nine to five; he worked all hours of the day and night with Danny, Jules, and Mickey Sanford, and then Joey.

Howie comes to a stop at the building and looks up, sees his old window on the fourth floor, and puts a foot on the first step of the wide stone stairway leading up.

I can't believe I once lived here, he thinks. *Was that really me?*

The front door opens and a couple in a hurry comes out. The man is wearing a dark blue cashmere coat and a black suit, purple tie, and brown wingtip shoes, and the woman has on a furry black-and-gray shearling, a charcoal gray skirt suit, and black pumps.

"Call Chandra," the man says to his wife, "at three to make sure Jackson's okay."

"Will do," the woman says.

"Excuse me *please?*" the man arrogantly suggests to Howie.

"Oh, sorry," Howie says as he steps to the side, even though he's not in their way.

"No," the man says, getting up in Howie's grill and thrusting his jaw out. "I meant, what the hell are you doing on our property?"

"Uh . . . sorry . . . I used to live here, that's all."

"It's *our* place now, so you can beat it."

"The whole building?"

The man and woman look at each other and snort, then the man purposely bumps into Howie and brushes him aside—the violin case drops to the ground—and the couple gets into the Town Car that is waiting for them.

Howie dusts himself off, picks up the violin, and walks to Central Park West. The trees lining Central Park and inside the park are all bare, but the avenue's streetlights have been festooned for the holiday season.

Howie comes to a grand white-stone building. This is where Dr. Love works.

Is there a chance the doctor couldn't make it in today? It wouldn't be the worst thing in the world.

He takes out his cell phone and starts to dial Dr. Love's office number—he'd committed it to memory days ago—but then worries about caller ID. He doesn't want the receptionist to know it's him calling. He sees a pay phone on the corner and walks up to it, wishes he'd brought a can of Lysol so he could spray it, puts on a pair of gloves, and punches in the number.

"Doctor's office," a woman answers.

"Uh, yes," he says. "I have an appointment tomorrow but I'm calling to make sure that the . . . is the doctor in today? When I saw him last week he said something about . . ."

His voice dies off and a few seconds later the woman says, "Yes, the doctor is seeing patients today. Do you wish to—"

He hangs up and stares across the street at the trees in the park until they fade into crosshatching, then he takes off his gloves, takes out the Purell, and rubs his hands clean.

What am I going to say to him? Howie wonders. He still has hours before the appointment. *Doctor, it's been more than thirty years since I've gotten more than two hours consecutive sleep and it's killing me? Doctor, I worry that I am worrying myself to death? Doctor, are you laughing at me and at all your patients?* Is that what he tells him?

He walks back to his old building and, careful not to put his foot down on the stoop this time, looks up at the fourth-floor window again.

*

It was the hardest Howie had ever worked: rehearsals, gigging in clubs from Baltimore up to Massachusetts (and believing they saw Mickey Sanford in every crowd), then recording the album, often not showing up at the studio until past midnight. Working and surviving on three hours' sleep or less, eating junk on the fly (and always eating it standing up; he cannot remember eating one meal

179

sitting down). The band would leave the Lone Star Café, Kenny's Castaways, or Vagrants at two in the morning, show up at Electric Lady Land at two-thirty, and then leave there at noon and have to perform somewhere at eight that night—and then do it all over again. Every day, every night, for months.

And all because of his violin.

Two days after Jules Rose had called him up, following the demise of anaesthesia, Howie was putting his two basses into the trunk of Melissa's yellow VW Bug, about to drive to Long Island to audition, when Melissa said to him: "Maybe you should bring a few other instruments, too?"

Howie was already anxious enough and this didn't help.

"Just so they know what else you can do," she added.

The doors to the Beetle were open, and now Howie didn't know what to do. He just stood there, teetering from one foot to the other with his hands in his pockets.

"I don't know."

Melissa told him to hold on and that's what he did, just staying in the driveway of the house in Fairview on the edge of the woods. It was sunny out, no breeze at all, a crystal-clear summer day. Jules really hadn't imparted much information to him over the phone; he'd just mentioned the Tarnished Angels, Avalanche, the Mud Lushes, and something about earthiness and grittiness. Howie was coming from the entirely wrong direction. *Why* me, he wondered. *I'm prog rock! I'm Edgard Varèse and John Cage and Van der Graaf Generator. They want* Exile on Main St. *and I've never even* been *to Main Street.* And, just as he realized his girlfriend might be right, he saw her stumbling out of the house overloaded with instruments.

He went over to her and grabbed a few. A tenor sax and an alto, two flutes, a bassoon, an accordion, and more.

"This isn't going to fit," he said.

180

In the end he only brought the two bass guitars, the tenor sax, and a piccolo. A violin, though, was already in the car, and Howie, not really thinking about it, just left it in there.

Two hours later, after an uneventful but nerve-wracking ride over the wobbly Throgs Necks Bridge and Sunrise Highway, he was sitting outside Danny's house.

When he showed up, the others had already been there a while. Mickey Sanford, whom Howie had never met but had heard of, was in the process of setting up a small, simple drum kit. He was tall, Howie saw, and sinewy and had long wavy black hair and reptile tattoos. Right away Howie was scared of him. It was just the way he moved . . . that and the leather wristbands. He was cocky, unkind, and foul.

Jules was there with a girl named Tara O'Neill who had porcelain skin and beautiful blond hair that went all the way down to her narrow waist, and had there been an American Ass Hall of Fame, hers would have been a charter member. Jules had a Les Paul and a National, and his golden brown hair was shoulder-length and he liked to whip it around when he spoke and walked. Howie and he had met a few times, and when Jules saw him he came over and gave him the power shake. "Thanks for showing up," Jules said. "Don't worry—they're gonna love you."

Jules introduced Howie to Danny, and the two of them weren't sure if they'd ever met before or not. Right away, Howie could tell that Danny was the brains of the operation, even though it was Danny who spoke the least and who helped Howie take his basses, sax, and flute out of the car. When he saw the piccolo he grimaced but didn't say anything, and Howie could tell from his stony countenance that Danny wanted to say to him: *Hey, you can forget all about your Robert Fripp, your mellotron, and your Soft Machine shit if you wanna rock with us. When the Piper at the Gates of Dawn sees and hears us, he's gonna slam the gates shut.* (Howie was glad Danny hadn't noticed the violin in the trunk.) Allison,

181

Danny's girlfriend, was there, too: she and Tara sat at a small white table and drank iced tea and watched their would-be rock-star boyfriends attempt to form a new band.

While they tuned up, Danny and Jules were trying, in vain, to explain what their group, the Ventilators, was going to be about, and Howie, who wasn't really getting it, nodded and said, "Uh-huh" a lot. Finally, Mickey twirled his sticks and said, "Can we just cut the verbal shit and play something?" Danny, who was quite aware that he and Jules weren't the most eloquent people around, said, "Yeah . . . good idea," and Danny, Jules, and Mickey launched into a slow, painful countryish song called "Waiting and Wilting." After a few bars, Danny stopped and asked Howie, "You can read music, right? That's what Jules said."

"Yeah, definitely."

These guys, Howie thought, *don't like me already. I'm sunk.*

They started over from the beginning and this time Howie joined in. It took only a minute but . . . *he got it.* He got all of it. He got the grungy, achy, 5-A.M. sound and groove that Danny was looking for, and what Jules had brought to the table to engender it. This band was going to be the polar opposite of everything that anaesthesia had been, and it was a miracle that the issue of the two bands even fell under the same category, that category being music. anaesthesia was way out there in the dark, empty, chilled space of Pink Floyd's "Set the Controls for the Heart of the Sun" and "Astronomy Domine." The Ventilators, though, were not in outer space and had probably never even looked up to see it; they were in the gutter, or soaking in damp sheets in a bug-infested room littered with used rubbers and dirty needles. The music of the spheres that anaesthesia had tried to emulate—Danny and Jules had taken it and tossed it into the toilet.

They went through six songs. Mickey's girlfriend of that month—a dark, top-heavy Italian girl named Susan—drove up in a Chevy Nova and sat with the other girls, and Danny, Jules, Mickey, and Howie started jamming, fucking around, going from song to song, and having a good time. Songs of their youth, songs they'd heard on the transistor radios they'd hidden under their pillows at night. They did "Summer in the City" and "The Tracks of My Tears" and "98.6," and worked their way forward in time. They took a beer break and cooked some hot dogs on the grill and smoked a joint that had been rolled in Mickey's hash oil. Howie abstained, of course.

"What, you're not into this?" Mickey asked him with an accusatory tone.

"Not right now," Howie said, feeling all eyes on him.

"You sure?"

"If he doesn't want to," Tara said, "don't push him."

"Yeah, really," Allison said.

After the Buds, hot dogs, and the joint, they sat back down and ripped through a few more songs. Pleasantly surprised about the country element in the music, Howie did his best but he wasn't sure he was impressing Danny, whose socks it were he knew he had to knock off. But stone-faced Danny Ault didn't give away much, not that day or in the years to come.

Tara said she would drive to the IGA to buy another two six-packs and got in her beige Buick Riviera. For no reason at all she honked her car horn two times as she was driving away, and when they heard it, Jules and Danny and Howie all looked at each other and grinned. They *knew* that sound, and each one of them knew the others knew it, too: It was the same exact honk as the one that began "Country Honk" on *Let It Bleed.* The three of them laughed and went into that song and, a few bars into it, Mickey said, "Too bad we don't have a fiddle."

Howie set down his bass and said: "Hold on."

He walked over to his VW and got out his violin and bow.

"Ready when you are, gents," he said, sitting back down with them.

"Honk-honk!" Danny said, and they started playing again, this time with Howie playing violin, Jules deftly sliding across his National and making it peal through the summer air, Danny singing as if he'd been born and raised in a shack outside Nashville, and Mickey keeping time. While Howie played, he noticed Danny sneaking a few glances over at Jules.

After the song was over, Mickey said, "Fuckin' A, that was pretty good."

"So," Danny, lighting up a cigarette, said to Howie, "when can you start?"

Two months later Howie and Melissa moved to Seventy-first Street. Worrying all the time that it might not work out, they kept paying rent for the Fairview house. Melissa would wake up at seven in the morning and often Howie would still not be home . . . he was either recording or had wound up crashing on Danny's floor or Jules's couch. Jules was a slob and Howie always made sure to take long, hot showers after he stayed over there—you never knew what sort of spirochetes might be squirming across the sofa. (Howie could not believe the women Jules brought home. Skanks of every shape, height, and weight. Girls with skin so bad you couldn't even see what their faces looked like.) He liked the songs Danny and Jules were coming up with and eventually began chipping in with suggestions and writing with them . . . and unlike his time with prior bands, Danny and Jules were open to ideas. We can add a few horns here, Howie would say, or why not put in a barely audible electric piano right here? Or let's cut the sax solo in half, save time for another verse or more guitar. Much to his surprise, not only was Danny listening, but most of Howie's suggestions were actually tried out. As the months passed, Howie felt more comfortable, he got to know the huge foibles and tiny quirks of his bandmates—and they picked up on his—and one night at Vagrants he told Danny and Jules he'd heard a few high-school kids talking about the test they'd just taken and how there was this dangerous strait in Canada named

184

the Furious Overfalls . . . and as soon as Howie said it, Danny and Jules looked at each other and they slapped him on the back. As of that instant that was who they were: the Furious Overfalls.

But it wasn't until they began working on *Come and Git It* that Howie really made his bones. By this time, Mickey had fled the scene and Joey Mazz had replaced him. (Howie was so glad that Mickey had split town that, the night it happened, he went home and nearly cried into Melissa's arms. He'd been petrified of Mickey and he liked Joey, who, though he read comic books and had to struggle to finish them, was a very sweet guy.) AaZ Records had tried to get Jimmy Miller or Al Kooper to produce the record but couldn't, so they hired this hack named Hal Clay, who'd produced about thirty albums up to that point. Hal knew what TFO was trying to do but his sole concern was squeezing one or two hit singles out of the album, something Danny wasn't really interested in. ("I don't want a hit single," he said. "I just want to be good.") Glum, seasoned session men—sax and horn players, pianists, organists—and unsteady, coked-up backup singers came in at god-awful hours of the night, played and sang, and then left without uttering a word.

Sometimes the atmosphere in the studio was toxic: Danny wouldn't talk to Hal so Hal had to talk to Jules, who had to relay it to Danny; Danny was so pissed that Jules was talking to Hal that he had to talk to Howie, who had to talk to Jules, who had to relay it back to Hal; and on the occasions when they *were* talking to each other, Danny was yelling his lungs out (and wrecking his voice) and threatening to beat the shit out of Hal. "You're fucking the whole thing up, Hal!" he'd yell, and Hal would yell back: "But it's for a good cause!" Howie became the quiet voice of reason. When Hal and Chunky Scrofa, the engineer of that disc and the next four TFO albums, couldn't take the long hours and the arguing anymore and split for the night, Howie would take over the mixing board and, with nobody else there but the band and a few hangers-on, that was

185

when they did their best work. That's when they sizzled and soared and lived up to their name.

After five months TFO had hours and hours of tape for Hal and Chunky to mix. Then came more arguing, more petulance and tantrums and turf battles. Lew Aaronson, the head of AaZ Records (his nickname in the business was "The Lizard of AaZ"), told Velcro Pravda to make peace, but Velcro was weak and ineffectual and would have had a better chance with Menachem Begin and Yasser Arafat. Hal even started bringing some muscle along with him, two huge guys—one of whom was nicknamed Rev—who only wore black and who packed sleek, silver handguns.

"Can't we just do it the band's way?" Chunky asked Hal.

"No," Hal snapped, "we cannot!"

But Danny wore Hal out, and Hal caved easier and easier, and when the album came out—to a tepid three-star review from *Rolling Stone,* and better reviews from the *Village Voice, CREEM,* and *Trouser Press,* and a flat-out rave in *Crawdaddy!*—it contained the type of songs, for the most part, that TFO had wanted to put out in the first place.

It wasn't their fault that when their record came out, David Bowie had already come out with *Station to Station,* and the Ramones released *Rocket to Russia,* and Elvis Costello put out *My Aim is True;* that Talking Heads and the Clash also released their first albums, and that *Saturday Night Fever* had come out, too.

"There's just not a hit here," were the last words Hal Clay ever said to the band.

Hal was right, but the album still sold a respectable 200,000 copies.

"It's too polished," was Danny's major complaint about *Come and Git It.* He was looking for something rougher: he wanted less gleaming titanium and more raw ore and slag. Next time, he vowed to the band, we won't be so goddamn agreeable.

186

All the reviews, Howie noticed, mentioned the fact that the band hailed from Long Island and seemed to hold it against them. "The suburban Long Island–based quartet," *CREEM* called them. "This seemingly gritty rock band," *Rolling Stone* wrote, "emerged from the very same narcoleptic 'burbs of Long Island that brought you none other than Billy Joel." (It was like John 1:46 all over again, when Nathanael asks Philip: "Nazareth! Can anything good come from there?") And not one newspaper or magazine ever pointed out that the band's bass player was not even from Long Island and had never once lived there.

Howie will never forget it, though, for as long as he lives: Walking up Seventy-first Street with one advance copy of *Come and Git It* under his arm. He'd gotten two hours' sleep and it was just past seven in the morning, and Melissa was about to wake up to go to work. He crept up the dark, carpeted stairs of the rooming house, smelled the stale cigarette smoke and cat pee, and put his key in the flimsy lock of his door. The lights were off and Melissa was asleep in their small bed in the corner of the cramped but orderly one-room they lived in.

He pulled the blinds up, the morning light streaming in from Central Park, and he sat down on the edge of the bed and stirred Melissa, then pulled out the LP. On the cover, in spectacular grainy black and white, was a photo of the Overfalls lined up against a small building on MacDougal Alley, food wrappers and cigarette butts and broken bottles and squashed cans at their feet. The picture was taken at six in the morning, and the band had been up for thirty hours straight and looked it. (After months of working on the record, it was decided they needed one blistering number to liven up Side 2, and they had come up with "Dog Water Girls" and then spent three-and-a-half days getting it down right.) In the photo, they exuded pain, bleariness, and hunger: Danny had puffy bags under his bloodshot eyes and sweat on the armpits of his shirt; Jules looked pale and emaciated and was nonchalantly displaying the makings of

187

a hard-on; Howie looked spent, dazed, and confused; and Joey was a corpse, the ghost of a war casualty. Even the photographer, you could tell, had been up all night doing things she should not have been doing (which, in this case, was one gram of cocaine, three poppers, five Dixie cups of Courvoisier, and eight-and-a-half inches of Jules Rose). Still, to Howie and Melissa that morning, the album smelled like freshly cut lilacs.

"Here," he said as she sat up and rubbed the sleep from her eyes. "Look at this! Unbelievable, isn't it? We're gonna make it!"

*

On the other side of Long Island Sound, Danny's Christmas tree is finally in its stand, it still hasn't been decorated, Jessica and Lily have gone to the mall, and now Danny and Emily are alone in the house on Shady Lane. This doesn't happen so frequently anymore, and neither of them feels too comfortable when it does.

Especially lately.

A son. Here comes the son. "Father and Son"—the only decent song Cat Stevens ever wrote. That terrible song Harry Chapin did about a father and son, whatever the name of that was. Sonny Boy Williamson. Sonny, once so true . . .

(There are, Danny knows, not too many rock songs about grandparents.)

"I'm making tuna salad," he says from the kitchen to Emily on the couch. "You want some?"

Emily mutes the makeover TV show she's watching and says, "You can't be serious, can you?"

He shakes his head, not getting it.

"Tuna?" she says, turning the sound back on. "The mercury???"

Oh yeah. Mercury. And then he wonders if Hot Tuna was ever a Mercury Records band.

188

From his vantage point in the kitchen, all he can see of Emily is the top of her blond head. He opens a can of Bumble Bee and nearly slices off the tip of the index finger on his left hand. About to go to the fridge to get some mayo, he drops the can of tuna on the floor. He's on edge today . . . there's too much going on. Joey's operation, the holidays, having to deal with Melissa Grey and TFO finances, and Emily. Sometimes it's better to be all alone in a hotel room in a faraway town whose name you don't even know. He knows he could see his GP and the guy would prescribe tranquilizers, but then he'd be taking them every day, three times a day. And he'd be right back where he started.

Emily—for whatever foolish reason—didn't want to know the gender of the kid, but the technician doing the sonogram screwed up and spilled the beans. For a minute, Jessica told Danny, Emily was upset that the surprise had been spoiled, but then she calmed down. She was delighted she was having a boy. (Of course, Danny knew, she'd have been equally as delighted if she were having a girl—they should invent some third gender nobody wants just so you can quantify your glee.) *But it was a boy,* he wanted to remind Emily, *who got you into this fuckin' mess! And you want* another *one around?!*

Staring into the fridge, Danny has forgotten why he's looking in there in the first place. Was it jelly he wanted? He turns back, sees the Bumble Bee on the counter, and realizes that he wants mayonnaise, then looks back in the fridge and sees they don't have any.

"How about peanut butter and jelly?" he says. It's at the "reveal" part of the makeover show: the family's house has been overhauled from the ground up, their hair has been remodeled and their wardrobes restocked, and people are sobbing tears of joy.

"On whole wheat please," Emily says.

Five minutes later, Danny is on the couch with his eldest daughter, both of them eating sloppily constructed peanut butter and

189

jelly sandwiches. The makeover show has ended and the next rerun, with a different lumpy family living inside a different lumpy house, has come on.

"So now," he says, "that you know it's a boy, have you come up with any names for the kid?"

She tilts her head cryptically . . . it's something between a positive nod and a negative shake.

"You haven't even thought of it?" he pries further. "You must have."

"Of course, I have some ideas," she says. Neither of them looks at each other.

Danny's cell rings. Thinking that it might be her phone, Emily takes out her phone and looks at it while he takes his out of his jeans pocket. He sees that it's Melissa calling and thinks, *Man, I really do not want to talk to her right now,* and pushes the button so the call goes straight to voice mail. Out of the corner of his eye, he notices that, rather than put her phone back in her pocket, Emily has set it by her feet on the coffee table.

"What do think of the name Raymond?" she says. "Or Derek?"

Raymond? Ray Davies. Stevie Ray Vaughan. Ray Charles. Ray Manzarek. Link Wray. Derek? Derek and the Dominos. Derek Trucks. That guy Derek Somebody who had something to do with the Beatles. Derek Smalls from *Spinal Tap.*

"They're both good names."

"You're just saying that. I could've said Igor or Adolf and you would've said you liked it."

"No. Ray and Derek are good names. Igor I'm on the fence about."

"What about Jaden or Cody?"

"You want me to disown you? Nah, no good."

This is the longest conversation they've had in quite some time and Danny doesn't want it to end.

"You're just saying that now, too, so you look more objective."

"Yeah, you could be right."

Danny puts his feet on the coffee table. For the first time since he brought the tree into the house, he catches a bracing whiff of it.

"So . . ." he begins, "have you told whoever is the lucky dude who happens to be the father of this Adolf Ault that he's going to have a son and not a daughter?"

She turns to him and says, "Yes. He knows."

He waits a few seconds and asks: "And he's happy about that, I hope? Assuming it's a he who's the father?"

"Yes, *he* is happy . . ." is all she says.

"Okay . . . no more questions in the next hour. I promise."

He takes his plate to the kitchen and dumps it in the sink. Emily stands up, amniotic fluid, umbilical cord, male fetus and all, and stretches with a deep groan that shakes a few more needles off the tree. She turns off the TV with the remote, tells her father she's going to lie down up in her room, and slogs upstairs as though she's dragging a Hammond organ and Leslie speaker behind her.

When she is safely out of sight, Danny looks at the coffee table.

Her cell phone is still there.

He picks it up, glances up at the stairs, and goes through her Dialed Calls list. But it's empty. He goes to her Received Calls and that's empty, too. According to this phone, then, Emily, who spends half her waking life talking and twiddling around with it, has never once dialed or gotten one single call, or sent or received one single text message. If she really did inform Mystery Man that he's having a son, then she was smart enough to erase any trace just in case one of her parents were a snoop, and for a few seconds his heart fills with pride over his daughter's guile. *Maybe,* he thinks, *I did raise her right after all.*

191

He hears his SUV grinding to a stop on the gravel outside and two doors opening and closing, and a moment later in walk Jessica and Lily, flushed from the cold and bearing T.J.Maxx shopping bags.

"Any news about Joey?" Jessica asks him.

"What are you doing with Em's phone?" Lily asks him.

"Uh . . . oh yeah," he says, putting the phone back down on the coffee table and feeling the sudden urge to go back to the garage, play guitar, and maybe get in a nap. "I thought it was mine." He turns to Jessica and says, "No. Nothing yet. I guess that's good news."

Jessica tells him that the Christmas tree looks nice, Lily skips up the stairs, and then Danny hears another car pull into their driveway. He and Jessica see through the living-room window that it's a blue Malibu.

"Uh oh," he says. Something must be very wrong.

Angie, carrying a Burlington Coat Factory shopping bag, gets out of the car and slams the door. The wind sends her curly black hair and thick black scarf blowing into each other until they become one.

"Maybe you want to go upstairs?" Danny whispers to his wife.

"Why?" she says.

Maybe she's not scared of Angie, but right now Danny is.

He opens the door. Angie looks like she's already been through too much for one day. And it's not even two o'clock.

"Why were you," Emily asks her father from the top of the stairs, "looking at my phone?"

"I wasn't!" he calls out to her with his back turned. "It was an accident!" Then he tells Angie to come in.

Angie and Jessica offer each other tepid kisses on the cheek. Not quite an air kiss but not full contact either. After the kiss Angie looks at her and she looks at Angie and, for the millionth time, they size each other up disapprovingly. Five-foot-nine college graduate Jessica, with her long blond hair, camel pants, chunky beige sweater tied over her shoulders, and teal ankle-high boots, and five-foot-three high-school dropout Angie in rocker black.

"Can I get you something?" Jessica asks.

"No," Angie says, turning away from her. "Danny, it's bad. They opened Joey up, they scoped around, and they can't operate. Fucking butchers! It's 'useless'—that's the word the doctor told me. *Useless.* The awtuhries . . . they're too blocked up to operate on. There's nothing they can do and it's just a matter—he could go any time."

Danny puts his hands in his pockets, feels the material, and grabs it. *Why couldn't she have called,* he wonders. *Why do this in person? And why come to me?*

"Oh, Angie," Jessica says, "I'm so sorry."

Danny takes his right hand out of his pocket and covers his closed mouth, grabs his jaw and cheeks, and feels the floor quaking beneath him.

"Where is he?" he asks.

"He's at the hospital. He's not conscious yet, but he's not really unconscious. He's havin' a ball."

Why couldn't you have called me with this? Why does it have to be me you come to? He's a drummer in the band I'm in, that's all. A drummer. *You come to me because I write the lyrics?! That makes me responsible? We are a band, we're a company, we're not a family. This isn't the Monkees, where we all live in the same fucking house!*

"Angie, are you sure," Jessica asks her again, "I can't get you anything?"

"You have no right," Emily says, still at the stairs, "to pry like that!"

"Emily!" Jessica says, turning around. "*Please!* Now isn't a good time."

Emily walks back to her room.

"Here," Angie says, handing Danny the shopping bag. "One extra-large faux-fur coat. Larry Levine. You owe me a hundred and eighty-three dollars."

"So he doesn't know yet?" Danny asks Angie softly. The floor isn't quaking anymore . . . now one half of it is mechanically pulling away from the other half and he feels as if he's about to plummet to the churning core of the planet. "He has no idea?"

She shakes her head, takes a step toward him, and buries herself in his chest. He puts his hand on her head and grabs her scalp. She feels ice cold. He opens his eyes and sees his wife looking at him. She doesn't look happy but he can't tell if it's because of Joey or Angie or Emily, or because of all of it.

Angie pulls her face away from his chest and says: "Danny . . . I was hoping you'd be the one to tell him."

*

Howie doesn't feel like taking an elevator right now, so after telling the doorman he's going up to see Dr. Love, he walks up the ten flights of stairs, avoiding the second step and the next to last step on each landing. By the time he makes it to the eighth floor, still in a sweater and his winter coat, he's clammy and out of breath. He's also one hour early for the appointment.

He opens the door to the tenth-floor stairwell, sees the hallway, and makes a left. After wiping his brow with his sleeve, he comes to Suite 10D. There are three other doctors, Howie sees, who share the offices with Dr. Love.

PLEASE RING, a small sign beneath the buzzer says.

Howie lifts his hand to ring but brings it back down to his side. He tries again but can't do it. He keeps his glove on so that, in case he *can* ring the bell, he won't have to wash his hand.

Okay, he thinks, *this time I will ring the bell.* But he still cannot lift his hand.

He walks back downstairs, checks to make sure he still has his wallet, phone, keys, and Purell, gets his breath back, and walks around the block. It's gotten sunnier and colder outside. He goes past his old building on Seventy-first Street, winds around Columbus Avenue, and comes back to Central Park West. The light is so bright today he cannot tell if the holiday lights on all the trees along the avenue have been turned on or not.

"Suite Ten-D," he says to the same doorman as before. "Doctor Love?"

"Go right ahead," the doorman says, raising an eyebrow.

I've got to do this, Howie says to himself, going up the stairs. *I have to. It'll be good for me and for Melissa and Michelle. I have to get myself right.* The longest journey, he remembers as he skips the second step on the ninth floor, begins with the first step.

This time he cannot even make it to the door. So he goes back down again and walks around the block, still clutching the violin case.

"Suite Ten-D," he says to the doorman, who now raises both eyebrows.

Ten flights up, after deliberating for ten minutes, he rings the bell. He's prepared to hear, "Who is it?" and then answer "Howie Grey!" He's been rehearsing it for days. But instead of someone asking who he is, the buzzer sounds and he opens the door and walks in.

The waiting room is nearly a perfect square. There are two green couches and four blue chairs and, behind unsullied sliding panes of glass, two receptionists. Two people are waiting in the room presently, a woman in her late fifties with thin brown hair and a hook nose, and a man about twenty-five who's reading the *Times.* They both look at Howie for a second, then look away. Being seen in this office . . . it's like having a sign around your neck that says: I

195

HAVE A LOT OF PROBLEMS. Howie looks down—he doesn't want the other patients to know that he's seen them—and walks to the receptionist.

"Grey," he tells them.

"You're very early," one of them, a round Hispanic woman, says.

"Yes. I know. That's because Howie can't make it today."

"Excuse me?"

Howie hears his cell phone buzz. He takes it out of his coat and sees that Danny is calling him. He lets the call go to voice mail and resumes.

"I'm his brother," he tells her. "Howie couldn't make it today and I live on Seventy-first Street so I thought I'd tell you personally."

"Okay," the woman says. "Please have him call and make another appointment."

He nods, tries not to look at the other patients as he walks out, and gently closes the door behind him.

Did the receptionist believe him? He doesn't think so. The patients in the waiting room probably overheard him. Did they believe him? Probably not.

He checks to make sure he has his wallet, cell, keys, and Purell and starts walking down the stairs again. *What happens,* he thinks, *if I gather up enough nerve to call and make another appointment, and this time I'm able to go through with it and show up? Do I have to now lie to the doctor and tell him I have a brother who lives down the street? What do I name my brother? Is he older or younger? Did we get along as kids? But the receptionist will remember me and will know what I look like. So do I tell them I'm an identical twin?*

And so on . . .

He heads west down Seventy-first Street. He'll walk downtown to Grand Central and get a train home. He tries not to

196

whimper. *I fucked up,* he thinks as he makes sure he has his wallet, keys, phone, and Purell. *I fucked up again.* Shaking his head more with resignation than disbelief, he's barely aware of anything and anyone around him. On Sixty-fourth Street and Broadway he's suddenly jarred back to life when someone—he has no idea who it is, how big the person is, or what he looks like—runs right into him and knocks him over, then runs away.

Two strangers help Howie up. He thanks them and looks down.

From the impact of being struck, the violin case had been knocked out of his hands. The case hit the ground and, he sees, the violin has tumbled out.

"You okay?" someone asks him.

"Yes . . . thanks," Howie answers.

He bends down and picks up the violin, examines it closely, and sees that it's broken.

Nine
Where We All Belong

Four-day-old January snow covers the asphalt outside the Parkway Diner, which lies 500 yards south of the Sunrise Highway where Lindenhurst fades into Babylon. The diner, whose facade drips melting ice to the snow, is a dull re-creation of a more lustrous re-creation of a genuine Depression Era diner; it seats a hundred and the wait staff wears powder blue uniforms. In the parking lot a man in stained kitchen whites shovels snow, and across the road stands a gas station, a Burger King, and the plywood-covered shell of a Blockbuster that closed a year ago. It's just past one in the afternoon, and seated in a booth at the window are Danny, Jules, and Howie.

"I call," Danny says, methodically ripping up a paper napkin, "once a week or so. He sounds good. You wouldn't know anything was wrong."

"Yeah, my old man," Jules says, "sounded great the week before he died, too."

Howie sneaks a peek at his watch. Melissa drove him here and will be back to pick him up at exactly one-thirty. The roads from Connecticut to Long Island were slick today and there was no way Howie was going to drive. After he checks his watch he stirs around the straw in his Sprite once clockwise, then twice around counterclockwise.

"I should call him," Howie says.

The waitress comes and refills Danny and Jules's coffee mugs. The door opens and a short girl about eighteen years old with frizzy brown hair rushes in, stomps the snow off her shoes on the mat, then goes behind the long counter.

"Not bad," Jules says.

"She looks like she's twelve," Howie says.

"Hey, if twelve was good enough for Jerry Lee Lewis, it's good enough for me."

Howie again stirs his drink once clockwise and twice counterclockwise and says: "I don't know . . . If I had some disease and were going to die, I'd want to know about it. I'd want the doctor or my wife or someone to tell me."

"We'll remember that," Jules says.

"I guess Joey doesn't want to know," Danny says.

"But he doesn't know," Howie says, "so how can he know he doesn't want to know?"

Danny rubs the gray stubble on his chin and says, "Angie assumes he wouldn't want to know. She knows him a whole lot better then we do, right? The doctor said he was going to tell Joey and she lit into him and scared the piss out of him."

Jules thinks about it quickly. Suppose a doctor told him he had a year to live: what would he do? Sure, he could try to round up all the pussy he could in the remaining 365 and a quarter days and go out in a real blaze of glory. Or he could track down Rhonda Wentworth and spend the last months of his life with her, as long as her husband wouldn't mind (and he would, which would only make it better). But what if whatever disease he was dying of made him so weak he couldn't have sex? Either way, he'd want to know the truth. And he's glad he doesn't have a wife around to not tell it to him.

"Okay," Danny says, eager to change the subject. "Here it is. And it's a doozy."

He reaches into one of the twelve pockets of his parka and takes out three printouts of their upcoming tour schedule. The Furious Overfalls Winter Tour 2012—as usual, in the cold months the band heads south and southwest, and this year will be no exception. Howie reads the printout; Jules barely looks at his. The tour begins in D.C., goes to Philly and Atlantic City, and cuts due south; then they swing over to New Orleans, Austin, and San Antonio, then head farther west to Arizona, California, and Portland.

"You trying to kill us?" Jules says.

200

"This is a lot," Howie says. (He notices that the band is booked to play San Francisco . . . He thinks of saying something about it but then thinks better of it.)

All these cities and towns and highways full of drunk drivers. Hotel rooms, motel rooms, linens and bathroom floors and showers that barely get cleaned. Fungus, mildew, bedbugs, and bacteria. Howie looks at his watch, stirs his Sprite the same way as before, and when he looks back up he sees that Danny has been noticing it.

"And so, uh, *what* are we doing for a drummer again?" Jules asks.

The frizzy-haired girl, still toting around some baby fat in her cheeks, has slipped into her waitress outfit. She glides by the booth and Jules checks her out.

"We have two problems," Danny says, transplanting the surviving remnants of his omelet with a fork. "One, we need a new drummer. And two, we'd have to tell Joey this."

"There are tons of drummers out there," Jules says. "I bet a lot of 'em would *kill* to play with us."

Danny doesn't know if there's one drummer out there who would kill or even injure to play in the Overfalls, but he doesn't want to burst Jules's bubble. This is the first time in years that the group has sat down and had a serious discussion. Usually when they eat together, most of the meal is spent either sitting in silence or getting on Joey's case (like the time Joey told them Mallomar cookies were grown and not manufactured—they didn't let up on him for months after that). Danny knew this meeting had to happen and kept putting it off. And when he left his house today to come here, he resolved he was going to tell the others he was leaving TFO. But now he doesn't know if he can go through with it. And if he can go through with it, when? When does he drop the bomb?

"How would we even get one?" Howie says. "I forget how it's done."

201

The waitress comes over and asks Howie if he wants coffee, and he looks up and says no.

"Are you on the menu?" Jules asks her. "'Cause you look kind of delicious."

Danny asks her to bring him a baked apple. He knows it's going to give him heartburn but it's cold out and there isn't much else to look forward to. Somewhere in his parka, in pocket four or nine, is a tube of Rolaids.

"Does *Rolling Stone,*" Jules says, "still run ads for musicians?"

Danny and Howie look at each other and Jules lets out a burp that renders whatever is currently on the jukebox inaudible for four seconds.

"They haven't run ads like those," Danny says, "since Grace Slick was sexy."

"There's always Mickey Sanford," Jules says.

"Well, he's dead most likely. And would you really *want* him in the band?"

"Oh no. No fuckin' way."

"Can you imagine," Howie says, "if Joey ever found out that Mickey replaced him?"

"Man," Jules says, "if Mickey ever came back, I'd start another band. I—"

The waitress sets down a brown bowl with an equally brown baked apple jiggling around inside it. The three of them don't say anything for an uncomfortable few seconds, and Jules knows why: he once *did* try to start another band . . . The wheels were in motion; he had Bob Smith on drums, a bassist, and his buddy Ike Kates on keyboards and vocals all lined up, and he had songs he'd never shown Danny or anybody else. Jules Rose's Raging Blue Balls— that was what he and Ike were going to call the band. It was a year after *Dead End Road,* after AaZ Records dropped TFO. Jules hadn't told anyone . . . he was just going to do it. But Danny found out and told Jules that he was more than welcome to form his own band and do side projects, but if he did, he'd no longer be welcome in TFO and that the door would never be open for him again. That was the end of Jules's solo career, and not one time since then, in all the decades, has it ever been mentioned. It never happened.

"So we don't know anyone, is that it?" Jules says.

Forty years making music and they do not know where to find a new drummer. Do they steal one from another group? Put an ad in *Modern Drummer or Snare Tri-Quarterly* or some other drum magazine? But what if Joey were to see it?

"I could call Chunky Scrofa," Danny says. "He might be able to help."

Howie, without even thinking about it, puts the straw back into his glass of Sprite and says, "You know . . . we could always use a drum machine. They're not expensive at all, they're certainly reliable, and I could figure out how to program it in a day. They're really just sophisticated metronomes with brains."

A sophisticated metronome with a brain, Danny thinks. *That's more than Joey is.*

"Man, I don't know," Jules says, leaning in toward Howie. "A *machine?* I mean, like, how impersonal can you get? That shits in the face of everything we're about."

"Your guitar is electric," Howie says. "Your amp and speakers are, too."

"Yeah, but I'm doing the playing . . . It's me telling 'em what to do."

"And it's us telling the drum machine what to do."

A *machine?* Replacing Joey with a machine? Then there would be three of them. Danny, Jules, Howie. And a fuckin' box. Danny thinks about it, but at the same time he's pleasantly surprised with Jules. *How impersonal can you get?* (Jules hasn't come out with something like that for years.) If the three of them went on tour with . . . with this dumb black box (for some reason, Danny pictures

203

a drum machine as a gleaming black cube), then the whole dynamic would change. Instead of getting two rooms for four people, they could get three rooms, one apiece, and the per diem they sometimes charged venues would now be divided by three, not four. In fact, *all* the money they earned would be divided by three. For every thousand dollars the group brought in, $250 per member would now mean $333.

"And who's going to tell Joey he's being replaced by a machine?" Jules asks. He looks at his watch. He knows that Melissa is coming back soon to pick up Howie and doesn't want to be around when she does.

"Well," Danny says, "that'd probably end up being me."

"Yeah," Jules says, looking right at Howie, "but Joey would know that it was *you,* Mister Mellotron, who brought the gizmo into the band."

Howie winces and stirs the Sprite clockwise and counterclockwise, and Danny says, "Can you please stop doing that with the Seven Up for Christ sake?"

No, I can't . . . I want to but I can't stop, Howie wants to say. But instead he says: "It's not Seven Up, it's Sprite."

"I've got another idea," Jules says, sitting up straighter in the booth. "Okay, it's way outta left field but hear me out. Remember when one night Keith Moon was either too sick or too fucked up to play? I think he passed out or something? And so Pete Townshend goes into the crowd and says, 'Hey, anybody here know how to play the drums?' And this guy raises his hand and they get him onstage and before you know it the four of 'em are playing like they'd been doing it for twenty years."

Danny and Jules know the story. Everyone of a certain age and mentality does.

"So your suggestion is . . . ?" Danny says, slurping up the last bit of baked apple.

"Okay, for every gig we play," Jules says, "right at the start we say to the crowd, 'We don't have a drummer anymore so what we'd like to do is bring one of you up onstage to drum with us.' And it'd become, like, a *thing*, you know? Drummers would hear about it and they'd come to our shows thinking that, hey, maybe they'll pick *me* this time. And the other thing is we wouldn't have to tell Joey he's being permanently replaced. 'Cause he's not."

Jules looks at Howie, who's still feeling guilty he suggested replacing Joey with a machine. Joey is not only still alive, he's alive within twenty miles of where his fellow band members are sitting and discussing his eventual demise.

"And what if," Danny says, "one night we try this stunt and there's not one person in the house who knows how to drum? Then what do we do—just give someone a pair of sticks and say, 'Okay, pal, sit down here and bang'?"

Jules thinks about it and says, "Well, if that happens, then maybe that's when we whip out Howie's gizmo. As like a last-resort type thing."

"It's not my gizmo," Howie says.

Danny signals for the check to the frizzy-haired waitress, who nods to him while at the same time avoiding eye contact with Jules.

"Look," Danny says. He stands up and the rest of them follow. "This may seem a little cold or a lot cold but I'll say it. With Joey gone . . . well, there'll be only three of us in the band. That means each of us gets a bigger cut. I'm sorry to say it, but there it is. The drum robot or whatever it's called—it doesn't have to eat or pay rent or pay alimony, and it doesn't have any kids to support. It's reliable and will always show up on time and it won't die on you. Or if it does, you just go to a store and replace it."

They go to the register and Danny pays, then they go outside and feel the cold right away. The sun is high in the sky but only brings out the grayer hues in the darkening snow.

205

"Look," Jules says, "I like the part that all the bread is divvied up three ways. I won't deny it. But—I don't know—a *machine?* Something you program? It's just not right. When I die are you gonna replace me with Guitar Hero?? I still like my Keith Moon idea the best."

"What if," Howie asks, "we're somewhere in Eastern Europe in October and we ask for a drummer in the crowd and nobody there happens to speak English?"

Now, Danny knows, has to be the time.

"I don't know about Europe in the fall," he says.

The three of them stand facing the quiet parking lot, waiting for Melissa to drive up.

"What do you mean?" Jules asks.

"The whole Joey thing," Danny says, making it up as he goes along, even though he'd rehearsed a dozen different speeches. "Maybe the band needs to take a break."

"What kind of a break?"

"I don't know. All I know is, the band is the four of us. It's us and Joey. It's not going to be the same without him. And, to be honest, I'm really tired. So maybe—maybe this is our last tour. Okay?"

Howie and Jules look at each other. Howie looks like he's going to cry, and Jules cannot believe what he's hearing. Danny can't bring himself to look at either one of them and, just in the nick of time, a dirty white Volvo appears on the road.

"Hey, I gotta scoot!" Jules says. "I'm already running late for—"

By the time he's finishing the sentence he's already getting into his car, so neither Danny nor Howie can hear which of his women or what spa treatment he's going to be late for. The Volvo slowly turns toward the diner and Jules's car passes it going the other way. Melissa drives up and says hi to Danny, and Howie gets in and fastens his seatbelt before closing the door. He's two hours

206

away from his front door in Fairview but he looks like a condemned man fluffing his pillow the night before his execution.

Danny watches the Volvo pull away, sighs, and pops two Rolaids into his mouth. He walks toward his black Suburban, then realizes he's going in the wrong direction and turns around. Seeing his distorted blue reflection come toward him as he opens the car door, he thinks: *Okay, I did it. I did it. Whew. But now what . . . ?*

*

"I'll tell you what the problem is with your first LP," Owen J. Crowe said to Danny and Jules in the Grassroots Tavern on Saint Mark's Place three months after *Come and Git It* disappeared off the *Billboard* charts. "And you tell me if I'm wrong or not. It was too . . . 'good.' Right? You guys didn't sound nearly as fucked up enough as you should've. That was it, wasn't it?"

Danny and Jules looked at each other: maybe this guy had them figured out. It was the middle of a Saturday afternoon, but still there were plenty of drinkers around; the light was dim and on the jukebox the Clash's "I'm So Bored with the U.S.A." was playing. Danny, Jules, and Owen, a record producer Velcro Pravda had set them up with, were sitting at a corner table in the back drinking Jack Daniel's and ginger ale. Neither Danny nor Jules had done any coke that day but it was obvious that Owen had been doing it since the second he'd woken up. Although he was sitting in his chair, he was so jumpy that he wasn't. Once in a while he even had to hold on to the bottom of his seat just so he wouldn't blast off out of it.

"That could be it, yeah," Danny said, not wanting to tip his hand. This was just a get-to-know-each-other meeting. Danny and Jules had enough songs—more than enough songs—to record a second album; they just weren't sure who they wanted to produce it.

"Nah, man, it *is* it." Owen sniffled a few times. "I know it. And so do you. I heard that record, I listened to it a dozen times, and

207

the first thing I thought is, Hey, this is kickass material, rock-solid shit, these cats can wail, but this sounds way, way too fucking slick. This thing isn't near *raw* and ugly enough. I mean, you guys have this hard, emery-board, rabid-alley-cat-in-heat-scratchin'-your-eyes-out vibe, but the last thing you want is to sound *polished*. That kills the whole fuckin' thing. It's just a waste." He sniffled again, ran his arm under his nose, and went on. "I would have made that thing sound so rough and raunchy that people wouldn't have been able to stand it. But not stand it in a good way, you dig?"

Danny and Jules looked at each other again. Was Owen J. Crowe just the man they were looking for? He had on blue leather pants, mirrored aviator shades, tasseled magenta snakeskin boots, and a silk maroon cowboy shirt open at the top to reveal four gold chains dangling from his gristly neck. His cheeks looked partially caved-in and his face was badly pockmarked, but he'd grown a beard over it where the hair would grow. Owen was forty years old but could pass, depending on the light and how stoned he was at the time, for either half or twice that. He'd produced a lot of good albums and even been nominated for a Grammy. He was the fifth producer they'd met in the last two weeks.

"Some of the songs," Jules said, "on that album I'd love to do all over again. Make 'em sound like the way they do live or in my head."

"Well, that ain't gonna happen, chief," Owen said. "Nobody gets a second chance in this goddamn business or in life, and it sure does bite the big one. So it's time to move on. Hey, I gotta go see a man about another horse."

He got up and went to the men's room. His third trip so far.

"Well?" Jules said.

"I wish he'd take me in there to meet some of these horses," Danny said.

"I think he completely gets us."

"Maybe he just wants a job."

Danny didn't trust anybody and, back then before he was used to it, it annoyed Jules. Danny believed, Jules thought, that every single person in the world was out to take advantage of them (the Overfalls) and of him (Danny), in particular. Nobody was ever sincere, everybody was fawning and lying all the time, every positive word written or said was mere flattery, and nobody ever truly liked the group . . . Everything people did or said was just a tactic to get into their good graces so they could rob them of something. What that something was—money, fame, talent, integrity, their souls—it didn't matter. It was just the idea.

"He doesn't need us. Maybe he we need him more?"

"Could be."

Jules wanted to say, *Come on, buddy, talk!* but getting anything from Danny Ault was close to impossible.

Jules glanced at the clock above the bar. After he left here it was just a short walk to the Yodel Chick on Sixth Street between Avenues A and B (she sounded like she was yodeling when she climaxed), or to the Blind Faith Chick, who lived on Fourth Avenue and Twelfth Street and looked like the naked girl on the cover of the Blind Faith album, plus ten years.

Danny finished his drink. It was his fourth Jack and ginger that day. He was married now and had moved to a modest two-bedroom apartment on Bank Street, a block up from the Hudson River. Allison was his wife and already they were having problems—Allison's main problem being Danny, and Danny's being Danny, too. They had even fought on their brief Jamaican honeymoon (Danny spent a good portion of the time working on songs and recording them on his cassette player). Jules, for his part, was getting (in his own words) more gash than a hospital emergency room on Saturday night.

After two long-haired kids in their late teens came over and told them they loved the Overfalls and had seen them at the Beacon Theatre, Owen came out of the bathroom wiping his nose with his arm again—that silk cowboy shirt was not long for this world. (And did he seriously believe that Danny and Jules were buying it, that he was really going into the bathroom to take a leak every five minutes?)

He sat down and took a sip from his drink.

"So, uh, you know Chunky Scrofa?" Danny said, referring to the engineer of their first disc.

"Sure, I know him. I haven't worked with him but we've crossed paths. He's good. Last time I saw Chunk it was in L.A. at the Sunset Grill. Chunky's all right."

"'Cause we'd like to stick with him."

The jukebox was now blasting "Janie Jones" and it was making the dust skip across the Grassroots' floorboards.

"Hey, as I said, Chunky's cool. One of the best. Been dying to work with the cat for years."

Owen frisked himself for cigarettes but couldn't find any, so Danny flicked him a Marlboro, and Jules finished his drink. Jules had only had two: he wanted to be in fine fettle for either Yodel or Blind.

"I've got an idea," Danny said. "If you're not doing anything, why don't you come over to my place tonight?" Owen nodded, to indicate he was free, and then sniffled a few times, and Danny continued. "You could see what we're working on now and tell us what you think is right and what's wrong and what you'd do with it. Nobody but me, Jules, Howie, and Joey has heard this shit yet. It's all new. This is a big decision for us. I don't want us putting out another record like the last one. It's occurred to me that if I ever have kids and I died and they *only* heard that record, then they'd never have any idea what I was really like. Anyway, I think you might— It looks like you know what we're after."

"Janie Jones" ended, and Jules stood up and said he had to scoot. Right then he was leaning more toward Blind Faith than Yodel. Yodel was decent looking but it really did sound like she

210

should be wearing a dirndl when she came. The Blind Faith Chick was fun and had a hyperactive tongue. Plus, after you were done with her you could just put on your clothes and leave, if you had even taken off your clothes in the first place.

"Great," Owen said, standing up and putting on his black-and-gold cowboy hat. He shook Danny and Jules's hands. "I'll come over. Can't wait to hear the new stuff. And I really do think I know what you want, but if I'm wrong, I wouldn't shove it down your throat. The music is the thing . . . I'm just there to bring it out. You want harsh, you want hard, and you want a mean and grungy, rockin', country-bluesy and a just totally fagged-the-fuck-out feel and all that. I get it. I dig it. I'm there. And now, if you don't mind, boys, I gotta go consult another male of the species about yet an entirely different equine beast."

Back into the bathroom, swiping his arm across his nose, went Owen J. Crowe.

"He's our guy," Danny said to Jules.

*

"Okay," Danny says. "Go out and get the next one."

Howie puts down his bass, stands up and goes to the door, discretely wipes off the doorknob's germs on his pants, and says to the person waiting outside, "You're up."

The Overfalls, minus Joey, have rented Studio B at Moonrise Sound Studios in Brentwood for two days and have been auditioning drummers. After their meeting at the Parkway Diner, Danny called Chunky Scrofa, who, after telling Danny how sorry he was to hear about Joey's condition, said he'd get right on it. "Sure, I know a few dudes I could shoot your way," Chunky said.

Moonrise Studios is an anonymous, one-story, beige rectangle of a building sandwiched between a McDonalds and a Rite Aid Pharmacy; only a mustard yellow crescent moon rising off the

211

flat roof gives it away. Fledgling bands, starstruck singers, rappers, and wannabes come to Moonrise to record demos, to rehearse, or to record vanity CDs that only their friends and family will buy or listen to. The equipment is pretty much state of the art, though, and the acoustics are good enough so that Moonrise was where *TFO 8,* *TFO 9,* and *TFO 10* were recorded and mixed.

Howie comes back into the studio with a skinny kid about eighteen years old in a North Face down coat and blue jeans. He has long black hair and the makings of his first goatee.

"Meet Sal," Howie says. "Sal Kaplan."

"It's Saul," Saul says.

Uninterested right off the bat, Danny signals with his hand to the drum kit. Howie and Jules rented it . . . they did not want to alarm Joey (or Angie) by asking to borrow his drums.

Saul is the ninth drummer that Chunky has sent. Yesterday, seven were supposed to show up and only five did. The first guy today was all right, was in his late thirties and had kicked around a few jazz bands, but he didn't really like the music the Overfalls had done and were doing; the second guy was a younger rocker but wasn't any good.

"So, Saul, tell us," Jules says from his seat, a cigarette smoldering at the tuning knobs of the Les Paul on his lap. "Who are you, what do you do, where do you live, what have you done, and what's up?"

Saul tells the band that he hasn't ever really played in a band but has been playing drums since he was six. "I've jammed with friends a lot but that's it," he confesses sheepishly. He just dropped out of Hofstra and lives in Mineola with his parents, who are getting on his case all the time to get a job.

"So this is the job?" Jules says. "Drumming for us?"

Saul shrugs and nods. He's nervous. This could be his first job interview or audition ever, and there's no way, each member of the band knows, this kid is going to join TFO, no matter how good he is. The only question is: Are Danny and Jules going to take it easy on him or have some sadistic fun and make the kid cry? The first guy who showed up yesterday: Jules told him that they were not really the Furious Overfalls, they were a Furious Overfalls tribute band, and the real Overfalls had in fact perished in a horrific plane crash ten years earlier, but nobody knew about it. The guy believed him. Howie is already worrying about it going too far with Saul when Jules says, "All right, Saul, we want you to start with a thirty-five-minute solo. You give us thirty-five rockin', sockin' minutes, then *boom,* we're gonna break right into 'Beck's Bolero' and blow the roof offa this joint. Are you up for that?"

"Thirty-five minutes? Really?"

"To the second. I'll time it with my thirty-dollar Rolex. You know 'Beck's Bolero,' right?"

Saul Kaplan looks from Jules to Danny and then to Howie. He gulps and says, "I dunno. Is that Jeff Beck, right?"

"Pretty good," Danny says, stifling a yawn. "But actually Jimmy Page wrote 'Beck's Bolero.'"

"Hey," Howie says, standing up and setting down his bass, "can we speak?"

Howie takes Danny and Jules to a corner of the studio to confer while Saul sits petrified at the drums. In their sidebar Howie asks Jules and Danny to take it easy on Saul, but Jules says, "Aw, come on, let's just let the kid *think* he's going to do a thirty-five minute solo," and Howie compromises. Howie, Danny, and Jules go back to their spots. Danny remains standing, though: his back is killing him today and right now standing is better than sitting.

"Do you know any of our music?" Danny asks him. "Are you familiar with the ancient classic-rock bag the Fabulous Overhauls are into?"

"Well," Saul says with his nervous cottonmouth voice, "I didn't until two days ago when I knew I'd be coming here today. So I downloaded some of your songs and—"

"Okay. Got it."

"All right, Saully-boy, let it rip," Jules says. "Thirty-five minutes, baby, and we want you to really bang it out. You are Tommy Lee . . . starting . . . *now!*"

Saul draws in a deep, long breath, counts to three, and then begins his soon-to-be-terminated thirty-five-minute solo. He starts with no idea of energy conservation . . . Right away he's flailing insanely at the crash cymbal and tom-toms, he's banging the snare and high hat, and he's kicking the bass drum so hard that it almost tips over, and his long hair is flying all over the place; within fifteen seconds he's worked up a sweat from his forehead to his fledgling goatee to his fingertips. There's no rhythm, no method, no continuity; he's an octopus on speed . . . It's a monsoon of manic noise and, finally, after a minute and a half of this, Danny mercifully says, "Okay, Saul, you can stop now. Saul, you can stop! HEY, SAUL! YOU CAN STOP!!! STOP!"

Saul brings his hands down and says: "So? Do I have the job?"

Five minutes later, Saul is driving back home to his parents and the rest of his life, and Howie, Jules, and Danny are just screwing around with their instruments and saying little.

"So, uh," Danny says, "how much does a drum machine cost?"

Howie says they can get a solid professional unit for less than $500.

"And it's better than Saul?"

Jules says, "Can we just get through all these guys today before we talk about hiring a robot?"

Danny tells Howie to see if anyone new is out there. A minute later a short, dumpy bald guy in his fifties walks into Studio B. Agewise, he fits right into the Furious Overfalls demographic, but in terms of looks, the man is a schlubby disaster and resembles a rock-and-roll drummer the way Joe Strummer resembled a Speaker

214

of the House of Commons. His name, he tells them, is Mark; he was born and raised in Carle Place but lives in West Hempstead now. He's wearing khaki pants, desert boots, and a white oxford shirt under a green merino cardigan and a pillowy black down coat.

"So, Mark," Danny says, strumming his guitar absentmindedly, "tell us who you are and what you do and when you plan to stop doing it."

Howie waves to the drum kit and Mark sits there after taking off his coat (he leaves his cardigan on, though). He tells the band he's a CPA, married with two kids; he used to play in bands in high school and college, still plays the drums once in a while for a Yes cover band called No, and loves the Overfalls and has all their albums.

"*All* our albums?" Danny asks.

"The latest one," the guy asks, "is *TFO 10,* right?"

"Yeah, it is," Danny says.

"Dude's got all our albums," Jules says, hammering out a loud anguished chord from out of nowhere.

"Do you even have . . . *Dead End Road*?" Danny asks. Mark nods.

"What are you," Jules asks him, "some kind of stalker?"

"No," Mark says, "I'm just a fan, that's all." Then he tells them: "I actually liked *Dead End Road* a lot. It's my second-favorite record of—" but Danny, not wishing to reopen the old wound, cuts him off. Mark tells the band he's seen them more times than he can count (which means a lot, seeing as he's an accountant). He first saw them at The Garden and The Coliseum in '80, in New Haven in '82 and at the old Boston Garden the same year, and then again in Pittsburgh. If they were playing within driving distance, he saw them.

"Well, thanks," Danny says. "You're paying for my kids' college." Even though his one kid in college just dropped out of college to have a kid.

215

Then Mark says (and at this point he's gently shuffling the sticks over the snare and high hat): "So I gotta ask you . . . Is something wrong with Joey Mazz?"

Danny says that Joey is okay, he's still in the band, everything is all right, and that if Mark is truly serious about joining the Overfalls then he shouldn't ever ask too many questions.

Jules rattles off a few more angry chords and then says, "So, Mark, name that tune. You tell us what your favorite TFO song is and we'll do it."

Mark adjusts his wire-rimmed glasses and says, "I could do 'Borderline'?"

Danny feels his mild dislike for Mark metastasizing into an intense loathing. The oxford shirt tucked carefully into his pleated khakis, the undershirt underneath the oxford, the green cardigan, the chrome dome catching the studio's flickering light. *This guy,* he thinks, *could be the Second Coming of Charlie Watts, but no fucking way is he ever joining my band.* But what really turns Danny against Mark is: *Had it not been for this or that and the grace of God, I could easily have turned out to be him.*

"Okay," he says, sucking his animus back down into his stomach. "'Borderline' it is. Count us down."

Five minutes later they've finished their most famous song, the song that put them on the map . . . before punk, disco, MTV, and the Human fucking League redrew that map. Mark did a credible job, he kept at it, he managed to roll along and come up with some okay fills when Jules launched into his solo . . . he wasn't great or even very good but he didn't suck. No, the Yes cover band he played in, had an okay enough drummer. At one point, however, he got too enthused—about the song itself, about the fact that here he was, living out his dream—and swung his head and his glasses went flying. But still, he played on.

"That was pretty competent," Danny says while Howie hands back Mark his glasses. "If you don't hear from us, it means you don't have the job."

Mark puts on his coat and asks: "Any idea when that might be?"

"Any idea when you won't be hearing from us? I'd say, as early as Monday."

Mark leaves and Danny mutters, "Goddamn fantasy camp," walks to a corner of the studio near the soundproof glass, and puts his head against the wall like a student who got caught being naughty.

"Only two more today," Howie says to him. "Then we're done."

"We don't have a drummer," Danny says so low that maybe nobody hears him. They hit the road in two weeks and they have no drummer.

"Maybe," Jules says, "my pull-some-random-jaboni-outta-the-audience-every-night idea wasn't so bad after all."

Danny pulls his head out of the corner, sees himself, Howie, and Jules dark in the glass, and says, "Howie, see if anybody else is out there . . ."

*

Owen J. Crowe was just what the doctor ordered. For months the band spent whole days at a time in the studio . . . they slept there and worked and worked and seldom saw the sun. They flew down to Muscle Shoals and then to L.A. to record and lost track of what month it was. It was grueling work and there were moments when it seemed as though everything was wrong and they'd never be able to make it right, but then they saw a thread of white light leading toward the end of the tunnel and followed it out. When the album was done it sounded just like they wanted it to sound. There wasn't,

217

as far as they were concerned, a bad second on the whole thing. If anything, the album was ten minutes too short.

Borderline never made it to number one on the Billboard charts but went Gold within four months of its release and, miraculously for its time, yielded three songs that cracked the top twenty. The Overfalls had made the record and the record made them. Soon, Danny and Allison went their separate ways, Howie and Melissa got married, and no longer would TFO be opening for Marshall Tucker or ZZ Top or Little Feat . . . they were headliners now. Rolling Stone gave the album four-and-a-half stars; Newsweek, Crawdaddy!, the Times, Trouser Press, and CREEM loved the record, too. And they'd even nailed a great grade from the fussy Village Voice:

Whereas TFO's first effort impressed but never awed, Borderline is a different animal. From the first nanosecond that the needle hits the groove, it transports you to a dark, primal Midnight in Your Soul chasm you might not ever wish to visit. The gritty blues-rock quartet hails from Lawn Guyland (but seldom sounds it, thankfully) and channels the Stones at their most fucked up. "Don't Want Your Help" and "You Can Go" sound more deep Southern fried than "Sweet Virginia," and "Waiting and Wilting" is "No Expectations" crossed with something too sad for even George Jones to contemplate. The eponymous track is the Stones' "Live with Me" meets the Temptations' "Get Ready" meets a bag of surefire Avenue C poison. Maybe they're merely faking their exquisite torture, but, really, who cares? You get the sense that tunesmiths Danny Ault and Jules Rose have not only played their Robert Johnson, Howlin' Wolf, and Lightnin' Hopkins records bare, but have also read their Barthes and Derrida. Nasty? Sharp? Ferocious and strung out? Yep. Almost too agonizing to listen to. Hell, yeah. A-PLUS.

Less than a year after *Borderline* came *Wasted and Tasted*—another Owen J. Crowe and Chunky Scrofa production that squeezed every bitter rotgut ounce of disheveled life out of the band—and their next hit, "Hurt," and by that time the band had roadies, including Rev and Sweet Lou and Big Bob, and stylists, photographers, attorneys, hairdressers, publicists, gofers, a song-publishing outfit, accountants, personal assistants, dealers (and their personal assistants), as well as stylists, crazed stalkers, an astrologist for Joey named Zeldina, a British tour manager whose father was in the House of Lords and whose mother was in a straitjacket, two guitar techs, and the usual other nameless hangers-on, parasites, and starfuckers. Danny got a Mercedes and moved to a bigger apartment, this one in SoHo, and bought a small house in Amagansett; Jules got a red Corvette, moved into a four-bedroom spread in the West Village, and bought a house in Westhampton; Joey bought his house in Bay City; and Howie bought the house in Fairview, but also kept a studio apartment for Melissa and himself on West Fifty-second Street in Manhattan.

The Overfalls played on *Saturday Night Live,* but at the after party, Steve Martin said something snotty to piss Danny off, and Danny called him out and starting punching him . . . Sweet Lou and an NBC bodyguard had to pull him off the zany ~~comedian~~ novelist. (In those days, Danny still allowed himself to vent his rage and had no idea that Sweet Lou's chief assignment was not to protect Danny from the world but to protect the world from Danny.) Danny also got into tussles with Alice Cooper and Bunny Wailer; the drummer in Foghat; Dickey Betts; Earl Slick and Carlos Alomar; a Norwegian roadie for A-ha, and ZZ Top's hairstylists; Bill Graham; the drummer from Ian Dury and the Blockheads, and Dave Blockhead from the English Beat; Luther Vandross; Davids Byrne, Crosby, and Lee Roth; every single one of the Eagles; and Laurie Anderson and Joni Mitchell. The word on Danny Ault throughout the business was: Either do what he wants, or pretend to do what he wants and hope he forgets, or stay

219

the hell away. He wasn't a diva, he never got lost in the whole rock-trip role—he was just a time bomb who couldn't bother to tick. Success made him uncomfortable, and he'd been much more content when he was struggling and failing. People in his inner circle knew not to be around him if he was doing blow or speed; on the other hand, if he was on Seconal, Nembutal, Demerol, or Valium, he was an absolute doll.

As for Jules, the year *Wasted and Tasted* came out he spent more days on antibiotics than off, and often he would get envelopes in the mail filled with photos that women had taken of their bodies or of their friends' bodies. He'd also get photos that men had taken of their wives' and girlfriends' bodies. Some of the women looked pretty good and a lot of them didn't look at all good, and Jules wondered, *Whoa, Jack, if these are the ones that the publicist is passing on to me, then what about the photos they're not showing me?!* "I could tell, Julie-boy," a letter from an eighteen-year-old (or so she claimed) Manchester lass named Lizzie went, "even from the fifteenf row that you got such a luverly plonker in yer trousers. Next time you cum to Merry Old I'd rilllly like to shake that thing around." Lizzie had enclosed with her handwritten missive a Polaroid of her naked self, with her "Borderline" and "Babylon Boogie" 45s covering her young breasts, but with her flaming red bush on full display. "Me Auntie Meg took this pitcher," she added, "and she'd like to meet you to [sic]."

When TFO toured England that year, sure enough, Jules took Lizzie up on her offer. (Auntie Meg was on holiday in Bournemouth and could not join the fun.) He happened to be off the antibiotics that week but soon was back on. There were all kinds of freaks out there. Like the Spunk Collector in Liverpool (she had a Julie Christie face but a Benny Hill body and saved the ejaculate of every rock star she'd been with), Exhaust Pipe Mouth

Girl in Stockholm, the Iguana Lips Chick in Sydney, and the resourceful Contessa Vanessa van Vaseline in Amsterdam.

They saw the country and the world, went to places and cities they otherwise never would have visited, and met people they otherwise never would have gotten close to.

I cannot believe, Howie thought as he walked past the graves of Chopin and Poulenc in Père Lachaise Cemetery, *I am in Paris.*

So this, Danny thought as he visited what was left of The Cavern Club in Liverpool and The Marquee Club in London, *was where it all began.*

Holy shit, Joey thought when he met Ginger Baker in England, *I am meeting one of my idols! I am talking to Ginger fuckin' Baker.* (And then he thought: *Jesus, what a disappointment this is.*)

I cannot believe, Jules marveled while waking up one afternoon at the Hôtel de Crillon, *that I just banged two French chicks. Sisters, too.*

Little by little, their idiosyncrasies came to the fore. It was all about exposure. Months on the road, months in the studio, for years . . . they couldn't hide their tics from one another. Danny was the first to realize that Howie might have serious psychological problems; when he brought it up to Jules, it all became clear to the both of them. Howie had had these issues from day one but he was getting worse. He wasn't yet setting down towels on the floors of his hotel rooms but he was washing his hands all the time, he was avoiding driving, he was terrified of flying, and he rarely let anyone touch him.

Jules couldn't pass up a piece of ass and it drove Danny, who preferred unsuccessful, unfulfilling six-month relationships to one-night stands, up the wall. There was no woman too skanky for Jules. A few missing teeth, a few extra twenty pounds, asymmetrical body parts . . . unless birthmarks, freckles, or moles

221

were involved, it didn't matter. (Jules would have passed up Cindy Crawford for Mama Cass.)

As solid a singer and songwriter as he was, as big and tough as he was, Danny turned out to be incredibly thin-skinned, and it wore on the other three band members. When the records were selling, when the raves were pouring in, if there was one single blemish or slight bump in the road . . . that is what he would seize on and not let go. *Wasted and Tasted* was only begrudged four stars from *Rolling Stone* (only half a star more than *Come and Git It* had merited), and *CREEM* said the record was good but nothing more. "Good but nothing more"—when Danny read that, the words branded themselves onto his soul. "If it's possible for a band to sound too derivative of itself," the buffoon in the *Village Voice* wrote, "then TFO is that band. They simply refuse to improve. B-MINUS." Danny told the people who handled TFO publicity to forget about sending him the positive record and concert notices . . . those no longer interested him. "From now on," he instructed them, "only send the bad ones."

In the days when they could afford their own hotel rooms, Danny would barge into Jules's room waving a newspaper article or the latest telex he'd gotten from the publicists.

"Did you see this?!" he'd yell. "Have you read this thing?!"

Of course Jules hadn't read it. He cared little what people wrote or said about the band.

"Now what?"

Danny would sit down on the edge of Jules's bed—the woman Jules was with would either pull the sheets up to her neck or run to the bathroom to get dressed—and he'd read the article. "'TFO's "Hurt" is a very good song,'" he'd read to Jules, who was only half listening, "'but only if you haven't heard "Wild Horses" in ten years.' Can you believe this? Who the fuck wrote this?! I bet"—he'd look at the article and find the name of the "journalist"

222

who'd reviewed the album—"I bet Mitch Katz has never once even tuned a guitar. Ten weeks to get one song the way we want it and this turd-bomb writes this."

"Yeah. It's bad."

"Hey," the girl of the hour would say, emerging from the bathroom with a top and panties on, "do you want me to stay?"

Jules and Danny would look at each other and Jules would say, "Nah, you can split."

On the Wasted Tour, one evening Danny was griping to Joey at the hotel bar about the review in that day's *Des Moines Register*. It was just the two of them: Howie was off by himself somewhere and Jules was on someone somewhere else. *Rolling Stone* had been planning to send a reporter to interview them, but Velcro had called Danny from New York only an hour before to tell him that the story was off. "For now?" Danny asked Velcro. "No," Velcro told him, "for good." Danny popped one red after hearing that and then another one twenty minutes later, so he was on the subdued side.

"*Fuck* 'em," Danny said to Joey at the bar, which was, including the people working there, unchanged from the Eisenhower era. "Who the hell needs *Rolling* goddamn *Stone*?"

"Yeah, who cares what they think?" Joey said, knowing he was addressing someone who did.

"I mean, do we really want some kid fresh out of Harvard who couldn't get a job at *Time* or *Newsweek* following us around from city to city and writing about the way I wipe my ass, or about you and Zeldina?"

Joey was hoping that the second Seconal would soon start making its presence felt.

Danny signaled for another drink.

"If I ever meet the guy," Danny said a drink later—but by this time Joey had lost track of just who the guy was—"seriously, I'll have to let him have it."

223

"You know, instead of that, bro, why not just like—"

"Just like what?"

"Write a fuckin' song about it. That's what you do, right? Check it out . . . my Uncle Jimmy, he lays bricks in Bay Shore. Someone pisses him off, what does he do? He goes and lays some bricks. Someone *really* pisses him and he'll go lay even more. Someone pisses you off, write a song about it. Hey! There's Zeldina! Gotta cut out . . ."

Joey leapt off his stool to get that night's reading and to get away from Danny.

Danny seethed into his Jack and ginger for a while, finished it, took the elevator up to the top floor—by which time the second red was finally kicking in—went into his room, turned on his cassette recorder, and picked up his Martin and commenced to write "Your Bleatin' Heart," which wound up as the third track on Side 1 of *West of Babylon,* their fifth album, and which the *L.A. Times* called "the best hate song this side of the Stones' 'Dead Flowers' . . . Why, it positively makes 'Idiot Wind' sound like 'Unchained Melody.'"

The *L.A. Times,* however, didn't like much of the rest of the album.

*

A week after the first two days of auditions, and a day following another fruitless two days of them, Danny pulls the black Suburban up to the strip mall between Bay City and Pleasant Valley. This time he's parked right outside a Payless shoe store. It's Saturday and he couldn't wait to get out of the house. Even though Emily is several months away from delivering, were someone to drop off a baby on the Ault doorstep, the house would be ready for it. Everything is in place: bassinet, breast pump, fifty boxes of wipes and Pampers, the onesies and sockies. Everything is there but the baby. And the father.

It's not too cold out today and he gets out of the car, walks right up to the Payless window, and looks in. All women inside. And girls . . . either teen girls together or younger girls with their moms. Or moms together.

How could Emily have a boy, he thinks. It just doesn't seem possible. She's so girly and her mother is so girly, not half a chromosome of tomboy between them . . . you'd think it was genetically impossible she could ever have a boy.

A woman in her thirties walks out of the shoe store with her teenage daughter. They look at Danny—does the mom recognize him?—then they keep walking, and Angie's blue Malibu pulls up near the Suburban.

Angie gets out of the car, slams the door. Ever since he's known her, he's never seen her close a car door gently. She has on a black leather coat, black tights, and black leather boots with eight-inch heels. *Is it possible,* he wonders, *that the sicker Joey gets, the better she looks? Is she already a foxy rock-and-roll widow even though Joey has yet to die?*

He is about to offer her a cordial hello and an innocuous kiss on the cheek, when she speaks first.

"Do you wanna tell me how the hell you haven't come over to see Joey? Where do you get off? And Jules and Howie, too? Okay, Howie I understand . . . but *Jules? You?* After all this time and everything you've been through togethuh? Jesus Christ!"

"I'm sorry," he says. "I've been really busy. Getting the house ready for—"

"Ffffffffffff," she says. "Using an unborn fetus as an excuse, that's low."

She has on a lacy black top beneath the leather coat. You can almost see through the lace but not quite. Or maybe you can.

225

"You're right," he says. "I'm terrible. I'll come over soon. Is he up for it?"

"Yes! He's just like he was a year ago or three years ago! Except he's lonely and he's going crazy from cabin fever. Are you really going to come over?"

Joey in a daze, his house in Bay City the usual dark and decrepit mess. Little Joey and his kid sisters. Danny was not planning on visiting and he doesn't want to. But he knows what he has to do.

"How about tomorrow at noon?"

"He'd love to see you. Jules, too."

"Him I can't promise."

They go inside Danny's car and sit close. Angie is not as pretty as Jessica is (and Angie knows it) but she's about five times sexier (she is aware of that, too).

"Look, I don't know," he begins, "how to tell you this, but—"

"Just say it."

He collects himself and says: "We're going on tour. And it's a long one. This thing was planned months ago. And we don't have a drummer. I'll be honest. We auditioned people, some serious losers. All right? I mean, we went below the bottom of the barrel and couldn't find anyone. But I just want you to know what's going on. This is a—"

"This is a business, right?"

"Right."

"I've got a drummer for you. You should've come to me first. I know a really great one."

"Who?"

Danny hopes she's not going to throw out Little Joey's name.

"His name is Joseph Mazz, Senior, and he's been your drummer for thirty years already."

"Aw, come on. He's not up for that."

"How would you know? You haven't seen him for months!"

"It hasn't been that long." He waits and says, "He's really up for it?"

"Yes! Even his doctor says so. Danny, it'd be the best thing you ever did in your life if you took him along. It'd make him so happy." Whether manipulatively or sincerely, tears well in her eyes. "And if you don't, it would crush him."

Danny takes his eyes off of Angie's face—and her calves—and looks out the window. A few women and girls go into the Payless, a few come out. Soon his house will be awash in blue shoes, blue clothes, blue pajamas. He'll be living inside a giant blueberry.

He looks back at her and she adjusts her coat so that it covers up some of her leg.

"Honest to God, on the lives of your kids," he says, "you're telling me that Joey is strong enough to go on the road with us? He's not going to drop dead during 'Babylon Boogie'? You know how grueling these things are."

"He is strong enough to play for you. I wouldn't tell you this if he wasn't. You think I *want* him to die? But you have to promise me you'll at least try to bring him back alive."

Danny takes his hands out of his coat pockets and puts them on the wheel. Angie has twisted her body so that she's facing him.

"I promise," Danny says. "I guess he's got the gig. Well, that was easy!"

"Just make sure," Angie says, grabbing his right arm with both her hands and giving it a suggestive squeeze, "that he doesn't overdose on Cheetos when he's out there, okay?"

Two minutes later, they kiss on the cheek, close to the lips—it lasts a few unsettling seconds longer than their usual kiss

227

good-bye—and she leaves, and suddenly Howie's drum machine, Jules's idea to pluck random people from the audience, and a few of the lousy loser drummers they auditioned aren't looking so bad.

Ten
What's Cooking

Angie's Malibu comes to a stop outside Moonrise Studios, and Danny, Jules, and Howie stand huddled together in the building's front doorway with their hands in their coats and pants pockets. The weather has turned cold again and smoke pours out on their breath. Three car doors open in unison: Angie and her black high-heeled boots get out of the driver's seat; Joey, looking no better or worse than he did before his aborted surgery, gets out of the shotgun seat; Little Joey, in jeans and a studded faux-leather jacket, gets out of the back. When they see their old drummer, Danny, Jules, and Howie clap in unison, and Joey clasps his hands over his head like a boxing champion and takes a bow.

Then he groans, "UH-OH! AW, FUCK!" and puts his hands over his heart and begins to keel over. But it only lasts a second and he stands back up and winks at his bandmates, who now come walking toward him.

"Sonuvabitch," Danny says. He thinks of mussing Joey's hair with his hand but that seems just a bit too close, and Joey's long, stringy hair is already mussed up enough as is.

Joey and Jules hug for a few seconds, however, and after that, Danny and Joey shake hands. Joey, knowing Howie well enough, does not commence to engage him in a hug or a handshake, but the two men acknowledge each other with a few nods and smiles.

"Hey, Angie," Jules says. "What's up?"

"It's been a while, Jules," she says. When they kiss on the cheek they make a brief stark contrast: she is as olive and dark as he is buttery and golden.

"I was gonna come by."

"When? Labor Day, Three thousand and ten?"

229

"Aww, lay off," Joey says to his wife. "He didn't wanna see me looking like I was gonna die."

Nobody says anything for a while and the words just hang in the air.

"Hey, guess who's inside?" Danny says.

Joey says, "Well, it can't be any of us, so who's left?"

Who's Left, Danny thinks. That should've been the name of the Who album right after John Entwistle died.

"Chunky Scrofa's inside," Howie says, "waiting to see you."

Angie says she's going to head home now and tells her son to stay and keep an eye on his father, and Little Joey commits to that with a nod. She walks back to the Malibu—Jules remembers how tight she was way back when, as well as the chimes of her bracelets and necklaces when she bounced up and down—and slams the door and drives away.

"All right," Danny says, "let's do us some home cooking."

The five of them—the Furious Overfalls plus Joey Junior—walk toward Moonrise and Danny thinks: *Home Cooking. That's a great name for a song. Could be about coming back home after ten months on the road. It could be about making music in your garage or on your porch. It could be about anything.* But he can't think of what the song should sound like, its melody, lyrics, tempo, or groove. Maybe, he hopes, it will come to him and Jules later, right out of nowhere, the way most of their best songs usually did. Or maybe it will just drift off into the deep blue yonder, where a million other songs he never wrote exist.

"Dude!" Chunky Scrofa says to Joey back inside the warmth of the studio. "I knew you'd pull through!"

Chunky Scrofa, when he worked on the first five TFO albums, used to be only twenty pounds overweight, hence the nickname. Then he took up several harsh diets, ran marathons, and studied a martial art or two. When people met him during this

230

period they couldn't understand why his nickname was Chunky. Eventually he gave up the diets, the running, and martial arts, and now nobody ever questions why he is called Chunky. Since the days of *Come and Git It,* Chunky, who claims to be half Italian, half Welsh, half black, and a third Brazilian-Jewish, has gone from 230 pounds to 160 pounds to 360 pounds. He still has a full head of hair but it's mostly gray now, as is the long bushy beard that falls halfway down his chest.

All the amps are set up. Jules sits down in a chair and lights a cigarette, and Howie walks as far away from him as possible and picks up his bass. He plugs in his Fender and, on low volume, rips off a few notes.

"So, uh, Joey," Danny says, "you remember how to play the drums? You sit right here, I think it was. And you just, like, make any noise at all."

Joey takes his seat on his throne, spins around two times and picks up his sticks, and Chunky sits in a chair near Jules and sucks on a black-and-white milk shake. Danny had tried to get him to work on *TFO 6, TFO 7,* and *TFO 8,* but, according to Chunky, something always kept popping up (a previous commitment, a health issue, some family crisis) and he could never make it. By *TFO 9,* Danny had gotten the message.

"So you're up for the road?" Chunky asks Joey.

"Hey," Joey says, twirling his sticks, "after the last couple-a months I'm ready to play the Black Hole of Calgary. Just get me out there, dude."

Danny, growing warier of Joey's fragility by the second, suggests they start with a slow number, which is something they never do. Usually when they practice—and they almost never have to practice anymore—they start with either "Rip this Joint" or "Crossroads" (the Cream *Wheels of Fire* version). Not only has it become something of a ritual, but it also gets the blood pumping and the adrenaline surging right away. But today Danny suggests they start off with "Ventilator Blues." Catching the drift, Howie and Jules nod, and Jules says, "Good idea," but Joey says, "Huh?" Danny tells him it's cold out and that his bones and joints are stiff, and he wants to start off slow and work up to speed. Joey says, "Sure, bro. Anything you say."

A second later Jules starts it up, Danny and Howie join in, and Joey, as though he'd never had a heart attack, been cut open, and been handed a death sentence behind his back, is keeping time and banging away as well as he always did. "Ventilator Blues." The Ventilators: Had Howie never listened in on those two kids talking about their geography test, that would have been the band's name. Would things have turned out differently? *TFO 7* would instead be called *Ventilators 7,* the same with *TFO 8,* and so on. The Furious Overfalls was a good name for a band: it made people look twice. Danny and Howie were for it, Jules preferred the Ventilators, and Joey, who was What The Fuck before WTF was cool, didn't care either way. It took years for the truth to sink in but Danny has come to realize that Jules was right. The Ventilators would have sounded better and more au courant at the time, like the Heartbreakers, the Destroyers, the Dictators, the Cars, the Pretenders, and the Replacements. People would have seen the words "The Ventilators" and assumed, incorrectly, of course, that they were a hot new punk band. And had they seen the name and then heard the songs they would have thought, *Ah, this is a retro-blues/rock punk band.* It would have given them more cachet and maybe the bottom would not have fallen out the way it did. Goddamn Jules Rose was right.

After they finish, Chunky applauds in his chair, tosses out his second milk shake, and says, "You motherfuckers ain't lost a step. Still hot like always."

Oh yeah? Danny thinks, *then why won't you be our engineer anymore?*

232

Joey Junior shifts in his chair. Danny looks at him and wonders why he elected to hang with the grown-ups today. He wasn't even keeping the beat with his boots, and if you don't keep the beat to "Ventilator Blues" it means you were born without a pulse.

"Everything okay?" Howie asks Joey, who's worked up a little sweat. "Should we get Eddie to turn down the heat in here?"

Joey tells him he's okay but says he's thirsty, and Jules dashes out and comes back a minute later with a bottle of Deer Park water, which Joey drains in two gulps. A year ago—before Joey's heart attack—there was no way Jules would *ever* have gotten Joey water.

"What's next?" Jules asks, but before anyone can answer, Eddie Le Vine, the seventy-five-year-old sleazebag who owns Moonrise and enjoys busting any pair of balls he can get away with, comes in without knocking.

"Next time, Julius, you want some water," he says, "*ask, don't take.* Okay?"

"Yeah, yeah," Jules says with a dismissive wave of his hand.

"What, you think I'm fucking around here? Had you asked me I'd have maybe given you the bottle."

Eddie closes the door behind him and Joey throws a drumstick at the door. He starts to get off his chair to retrieve it but Danny hastens over and gets it for him, feeling a sharp pain in his lower back in the process; it's the first time in their thirty-plus-years acquaintance he's ever picked up anything for his drummer.

They work through "97-3 Strut," a bouncy boogie-woogie and the third single released from *Wasted and Tasted,* and at the end Joey again has to wipe off his sweaty forehead with his arm. They do "Dog Water Girls" and then Danny suggests they take a break. He goes outside to call Angie on her cell phone but she doesn't pick up. Her two daughters are in school right now, Little

Joey is here at the studio, and so is Big Joey—it's probably the first time she's had more than an hour to herself in months. Just when he's about to head back in, a familiar gray Honda Accord pulls up right next to his SUV, and Emily, struggling with her new increased dimensions, gets out.

"Everything okay?" Danny asks her as she waddles toward him, her blond hair blowing around. He'd asked her over breakfast if she wanted to come and watch them rehearse, never once thinking that she'd take him up on the offer. Yet here she is.

She tells him everything is fine and that she was going stir crazy, that she and Mom were snapping at each other, and with nothing else to do had decided to come by.

He opens the door for her and sees Eddie Le Vine in the hallway. Eddie has on an aqua blue Adidas tracksuit and pinkie rings on both hands. He's six foot two, liver-spotted all over, and wears a lopsided brown toupee that looks like week-old roadkill. Presently he's standing with five kids in their late teens or early twenties, all with lousy posture and horrible skin. Danny takes one look at them and tries to guess the genre: rap-metal-emo. Or whatever they call that stuff. He looks at them and can almost hear it hurting his ears.

"What is this, Family Reunion Day?" Eddie says, taking in Emily and her belly and the coat failing to hide it.

"Yes, it is," Danny says.

"Hey, at your age, *mazel tov,* right?" He pinches Danny's cheek much too lovingly for Danny's taste.

"She's my daughter, Eddie. Not my wife."

For a moment, he wishes he were back in high school and that Eddie played for one of the football teams Danny's school used to face regularly. A nice forearm shiver to the helmet or a helmet spear into the sternum—that's the way he handled players he'd taken a loathing to. He loved to watch their eyeballs tumble around like tossed dice.

"Oh, yeah? Then even more *mazel* to you. Hey, I want you to meet— These kids are from Yaphank and they are gonna be so freaking h-o-t, hot, it's scary." Eddie, his lips slick with his own saliva, puts his arm around the tallest of them, whose face could easily double for a mushroom and anchovy pizza in a Domino's Pizza ad. "They did their first demo here. They're called—what's the name of your outfit again?"

Mushroom Anchovy Pizza says, "Phankay. It's like an anagram of Yaphank."

"People already have enough trouble," Danny says, "saying Yaphank the right way and now you're going to ask them to mix the letters around?"

Another of them, this one with pink eyeliner and teal streaks in his oily brown hair, says, "But peeps won't even be knowin' they sayin' it mixed up so it's aiiiiiiiiight."

You're not black, Danny wants to say. *You're a scrawny white Irish kid from the Guyland and you're trying to sound like Ice-T.* He wants to push this kid right up against the wall and squash him, even if it's in front of his daughter . . . *because* it's in front of his daughter. It's practically biblical: Each generation comes along and creates music their parents detest. His old man liked swing, *his* old man liked Bach, Danny likes rock 'n' roll. He knows this is the way it's always been and always must be . . . but the music that comes out today really is very bad, and whatever the kids of Yaphank-Hankpay churn out is most likely atrocious.

Teal Streak tells Danny their first CD, on Thrill Kill Records, is going to drop on iTunes in about eight weeks.

"Danny, they're gonna be huge," Eddie chimes in. "They're the shit. You're looking at the next Jonas Boys and Great Charlotte here." He turns to the boys of Knaphay and says, "This is Danny Ault from the Furious Overfalls."

The five of them show no signs of recognition at all and just scratch their blackheads.

235

"Yeah," Eddie says, "it wouldn't mean anything to me either." The band heads down the hallway, and Eddie asks Danny, "Hey, you met my nephew Dave, right? Dave Litt?"

Danny shrugs, and Eddies reaches into a tracksuit pocket and pulls out his wallet, then pulls out a business card and hands it to Danny.

"You met Dave here," Eddie says, "when he was just a kid, but you were probably too stoned to remember."

"Hey!" Danny says, reminding Eddie his daughter is right here.

"Dave is doing the whole satellite radio deal now . . . He's a vice president of programming over at Sirius."

"Great. I'm happy for him. I have to—"

"He works with lots of old rock and rollers like you. You sit down for a few hours in a studio, play some songs, and tape a month's worth of shows in one day, then get your check and leave. It's quite the racket, let me tell you. I told Dave you guys were coming here today and he wants you to give him a call. You know who does a show for him? What's-his-face, Eric Birnbaum, the main guy from the Animals! Can you believe it?"

Danny looks down at the business card then inserts it into his wallet. When he looks back up he catches Eddie checking out Emily's chest and pulls her away. With his arm around her, they head down the hall to Studio B.

"Guess who's here today?" Danny says. "Joey Junior."

"Who?" she asks.

"Joey Mazz the Second. Joey Mazz's son. You've met—"

"Yes, many times. You could've told me he was coming today."

"I didn't know until he showed up. And I didn't know *you* were coming!"

They come to the door to Studio B. Danny has no doubt that Studio A is where Phankay will be working today and that in

236

a year they will be millionaires and in two years flat broke and not talking to one another. He opens the door and everyone stops what they're doing—which is just fucking around in a studio, strumming and chatting—and straightens out when they see a pregnant woman in their midst. Joey Senior stands up, comes over, and kisses Emily on the cheek, and Joey Junior stands up, too, but then thinks better of it and sits back down in his chair near the soundproof glass.

"So you have any names picked out?" Jules asks her, just for the sake of making conversation. Emily shakes her head. She's a terrific-looking girl, tall and angular and perky, but if anyone were ever off-limits to him, it's her.

Just for a cheap laugh Jules strums his guitar and starts singing "Having My Baby" by Paul Anka, doing a credible imitation.

"Hi, Joey," Emily says with a wave to Joey Junior.

"Hey, Em, what's going on?" the kid asks.

She pats her tummy and says, "This is."

"Yeah, I heard . . . congratulations on that."

Chunky, the only one present whose belly is bigger than Emily's, pulls up a chair for her to sit on, and she lowers herself into it with a sigh. Jules sings more songs with "baby" in them: "Wild World" by Cat Stevens and "Ooo Baby Baby" by the Miracles.

"Okay, maybe you can cut it out now, Jules," Howie says.

The band breezes through four more songs, this time doing their own numbers, and all the time Danny, Jules, and Howie keep a watchful eye on Joey Senior, who, despite the illness and layoff, hasn't lost a beat. They get him more water—Jules purposely now takes it without asking Eddie—and tell him to take it easy, that he doesn't have to go all out on the drums. But they don't want to be too obvious. Emily and Little Joey seem to be having an okay time, and Chunky says it's time for lunch. They get a menu from

Gloria, the receptionist—a skinny fiftyish Latina (she looks like Olive Oyl) with a quarter-inch chin and a lot of gold jewelry, who's obviously having an affair with Eddie—and write down their orders. Joey Senior says he wants two cheeseburgers deluxe, and Howie's face goes as white as the studio wall panels around him.

"Two?" Howie asks.

"Yeah. Medium rare. Takes Swiss. Nah. Make it chedduh."

"Aren't you supposed to be eating healthy?"

"Well, I really want three but I'm only ordering two. So that's healthy. And sure, have them throw in a house salad. Russian on the side."

Chunky Scrofa doesn't make matters any better: he orders a cheeseburger deluxe, too, plus a BLT, extra bacon, and two more black-and-white milk shakes. Howie and Danny go out into the hallway, ostensibly to give the menu to Gloria so she can call the diner, but more to converse about Joey.

"Two cheeseburgers deluxe?" Howie whispers. "That's insane."

"Don't put the order in yet," Danny whispers back. "I'm gonna try Angie again."

Down the hallway one of the guys in Yaphank-Knahpay-Phankay comes out of a bathroom and goes into Studio A. When he opens the door, a roaring tsunami of death metal spews out—it sounds like trucks hauling oversexed animals crashing into one another head-on—and then the door is closed and all is quiet again.

"I have seen the future of rock and roll . . ." Howie begins.

". . . And there isn't any," Danny ends.

Outside the air has turned much rawer, and Danny's hands are numb and he can barely work his cell phone. It's been years since Emily showed up to watch the band . . . he cannot even remember the last time. Jessica knows that Joey doesn't have much time left, but Emily doesn't, unless Jessica spilled the beans. It's good having her in the studio, though. She can see that her old man actually has to work.

Angie doesn't pick up. He tries her at home and she answers.

"Hey," he asks her, "isn't Joey supposed to be eating healthy?"

"Why?"

"He wants two cheeseburgers deluxe and fries. With cheddar."

"Chedduh? Tell me you didn't order that!"

Does it matter? The man doesn't have much time left. Maybe they all should just let him eat what he wants. Condemned murderers get one good last meal on Earth—can't a condemned man who's never killed anyone have all the good meals he wants?

"We're about to. What do I do?"

"You really need me to tell you?! If this is what it's like now, what's it going to be like when you're in Alabama in deep-fried ice cream country? Get him *one* cheeseburger deluxe and make sure he doesn't eat all the fries! And for God sake, make it Swiss!"

They say good-bye and the notion strikes him to go back inside and play until midnight, just to show Emily how hard her pops works, to show her what he's been doing since he was seventeen. *You think it's easy, honey, being a has-been rock star— here, take a look at this.* He looks at Moonrise. It's not the worst studio in the world. But still. What a long way down he's come. The Overfalls have recorded at Electric Lady, the Hit Factory, Muscle Shoals Sound, Record Plant in L.A., and Olympic in London. He's visited Sun, Chess, Stax, and Abbey Road. And now look where he is. In twenty years will there be a plaque outside that says MOONRISE SOUND STUDIOS: THIS IS WHERE YAPHANK-AHPANKY RECORDED THEIR SEMINAL FIRST ALBUM, WHICH WAS

239

NOT EVER RELEASED ON VINYL, CASSETTE, EIGHT-TRACK, OR CD,
BUT WAS DOWNLOADABLE TO A CHIP IN YOUR iBRAIN?

Howie is still in the hallway waiting for Danny, wearing
that perennially lost look of his. He had that look when he came
out to Long Island for his audition and it hasn't changed since. He
asks Danny if everything's okay, and Danny tells him to have
Gloria only order one cheeseburger for Joey, with Swiss not
cheddar, and that he (Danny) will take the heat for it. "Or better
yet," he says, "we'll blame it all on Gloria."

The band runs through three more songs and Chunky, just
to feel more comfortable and in his element, goes behind the glass,
sits at the console, and leans back in his swivel chair. Joey is out
of breath but says he feels okay. When lunch comes he forgets that
he ordered two cheeseburgers deluxe and all is well, until Chunky,
coming back into the studio to grab his chow, says, "Hey, what
happened to my boy's second burger?" and offers Joey half of his
BLT.

Danny asks Joey if he's up for more rehearsal, Joey says
yes, and they coast through four more tunes. Every few minutes
Danny sneaks a peek at Emily; she seems to be having an okay
time and Joey Junior is finally moving his feet to the beat. They
take another break and Howie asks Danny if maybe they should
stop for the day, to give Joey a break, but Danny tells him that
Angie said he could put in a full day. While they're talking Jules
plugs in his fuzzbox and, out of nowhere, breaks into the piercing
baroque opening of Janis Joplin's cover of "Summertime," and
they all pick up their axes and join in.

"Hey, Emily," Danny says, "you wanna sing?"

Emily has a great voice—what she lacks is confidence and
ambition—and her father knows she knows the words. She shakes
her head and Jules says, "Aww, come on! We need a female touch
here." She looks at her dad and he signals her over to his mike.
She stands up and joins him and, on the coldest day in Long Island

240

in four years, starts "Summertime," singing it more like the Zombies' jazzy version than Janis's and Big Brother's bluesy cover. A quarter of the way through the song, Joey beckons over his son to sit in for him, and Little Joey has no choice but to say yes, so he finishes the song at the drums. It's a family affair now, and with each bar Emily gets more confident, and Danny feels his heart warming for his lovely, talented daughter. *So what if she's pregnant, so what if the baby's father is some zero working in a Dairy Queen? . . .* He loves Emily and would do anything for her. *Jules, you skirt-chasing idiot,* he thinks, *you will never in your life know this joy. You fuckin' blew it, pal.* The song ends and Danny only notices now that Em had both her hands on her belly the entire five minutes.

The band applauds Emily and Little Joey, who sit back down, and Howie tells the two kids they were great.

"She's got a better voice than you and I do," Jules says to Danny, who agrees.

Howie asks Big Joey if he's up for a few more songs, and Joey says yes. But does he know his limit?

Danny says he needs to take a break, coming up with the excuse of giving his back a rest, and Joey buys it easily. He goes outside and calls Angie again, at home and on her cell, but she's nowhere to be found. *I can't do this all the time,* he thinks. *If he's going on the road with us, I can't be checking in with his wife or his doctors every five minutes. If he's going to die, he's going to die. And he* is *going to die.*

He goes back inside and opens the door to Studio A, and in an instant, as the cataclysm of screeching noise smashes into him, he realizes he's walked into the studio where Phanyak-Yaphank is rehearsing, recording, or just venting its teen angst. He closes the door and it takes a few seconds for him to recapture his breath.

Back in Studio B, they resume. They do two more TFO songs and then Danny asks Joey Senior what he wants to do. Joey

241

thinks about it and, before he can answer, Jules has started a song. It sounds familiar at first but Danny cannot place it . . . then he looks over to Jules, who mouths the title of the song: "Theme . . . Imaginary Western . . . " Danny gets it and nods, and in a flash the lyrics come back to him as though he and not Jack Bruce and Pete Brown had written the song. Howie and Joey join in and Danny begins to sing: "When the wagons. . ." If he'd heard this song 500 times, 480 times he was stoned, but still he nails the lyrics. And he sees—and Howie and Jules see—that Joey is having the time of his life. For decades Joey has wanted the band to cover this song and finally, even though it's only inside a shitty studio in Brentwood near a McDonald's and not in front of 20,000 fans, they're doing it.

An hour later, worrying about Joey, they call it quits for the day, and Jules elbows Howie in the ribs and points across the studio. On the other side of the glass, Chunky has fallen asleep at the mixing board. For all anyone knows he's been asleep for the last forty minutes.

It takes a while to unplug (and to wake up Chunky), but they pack up their gear and go outside. It's 2 degrees out and getting darker. Chunky squeezes into his black Mercedes and drives off, and Emily gets into her Accord and follows Danny's Suburban home; Jules is going to give Joey and Little Joey a lift to Bay City, and Howie has to wait by himself for an hour and a half until Melissa comes to pick him up and take him home.

On the road to Bay City, Little Joey rides shotgun and says little, and Big Joey sits in the back, behind Jules.

"Man, Emily's got some decent pipes," Joey Senior says.

"Yeah," Jules says, "and her voice ain't bad either." He turns to Little Joey and says, "Bet you never had a piece of ass that sweet, huh?"

Jules adjusts the rearview mirror, for a second catches sight of himself and the faint crow's feet around his eyes, and drives on.

At first the four of them were all in agreement—they would not make music videos. Even Joey agreed. It didn't matter what it meant for the band's success, it didn't matter if they could get Martin Scorsese or Ingmar Bergman to direct—they wouldn't do it. The very idea of a video for MTV was anathema to them, especially to Danny, who told people he wouldn't lip-synch a song even if someone offered him a million dollars in cash. The first to cave, naturally, was Jules: he had watched MTV and seen all the willowy foxes who appeared in videos. That seemed to be the whole point: Come up with a lame idea, have a casting call and pick five women out of the thousand who show up, bump them, make the video, and go home. Velcro Pravda told the band it would be a breeze: someone would come up with some idea or "plot" wherein Danny and Jules would not have to lip-synch, and they could knock off the whole thing in a day or two.

Wasted and Tasted was not selling as well as *Borderline* had; it was only moving slightly better than *Come and Git It* did, which wasn't bad, but after having gone Platinum with their second LP, wasn't good either. Velcro kept pressing, Jules kept nudging, and Howie and Joey were now on the fence. With Lew Aaronson and AaZ Records pressing as well, Danny could see the writing on the wall. They *had* to make a video. It was one thing to despise the Thompson Twins, the Human League, and Duran Duran . . . but you had to at least try to keep up with them. Otherwise, you could never beat them.

It was decided that they'd make a video for "Hurt" and that they'd get an unknown, pretty young actor and actress to appear in some sort of three-and-a-half-minute teen love story, that TFO would appear intermittently, and that Joey, of all people, would do

243

the lip-synching. Joey . . . the only person in the Overfalls whose voice never once was heard on any of their albums.

The whole shoot cost less than $70,000 and was done out in Montauk—on the beach, in the town, and along deserted back roads—on a gray November day. When Danny was told, a week before filming commenced, that the director, a temperamental punk two years out of NYU film school, had also made videos for A Flock of Seagulls, he called up ten different people at AaZ and threw a fit at each of them, then took two Valium, calmed down, called everyone back, and said, "Okay, sorry . . . let's just get it over with."

That was how Jules met Rhonda Wentworth. She was one of two stylists on the shoot. She had dirty-blonde hair kept in a pixie cut, was slim, and had a button nose and juicy Jean Harlow lips, big baby blue eyes, and a husky voice for someone only five foot two. The first time Jules saw her was when she came into his trailer, and as soon as they set eyes on each other, they knew something life-changing would happen—they just locked into each other and couldn't wipe the smiles off their faces for the rest of the day.

Rhonda was from Syosset but was presently living on the Lower East Side on Clinton Street with two roommates. As she worked on Jules's eye makeup ("Do everything you can to make me look like Boy George," he joked to her), she told him how she'd once sneaked into Vagrants and seen the Overfalls when she was only fifteen and the band was still called the Ventilators. "Fifteen?" he said to her. "It's a good thing you didn't come up to me—I'd still be in jail now." Everything she said and the way she said it rubbed him the right way. From their vantage point in the trailer they could see the pretty young actor and actress filming a fifteen-second scene—the boy pleading, the girl fuming (they nailed it in only ten takes)—and Jules told her how against the idea of videos the band was, but that this was what they'd been reduced to. Their label, he also told her, really wanted them to "totally New Wave it up" on their next album.

"Well," Rhonda said, "everyone sells out. Even the Who, you know?" She worked on his shirt and he took the cigarette out of her mouth, took a puff, and put it back in.

"Have dinner with me tonight, blondie," he said. "Okay?"

She said she would and then asked him, "So, do you ask out every single pretty girl you meet?"

"Just about, but not for dinner," Jules said. "And do you say yes to every single stud rocker who asks you?"

"Yes, but not for dinner."

Someone knocked on the trailer door, it was time for the band to film their scene, and ten minutes later, as he trudged along the chilly dunes of Montauk, while Joey played air drums and dreamily lip-synched, Jules could not stop thinking of the sexy blond stylist who'd just dressed him up while charming the pants off of him. (An attentive eye can espy his arousal in the "Hurt" video in some scenes.)

They looked somewhat alike—that could have been part of the attraction. They had the same lips and eyes and hair color (before Jules started dyeing it blonder) and were built the same way, with their long legs and narrow waists and shoulders. She had the most beautiful skin of any woman he'd ever been with . . . it was absolutely pristine. "Oh my God, you're so perfect," he cooed to her many times when they caressed each other into narcotic oblivion for hours in dark rooms. Her skin was so luminescent that whenever she appeared in photos, she leapt off the paper.

The "Hurt" video boosted record sales, but only a bit, and within six months of their meeting, Rhonda and Jules were shacking up. Photos of them appeared every now and then in *People* and *Us* and *Rolling Stone*. They were an It Couple, and the more time they spent with each other, the more alike they looked.

245

Jules cut his hair and she grew hers, and now both their coifs were shoulder-length. Under her sway, he began to dress more colorfully. Gone were the torn jeans, work boots, and plaid shirts (they'd been handed down from Creedence Clearwater Revival and would later resurface on Nirvana and Pearl Jam) . . . now it took him an hour to get dressed and leave the house. He spent more money on clothing than the rest of the band did on food, housing, drugs, and accountants combined. Jules and Rhonda moved to a larger apartment so that his wardrobe could be contained, but the greater space only meant more room for new clothes. Danny was happy for Jules—he liked Rhonda and knew she was a stabilizing force in his life (in the whole time Jules and Rhonda were together, Jules didn't catch one single social disease)—but he could not believe the outfits Jules was wearing. He'd show up for gigs and recording sessions in a patent-leather motorcycle jacket; in velvet, brocade, organza, silver-lamé, and ombré-dip-dyed silk scarves; in taffeta, sheared beaver, iridescent silk, even sequins and beading . . . all at once. The dazzling shoes and boots he wore were made of the hides of exotic animals most people had only seen on PBS nature programs. Danny and Howie wrote a song for *West of Babylon* called "Pretty as a Peacock" and Jules had no idea it was about him.

For the first and only time in his life, Jules was true to a woman. The two lovebirds had an agreement: he could bang all the women he wanted as long as he didn't fall in love with any of them and never embarrassed her, and she could bang any guy she wanted as long as she told him about it in excruciating blow-by-blow detail. With that entente in place, though, nothing happened (after they got a few unexciting threesomes out of the way in the first year of their courtship). He would meet women and flirt with them but he always nipped it in the bud before it turned into something; also, Rhonda would often travel with TFO on the road as their stylist. So they always kept an eye on each other.

Rhonda handled The Life: she could deal with waking up at one in the afternoon and going to bed at five in the morning, and she could deal with the travel and the hotel rooms and the eighty cities in ninety days. She never complained about the rotten food and unsavory people. "She's a keeper," Howie told Jules many times, marveling at her stamina and ease at adapting to a rocker's life. She could also tell when Jules needed Man Time with the boys and was never suspicious when he'd vanish for a few days. One year, the band was touring Europe, about to play Rome on the West of Babylon Tour, and, on a rare four-day break between countries, Jules and Rev took off and never told anyone where they were going. When they resurfaced, looking bedraggled and wasted, at the Hassler Hotel, Rhonda coolly acted as though he'd never left. It turned out that Jules and Rev had rented a Maserati, driven to Geneva and, after draining the city of a good portion of its controlled substances, Jules had bought a five-carat diamond engagement ring, which he sprung on Rhonda on the Piazza Navona at four in the morning. (He didn't get on his knees because he didn't want to ruin the claret-color crushed-velvet pants he was wearing at the time.) She said yes and soon they set a date for the following summer.

A lot changed in that year. *West of Babylon* sold poorly, TFO had only one album remaining on their contract, and they weren't coming up with any strong material. People were forgetting about them. When the band wasn't on the road—and sometimes when they were—Danny and Jules would snap at each other, sometimes going days without speaking, or just go through the motions of getting along. Danny was doing lots of drugs and drinking heavily, getting into arguments with anyone he could, and just being an all-around pain in the ass. He and Jules would work for weeks trying to write a song only to realize it just wasn't that good . . . then Danny would disappear for a few weeks. Truth be told, his songwriting was better when he was on drugs. (If he

247

was a little drunk, he was good; if he was drunk and on coke, he was very good; but when he was drunk and on coke and pills— that was the best Danny Ault you could get.)

Meanwhile, Jules and Rhonda were gearing up for their July wedding, and Jules went to Las Vegas in June for his five-day-long bachelor party. "It's gonna be total, complete, utter debauchery," Joey had promised him. "It's gonna make the Roman Empire look like ancient fuckin' history."

It never came close to that. Of the fifty-five people invited, only fourteen showed up. Chunky Scrofa and Owen J. Crowe did not attend; Danny showed up but only stayed for two days, got bored and morose, and left. (No matter what they did to it, he always hated Las Vegas.) The MGM Grand had half a floor booked for the party but eventually gave them seven rooms. Jules lost ten grand shooting dice and was too petrified of his upcoming nuptials to party hearty, and it fell upon the bachelor roadies Rev, Big Bob, and Sweet Lou to remind him every five minutes he was doing the right thing marrying Rhonda. (Rev was none too convincing: "Yeah, she cool . . . Rhonda's all right" was the best he could come up with.)

One night at 3 A.M., after dumping 2,000 bucks at blackjack, Jules came into Joey's room and tried to get Joey to talk him out of the wedding. But Joey wasn't having any of it. He kept telling Jules how great Rhonda was, that they were perfect for each other, that he hoped one day to meet someone just as great, and that Jules would never be able to find anyone else so good.

"This isn't what I wanted to hear, douchebag," Jules, sprawled out on Joey's floor, said.

"Man," Joey said, stuffing his mouth with Doritos, "you two are gonna have some great kids. Think about it. One day you could teach your son how to play guitar. And the both of yous could sit around your living room playin'. It doesn't get any better than that."

248

Jules mumbled that maybe it didn't get any *worse* than that, but Joey could not hear it above the racket of his crunching Doritos. "Besides, Joey," he added, "she never said a thing to me about ever having kids."

A few minutes later, Rev and Sweet Lou burst into the room with their bachelor-party gift for Jules. Her name was Robin Marie and she was a platinum-blonde showgirl from the Folies Bergere show at the Tropicana. She was stacked like Anita Ekberg from her *La Dolce Vita* days, and when she stood before Jules in her gold high heels, all she had covering her private parts were three dollops of whipped cream. Naked, tall, and built like a goddess, she was too plentiful to look at for more than three seconds at a time.

"Hey," Lou said to Jules, "this is for you, dude . . . on us."

Robin Marie, who was from Quebec, said, "Hi, Jules. In ze mood for some whipped crème?" Jules's heart was pounding, his blood was surging . . . this creature before him was almost too voluptuous a specimen to be human. She did have a mole near her navel, though. Jules looked to Joey, who shook his head warily. *Uh-uh,* Joey was signaling, *I wouldn't do this.* All he had to do, Jules knew, was take Robin Marie back to his room, do the deed, and send her packing. The whole thing could go down in three minutes.

"Well?" Rev said. Robin Marie dragged an index finger across one of the lumps of whipped cream and then sucked it off her long fingernail. Now Jules could see how very bubblegum pink her nipples were. But he kept fixing in on that mole near her belly button, and it grew to the size of a casino chip.

Jules said to Rev and Lou, "Nah . . . I'm gonna pass. But thanks. I appreciate it." He apologized to Robin Marie, who, perhaps more relieved than insulted, was quickly hustled out of the room.

The wedding was only a month away, and *West of Babylon* had been off the charts for quite a while.

*

By the time Jules pulls his car up to Joey's house, it's evening. Little Joey has said hardly anything, Joey Senior slept most of the way, and three times en route Jules had to pull into gas stations to urinate. It's been a while since Jules has been to Joey and Angie's, a creaky two-story shingled house sorely in need of a new paint job. It's one of those houses that, even on a summer afternoon with the sun flooding in and all the lights on, still always seems dark inside.

The front door flies open—which, of course, means it's Angie opening it—and the three men drag themselves out of the car. The Christmas lights have not been taken off the windows outside and they flicker in the frigid air.

"What took so long?" Angie asks. Even when she's not remotely angry, she can still come across as furious.

"Nothin' did," Joey tells her as he, his son, and Jules step inside.

Angie takes Jules's leather coat and drapes it over a living-room chair, and right away Jules sees Joey's two daughters, Suzanne and Marianne, and feels something lukewarm and disturbing in the pit of his stomach. The two girls, eighteen and sixteen, aren't doing anything, just sitting on the tattered gray couch drinking hot chocolate and watching TV. Suzanne sees Jules and smiles, and Marianne doesn't even look up at him— she's either too shy, too involved in the text she's composing on her cell phone, or hasn't noticed he's there. There's a fireplace but no fire going presently, and the living room, though not tidy, is not a mess. *I have to get out of here,* Jules thinks, *as quickly as I can.*

"You staying for spaghetti?" Angie asks him from the kitchen, wrapping a black apron around her waist. "It's soon."

"Nah," he lies, "I got plans tonight."

"Plans, huh? With you, I know what that means."

"You should stay," Big Joey says as his son darts up the stairs. "Angie makes a mean Bolognese."

It's tempting. Jules remembers Angie's pasta from his three-week fling with her before she and Joey got married. He's quite familiar with her cooking.

He sits down in a bulky beige chair near the couch that smells like beer farts and thinks he can feel a spring digging into one of his ass cheeks. The floor in the living room is warped and the wood tilts toward the front door. Jules's feet are only inches away from Suzanne's. She's the better-looking of the two sisters, but still neither daughter is that attractive—they both inherited their father's potato nose. She's thumbing her way through *Glamour* and Marianne is still texting someone.

The TV is on mute and the only background noise is a loud clock ticking in the kitchen: it sounds like a heartbeat in a TV hospital drama. Jules stays in his chair and the warm, unsettling feeling only gets worse. Suzanne's bare foot inches over to his ankle and, for a few seconds, rubs it. Slowly, so as not to offend her, he pulls his foot away. But was she really playing with him?

Joey Senior goes upstairs and Jules stands up, drifts into the kitchen, and helps himself to a chunk of Italian bread.

"How'd the patient do today?" Angie whispers.

"Who?"

"Who do you think?"

"He was fine. He got a little tired. But it was cool—he's a serious trouper."

He tells her they're going to rehearse a few more times before the tour and he'll play himself into shape.

251

"Little Joey played too," he says. "Emily Ault showed up and sang. It was nice."

She stirs the sauce with a big wooden spoon. Tomatoes, onions, carrots, red wine, ground chuck, olive oil . . . it all smells good. The pot of pasta is boiling furiously and foaming on the surface, and he's dying to leave.

He looks at the back of Angie's long neck. She's still in great shape. She was wild in bed and loved to get on top and pinch or pull on Jules's nipples. Or she'd spin around reverse cowgirl–style, grab his nuts, and pull on the skin of his sac and let it snap back. Now that is a real pro for you—how many chicks know to do that? Did Angie ever tell her husband about her and Jules? For years he's wondered about that. (He knows *he* never told him.) If she did tell him, Joey either didn't care that much or did and forgot all about it.

"That clock is really loud," Jules tells her, and Joey Junior comes down the stairs and grabs a piece of bread, never making eye contact with anyone. Just for something to do, Jules pulls his hair, and Angie looks at her son and then at Jules and grins. Even though he took his last leak only twenty minutes before and hasn't had anything to drink, Jules's bladder feels like a plastic sandwich bag filled with ten gallons of water. Angie, slowly pouring him a heaping glass of Chianti, isn't helping.

"Hey," Angie calls out to Suzanne, "are you gonna set the table or what? Marianne, pull your nose outta that thing and run up and tell daddy dinner's on in five."

It's now or never. He can't stay here, he'll go nuts. He has to take a whiz and cut out. Or he could just grab his coat and leave and pull up to the side of the road and piss there.

He makes for the bathroom, which is just beneath the staircase. Each step of the staircase looks lopsided—the whole house looks as though van Gogh painted half of it then gave up and handed his brushes to Edvard Munch. Joey Mazz bought the place when the band first started to make it. It was shitty then and it hasn't gotten much better. He could have gotten a much better house but wanted to stay in Bay City, close to his parents. When they died he still could have moved to a better home in a more upscale area. But now, with three kids and no record deals, they're stuck here. Even in the bathroom Jules can hear the kitchen clock . . . *Maybe,* he thinks, *in a drummer's house all the clocks have to be this loud.*

If I leave now I can make it home in forty-five minutes. Or I can call and maybe stop in at Princess Pink's place in Oakdale. Last time I tried that, though, she wasn't into it. "I have a boyfriend now, Jules," she told him proudly. "It's like really serious, too. We can't keep doing this every few months whenever you get horny." They had sex anyway, but it just wasn't the same.

He hears, on the other side of the bathroom door, the table being set, the clinks of plates and glasses and silverware. Chairs being pulled. It's now or never.

He opens the door and, keeping his head down, walks to the chair where Angie had tossed his coat. But it's not there and he has to look up. Joey Senior, Suzanne, Marianne, Little Joey and Angie are all seated and passing around bowls of pasta and Bolognese sauce. There's a bowl of salad on the table, too. And an empty chair.

"Come and join us, bro!" Joey Senior says.

"I can't. Anyone know where my coat is?"

A minute later he's outside opening the door to his car when the front door opens and Little Joey comes out.

"Yo, Jules!" the kid says.

"What is it?" It's so cold out that Jules's eyes are tearing up.

"I got this for you. In case you want."

Joey Junior hands him a small baggie. The Christmas lights flicker red and blue and Jules can see there's weed inside.

253

"How much?"

"Fifty."

"Sure. I'll pay you the next time I see you."

Jules gets in his car and is just about to drive off but then summons the kid back.

"You should drum more," he tells him, "you know that? You could be really good. You're not as good as your old man but don't give it up. You'll get better."

*

Two weeks after the Vegas bachelor party, Jules was at the Wentworth house in Syosset having lunch and making nice with her folks. Rhonda's old man was a policeman, a Brooklyn narcotics detective, and the mom was a high-school principal, but despite that and all his boyhood prejudices, he still liked them and they were polite and making an honest effort to like him, too. They knew their daughter loved him and that he worked his ass off. Their house was small and unassuming and reminded Jules of his family's place in Green River. Rhonda had an older brother and a younger sister and they were there that day, too, discussing the upcoming wedding over tuna salad sandwiches. The wedding was to be on the beach and, in case of rain, there was a contingency plan to take it inside. Everything was set. Two hundred people were coming and Jules was letting the Wentworths off the hook by paying for it out of his own pocket.

After lunch, Jules went out alone to the small backyard and sat in a deck chair in the sun. The Wentworths were good people. Sure, had he been carrying some coke or pot and run into the old man a few years earlier, he'd have been busted, but everybody's got to do something for a living. It was hot and bright that day and Jules opened the top two buttons of his shirt. Rhonda had gotten him the shirt—silk tangerine-and-violet paisley—in London on the last European tour. Rosanna, her kid sister, came outside and asked him if he wanted a beer or iced tea, and he said no, he was all right. Rhonda did not have the Silver, but Rosanna sure did. That liquid sparkle that told you she could light a fire in a bed just by lying down on it. She was a five-minute chick. Another time, another place, another universe and Jules would be in the parents' bed poking her right now.

Sweat began to form on his forehead, and he took out a pair of sunglasses, put them on, and stretched out. In two weeks, it would all be over. Rhonda had no idea, but right after the ceremony and just before the reception, the Overfalls were going to get on a makeshift stage on the beach and Jules was going to sing "Gimme Some Lovin'." He knew his sassy, sexy bride would eat that up, maybe even swoon.

The sun hid behind some clouds, then came out brighter and hotter. It was two in the afternoon. He reached for his sunglasses, then remembered they were already on.

He closed his eyes and thought of women he'd known and been with. There were girls in high school he had crushes on but who never noticed him. When he started playing in bands, though, everything changed. Avalanche, Brittle Cringe, and the Stoning Rolls weren't any good and never made it, but the chicks were always there and he was always there for them. If you turned anything down, you were a fool. There was Tara O'Neill, when the Overfalls weren't yet the Overfalls. What an ass on her. Like two cantaloupes joined together. No pair of blue jeans could contain that thing. And that hair. Genuine blond, all the way to her waist. There was Patchouli Julie with her mile-long legs, and the way she dug her nails into the back of his neck and the sexy noises she made. There was Contessa Vanessa van Vaseline in Amsterdam and her bottomless bag of tricks. Not the best-looking woman in the world but you never knew what she'd do.

255

A squally guitar riff came to him, then vanished. He dozed off for a minute and when he awoke, Rhonda was sitting on the grass beside him talking about babies, about how her folks couldn't wait to become grandparents and wanted them to have three or four kids. *Three or four,* Jules thought. *Huh? What the fuck? I'm not even sure I want to have* one *or even* half *of one, and you're talking* four? "They're so excited," Rhonda said, "and Daddy really wants us to have boys. But it's okay," she asked, "if they're girls, right?" Sure, Jules said, that'd be fine. His forehead and shirt were soaking and he undid a few more buttons. *Would your folks also like it,* he wanted to ask her, *if I slipped my dick into a bear trap?*

As planned, Rhonda spent that night at her parents' place in Syosset and Jules went back to Manhattan. They had eight rooms—if you cleared the clothing out you had enough space for four kids. He thought of calling up Danny, but they hadn't said a word to each other since Las Vegas—he didn't even know if Danny was in New York. He called up Big Bob and hung out with him for a while at a bar on Columbus Avenue. A skinny woman in her late thirties, a garmento with straggly brown hair, recognized him and told him she was a fan; they made out in the bathroom, he got his fingers wet, and she gave him a clumsy hand job. He got home at three in the morning, played guitar for a while among the racks of clothing, and called Rhonda the next day and told her he couldn't go through with it—he didn't want to have kids. "Marriage is scary enough," he told her, "but kids? Forget it . . . I can't do it."

She was sobbing on the phone, and when she wasn't sobbing she was whimpering and pleading, but nothing she said could change his mind. It was the worst he'd ever felt and it was the worst thing he'd ever done, but he was doing what he had to do. They were on the phone for over two hours and half the time nobody said anything. He tried everything he could to make it

256

better for her, but in the end she hung up on him and that was it. Except for one chance encounter a few years later on Bleecker Street, they never saw each other again. He left town for a week so that she could clear all her stuff out of the apartment and move, and when he returned it was like living in an empty meat locker.

Three weeks after he called the wedding off, he called up Sweet Lou at one in the morning and asked him: "Hey, remember that chick Robin Marie? The one in Vegas with the whipped cream? Would you have any way of getting back in touch with her?"

*

Jules isn't driving home—he's just driving around with *Layla and Other Love Songs* playing low on the stereo. Hardly anybody is on the road tonight and the signs and towns and houses go by. Hauppauge, Wyandanch, Bethpage. He banged a girl from Bethpage once, on the famous golf course there. Two in the morning, par four, dogleft left. He stops in Hicksville at a Wendy's and they won't let him use the bathroom unless he buys something. He gets a small french fries and then they tell him that's not enough, so he goes outside, tosses out the fries, and whizzes on the back of the building. Take that, Wendy.

"I don't know about Europe in the fall," Danny had said at the Parkway Diner. "Maybe this is our last tour."

How the hell can he just do that, Jules thinks as he zips up. He gets back into his car and sits there for a while.

"Why the hell is it up to *you*," Jules hears himself say aloud, "if the band breaks up or not. *I* don't have a fuckin' say in it?"

Would he really do that to me? he wonders, turning *Layla* back on. Could Danny really do that? *After all the shit we've been through together . . .*

257

Back on the road. He knows a chick in Hicksville he could call. Big thighs, poochy tummy, a face that only a prison matron could love. *What the fuck is her name anyway?* He cannot remember. Signs for Plainview, Melville, Huntington Station. THE HAMPTONS 45 MILES, a sign reads. Yeah, right. He had to sell his sweet little place in Westhampton after *Dead End Road,* after the band had to cough up two million to Alan Wilbur Murdock and another few hundred thousand to the band's team of legal experts. Some goddamn team—it was as if they'd retained the services of the '62 Mets. He always wondered what it was exactly that did the band in—was it Alan Wilbur Murdock in the hotel parking lot or was it *Dead End Road* and the fact that they just could not come up with any decent songs anymore?

SYOSSET 5 MILES, a sign says.

Did Danny mean no more touring or no more recording? Or both? Is that it? Is he killing the band? And it was just like him to not say whatever it was he was really saying.

What the hell am I going to do, Jules thinks as he takes the road to Syosset. The sky overhead is icy silver and there are few other cars out now—it's just him in the arctic suburbs. He remembers that the Wentworth family lived on Cheshire Avenue but doesn't remember the number, and it takes him ten minutes but he finds Cheshire Avenue. His bladder buzzing like crazy again, Jules slows down the car and drives up and down the street and comes to the house he thinks it might have been. One story, cream-color siding, flat roof, small front lawn. Yes, this is definitely it. All the lights are off inside; most of the lights are off in every house on the street. He gets out and walks onto the rock-hard soil and comes up to the house. He looks through the living room window but the curtains are drawn. He could creep around to the back and check out the backyard. Maybe the deck chair is still there, where he sat in the sun and Rhonda talked about having kids. He decides to go back to the car and on the way he sees the name on the mailbox.

The Wentworths do not live here anymore. Gone.

Heading east now, after a stop at an Exxon station, he suddenly remembers that the chick in Hicksville is Sexy Sadie. Her name isn't really Sadie and she isn't sexy, but for some reason that's what he calls her. He finds her number on his cell and calls, and she picks up on the first ring. She lives alone and he could be over there and in her bed in twenty minutes, and out of her bed in twenty-five.

She says, "Hello?" and he says nothing.

"Jules?" she says. "Is that you, honey?"

He hangs up on her and drives home.

Part Three
On the Road Again

Eleven
Roadwork

Manhattan, just before noon. Howie waits inside Penn Station for the train to D.C. with his duffel bag, bass guitars, and electric violin. In Kingstown, Danny, Jules, and Joey load the Suburban and U-Haul with the gear and a box of 1,000 *TFO 10* CDs. The smell of the Dunkin' Donuts ten yards away from Howie is already starting to seep into the ruff of his battered sheepskin coat. Somewhere in the knapsack on his shoulder is the printout of the band's itinerary, but Howie doesn't really need it: he has most of it memorized. He knows that Danny will drive the Suburban down to D.C., with Jules and Joey in the U-Haul, or that Danny and Joey will be in the Suburban, with Jules alone in the U-Haul. Any permutation is possible so long as it's not Danny and Jules in the same car.

He's been here twenty minutes and has already washed his hands in the men's room and then doused his hands with Purell three times. It doesn't matter how hot the water is or how much Purell you rub into your hands . . . because it's still a bathroom at Penn Station. One square inch of sink is like Times Square on New Year's Eve for bacteria.

His train will be departing on Track 21.

I should have bought two tickets, he thinks now. That way, no stranger could sit too close to him on the train. He could just put his instruments on the next seat and flash the tickets to anyone who wanted to take it. But it's too late.

His train has been ready to board for five minutes now, but Howie is so worried that he's going to forget all his stuff that he's stuck and cannot move.

By now, he thinks, *the rest of the band is already on the road.* But maybe not. There's always the bickering, unforeseen glitches, kidding around; there are Jules's three suitcases of clothing and Danny's bad back. If they only had a roadie, things would be a lot better. But then there would be five of them and the whole dynamic would shift.

And this is it, he thinks. *After this tour, that will be it. It's all over.*

He looks at the hundreds of people surrounding him, most of them hurrying to and from work, and thinks: *What am I going to do? I have to do something.* He told Melissa a few weeks ago that Danny was leaving the band, and she tried to be encouraging; she said something about this being a good opportunity, about how when one door closes another door opens, but Howie told her that this was more of a case of one door getting slammed shut and all the other doors in the world breaking at once.

"Well," she promised him, "I'm going to think of something."

Two men in blue uniforms are working on the outside of a newspaper store, and to get to Track 21 Howie will have to pass either beneath or near some scaffolding. It's unavoidable. Or he could take the long way around, go way out of his way to avoid it.

"Eleven-fifty-five Acela Express to Washington, D.C., stopping at Philadelphia . . ."

He sticks his iPod buds into his ears. His tastes have come full circle: he's back to listening to Van der Graaf Generator, Amon Düül, and John Cage. He looks around to see if anyone is looking at him. Nobody is. So he moves: He lifts up his right foot and takes a step, then lifts up his left. He takes five steps, then realizes he left his instruments and duffel behind him. He darts back to pick them up, another minute ticks off on the Arrivals and Departures board, and he runs to Track 21, taking the long way to get there and avoiding the scaffold.

"Anyone sitting here?" a man with a runny nose politely asks him fifteen minutes later as the train chugs south.

Howie pulls out his earbuds—"Imaginary Landscape No. 1" fades out—and picks up his guitars, stowing them on the rack above his head so that the man can sit down.

Love Street, Kingstown, Long Island. Early afternoon.

Howie was right: the others haven't even left yet. On the way to Jules's house, Danny saw Wendell, Emily's most recent boyfriend, standing outside of a Starbucks cramming a muffin into his mouth. Without even thinking about it, Danny double-parked the SUV, slammed the door, grabbed the kid by the jacket and got right up into his grill and said, "I know you, Wendell! You remember me?! Emily's father?!"

Crumbs falling out of his mouth, the kid replied, "Yeah, but my name isn't Wendell, it's Wyatt."

"Whatever your name is . . ." Danny began, and then proceeded to rip into him for knocking up his daughter and abandoning her. Some passersby stopped to look at them, others hurried away, and Wyatt said, "Mr. Ault, I swear to God I'm not the father. I *swear* it." Danny let loose his crumb-speckled collar and realized someone so dense probably could not be that convincing a liar, so he got back into the Suburban. Meanwhile, in Bay City, Joey couldn't get out of the house . . . Angie was nagging him about his health and reminding him to eat healthy on the road; Little Joey was being a slug and wouldn't get out of bed to say good-bye to his old man. Danny and Joey arrived at Jules's house within minutes of each other but were still twenty minutes late, and Jules hadn't even woken up yet.

Bleary-eyed and unshaved, Jules made coffee for the three of them, squeezed into some holey black leather pants, and threw on a shirt and a sweater.

"Are we ready to roll?" Danny asks now, his fingernails digging into the fabric of the chair he's sitting in. Somewhere beneath all the dust bunnies in the corners of this living room are more dust bunnies, and more beneath those; the windows are only nominally transparent and the appliances in the kitchen look as though they are going to collapse under the weight of their own grime.

"I haven't packed yet," Jules confesses.

He heads into his bedroom to start packing, and Danny groans, digs his fingernails further into the mint green chair, and looks at the lopsided framed poster of Jimi Hendrix on the wall. Joey just lingers about and swigs his Martinson's. Had Hendrix lived, millions of people have wondered, what sort of music would he have ended up making? But right now all Danny wants to know is that if Hendrix had lived, would he have gotten married and wound up with a woman who wouldn't have permitted him to dwell in such squalor? Does Jules even realize the poster is lopsided?

"This place makes my crib look swank," Joey says.

"Must he always bring fifty different pairs of snakeskin pants?" Danny says. "Are there even fifty different kinds of snakes?"

"Hey, I got this for you. It's pretty cool."

Joey pulls a cheap, plastic, nine-keyed piano toy from out of a Babies R Us bag.

"What the hell's that for?"

"For your future grandkid, bro. It'll attach to his crib. Check it out."

Joey pushes a pink button and the toy keyboard lights up. He pushes a blue button and the toy starts jingling "Twinkle, Twinkle, Little Star," and he presses a few keys and begins playing along. The thing is shockingly loud for it being so small, and Danny snatches it away and turns it off.

"And we're taking this on the road with us, Joey?"

"Hey, it only needs two C batteries and it knows six different songs. Including 'Whole Lotta Love'!"

"Almost there . . . having a slight sock crisis!" Jules calls out. The house has three bedrooms, two downstairs, one upstairs; Jules sleeps in one of them, one of them is just for clothing, and the other one—nobody knows what goes on in there.

Danny stands up and looks out through the whorls of dirt on the living-room window. The U-Haul is here . . . at least Jules remembered to rent it. Two years ago when they began their tour, Jules had forgotten and it screwed up everything for days.

"He shoulda gotten married," Joey says. "Then he wouldn't be living inside a freaking roach motel. A chick would've set his ass straight."

A few years ago the band still took planes on their tours. A few years before that, people would recognize them at airports and on planes and in hotel lobbies. As recently as fifteen years ago they would even check into their hotel rooms under cheeky aliases: Danny was John B. Sloop, Joey was Ludwig van Yamaha, and Howie was David Watts. (Jules usually checked in under his own name—that way the girls could find him.) One time they were flying from New York to L.A. and a flight attendant recognized them and told the pilot; after the plane landed the pilot got on the PA system and told everyone that the Furious Overfalls were on the flight, and Danny could hear awestruck *Ooohs* coming from the coach seating behind him.

But that was a long time ago.

"Two more minutes, no shit," Jules calls out from upstairs.

"Remember Rhonda? The Syosset chick?" Joey asks from the kitchen. "She was perfect for him."

Danny turns around, sees Joey scouring his coffee mug in the kitchen, and says, "Sure. She was."

Had Jules married Rhonda, though, they would have been divorced by now—there's no question about that. There's just no way that could have worked out. And so nothing would have changed. Jules Rose would still be rifling through his fraying faux-fur vests and Joey Mazz would still be in the kitchen dying and Howie Grey would still be on a train and Danny would still be

267

standing near the window grinding his teeth. Nothing would have changed. The band would still have crashed into a wall and time would have passed them by. The incident outside San Francisco would still have happened; so, too, would have *Dead End Road,* and their record label would still have dumped them. Danny remembers now talking with Jules at the bar at Vagrants—talking about Springsteen, the Ramones, and the Clash, and about how maybe they (the Overfalls) had come along too late, were perhaps too *this* and maybe not enough *that.* Over the years, Danny has sometimes felt like a kid who'd hopped onto the carousel with the quarter running down. And besides, Rhonda and Jules breaking up—it kept Jules miserable for two years and the band got a few more good songs out of him as a result. Danny doesn't know about writers and painters but knows that happy, content people do not write songs like "Bell Bottom Blues" or "Hellhound on My Trail."

Jules comes down the narrow staircase, carrying his suitcases and scrolling through his cell phone. "Just making sure," he says, "I've still got the Shut Up Girl's number in San Antone."

"The Shut Up Girl," Danny says. "I almost forgot about her."

"Shut *up,*" Joey says, imitating the Shut Up Girl.

Sensing something crucial missing but not having any idea what it is, Jules says: "Who's gonna help me get the gear up from the basement?"

The gear. Amps, drums, speakers, cables; Howie's accordion, violin and alto sax. Danny took three Tylenol before leaving in preparation for this, but he's not looking forward to bringing everything up and then loading it into the U-Haul.

This is the last time, he thinks, *I will ever leave on a tour. Thank God.*

"Let's do it," Joey says.

"No," Danny says. He doesn't want Joey lifting anything heavy. "We've got it. Okay?"

"I could—"

"No, you couldn't," Jules tells Joey.

Jules and Danny walk to the kitchen, where the stairway to the basement is. Walking down, one dangling lightbulb shining feebly over the steps, Danny swats away a cobweb.

"Let's try not to have Joey lift anything," he whispers.

"Definitely," Jules whispers back.

Jules flicks the light on and Danny sees something gray scurry into a crack in the wall.

"When's the last time you were down here?"

"When we got back from Maine."

It's going to take an hour and every fiber of muscle they've got to get all the gear upstairs. Howie is going to beat them to D.C. and end up by himself for a while. But that's Howie.

"You have any neighbors who'd help us?" Danny says. "I'll give them some bread."

"Yeah . . . there are two big teenage boys across the street who might help for like twenty bucks total. I'll try and get 'em."

Jules darts up the stairs. "Hey," Danny hears him say to Joey, "come with me . . . I wanna get two kids to help us. Don't say anything though."

They used to play pranks on Joey and it could get cruel. The usual short-sheeting his bed, TPing him and his bed while he slept, sending fugly groupies up to his hotel room. Rev once even put a real python inside his snare drum case—when Joey opened it, the snake sprang up, and Joey jumped three yards into the air. If they did that to him today it would probably kill him. *Try to bring him back alive* were Angie's instructions.

Danny hears rodent nails inside the walls and then hears human footsteps. The basement door opens and Jules's head hits the dangling bulb as he peers down to talk.

"The boys say they'll do it," Jules says. "But they want forty each."

"Forty? *Each?*"

Danny looks at all the crates and equipment. It looks like mourners gathering in a foggy cemetery. Each year it seems to weigh a ton more.

"Sure," he says. "Why not . . ."

*

Wilmington, Delaware. A Roadhouse Blues club. Eleven at night. Their fourteenth show in fifteen days, their third in Wilmington. They're breezing through "Too Little Too Late" from *Come and Git It*.

The four of them on the stage, the silhouettes of the sound and light men just offstage, 200 souls in the crowd, the smell of beer and french fries from ceiling to floor. Last night, a Saturday, they drew almost 300. (The Overfalls know that the vast majority of the crowd is not true TFO fans: they come here to see a band perform, any band. If Lothar and the Hand People had shown up, they would still be out there.) The monitors are blasting the music back at the band . . . The stage is small but they're tight tonight, cruising along, and the joint, if not exactly jumping, is at least not stationary. Danny's voice is in good shape and Jules is ripping away, playing every furious lick as though for the first time. Sometimes he cannot stand the sight of him, but Danny has to give that to Jules: he can make the stale smell fresh as good as anyone.

For the four shows in D.C. they weren't at their best, and the crowds were sparse and surly. The opening band was a local trio called the Five Fourths; they seemed to have learned how to play their instruments only a month earlier. (They did a cover of "Summertime Blues" but, amazingly, got the words wrong: they thought it was "Simmer Down Blues.") Joey made it through the first night in Wilmington okay, but last night he couldn't last more than two songs for the encore. So they ended the gig four songs early, Howie filling in on drums for the finale. The opening band

270

tonight was a not-so-bad Fleet Foxes– and Iron & Wine–like quintet called the Backwoodsmans. Red plaid shirts, blue jeans, Timberland boots, long beards. Their mandolinist/accordionist, who looked like he bottled moonshine to make extra money, told Danny he liked a lot of TFO songs but, when pressed to name one, couldn't.

Danny ends "10 Day Load" now to healthy applause and turns around to sneak a peek at Joey and see what kind of shape he's in. He looks a little drained as he takes a long pull of Poland Spring water, then Danny sees that both Jules and Howie are checking out Joey, too. The applause dies down, and Danny walks over to Joey and asks, "You all right?" He gets a confident nod and walks back to the mike. But, before he can introduce "Dog Water Girls," Jules has begun "Theme for an Imaginary Western." Danny makes a What-the-fuck-are-you-pulling? face at him, but by now Howie and Joey have joined in and Joey is beaming. Danny shakes his head, momentarily bewildered, but then starts singing about wagons leaving the city. Jules breaks into a fuzzy two-minute solo, and Joey has never looked so happy. When the song ends, it gets a decent amount of applause and nothing more, and then Danny and Jules cut lose with "Dog Water" and all is well again. As he sings the silly lyrics he's been singing for almost four decades ("Loud squeakin' and drippin' and leakin' / need some grease / not just some tweakin'"), Danny thinks about lacing into the band for going off the sacred, untouchable set list but then realizes that Joey had fun and maybe—just maybe—it wasn't such a bad thing to do. *Fuck the crowd, let's keep Joey happy while we can.* The only thing to do is maybe work on the song and tighten up their version of it. Otherwise, sure, keep it in the act. But no more stunts like this.

One more night staying at the Marriott Courtyard and then first thing tomorrow—if they can wake up Jules before 11 A.M.—it's off to Atlantic City. The Borgata, three nights at the 400-seat Platinum Pier Lounge . . . The opening act is an all-woman rock band from Philly called Barely Beagle. Jules has scoped them out online and has his eye on the doe-eyed, built-for-speed, twenty-three-year-old guitarist, who looks like Jane Fonda circa *Barbarella.*

Danny is cleaning his face in the sink in the cramped dressing room backstage when he hears someone say, "Hey . . . that was really cool stuff you guys did."

He stands up, feels an ice pick plunge through his lower spine, and sees the guitarist/lead singer of the Backwoodsmans, maybe thirty-five years his junior, standing right next to him. Howie is in the room, too; so are two other Backwoodsmanses. They look just like the guys on the Smith Brothers Cough Drops box, plus one.

"Thanks," Danny says.

"It was great opening for you."

Danny doesn't say anything. More than anything right now he wants a two-hour-long massage. And a beer. And a few shots of Jack. But he'd settle for just the massage.

"Do you guys have a record deal?" Howie asks. One of the other Smith Brothers, the drummer, says they might be close to one with a small local label. "Right now," he says, "we're just trying to survive."

"I hear you," Danny says.

"That tune, the, like, western song about the wagons?" the other Smith Brother, the mandolinist/accordionist says. "That was good. Which CD is that on?"

Danny and Howie look at each other for a second and grin.

"Uh, that'll be on our next one," Danny says, knowing there won't be a next one.

Wait, Howie thinks, *does this mean the band isn't breaking up?*

*

Two-thirty A.M., somewhere between Norfolk, Virginia, and Greenville, North Carolina, Route 258. Heading down to Chapel Hill and a Hampton Inn. Or is it a Holiday Inn Express? Danny has the U-Haul tonight, and Howie rides shotgun, his head resting against the cold window. Jules and Joey are up ahead somewhere in the Suburban . . . It's a wet, foggy night and every once in a while the U-Haul's tires send up black rain swooshing along the windows. Howie has the road map on his lap, and on the car stereo *Sticky Fingers* plays, but the volume is low and they can barely make out which song is on.

"Are they still up there?" Howie asks.

"I think I see 'em," Danny says. He has his glasses on but squints anyway. "Or maybe I don't. But they know where to go."

Howie wonders if they do. Joey already lost his copy of the itinerary but Jules claims to still have his. They have a map, too; Howie knows that because he made sure they did. As a matter of fact, there are three maps in each car—Howie bought them and secreted them inside both vehicles (the glove compartments, under the seats, etc.).

The Borgata gigs went well and Joey was strong enough to play the regular hour-and-a-half set the final night. Jules didn't score with Barely Beagle's guitarist but did, sort of, with her mother, and it was that night when he finally realized what he'd forgotten to pack: Blue Magic, his Viagra. (He still has three 100-miligram hits in his wallet, though.) "Theme for an Imaginary Western" is now on the set list and it was agreed that "97-3 Strut" had to go. Danny wasn't wild about the idea and the rest of the band knew it, but by the time they were in Philadelphia they had "Theme" down pat and it was a done deal.

"We always get good crowds in Raleigh," Danny says to Howie now.

"Yeah," Howie says. But then Howie realizes: Danny thinks they're going to Raleigh, not Chapel Hill. They *are* going to Raleigh, but Chapel Hill is first. Does he correct Danny or just let him go with it and hope he doesn't take a wrong turn?

"We're not going to Ra—" Howie begins, but before he can make it to "leigh" the U-Haul's engine lets out a series of loud belches and dies.

"Aww, shit!" Danny says, coasting the vehicle over to the side of the road.

Howie looks at Danny, whose face has turned crimson. *Please don't have a fit,* Howie thinks, *please don't have a fit.* And then he thinks: *I hope nobody slips in a puddle and falls and fractures a hip.*

Danny squeezes the wheel so tight Howie thinks it's going to snap. They sit in silence, other than "Sister Morphine," for two minutes.

"Okay," Danny sputters. "Now what?"

"We should call the others. Then we get some professional help. You know, the Triple-A kind."

Danny looks over at Howie. Poor little nutty Howie Grey. There have been so many times when he's wanted to clobber him or hug him or clobber him *and* hug him. He knew Howie when Howie was in his early twenties; he's the same now as he was then, and Danny thinks that Howie is probably the same now as when he was four.

Danny digs into his pocket, pulls out his cell phone, has to turn it on, and calls Jules. Jules's phone doesn't ring and the call goes straight to voice mail.

"That dumb fuck!" Danny yells, hanging up. "He doesn't even have his cell on!"

Howie looks at him and Danny knows why: *he* didn't have his on either.

"Try Joey . . . his is always on."

Howie's calmness—even though who knows what nightmarish furies are plaguing him inside right now—is really bothering Danny. *How can he be so fucking calm? It's raining, the car is broken, the others might get lost, this is bad.*

Danny tries to call Joey but his hands are shaking and his big fingers cannot complete the task. He yells and throws the thing against the windshield. Nothing breaks.

"You do it! Please!"

Howie picks up Danny's cell and makes the call. The phone rings once. Then, on the second ring, all of a sudden Danny and Howie hear behind them—loud enough so that they both jump out of their seats—the beginning of Led Zeppelin's "Kashmir." For the first guttural "Duh-Dah-*Dah*" they have no idea what the hell is going on. When they hear the second "Duh-Dah-*Dah*," they both realize: Joey's cell phone is in the U-Haul, probably inside a drum crate. ("Kashmir" is his ringtone.)

Danny takes his hands off the wheel. He opens the door and steps out, and Howie stays in. The rain slashes down, the mist is blinding. Danny lifts up the hood and "Kashmir" dies out. On the car stereo, "Moonlight Mile" plays. Danny gets back in the car, his hair and jacket dripping with rain, and slams the door.

"We're fucked," Danny says. "Now do you see why I can't do this anymore?!"

Danny's words echo in the car for a few seconds. Then Howie says: "Hey, I never said anything."

So that's it, Howie realizes. *He really means to end it.*

Danny bangs on the car horn three times and yells, then sits back in his seat.

Little by little he calms down, and the lavish string coda of "Moonlight Mile" plays throughout the car. He tells Howie that they'll get there. They'll call Triple-A and get to Raleigh and hook back up with Jules and Joey at the Hampton Inn.

"We're not going to Raleigh," Howie tells him. "It's Chapel Hill."

As Danny fumbles to call Triple-A, Howie watches cars blur past, and the rain, now coming down harder, pelts the windshield.

West of Babylon did not go Gold but did yield two songs that cracked the Top 100 for a heartbeat before vanishing. It was the third album they'd made with Owen J. Crowe and Chunky Scrofa— they recorded it in New York, Memphis, L.A., and Notting Hill, London—and they were sure it was going to be big. But it wasn't. In the B-minus review that ran in the *Voice,* it was suggested that "even though the nastiness still yowls hoarsely from every groove, perhaps this band's time has come and gone."

Howie was the only married member of the group. Danny's first marriage was a short-lived, crockery-throwing disaster, and he'd yet to meet Jessica. Jules was bedding anything that moved and a few things that didn't; Joey hadn't yet met Angie (and neither had Jules). There was a tour to push *West of Babylon,* but by that time MTV was where kids got their music, and Madonna, Michael Jackson, and their ilk were what they wanted to listen to. Singers— who now, thanks to filters and clever producers, not only had to know how not to sing but also how not to dance—wore headsets; their "rock concerts" resembled Vegas-style extravaganzas with backup dancers and costume changes; tours required more planning and personnel than Desert Storm. Radio stations that would have played *West of Babylon* had changed their formats; some cities no longer had authentic rock stations, and there was nowhere to promote the album. *Rolling Stone* and rock journalism had moved on to other things: reporters were not granted needles-and-all access but were given press releases instead. The industry had wised up.

Howie saw it happening before the others did and he knew it, but while they clung to the last vestiges of their fame, he kept the information to himself.

There were times when the band was so soaked with sweat after a show that they'd return to their rooms—and this was when they each got their own room, and the rooms were on the top floors of very good hotels—and strip, bunch up their shirts, and throw them out the window, just to watch the loud splat they'd make. Joey once made a young gofer go out at four in the morning to get him a banana and then, when he didn't approve of the banana the poor guy had brought back ("I like 'em with an even number of spots, not an odd number . . . didn't you know that?"), he sent him back out again. Howie just never got into being a star. He had Melissa at home and passed on all the women. He caught giddy contact highs off of all the weed in the tour bus, dressing rooms, recording studios, and hotel rooms, and that was enough for him; he always got strange looks when he turned down booze, pot, coke, and pills. People thought he was a freak.

Nobody was really aware of what was germinating inside him. It was getting worse by the year.

Owen J. Crowe, of all people, was the first person to notice something was off. Howie will never forget it: It was at Electric Lady Studios on Eighth Street and they were mixing "Borderline," adding some overdubs. They'd been stuck in the studio putting the finishing touches on the final track, making everything right and trying to resolve the tug-of-war between Danny and Jules. Danny was drinking Jack Daniel's out of a bottle and doing lines, and there was a never-ending joint going around. For two weeks they'd been in the studio from three in the afternoon to four in the morning. Owen was being Owen, providing suggestions and direction but also bolstering morale: he'd pile metal chair upon metal chair until they reached the ceiling and then kick the bottom one so that all the chairs fell; he'd whip out one of his pearl-handled Colt 45s and threaten to shoot the ceiling and glass; he'd carry on a (relatively) normal conversation about a song and what they should do to it while wearing nothing but baggy boxer shorts with hearts on them. On the final evening, he spray-painted a brand new Steinway piano and carved his initials all over it with his ruby-encrusted jackknife. And so on.

277

That night, Howie kept excusing himself to the bathroom to wash his hands. By four in the morning everything was finally coming together and people were celebrating . . . Howie came back from the bathroom and Owen J. Crowe, a coke booger the size of a plum pit clinging to his left nostril, drawled, "Hey, how come you keep goin' to the shitter?"

Howie shrugged and hoped nobody was paying attention.

"That's like the tenth time you went to the can in the last hour," Owen said.

"No, it's not," Howie, literally caught red-handed, said.

"Yeah, it is. Maybe not the tenth . . . I ain't countin' but you been goin' there a lot. I mean, what the hell could you do in the shitter that you can't do in here? We got everything in here. We got reefer, blow, big titties, and a gallon of Kentucky's finest. You got a young boy in there, Howie, that we don't know about?"

The others laughed, not at Howie but with Owen, but it sounded like grade-C horror-movie cackling to him and made him dizzy. Twenty minutes later his hands began to tingle, then they began to burn. He could feel the bacteria multiplying—his fingers felt like the tunnels of toy ant farms. All he wanted to do was go to the bathroom to clean his hands, but he didn't want Owen, on the floor now twirling his pistols, to see him. When he was sure the producer wasn't looking he stood up, but just when he made it to the door Owen said, "There he goes again! That must be some piece of ass Howie's got waitin' for him in that shitter!"

A few weeks later they were on Long Island, holed up in what had once been a furniture warehouse, rehearsing for the upcoming tour, and Howie was scrubbing his hands in the bathroom. Joey walked in and went to the sink, turned on the water, and doused his hair and face.

"So, bro," he said, "what's up with all the washing?"

"Germs. I'm worried about germs," Howie said.

"All the time?"

"Yes. All the time. It doesn't stop."

The water dripping from Joey's hair, which was then black and wooly, looked like molten silver.

He slapped Howie on the shoulder and said: "Don't worry so much. You're a rock star! Life is good." Then he headed back to the rehearsal.

A few weeks later they were in Boston at the Copley Plaza when the fire alarm went off at three in the morning. The four of them got dressed and opened their doors at the same time. Jules and Danny went down the stairs, followed by Howie and Joey.

"Why are you always skippin' the second-to-last step?" Joey asked.

"Am I really doing that?"

"Yeah."

They kept walking downstairs and Howie kept skipping the second and penultimate steps. As instructed, they crossed the street and waited. Three fire trucks arrived but soon it was discovered that it was a false alarm. On the way back up the stairs Joey noticed that Howie was skipping the same steps again.

Howie put his key in his hotel-room door, and Joey—their rooms were across from each other—said to him, "So what was up with you and the steps?"

It was late and Howie was too tired to obfuscate.

"Joey," he said, "I'm afraid that the whole building will collapse and kill everyone."

The next person who caught on was Danny. It took Howie months to gather up the nerve to tell Danny that he would prefer not to fly so much with the band, that he would rather take trains or buses when possible instead. If that wasn't workable, he'd told Danny, he'd understand and would not complain if he was let go from the band. You're afraid of flying? Danny asked him, stunned. Howie was stunned, too: he thought for sure that everyone had seen him cowering in his seat any time there was even the slightest turbulence or an announcement from the flight deck. Danny thought he knew all there was to know about his band and had to collect himself, but then told Howie there was no way he'd ever be kicked out of the band. He told him they'd work something out with Velcro Pravda and the tour manager.

"What about our European and Asian tours, though?" Danny asked him. "I mean, you're gonna have to fly then . . . taking the *Queen Mary* across is out of the question."

Howie told him he'd suck it up and would fly to Europe and Asia. "But," he said, "you might have to spot me a Valium."

Soon everybody knew. The roadies, guitar techs, bus drivers, publicists, the people at their record company and music publisher. The only time anyone ever brought up the problem was many years later: the band's fortunes had plummeted and they were on the road in Albuquerque. *TFO 7* had just come out and they were now truly on their own, just as when they'd started. They were dragging their gear into a U-Haul outside a Motel 6, and Joey noticed that Howie was tapping the outside of the van three times before he got off the van and four times before he got back on.

"You know what?" Joey said to Howie, out of everybody's earshot. "I bet I could help you. You don't need to see a shrink about this, you need to see *me*."

Howie made sure nobody else was listening and said, "I'll keep that in mind."

*

The Red Rooster, Port St. Lucie, Florida. The Long Island winter seems like ten years ago. Three nights here, capacity: 375. Two nights ago was Daytona Beach, the 500 Club, the end of a Friday and Saturday set. The opening act there was the SinnaBons, a twangy Belle & Sebastian–ish quartet. Before Daytona was Jacksonville; a monotonous doom band called A Plunger Event led

280

off the bill. (Danny and Jules did a radio interview there to flog the gigs, and the DJ asked them, "So what is the secret of the band's longevity? How have you guys not broken up?" When neither of them could come up with an answer, the DJ, sensing their discomfort, moved on.) The Overfalls are working their way down Florida's outer thigh to Miami. They will then come back up the inner thigh to Pensacola, and then to Mobile, and a casino in Biloxi, and so on. Up into the fetid crotch of the Gulf Coast. And then onward.

Joey has good nights and bad nights. The second night in Jacksonville he lasted the whole gig and was terrific and fired up the band, but on the final night he could only make it through six songs. Howie, getting used to it now, took over and drummed for the rest of the evening. (The set list had changed as a result, and they smoked through eight minutes of "Crossroads," Joey cheering them on from the side. "Why the *fuck* do we keep adding these songs that aren't on the goddamn set list!?" Danny fumed afterward at Jules, who'd sprung the song on them during the encore.) They called for a doctor at the hotel and, in the hallway where Joey couldn't listen in, Danny told him the problem and showed him the meds Joey was taking. The doctor went into Joey's room and looked him over. He came back out, assured Danny that Joey wasn't going to drop dead any time soon, and said, "That one in there . . . he's a real soldier, let me tell you that."

Two big guys with shaved heads and prison tats had offered to help the Overfalls take their gear into the club tonight, but Danny, of course, turned them down. The Red Rooster is genuinely funky, not retrofunky, and the manager, a skinny pale dude named Travis, is showing the Overfalls to their dressing room now, taking them down an unlit corridor whose pitted blacks walls and ceiling seem constructed entirely of beer and tequila fumes.

"The band that opens for you is already in the dressing room," he drawls. "Hope you don't mind."

"No problem," Danny says. It's a good thing Travis's skin is so white—it's the only light there is right now.

"Who are they?" Jules asks, following Travis's neck.

"The Brothers Cousins," Travis says. "They're from Gainesville. Rock 'n' blues and a little country, more blues than rock. Kinda like Marshall Tucker, kinda like y'all's, too, but younger."

"Are there any Exit signs in this place?" Howie asks. "What if there's a fire?"

"Yeah, we had some signs like that here once."

Travis comes to the unlit red lightbulb that marks where the dressing room is and opens the door, and the burst of light from within is momentarily blinding.

A moment later, the two bands shake hands and get to know one another. The Brothers Cousins really are brothers whose last name really is Cousins (there are four brothers Cousins plus a cousin, the keyboardist, who isn't a Cousins), and they range in age from nineteen to twenty-six. The dressing room is big enough for both bands but only just, and the Cousins are nice enough to keep out of the way.

"Hey, you're Danny Ault, right?" Aiden Cousins says. He's tall and narrow and looks more like a young Viggo Mortensen than the older Viggo Mortensen does.

"Yeah," Danny says.

"We're huge fans . . . me and my brother Skeeter over there been listenin' to you since we wuz kids."

"Really? And why would that be?"

"Yeah," Jules says, taking off his jacket and stretching out and almost hitting someone's chin. "How'd that happen? Shouldn't you guys be into Kanye West and Justin Beaver?"

"No fuckin' way," Skeeter says.

Aiden laughs and explains. "Nah, our dad and mom was really into you, seen you all the time live in Atlanta and Miami. We grew up on you guys's records."

In the corner, Joey and the Brothers Cousins drummer are talking about drums. Two Brothers Cousins hangers-on, one of them the spitting image of a young Merle Haggard, walk in, both of them smoking cigarettes. They could take part in a Battle of Gettysburg reenactment without having to change much about their appearance.

"On vinyl, too," Skeeter says. He turns to Aiden: "You gonna tell him or should I?"

Danny looks at Skeeter, then back at his brother. He has no idea what it is they're not telling him but he can feel a scalding wave of anger rising up from his chest to his neck. What is it they don't want to tell him? *Cannot one day ever go by,* he wonders, *when I don't want to administer a good beating to someone?*

Aiden lights a smoke and says: "Well, we do a song of yours. We been doin' it for 'bout three months now."

"Oh," Danny says. "That's all?"

"You're lucky," Jules says to Aiden. "He was about to kill you."

"What song?" Howie asks.

"It's a slow one," Aiden says, avoiding eye contact with Danny. "'It's All Gone,' it's called?" He says it as though Danny might have forgotten a song he'd written and had once regularly sung, although he hasn't sung it for well over a decade.

"You're yanking my crank," Danny says.

To prove he means it, Aiden starts singing the first verse, then lets it die.

"Hey, that means you owe us some money! Where's the check?!" When he sees Aiden and Skeeter simultaneously flinching, Danny tells them he was only kidding.

"Of all our songs," Jules begins, "you cover that one . . ."

283

Travis knocks on the door, three more hangers-on come in (they're wives or girlfriends, and one of them must be related to one of the original hangers-on because she looks like Merle Haggard, too), and he tells them the place is filling up out there and the Brothers Cousins are on in ten minutes. An emaciated blonde with three nose rings climbs aboard Skeeter's lap and they start making out for a while. Aiden tells Danny they're going to do "It's All Gone" tonight and it would be great if he—Danny—would come on and join them. Skeeter pulls his tongue out of his girl's mouth, looks over to Howie, and asks him if he's got his accordion on him. Howie nods and Skeeter tells him that he plays violin during "It's All Gone," and that it would be great if Howie could play accordion behind Danny, but Howie looks at Danny and can tell he's not into it.

"Aw, boss," Joey says. "That's your best song ever when it comes to singin'."

Danny knows that Joey's telling the truth: on no song he ever wrote or covered did Danny ever venture out of his usual range and comfort zone except for "It's All Gone," and the effect of him singing tenor (he sounded like a cross between Richard Manuel and Thom Yorke) and fading out at the end was haunting to those few who'd listened to it.

"Do you do the Mansion version or the Memory Motel version?" Danny asks.

"Huh?" Aiden says.

"Nah, I'll pass. Good luck with it though."

"Are you—" Aiden presses.

"Don't press your luck, pal," Jules warns him.

An hour later the Brothers Cousins end their set with "It's All Gone" and the Overfalls take it in, watching backstage. They do a credible job, but when it ends, Danny whispers to himself, "Damn . . . maybe I should've done it."

284

An hour later, the Overfalls end their first set with "Hurt," but just when they're about to go offstage and grab their breaths, Jules launches into the beginning of Blind Faith's "Sea of Joy" and Joey yells, "Yeah!" Danny doesn't do anything for a while, just stands there flatfooted and angry, but Howie and Joey have joined in and are sailing along. Danny has no choice but to follow and start singing, and Howie grabs his violin and, three minutes into the song, breaks into a solo that matches Ric Grech's note for note.

As they file off for their break, Jules worries what Danny is going to say to him. *Don't you ever fuckin' do that to me again!* or *We're cutting this ad lib shit out as of today!* Or something to that effect.

But instead all Danny says is: "Hey, we did a pretty decent version, all things considered."

*

A Holiday Inn Express, Boca Raton. The band just finished playing; Joey made it through but was struggling so they cut the encore short. The equipment is still at the club and they're going to pick it up tomorrow at noon and move on.

They're not letting Joey do anything on this tour except play drums and play video games in his hotel room.

This morning he wanted to carry his kit into the club but Danny and Jules did it for him. He went out to get the amps and guitars but Howie told him to go get something to eat and he, Danny, and Jules took the stuff inside. Joey came back with three Nutty Buddy–like prefab ice cream cones, gave Howie one, and ate the other two himself, both at once. Two weeks ago it was decided—nobody said a word, it was just done—that Joey could eat whatever he wants, no matter how bad and no matter how much.

Howie and Jules are in one room tonight, Danny rooms with Joey. Danny cannot sleep because Joey is snoring up a storm. *Maybe it's the air-conditioning,* Danny thinks, so at midnight he gets up, goes to the thermostat (one of the newer square ones he hates), and tries to make sense of it and turn it off. The room gets too warm in a matter of minutes, and Joey's snoring gets even louder, so Danny turns the A/C back on.

Joey turns over onto his back and, in the pitch-black room, says, "You awake, bro?"

"Yeah."

"Any ice would be really nice. The cold kind. Yeah."

Danny sits up and wonders if Joey has a fever.

"You want some ice?"

"The place is on fire."

Danny pulls on a pair of jeans, which are still damp from tonight's show. He grabs the keycard off his nightstand and goes to the hallway, groggily heading for the ice-making machine near the elevator.

I'll do anything for him, Danny vows as he walks down the hall. *If he wants a banana with exactly six spots I'll drive all night to find it. If he wants a can of Mountain Dew and I bring one back and he says that 2009 was a bad year for Mountain Dew, I'll go back out and get him one from 2010. The guy saved my life in that hotel outside St. Louis—if he hadn't showed up that day, I'd be dead right now.*

The elevator doors open and Jules staggers out, and they pass each other and don't say a word. He looks like shit . . . his hair is all over the place, his eyes are bloodshot slits, his shirt is half out of his pants.

Danny goes into the small room with the ice-making machine and gets a bag of ice, then returns to the room and all is dark again. Somehow the room got cold all over again.

He sits on his bed and says, "Joey, you awake? I got your ice."

Joey snores.

"Joey! I got your ice."

286

"I didn't want any ice, bro. But thanks."

Danny rubs his stubbly jaw. *He must have been talking in his sleep.*

"Hey, where are we, bro?"

"Boca Raton. We go to Miami tomorrow. Three or four nights."

"The floor service good the fighting stairway up going games down."

"Uh-huh."

Danny takes the bag of ice over to the sink near the bathroom, dumps it out, and gets back into bed and eventually falls asleep.

*

Miami Beach. The Hard Rock Cafe, a Hilton Garden Inn near the airport, the screeching and thunder of airplanes landing and taking off. Greasy Cuban sandwiches, runny scrambled eggs, charred hash browns, and chicken-fried something with a sauce that looked as if it had squirmed out of a health-clinic sample vial. The marquee at the Hard Rock got it wrong the first two nights. First it read THE FABULOUS LOVERBALLS. Danny complained to the manager, but then on the second night the marquee read THE FURIOUS COVERTALLS.

"What the hell's the name of our band again?" Jules asked, rubbing his eyes, when he got out of the Suburban that night.

They were already starting to forget where they were when they woke up. Miami looked like Orlando, which had looked like Port St. Lucie and Jacksonville. The hotel breakfasts were blending into each other, too: the muffins tasted like pancakes and the pancakes tasted like cereal and the cereal tasted like the cardboard bowls they were ladled into. In Florida alone Danny has so far smashed three hotel thermostats, raising his lifetime count to 941. The Brothers Cousins were the opening act in Miami, too, but this time each band had its own dressing room. Skeeter Cousins asked Danny on the

287

fifth night if he was sure he didn't want to sing "It's All Gone" with Aiden, but Danny again told him he'd pass. This time, however, he gave it some thought.

"Maybe Florida isn't such a bad place," Danny said one night at an Arby's after a show. "Maybe I should retire here."

"Retire?" Jules said, looking up from his mushy dessert. "Oh, is that what you're doing?"

Danny, who didn't like Jules's tone, thought of getting into an argument about it but decided he was too tired. Besides, Joey is in the dark about the whole thing: he has no idea that TFO is in its final weeks.

"You really wanna be so far away from your grandkid, boss?" Joey asked.

"You had to remind me about that?" Danny said.

"Hey, if it's gonna happen, then it's inevitable."

Through the Everglades across Route 41 to the Gulf, a day off, and then three nights at a once-upscale but now broken-down theater in Naples. No longer a theater, the seats had been ripped out fifteen years ago. (But the club provided its own backline and so the Overfalls were spared some heavy lifting.) Joey couldn't handle the encore the first night but slogged his way through on the second and third nights. "Are we sure," Jules asked Howie as they drove up the Gulf Coast, "that maybe he's not sick and is just lazy?"

They're in Bradenton now, it's the second of two nights at a club called The Spanish Moon, and it's a warm, foggy evening—standing on the street overlooking the marina, you cannot see the boats, the nearby bridge, or the water. A decent-size room with surprisingly crisp acoustics . . . the band has played here a few times before and has a local following. (Last year and the year before, Jules banged a buxom mother of three, but so far this year she has not shown up.) The opening act was a morose Gang of Four–esque band called Youth Hotel that grew glummer by the minute; in the middle of their final song, even they couldn't take it anymore and

288

they put their instruments down and left the stage in tears. The Overfalls are two songs away from ending their first set when Danny sidles over to Howie and says, "Yo, check out the guy . . . at the bar, fifth on the right. With the aviators on!" Howie squints and finds the man in question. "Is that him?" Danny asks.

"Him" is Mickey Sanford, and the guy at the bar with the large aviators sure does look like Mickey Sanford—like Mickey Sanford the last time they saw him plus three decades and minus a lot of hair. Howie, as he checks him out, doesn't lose a beat on his bass, and Jules slides and soars on his solo and the Coricidin bottle he's using dazzles the lights back at the audience.

The solo ends and Danny hurriedly wraps up the song, and during the fifteen seconds of applause he goes over to Jules and tells him to be careful because Mickey Sanford is at the bar. Jules finds him and agrees. "That's him! *Shit!*"

Unbeknownst to each other, Danny and Jules have the exact same vision: Mickey, during the encore, is going to thread his way through the crowd, approach the stage, whip out a pistol, and start popping away at the band. Danny—shot in the heart—would go first, then Jules . . . By the time those two have been killed, Howie is either frozen in his tracks, which is his normal bass-playing stance anyway, or fleeing, and Mickey would bring him down with a bullet to the back. It's the ultimate irony that Joey Mazz, the dude who replaced Mickey and who's actually dying in real life, would probably escape intact.

"Do we stick around?" Jules asks backstage as they all slug down water.

"We could leave," Howie says, thinking, for the millionth time, of Melissa being a widow and Michelle being fatherless. "We could just say Joey got tired."

Danny tells them they have to finish the gig. Jules isn't pleased but he knows it's the right thing to do. They'll do only three more tunes, Danny says, and hightail it the hell out. If they see Mickey coming toward them, they'll drop their instruments and run.

Twenty minutes later the show is finished and they're all still alive. The four of them are relaxing in their dressing room when there's a knock at the door. Tommy, one of the owners of The Spanish Moon, comes in and says, "*Great* show, guys."

Jules thanks him . . . Danny doesn't want to engage in any conversation; he just wants to get everybody back to the Hampton Inn and then back on the road as soon as possible.

"You guys coming back same time next year, I hope?" Tommy says.

Jules and Howie look at Danny, who says, "We may not."

"Hey, there's someone out here," Tommy tells them, "who says he knows you from the old days. He insisted he gets to see you."

Danny, Jules, and Howie gulp simultaneously.

This is it. Mickey Sanford's Revenge. Thirty-plus years in the making.

"From the old days?" Danny says.

"He said from way back," Tommy says. "Dude sure looks it, too."

Howie thinks there's no point in even packing up his electric violin. It's all over. Danny lets drop the wet towel in his hands. He'll never even get to see his grandson.

"All right," Joey says, "so show the guy in."

Tommy opens the door and nothing happens for ten seconds. Then they see a squat, chocolate-skinned black woman in a tight purple dress with a crimson-highlighted updo backing her way slowly into the dressing room. She's pulling a cumbersome wheelchair, trying to get it over the saddle of the threshold. She finally makes it in and slowly turns around the wheelchair, and the four Overfalls behold the crumpled, liver-spotted, hunched-over mess sitting in it. The woman looks very familiar to Danny but the man in the wheelchair doesn't—he makes the decayed carcass of

290

Norman Bates's mom in *Psycho* look succulent in comparison, and what few teeth he has resemble dried lemon pulp. Danny looks back up at the woman and says: "*Viola?* Viola Williams??"

"Danny!" she says with her familiar rich voice. "I'm so flattered you reckinize me."

Viola Williams . . . one of the Moist Towelettes, the trio of writhing foxy backup singers for Jakey Gee and the Aerosouls. She was the one who'd told Danny that she wanted to slice off Jakey's "little mouse balls." And then one sultry night outside Memphis at the Commodore Hotel, Jakey was murdered and nobody had ever gotten arrested. Danny knows he told his band this story but it was many years ago and he doubts any of them remember.

He goes over to Viola and they embrace and kiss. Danny has put on thirty pounds since his Aerosouls days but Viola has put on twice that. He introduces her to his bandmates, omitting the pertinent information that she might have murdered the Aerosouls' front man.

"You remember Sy, right?" Viola says. "Jakey's father, Seymour Garfein?"

"Of course," Danny says. He realizes now that just because Viola Williams happens to be here does not mean that Mickey Sanford isn't, so he walks over to the door and shuts it. "Who could forget Sy? All his Mafia connections—that guy was as dirty as—"

"This is him."

"Oh!"

"We seen in the paper you was playing here and he insisted we come and see you." She bends down and raises her voice, right into the old man's ear. "Say hello, Sy . . . this is Danny Ault."

Danny looks down at the remnant of the human being in the wheelchair and now sees it: It is Sy Garfein, the old Garment Center trucking kingpin. With all his might, the old man lifts up a flecked, flaky, skeletal right hand, waves it twice, and drops it back to his lap. Viola wipes his chin and explains that after about fifteen more years knocking around as a singer she got a certificate in home nursing care and has been taking care of Sy for twenty years. When Sy moved to Florida fifteen years ago, she tagged along. She and Danny talk about old times for about ten minutes, even break into a few old Aerosouls songs . . . Viola can still sing up a storm and they both remember all the lyrics, such as they were. Howie tries to get as far away from Sy Garfein as he can while still remaining within the damp confines of the dressing room.

Viola kisses Danny good-bye and turns the wheelchair around.

"Bye, Sy," Danny says, putting his hands on the old man's shoulder. What skin Seymour Garfein still has barely stretches far enough to cover his bones.

Sy looks up, shakes his head as if he were declining poisoned food, and looks down again. Viola wheels him out and Danny, after checking to see if Mickey Sanford is out in the hallway, closes the dressing room door.

Nobody says anything and Danny feels a chill overtake him.

"So," Jules says, "was Viola Williams the one who sliced—"

"Yep . . . that was her!"

*

Up the Gulf Coast, the weather warming every day. The fog that settled in when they were in Bradenton is long gone, except all four of them still feel it between their eyes and ears. Hundreds of fried shrimp, hush puppies, french fries, and cans of Mountain Dew— Joey drinks it morning, noon, and night. "They're gonna fix you up," Jules said to him, "with a Mountain Dew drip if you ever wind up in the hospital again."

They played four nights in Pensacola at a club called The Sopwith Camel. The Marginal Way, a wussy eyeliner band trying to sound like the Cure but sounding more like the actual disease, was the opening act. Lots of U.S. Air Force personnel and college kids bouncing up and down. Jules picked up an air force lieutenant named Sharona and went back to the house she shared off the base with four other women (he saw that he'd gotten the cream of the crop). He was down to the last half of a Viagra in his wallet but fell asleep before it took effect, woke up five times to pee, did Sharona when they woke up in the morning, and made it back to the Holiday Inn Express just in time to move on. Route 10 northwest here to Mobile, over the Gulf. The A/C cranked in the Suburban, the windows down in the U-Haul, and Howie nervously grabbing onto his armrest as they went over the Battleship Parkway bridge, fearing its immediate collapse. Three raucous, exhausting, backbreaking nights at Shakespeare Alley, another old theater converted to a music venue. The first two nights the band knocked the crowd out; the final night—tonight—Joey was too tired to play and Howie had to cover for him again.

"After this is over," Danny whispered to Howie tonight after the show as they were reloading the van, "you'll never have to drum again. I promise you."

At first Howie thought that by "this," Danny meant this show, but then he realized it meant after Joey had died and the band was no more.

It's two in the morning in Mobile and Howie is rooming with Danny again; Jules and Joey are in a room down the hall, but Jules is out with the manager of Shakespeare Alley and her husband. There's a pathway of towels to the door and another one to the bathroom. Howie lies in his bed on his back and tries not to think. *What if Joey is dead?* He turns over on his side, faces the window. *He's in his room all alone . . . what if he's having a heart attack right this very second and there's no one in there to help him?* He turns over so he's on his back again and listens to Danny's quiet breathing. The room has gone from cool to hot to freezing. He thinks of standing up, walking along the towels to the door, tiptoeing down the hallway, and knocking on Joey's door just to see if he's all right. *But what if,* he thinks, *he* is *all right but the sound of my knocking at the door wakes him up, scares him, and kills him?* He tosses and turns for another hour and the room gets colder and then suddenly he hears a fist smash into the thermostat.

An hour later Howie still hasn't fallen asleep: the whole time he worries about Life After TFO. What will he do? *Do I,* he worries, *have to start auditioning again? After all this time and at my age? Who would ever hire me now?* Then he worries about Joey again. He gets up, tiptoes to the door along the towel pathway, grabs his keycard off the dresser, and opens the door. He leaves the door ajar, but after taking ten steps down the hallway he worries about someone creeping in and murdering Danny, so he goes back and closes the door. He's made it ten steps down the hallway again when he begins to worry that maybe he closed the door but it's not locked, so he goes back and checks. It's locked. Finally he makes it to Joey's door. He listens in for a minute, hears nothing, then starts to walk back to his room. But he heads back to Joey's door and listens again. Ten minutes go by . . . he cannot pull himself away. He hears nothing inside and wonders if Joey is already dead, that he arrived too late, that it was his going back and forth that killed Joey. He begins a countdown from 100—when he hits one, he resolves, he'll walk back to his room—but when he comes to one, he can't move, so he starts again, this time from 200. At a 175 he hears an elevator open . . . Thinking it might be Jules coming home, he darts up and runs down the hallway and makes it back to his room.

Howie lies on his back, but just when he's about to drift off, he comes to. Melissa told him she would think of something— something he could do for a living. But what is she going to come up with? The only thing in the world he knows how to do, he already does. He thinks of putting on his iPod and drifting off to Sigur Rós but decides not to. Tomorrow they head to Biloxi. *What if,* he thinks, *Hurricane Katrina II strikes while we're onstage and the casino we're playing gets washed out to sea?*

294

He stands up, walks along the towel pathway to the bathroom, closes the door gently so as not to wake Danny, and turns on the light. Grabbing some sanitary paper from the dispenser on the wall, he turns on the hot and cold water, his fingers never touching the faucets. He washes his hands, turns off the water, and, right before heading back to bed, catches a glimpse of himself in the bathroom mirror. The bags beneath his eyes are puffy, sagging, and some unnamed shade between brown and gray.

*

After *West of Babylon,* the band was in trouble. They had one more record left on their contract but Lew Aaronson had lost interest in them. Nobody ever called them and, worse, nobody ever returned their calls. Meetings were canceled and never rescheduled. The Lizard of AaZ reassigned people in his promotion and marketing departments to handle other artists and never appointed anyone to replace them.

West of Babylon CDs, cassettes, and vinyl were being sold in record stores for "The Nice Price." Had the disc come out ten years before, it would have gone Platinum, perhaps even been nominated for a Grammy; now you could get it for $3.99.

Howie and Melissa sold the Fifty-second Street studio and lived in Fairview year-round.

Jules and Danny knew there were songs on *Babylon* which were as good as any they'd ever written. It had been a war between the two of them to write the songs and then another war to get them to sound the way they should. And all for what—The Nice Price? They made a cheap video for the single "What Goes Around . . ." (it was about venereal disease and was recorded before Justin Timberlake's hit of the same name, which is not about venereal disease), but it didn't boost sales and MTV only showed it a dozen times before shelving it. Once again, Danny and Jules stuck to their guns and refused to lip-synch.

Howie worried about the band. Danny and Jules seldom interacted on the road and sometimes the performances suffered as a result. The road crew kept to themselves and gone were the stylists, guitar techs, and parasites. It was a bare-bones road show now. When they were on, when they were good, they crackled and popped as they always had. But too few people were interested.

Four months after the Babylon Tour gave up its ghost, it was decided that the band, without Chunky or Owen or Velcro Pravda, would meet at Jules's Westhampton house to discuss, in Danny's exact words, "what the fuck we can do to keep this ship floating." They would spend ten days there and no wives, buddies, or girlfriends were allowed; they'd bring their instruments, though (Jules had an upright piano in the living room). The place wasn't big enough to house all of them so Joey would drive in from Bay City each day. Jules came up with the idea that they all bring some of their favorite music—"stuff," he suggested, "that maybe we forgot and need to get back to." (Joey forgot about the request and didn't bring anything the first day. The next day he showed up with a few Bad Company, Led Zep, and Beck, Bogert & Appice LPs.) It was August, and the Montauk Highway on the weekend was clogged with traffic. Howie didn't feel comfortable staying in Jules's house, even though he had the tiny attic bedroom all to himself. The house was a quarter of a mile away from the beach but he could hear the ocean in the dead of night and he worried that a wave might roll in and destroy the house.

For days they listened to music and talked things over. They listened to everything the Beatles had put out from *Please Please Me* to *Abbey Road,* everything the Stones had done from *England's Newest Hit Makers* to *Exile on Main St.* They listened to the songs of their youth again, to the music that had propelled them to become musicians in the first place: the Animals, the Kinks, Four Tops, the

Byrds, Cream, the Temptations, Traffic, the Doors, Derek and the Dominos, Hendrix, Small Faces, and so on. While they listened they talked and it was the most that Danny and Jules had conversed in years. On the sixth day it was decided that they would fire Velcro Pravda. He had other irons in the fire anyway (he was managing a few post–New Wave bands and wasn't returning TFO's calls either—Danny knew that getting rid of him would not be a problem). That night, as Howie lay in his small bed, there was a thunderstorm and he worried about the house collapsing and Danny and Jules dying under the heap of furniture and wooden planks. The next day, Joey showed up with some Deep Purple and Uriah Heep albums, and the band gave them perfunctory spins on Jules's Thorens turntable, then immediately forgot about them. They decided the next day that Owen J. Crowe would not produce their next album. They couldn't settle on anyone to succeed him—Jimmy Miller, Eddie Kramer, Jim Dickinson, Glyn Johns, and Tom Dowd were all mentioned as prospects—but did agree that Owen was gone.

Whatever their next album was going to be, they knew, it had to be their best.

They jammed for a few hours the next day, a Friday. It was 90 degrees outside and, even though the A/C was on, it didn't do much. Danny, Jules, and Joey kept drinking beer, outside the sky darkened, and the weekend renters descended on the Hamptons. Danny whipped out a gram of coke and he, Jules, and Joey made short work of it, so then Jules whipped out a gram of his own. By this time, after so many years together, they knew not to ask Howie if he wanted any. Their exhilaration, as temporary as it was, was contagious and Howie felt reinvigorated vicariously.

"All right," Danny said, "what we have to do is . . . we have to maybe think about starting over, from square one. There's no way we're dyeing our hair pink, right?"

"No way," Jules agreed. "We are not the Inhuman League."

"What about you, Joey? You wanna put on a lacy black bustier and wear one glove and dance around like a whore?"

"No," Joey said, "but if it'd save the band, I'd do it, sure."

"If we're stuck being ourselves, then we've got to make the most of it. We know who we are."

While Jules and Joey kept agreeing and putting in their two cents' worth, Howie felt something like a severe coke crash. The band would go on being the band it was—Howie was all for that—but would it work? Had the Beatles stayed together, were they ever going to take a stab at reggae, disco, or punk? The problem, Howie knew, was that the world had moved on and, as much as TFO was committed to their mongrel amalgam of rock, country, and blues, maybe nobody else was. He remembered being in anaesthesia at Yale and their ridiculous arguments about Breton, Milhaud, and Genet. They could argue all they wanted—and they always did want to—and finally reach a consensus, but it meant nothing if nobody was going to produce it, listen to it, or buy it.

The following evening—after some jamming, talking, listening to records, and more coke and beer—they got into Jules's and Danny's cars and drove out to Amagansett to a club on Main Street called The Stephen Talkhouse. When they were just making their bones, first as the Ventilators and then as the Overfalls, they'd played a few gigs there and had returned many times over the years. It was a Wednesday night, still hot out and now stiflingly humid, and the place was crowded. A band called the Raincoat Crowd was playing and Jules knew the keyboardist. The Raincoat Crowd's set ended, and the Overfalls took the stage (borrowing the band's equipment and the club's backline), played five songs, and got a lot of applause. Jules picked up a German model named Ulrike who was staying in the Hamptons for a week with some very rich friends. She was in the U.S. doing some print ads, she told Jules, and was "The New Ass of Jordache" in their latest jeans campaign. Ulrike didn't want to go back to her friends' place in East Hampton so

Jules took her back to his house in Westhampton; Danny, Joey, and Howie drove back to the same destination in Danny's BMW. When they got there, Joey got into his yellow Camaro and drove back to Bay City. Not wishing to listen to the fucking noises, Danny and Howie went to a bar and finally made it back in at four in the morning when all was quiet.

The next day at eleven Howie was woken up by the noises he'd tried to avoid the previous night. It was loud, it was vicious, it sounded like ten people, not merely two, five of whom were Germanic. ("I think Jordache," Jules said later, "is going to have to get itself an even newer Ass.") After five minutes of the racket, Danny knocked on Howie's door, opened it, and said, "Let's split . . ." and in five minutes they were back in Danny's BMW, heading toward Montauk.

They grabbed a quick meal at a clam stand near the water. The roads going east were empty and it was still hot and sunny out. The wind, though, coming off the beach provided some relief. At a pay phone near a pizza parlor in Montauk, Danny called Jules and asked if he was done. *"Done?"* Jules said. "We're just getting started!"

Back in the BMW, they drove around, taking back roads, passing ponds, potato fields, and horse farms, and passing sandy hills and houses being built and houses getting torn down. They checked out mansions along the water they now knew they'd never be able to afford. A radio station from somewhere—Boston? Canada? Luxembourg?—was coming in faintly, and Howie kept trying to home in on it with the dial because the music it was playing was uniformly excellent and, other than pairing Rev. Gary Davis's version of "Death Don't Have No Mercy" with Hot Tuna's, had no method to its madness. It played a zydeco song that Howie was able to finger as Clifton Chenier, followed by "Black Peter" from *Workingman's Dead*. The music was all over the place: after Louis Armstrong's "Basin Street Blues" came "I Scare Myself" by Dan Hicks and His Hot Licks, and after that came Dr. John's "I

299

Walk on Gilded Splinters." They drove by some steep, sugary dunes and the station disappeared; then the dunes came to an abrupt stop and the station came in louder and clearer than before.

"I can't tell you," Danny said, "that I have any idea where we are right now. I think we're off the map. And we don't even have a map."

Bill Monroe's "Little Cabin Home on the Hill" played; after that came "What About Me" by Quicksilver Messenger Service, and Danny said, "I always loved the piss out of this song."

As they drove around, a crazy notion struck Howie: The four of them, the Furious Overfalls, should lock themselves in a house in the middle of nowhere—maybe in the Catskills or on Lake Superior or somewhere along the Gulf Coast—with all their gear and seal out the outside world. No contact at all. Not even a phone. Danny would have to do without booze and pills, Jules without pussy, Howie without hand sanitizer, and Joey without Spider-Man. They should stay in that house as long as it took; they would eat, drink, and breathe music from the second they awoke to the second they fell asleep and would emerge with the best music they could create. Maybe there would be some bluegrass, some folk, blues, rock and soul; it would be little bits of everything all thrown into a massive cauldron . . . It would come from the Mississippi Delta and Chicago, from Storyville and Detroit and Liverpool, from Highway 61 and Route 66 and Hitsville U.S.A., from the hills of Kentucky and the swampland of Louisiana, and from Memphis, Bakersfield, and East London, but the bubbling, tongue-scalding gumbo would be something bold, new, and strange, even though it was old, classic, and all-American.

The ocean was to their right and the sky was clear. Muddy Waters' "Rollin' Stone" played, and they came to a brown four-story house near the water. "This Is Where I Belong," one of Danny's favorite Kinks songs, came on, and he turned it up and said, "This station is in-fuckin'-credible."

God, both of them thought, *am I ever glad I'm a musician.*

They were in no hurry to get back to Jules's place in Westhampton . . . they just wanted to cruise around and listen.

They came to a crooked yellow sign announcing a dead-end road but took the road anyway, and Robert Johnson's "Me and the Devil Blues" came on. The road was narrow and bumpy; there were bushes on one side and white sand on the other, then suddenly right before them arose a stone-color three-story house that looked more Edward Hopper than anything Edward Hopper had ever painted. From their vantage point they could make out three turrets, but it looked as if there might be more turrets on the side facing the water, and an old Cadillac with a mangled fender was parked in the driveway. "King Harvest (Has Surely Come)" by the Band came on, and Danny pointed to a hand-painted sign near the mailbox that read FOR RENT THIS FALL. Howie said, "Why would you put your for-rent sign on a house at the end of a dead-end dirt road where nobody can see it?" and Danny said, "Because you don't really want to rent it?"

Danny lowered the volume and said, "So the Band . . . they secluded themselves in a house in Woodstock until they finally came up with their sound—with the sound they wanted. They went into that house one way and came out another and that was them. And the Stones did it in France, too."

Howie's heart started racing—he'd been thinking the exact same thing. Had Danny been reading his mind? Or had he (Howie) said aloud what he'd assumed he had only been thinking? And if he *had* said it aloud, what else had he said, not just today but over the past few years?

Danny got out of the car and walked toward the house, and Howie turned the volume back up . . . now Hank Williams was howling, as though he were undergoing painful gum surgery, "Moanin' the Blues." Howie watched the front door of the house open—he couldn't tell if it was a man or a woman talking to Danny,

301

it was just a gangly shadow moving its arms. Five minutes later Danny returned to the car—his powder blue T-shirt and burgeoning gut were soaked with sweat—and said to Howie: "I'm going to look around inside. You want to join me?" He knew that Howie would say no but he asked anyway, and Howie did say no. Fifteen minutes later Danny came back out of the house with a smile on his face and got in the car.

"They wanted ten grand a month, those fuckers, can you believe it?" he said as he turned the BMW around and began driving away.

"For the fall?" Howie said. "That's a lot considering nobody's ever here then."

"Yeah, that's what I told them. So I got it for three thousand. For four months, with an option for four more at the same price. HA! We move in the second week of September. Bring your bass, your accordions, all your saxes, flutes, violins, zithers, glockenspiels, contrabassoons, and kazoos. But no mellotron!"

Howie didn't think he had ever seen Danny Ault looking so jazzed. Not since the first TFO album had come out, at least.

"I'm going to rent a mobile studio," Danny said. "And I just thought of the perfect person to produce the album, someone we hadn't ever brought up: *US!* Ourselves!"

They drove back to the crooked yellow sign announcing the dead-end road and decided they were going back to Westhampton, whether Jules was through with the New Ass of Jordache or not, to tell him the news. "Gimme Shelter" began playing on the radio, Merry Clayton wailed with rapture, and the station faded out and in again. Howie said, "So how did you get them down to three thousand?"

"You're not gonna believe it. *They're fans!*"

*

The Hard Rock. Biloxi, Mississippi.

They haven't made it to New Orleans or Texas yet, and the end of the road is nowhere in sight. The fog in their brains has not lifted. There comes a point in every tour when it becomes grueling beyond all endurance, when the experience becomes an exercise in masochism and testing one's ability to withstand the long hours, the food, the boredom, the driving, the lodging, the work, and each other; every year when the Overfalls take to the road, that point starts to come earlier and earlier. Last year Howie first felt it in New Orleans at Jazz Fest (Danny learned months ago that TFO wouldn't be booked into Jazz Fest this year but managed to secure three nights at the House of Blues on Decatur Street); the year before it happened in Austin, but tonight at The Hard Rock, which is almost packed but not quite, he thinks they've already come to the threshold and maybe taken a step over it.

Howie and Jules have discussed the band's punishing schedule and Danny's stubbornness and they agreed that it's all about him testing himself and testing the band. This was the ultimate control-freak experiment. The money is coming in, yes, and they're keeping their name alive . . . but that's not it. Can they still do it, can they still eat the Styrofoam food, drink the Crayola drinks, endure the hotels and horrific hours and still be able to knock themselves out onstage every night?—that's what it's really all about. After weeks on the road, it was now more of a siege than a tour, a triathlon and not a sprint, and Danny was more like captains Ahab, Queeg, and Bligh, all rolled into one, than a dude from Pleasant Valley with a guitar.

Four nights in Biloxi . . . The hotel is putting them up and, for the second time since they set out from Long Island, they have their own rooms. Two songs ago they covered "Crossroads," which has managed to become a fixture on their set list, then did the much slower, achier "Waiting and Wilting," and they're pepping everybody back up now, including themselves, with "Babylon Boogie." (Bluesier than "Spirit in the Sky," rockier than Canned

Heat's "On the Road Again," it gives Danny a chance to display his considerable harmonica chops.) There are 200-plus men and women out there, Howie sees, and they're all keeping the beat with their hands and feet. This song always gets people up, gets them shaking and ordering more drinks.

In mid-song, Howie turns around and takes a look at Joey. Somehow, despite all the junk food, he's lost about five pounds on the tour so far and only now does Howie notice he looks paler than he did a few weeks ago. But he's drumming perfectly, banging his tom-toms and crash cymbal, keeping the groove. Howie winks and Joey smiles back. *Okay,* Howie thinks, *we are not Entwistle and Moon or Jack and Ginger or Sly and Robbie, but we've always been damned good.*

A few yards from Howie's feet, a foxy woman in a tight pink Hello Kitty tank top stands up and start swaying her hips and clapping her hands over her head to the beat.

Is it possible, Howie wonders as Danny blasts away on the harp, that Joey can drum all the sickness out of his system and work away all the gunk clogging his arteries? Maybe he himself can do what surgery could not, just by thrashing, smashing, and rocking and rolling.

Howie turns around again and sees Joey in his Neil Peart T-shirt, his eyes shut, his long salt-and-pepper hair flying east and west, the sweat pouring off. He's drumming as well as he has in the last five years. Nobody out there in the crowd would ever suspect this is a dying man. The next song is "Blue, Bluer, Bluest," a slow number from *TFO 8*—Danny came up with the idea a few nights ago to always follow a fast song, such as "Boogie" or "Crossroads," with something slower so that Joey can conserve his energy.

The song ends and Danny picks up his silver harmonica brace and puts it around his neck. He slugs some water from a bottle, swishes the water around, and drinks more. It's another tactic: Take a minute or more between songs to give Joey some downtime. He fiddles with the harmonica holder, tells the audience, "Don't worry . . . I'll get it right . . . I always have trouble with these things, ever since my night brace . . . Okay, this next song is from our first album *Come and Git It,* which is available on Amazon, iTunes, iPads and Maxi Pads, and wherever obsolete music is sold. It's called—"

Just when Danny is about to say "Long Way Down," Joey kicks the daylights out of his bass drum and hits his closed high hat, then hits just his high hat and then the high hat and snare together . . . He keeps going and it sounds vaguely familiar at first, but then, after another few beats, very familiar to Danny. He hears Joey laughing maniacally behind him and turns around, but by this time Jules and Howie have picked up on the cue and joined in. Joey has, without permission from anyone, launched into "When the Levee Breaks" by Led Zeppelin. Danny sees Jules, his legs spread wide and his guitar slung low, chopping away on his Les Paul, then turns and sees Howie, as always stuck on the stage as though the planks had been built around his feet, plucking on his Fender for dear life. *The harmonica is right in front of me,* Danny thinks . . . and then he stops thinking and starts honking right into the mike. Joey bashes, Howie plucks, Jules chops, and now Danny has joined in on guitar, too.

It's all a matter of whether he can remember the words or not.

From nowhere, from hearing it on the radio for decades, while he blows up a wicked tempest on his harp, the lyrics come back to him, and then all four of them work in unison and drive the song, which then drives them harder and harder in turn. The whole joint quakes . . . it feels as if levees *are* breaking all around them. Howie turns around and sees Joey pounding the life out of his drums. "Jump, Howie!" Joey commands. "Jump!" And Howie does jump. He hops around like the stud bunny on a rabbit farm . . . He thumps his foot up and down on the stage to the surging beat and wiggles his hips. For the first time in his life as a performer, he's *moving!*

After the soft bridge in the middle of the song, the lyrics slip away from Danny but he makes up new words on the spot and nobody except the band notices: *"Jules's bladder sure gonna burst tonight. I say, Jules's bladder sure gonna burst tonight. He'll take some Flomax, then he'll feel all right."*

Two songs later they set down their equipment and file off the stage for a five-minute break. When they make it into the narrow, neon-lit corridor, Joey puts his hand on Danny's shoulder and says, "Sorry about that one, boss. I was just kinda feelin' it, you know."

"'When the Levee Breaks,' Joey?" Danny says. "Jesus goddamn Christ!" He draws in a deep breath, looks his drummer square in the eye, and says, "You *ever* spring 'Stairway to Heaven' on me, I'll kill you."

*

One of the best parts of no longer being successful and of having to take cars from city to city instead of fly is that you get to see parts of the country you'd never normally see. Another plus is that you get to spend more time with one another.

Danny rides with Howie in the Suburban—Jules and Joey are either miles behind or ahead of them—and they're somewhere in the middle of a flat, sun-drenched limbo in Mississippi, the air rife with sweet, dizzying smells. Before they make it to Louisiana there's a detour, an unavoidable geographical loop built into their itinerary: they have to shoot up to Jackson, Mississippi, then go farther north to Memphis, but then drop southeast to Atlanta.

"Could you put away that map?" Danny says.

"This?"

"Yeah! That."

"I think we might be lost."

"Here . . ."

Danny swipes the map off of Howie's lap, where it's been resting for hours, days, weeks, and tosses it to the backseat.

They pass graceful willow and sycamore trees, sparkling emerald fields and shacks that look like Monopoly hotels made of aluminum, wood, and tin; green traffic signs for Rosedale, Clarksdale, Lula, Cleveland, and Helena shimmy like mirages and then vanish; churches and fast-food joints and cotton fields roll by. The sun bakes the car and the windows are open, Buddy Guy and Junior Wells are on the radio doing "Cut You Loose," and Danny's cell phone rings. He takes a look at it and sees it's Angie. He thinks about not answering the call but . . .

"Hey, Angie."

She doesn't even bother with the usual pleasantries.

"So how's he doing?" she asks. Howie can hear her from the shotgun seat. His arm is resting on the open window; he feels the sun on his elbow and, worried about skin cancer, brings it back inside the car.

"He's holding up really well," Danny says.

"And the diet?"

Danny and Howie look at each other.

"You know, we're watching him. But there's only so much we can do."

"What did he have for dinner last night, Danny? Do you wanna tell me?"

For dinner? Which dinner? The one *before* the show or afterward? Before the show he scarfed down a heaping portion of beer-fried shrimp, deep-fried pickles, and half a deep-fried catfish sandwich. The dinner after the show consisted of fried chicken from KFC augmented with fried chicken from Popeyes. For dessert Joey ate Reddi-wip-topped Double Stuf Oreos. But at least the Oreos weren't fried.

"I can't even remember . . . Howie, what did Joey have for dinner last night? Do you remember?"

"A vegetable salad, I think," Howie says, flipping him the bird. "No dressing."

"You hear that?" Danny asks Angie.

Danny, now believing Howie about being lost, pulls the car over to the side of the road. There is no traffic going either way. Howie reaches back and gets the map . . . he believes they've completely overshot Jackson.

"And he's strong?" she asks. "I don't know why I let him do this with you guys."

"Because he wanted to. This is our life. Look, we're—"

"Remember—you promised me he'd get home alive and not in an urn with the Mötley Crüe logo on it! Is he there with you now?"

"It's just me and Howie. He and Jules are—who knows where they are . . ."

Howie, the map on his lap again, makes a signal with his thumb, pointing behind them. They did overshoot Jackson.

"Good," Angie says. "Don't tell him this but . . . Little Joey got into some trouble a few nights ago."

Danny doesn't say anything, and Howie, as he watches a ribbon of red dust spiral through a row of pink-and-white willow trees, listens keenly. Joey Junior had been working as a bartender at some joint in Bay Shore, not too far from the Fire Island ferries. The owner of the bar suspected he was dipping his hand into the till at the end of each shift and set a trap for him; he found out Joey was pinching about fifty bucks each night. The guy fired him on the spot, then bitch-slapped him when he skulked out.

"Fifty bucks a night, Danny! Was he giving *me* any of the money?! No! And he's living here for free!"

Danny tells her that at least the owner of the bar didn't have the kid arrested, and Angie reminds him that Little Joey isn't a kid, he's twenty-two.

308

Danny promises he won't tell Big Joey about all this and they say good-bye. He turns the car around and says to Howie, "If she didn't want me to tell Joey, then why did she tell *me*?"

"Man, am I glad we had daughters."

"Uh, I don't know about that, brother."

A few miles later they come to a crossroads; there's a small nameless diner there near an old one-tank gas station and they go in and grab something to eat.

*

One of the worst parts of no longer being successful and of having to take cars from city to city instead of fly is that you get to see parts of the country you'd never normally see. Another drawback is that you get to spend more time with one another.

Jules and Joey are in the U-Haul. The windows are closed and the A/C blasts away, and so do AC/DC's greatest hits, and Joey air-drums in the shotgun seat. They managed to split Biloxi shortly after Danny and Howie did and are in no hurry to get to Jackson, wherever Jackson happens to be.

"Gimme one of those?" Joey says.

There's a pack of Marlboro's between them and Jules picks it up and flips a cigarette to Joey. He feels his cell phone vibrate, takes it out, sees it's Angie, and, not having any idea why she'd be calling him, lets the call go to voice mail. Joey asks him who's calling and Jules says that it was just some chick.

"I'm not supposed to do this," Joey says.

"Listen to AC/DC? Don't worry, I won't tell."

"Nah, I mean smoke."

"Yeah, I knew what you meant, bonehead."

"Where are we going again?"

"Jackson."

"We was already there, right?"

They pass a freshly painted Baptist church with a cluster of bone-white houses in its shadow. Jules thinks he might see a hill on the horizon to his right, but it may be a cloud.

"No. That was Jacksonville."

"I can't wait until this thing is over," Joey says.

Jules sneaks a glance at Joey. He has a few days of gray stubble on his chin and his skin is the color of dirty chalk. It seems as if every day he gets a shade paler, and Jules can see the network of blood vessels crisscrossing his temples.

"If Angie knew you gave me this smoke," Joey says, "she'd castrate your ass."

Probably she would. But she would have also sliced him, Danny, and Howie to pieces weeks ago for what they've been letting her husband get away with. Last night Jules and Joey were up until three in the morning drinking, smoking, and fucking around. Then they smoked half a joint in the hotel's indoor pool, hit the vending machine on the way upstairs, and Joey knocked off two Snickers bars before bedtime.

"Back in Black" ends and "Highway to Hell" comes on, and Joey turns it up, but then Jules turns the volume back down.

"You don't like this?" Joey asks.

"I don't like AC/DC."

"Yes, you do."

"No. I never liked AC/DC."

"I didn't know that. Then why'd you have all their records?"

A sign for Jackson pops up and Jules veers right.

"I've never bought or owned one single AC/DC record," Jules says.

"But you liked 'em . . . so why didn't you get any of their records?"

"I never liked them! I've told you that like a million times, shit-for-brains!"

"I thought you liked 'em."

"I don't. I never liked them."

"Well, you shoulda told me that."

"I did."

"Jeez, I'm sorry, bro."

"Why are you apologizing?"

"'Cause I just am. Sorry."

Is this what it's like having a kid? Jules wonders. He's seen people talking down to their sons and daughters and he always got a laugh out of it. *Thank God I don't ever have to do this.* But is that what he's been doing to Joey for the past thirty years?

"I coulda sworn we already played Jackson," Joey says. "Are you sure we're going to the right place?"

"That was Jacksonville. That was in Florida. This is Mississippi."

Joey breathes in deeply, then coughs, then flicks what's left of the cigarette outside.

"I gotta take a leak again," Jules says.

Jules, who does not really have to take another leak, pulls over and hears some of the gear in the van shift around. To his left are bright green fields that look to him like a sea of glass. To the right some clouds laze over the horizon.

He gets out, shuts the door, and walks around to the rear of the van and sits on the fender, which is hot—he feels the heat through his jeans. He looks down the road and sees miles and miles of gray, silver, and green. He hears that Joey has turned up "Highway to Hell" and lets out a little laugh, then feels a knot in his throat, which has suddenly become very dry. He puts his hands to his face and takes off his Wayfarers. It's sunnier out than he thought . . . even the Mississippi shade is bright. Tears start to stream down both cheeks and it feels as though someone is vacuuming the air right out of his lungs.

Joey is going to die, Jules thinks. *He's really dying. And the band will end. It's all over. The whole fuckin' thing is over.* He thinks of when he was going to form his own band. He had everybody ready to go. *I could try that again,* he thinks. *Get in touch with Ike Kates and round everyone else up.* Then he realizes he has no idea where the other would-be members of Jules Rose's Raging Blue Balls are anymore.

Joey, please don't die on me, you moron. I'm going to miss you too much.

From out of nowhere a white flatbed truck rumbles by and Jules waits until the song ends and until the tears stop. He clears his throat and watches the truck vanish.

"Bro?" Joey calls out from inside the cab. "Everything okay?"

Jules knows that, if something were wrong, Joey would always have his back. In combat Joey Mazz would be the kind of soldier who'd lose all four limbs to save a buddy, who'd lose them even though it turned out his buddy had never really been in peril in the first place. He is loyal without even knowing what the word means.

"Yeah!" Jules says. "Everything's cool."

He wipes his eyes, puts his shades back on, gets into the cab, and slams the door so loud that five sparrows shoot up from the roadside grass and scatter into the air.

A few minutes later, Joey asks him, "Did you rip one?"

"No. Wasn't me. Must've been someone else. But who?" He slugs his drummer in the shoulder.

"I'm hungry," Joey says a few minutes later.

Twenty minutes go by and they come to a small nameless diner and a one-tank gas station at a crossroads. When they walk in, Danny and Howie are already there.

*

Memphis, Tennessee.

Danny and Jules do a fifteen-minute radio interview that Jessica had set up from Pleasant Valley and, when the interviewer asks,

312

neither of them can remember the URL for the website that sells Overfalls CDs, T-shirts, and posters. They have a night off and Howie walks around in circles . . . He wants to venture away from the pattern he's set for himself but cannot. He winds up walking the same exact circuit fifteen times. Jules buys a sweet cherry-burst Hummingbird guitar at Strings and Things, then thinks about going online and ordering some Viagra but doesn't know where he'd have it delivered to: if he orders twenty hits and has it sent from Mumbai to New Orleans or San Antonio, where the Shut Up Girl is waiting for him, what would happen if by the time it arrives in the Big Easy or San Antone the band has already been and gone?

In Memphis, Danny thinks he's somewhere else in the Volunteer State. "Let's give a warm Tennessee welcome, ladies and gentlemen," the announcer says, introducing the band, "to—from Long Island, New York—*the* Furious Overalls," and then Danny says to the crowd, "Thanks! Thank you. It's great to be in Nashville!" When a few people in the crowd groan and correct him, he doesn't even believe them and wants to storm off (he also wants to punch out the announcer for dropping the Long Island bomb like that). On the fourth night, after the same introduction, he makes the same mistake and Jules whispers, off-mike, "Yo, Memphis! *Memphis!*" Danny glowers for a second but then laughs. Instead of kicking off with "Dog Water Girls," as they always do, he starts strumming the intro to "Theme for an Imaginary Western" and the band joins in. *Christ,* he wonders, *am I really starting to* like *this song?*

They were supposed to leave Memphis in the morning and arrive in Atlanta in the afternoon but there was a glitch: two days ago Melissa Grey FedExed a box of 1,000 more *TFO 10* discs from Connecticut but they haven't arrived. So they park their cars, split up, walk around Memphis, rejoin each other, split up again. Joey gets tired and gets into the back of the U-Haul and naps, and, a few hours later, only Howie remembers where they parked the cars. By

313

the time the four of them are back together, it's 7 P.M. and FedEx has the box of CDs that Melissa sent; also inside the box is a securely taped manila envelope intended for Howie's eyes only. But when the band pulls into Atlanta it's the middle of the night and the hotel won't let them check in, so they sleep the rest of the night in their cars.

At three in the afternoon they do an interview with a college newspaper, and Danny and Jules can tell that the nerdy kid interviewing them had never heard of the band until she'd been handed the assignment that morning. That night, again going off the list, Danny kicks off the set with "When the Levee Breaks" and gets the joint jumping, even though not one person in the house has come to see a Led Zep cover. The band opening for them, a local country-rock combo called Ambergris, had never heard of the Overfalls either.

"Do you know what Ambergris is?" Danny asked the lead singer in the dressing room they shared before the show.

"Yeah," the guy chuckled. "It's like whale vomit or something. They use it to make perfume. Cool name, huh?"

"And did you know," Jules joined in, "there already once was a band called Ambergris?"

"No frickin' way," the singer said.

Danny told him that Jules wasn't fucking with him. "It was sort of a rock and jazz outfit," he said, "like Blood, Sweat and Tears, Chicago, or the Ides of March."

"Or Blues Image or Ten Wheel Drive," Howie chimed in.

"Like *who*?" the drummer, a zit-spangled, redneck bull of a guy, said. "Ten Wheel *What*?"

"There's never been," the singer insisted, "another group called Ambergris before us!"

"On the graves of my parents," Jules said, "there really was a group called Ambergris. I think you cats maybe need to change your moniker."

314

The members of the soon-to-be-renamed band all looked like people who'd just been informed they *hadn't* really won 100 million in the lottery after having spent 25 million on tickets. "You got any other names for us?" the bassist asked.

"Ten Wheel What sounds good to me," Jules said.

"How about . . ." Danny began, "how about Iron Butterfly? I always thought that'd be a great name for a band. Like, how could a butterfly ever be made of iron, right?" The members of Ambergris all looked at each other and nodded, and thus was forged and hatched the second incarnation of Iron Butterfly.

Atlanta, up to Nashville (where Danny thinks he's in Memphis) for a night, then over to Shreveport, the U-Haul breaking down at 2 A.M. outside Grambling, a ten-hour ride turning into fifteen.

The Brothers Cousins pop up again, opening up for TFO in steaming, sweaty Shreveport for three nights, two of which Joey cannot finish. The final night, Aiden Cousins whips out a joint and Danny smokes half of it. Then he drains an ice-cold bottle of Dixie beer in twenty seconds. When the Brothers Cousins do "It's All Gone" to end their set, Danny comes onstage, followed by Jules with his brand-new cherry-burst Hummingbird, and Howie with his black-and-silver Hohner Panther accordion, and they join in. Danny nails it—but still isn't satisfied with his vocals (*not nearly soulful enough,* he thinks)—and the Brothers thank and congratulate him during the applause. It's the first time he's sung the song in twenty years and the words come back to him like it was yesterday, and Joey hugs him backstage and says, "I knew you could do it, boss."

Back into the U-Haul and Suburban. New Orleans, then Austin, San Antonio . . . each city a light-year away from the next. Howie thinks of looking at the itinerary and counting how many gigs they've played, how many times they've done "Hurt," "Borderline," and "One More Time," but thinks better of it. They're barely aware of what month it is and where they are, and at one point Howie calls home but it takes him a few seconds to remember which one is

315

named Melissa and which one is named Michelle. The fog hasn't lifted; it's only gotten thicker and more blinding.

"How many fucking towns named Jackson are there in this country?" Jules asked at breakfast somewhere, and Danny remembered that Jules had already asked that, possibly as recently as the day before.

"So who is Jackson named after anyway?" Howie asked, wondering if it was Andrew or Stonewall.

"Probably," Joey opined, "just some guy whose last name was Jackson."

Somewhere near Beaumont, Texas, they pull the two vehicles over and pile into a booth at a rickety roadside diner. Danny has six days' worth of beard going, Joey's eyes are bloodshot, Jules hasn't showered in two days or applied deodorant in four. The sky is big and blue and, other than the waitress and cook, they're the only people around.

"So we're doing this again next year?" Joey asks with a mouth full of hash browns, omelet and ketchup.

Howie starts counting the chocolate chips in his pancakes.

"Who knows what we'll do," Danny says. The last thing he wants is for Joey to find out about the end of the Overfalls—even Jules and Howie are in on that with him.

"Well," Jules says, pouring sugar into his coffee, "I'm up for it."

"How about we just change the subject?" Danny says.

"You can sign me up for next year," Joey says. "Bring it on, dude!"

Jules pours milk into his coffee but misses the cup by a good five inches.

"What about you?" Joey asks Howie.

"You know me," Howie says. "I was born to rock and I was born to roll. Plus we're making decent money."

316

"Yeah," Jules says, mostly for Danny's ears. "We've sold lots of CDs."

"A thousand CDs at ten bucks a pop . . ." Joey calculates. "That comes to . . ."

"Yes," Danny says, "I can do the math."

"Next year," Joey says, "I'll probably be in a lot better shape. Howie, you won't have to drum for me. I say add forty more shows. Or fifty. Just get me out there. The best thing about touring other than the money is it gets me outta the house and away from the balls and chain."

"You heard the man," Jules says to Danny. "Fifty more shows."

Jules takes a wad of chewed but unswallowable waffle and bacon out of his mouth and sticks the cud inside a used container of syrup.

"Fifty more shows," Danny says. Only Joey cannot sense the sarcasm in his tone. "Duly noted. Got it. Consider it done. Maybe I'll even make it a hundred."

The rest of the meal is eaten in silence, other than for Joey's burps. When the waitress hands Danny the check, the four of them look outside and see the sunset and realize the meal they've just eaten was dinner and not breakfast.

*

San Antonio, Texas. Home of the Alamo, the River Walk, the Spurs, and . . . the Shut Up Girl.

The cars pull up to The Turning Point at six at night and the four of them get out and stretch their arms. Danny and Jules go inside and re-introduce themselves to Jack and Cat Tirpak, the husband-and-wife owners and managers. The Turning Point can squeeze in 300 on a good night, and Cat tells Danny that tonight and tomorrow, a Friday and Saturday, the place should be packed. Jack

317

asks them if they need help bringing in their equipment, and Jules expects Danny to turn down the offer, but instead Danny tosses the U-Haul keys to Jack and says, "Yeah, we could use some help."

It nearly blows Jules off his feet.

An hour later they're back in their rooms at the Sheraton Gunter Hotel. Once again—and it's only the third time on this tour that it's happened—they all have their own rooms.

Howie has just washed his hands and feet. Showtime is in two hours and soon they'll head back over to The Turning Point. For the tenth time since he first set eyes on it, he opens the manila envelope Melissa had sent him. He takes out the six-by-eight-inch card, suitable for tacking up on bulletin boards all over Connecticut, that his wife and daughter had masterfully designed. He looks it over.

HOWIE GREY

[FORMER MEMBER OF THE FURIOUS OVERFALLS]

THE UNIVERSE'S MOST INCREDIBLY VERSATILE
ROCK STAR

WILL TEACH YOU HOW TO PLAY

THE ACCORDION

AND

THE ZITHER

AND PRETTY MUCH EVERY MUSICAL INSTRUMENT IN
BETWEEN

So that's his future. The first time he saw it, Howie was skeptical. But by the fifth time—and he hasn't shown it to anyone else, of course—he began to think it wasn't such a bad idea. Sure, he would have to meet new people; sure, some of these people would be in their teens and he would have to do some driving around . . . but he wouldn't have to audition and he wouldn't have to tour anymore. He would be his own boss. On the card was a press-kit photo of him from twenty-five years ago, his home phone number,

and the URL for his website,
HowieGreyMaestroMusicalInstruction.com, which didn't exist yet.

Could I really do this? he wonders. *Should I do this?* And,
just as he's about to come up with an answer to his own question,
someone knocks on his door and, just from the force of it, he can tell
it's Danny. He quickly hides the card underneath a pillow.

"Open up!" Danny says. "Something's wrong!"

Howie goes to the door . . . Danny is trembling.

"Have you seen Joey? He doesn't answer his door or his
phone, not his cell or the one in the room."

Oh no, Howie thinks. *He's dead. He died in his hotel room.*
Then he thinks: *I have seen Danny Ault angry, I've seen him happy,
I've seen him high and drunk and bored . . . but this is the first time
since I've known him that I have ever seen him* scared.

"Is he maybe with Jules?"

"Nope. I just called him . . . he's downtown buying a
cowboy hat."

They take the elevator to the lobby and talk to the hotel
manager, who grasps the situation—it takes five minutes of
explaining and threatening, though—and then accompanies them
back up to Room 405. Danny knocks again and says, "Joey? Are
you there? Are you okay?!" but there's no answer. The manager
slips the keycard in and they all hear the door click open. The room
is dark, the shades are down, and everything is quiet. They walk in
and Danny flicks on the light, and they see that the room is empty.
The only things on the bed are the room's video game controller,
which looks like a dead lobster, and the Babies R Us piano toy that
Joey had bought for Danny's grandson's crib.

"Jesus Christ," Danny says, picking up the plastic toy. "That
dumb fuck."

Just then they hear, behind them, Joey saying, "Hey,
whassup?"

The manager drifts away and Danny and Howie turn around and see Joey, as white as a ghost, about to dig into a prefab ice cream cone.

"We were . . ." Danny starts. "It's almost—we have to get going soon."

"I don't know," Joey says. "Howie, you might have to drum for me again. Sorry, bro. I don't feel so good right now."

Howie is about to tell him it's cool, but Joey's eyes suddenly flutter upward and he collapses into Danny's arms.

*

Danny called Jack and Cat Tirpak and told them he was on the way to San Antonio Community Hospital, and that there was no way TFO could play tonight. The Tirpaks understood, and two local bands called And Plus & Ampersand and Rabbit Vibe will hustle over to the club and cover for them tonight.

When they got to the hospital, a doctor and a nurse administered an EKG test right away, only a minute after he'd made it past the triage nurse. Further tests revealed that Joey had not had a heart attack tonight, only a mild arrhythmia, but had suffered a silent one perhaps a week or two ago. Danny, Jules, and Howie cannot remember exactly where they were a week or two ago.

The three of them linger outside Joey's room now, Jules wheeling himself back and forth in an abandoned wheelchair. There's another wheelchair right next to them but Howie wants none of it, nor does he want anything to do with the doctors, nurses, orderlies, and patients walking around, especially the patients strolling down the corridor wheeling their IVs.

"Do we tell Angie?" Jules asks.

"I don't know," Danny says.

He opens the door to Joey's room a slit and sees him lying flat on his back, the vital-signs machine flashing and beeping away,

320

the lines going into and coming out of his body. Danny sees Dr. Huerta, his attending cardiologist, looking Joey over. Joey is out cold and Danny closes the door.

"It's wrong not to," Howie says.

"When did being wrong," Jules says, "ever stop us from doing something?"

"The way I see it is," Danny says, "Angie didn't tell Joey about his condition . . . so maybe we don't tell Angie."

"I got no problem with that."

"I'm on board," Howie says.

Dr. Huerta, all of thirty years old, comes out of Joey's room, and Jules stands up from the wheelchair.

"Anything new?" Danny asks.

The doctor says that Joey is resting comfortably and isn't in imminent danger. He's about to walk away when Danny tugs at his lab coat and keeps him around.

"So it's not so bad, right?"

"No," the doctor says. "He's going to be okay."

"How long do you think he has to be here?"

"I don't ever like to put a time on anything—"

"Well, we all occasionally have to do things we don't want."

"He could be out of here in four days. Maybe even three. We don't like to keep people around here if they don't have to be. What's your relationship again to the patient?"

The patient is my drummer and I'm his singer, Danny thinks of saying. *He's my goddamn drummer; he's been my drummer since 1978. The four of us old dudes are so tight it puts actual blood brothers to fucking shame.*

"He's in our band," Danny tells him.

"Well, I'd say four days at the absolute most. And when he gets out, he's going to have to take it easy."

321

Jules snorts and Danny nods at the doctor, who swiftly turns, heads down the hallway, and nearly barrels over an old woman with a metal walker.

"Yeah," Danny says. "'Take it easy.' Right."

"Four days," Jules echoes as he takes his seat back in the wheelchair and starts spinning himself around and popping wheelies.

"Can we really," Howie asks, "ask him to take it easy? I mean, if you ask me, taking it easy is what would kill him."

Danny goes back to the door to Joey's room, opens it, peeks in again, and then closes it.

"So, Howie," he says. "What was it you were telling us a while ago? Something about a drum machine?"

Twelve
Farther Up the Road

"Shut *up!*"

"And he didn't even know it. He's had like four or five of these silent heart attack deals in his life. Only the machine knows that you had one. It's some scary shit."

"Shut *up.*"

"I'm telling you the truth, babe."

Carrie Anne, the Shut Up Girl, and Jules are sitting at the bar of a chain restaurant in San Antonio—he's eaten half of a Take This Job & Shove It Burger. There's a replica bull's head above the cash register, and Lone Star flags and Lone Star beer all over the place. Tomorrow the Overfalls head up to Austin for two days and then it's adios, Texas.

"But he's gonna be okay, though?" she asks.

Jules thinks about telling her the truth but then just shrugs.

Carrie Anne is forty years old and has long teeth and big brown eyes. She's never been married or engaged. She's wearing a skimpy halter top, tight jeans, and T-strap sandals, and her legs are a mile high. Jules espies more tiny freckles on her shoulders than were present the last time he saw her. *Too much sun out here,* he thinks.

He leans back on his barstool. On the jukebox, Glen Campbell's "Galveston" ends and "Jesus, Take the Wheel" comes on; in the back, pool balls clash against one another. *God, this song sucks,* Jules thinks. *It's not even real country.* He hates music like this more than he hates rap—which at least has some rhythm to it—and opera. If there really is a Jesus, Jules wants to know, then why did He send the car spinning out of control on the ice, and why would He ever allow a song like this to exist in the first place?

"You should've come and seen us last night," he says to her. It's four in the afternoon and from his barstool he can see the street outside. It's sunny and warm, and men and women go back and forth in short skirts, tank tops, and short-sleeve shirts. On this tour, he's gone from 8 degrees to 88.

"I couldn't get off my shift. Plus, like, you might have let me known you were in town before last night? Or maybe you didn't want to see me . . ."

"You and your freakin' shift." Then, affecting a cowboy accent: "Oh well, darlin', I got tons more chiquitas here deep in the heart of Texas."

"Jules, shut *up.*"

He leans in close and they kiss for ten seconds. When he backs away, her eyes and lips stay closed for five more seconds. This makes her look very stupid.

"So Joey still drummed for you?"

"That's the amazing thing. We only missed one gig. Dude checks out of the hospital the next *day,* that same night he's pounding the skins. I can't believe you couldn't come see us. It's not like I find myself in this neck of the woods so—"

"Come here, you," she says, closing her eyes.

"Nah. Meet me in the bathroom."

"Here?"

"No. At the freakin' Alamo. Yeah, here. I'll be in there in exactly one minute thirty seconds. Pick a nice stall and get yourself good and ready for me."

He turns away and faces the bar. She stands up. What a pair of pins on her.

She looks at him and says, "Men's or women's?"

*

Two nights in Austin at Stockton's Wing, a dangerous crowd of only a hundred the first night. Six fights, one including knives, broke out during the first set, and Danny told Jules, "Let's hurry up. I want to get out of here alive." They ended up shaving half an hour off the usual show. Joey struggled but made it through and he didn't want to stick around either. The following night, there were four times as many people but half as many fights. "Sorry, bro," Joey said as he handed Howie his sticks for the encore.

Up Route 85, through the desert, and an unplanned stop in Truth or Consequences, New Mexico, where they have to turn in the U-Haul and get a new one. Eighty degrees, not a cloud to be seen. Not *anything* to be seen. "Look at all this nothin' to look at," Joey says to Jules.

In the Suburban, as the outline of Albuquerque wriggles in the distance, Danny asks Howie, "Where are we staying tonight?" A Marriott Courtyard, Howie tells him. But when they get to the hotel, there are no reservations—the two women working the desk search their computers but there's no sign of them. Danny, Jules, and Joey are astonished that Howie had gotten it wrong. "Okay," Howie says, "maybe it's a DoubleTree."

With their new U-Haul, they check in at the Duke City King Club, capacity: 510, and learn that the band opening for them, the Scrappy Proctors, had not only canceled but had broken up—the keyboard player had thrown a hissy fit the night before and walked. "Can you guys," Billy, the club manager, asks Danny, "maybe do an extra-long show today and tomorrow? I'd make it worth your while."

At nine that night the place is packed and the band is backstage. Billy comes into their dressing room and asks Danny how they want to be introduced, and Danny tells him, "Oh, just come up with something."

A minute later, as they hear Billy telling the crowd that the Scrappy Proctors have broken up, Joey tells Danny and Jules he can't go on.

"I'm just not feelin' it."

"You're sure?" Jules says.

325

Joey nods guiltily and Jules grabs his shoulder and gives it a squeeze.

"Howie?" Danny says.

Howie, sitting on an old red couch, offers up a resigned nod. He hasn't said a word the entire tour but they all know he cannot stand spelling Joey at the drums.

"Nah, nah," Jules says. "Let's do this . . ."

". . . And we have a real treat for you guys tonight," Billy tells the crowd as a bolt of feedback shrieks for a second or two. "These guys are from Long Island, New York"—there are a few boos at this point—"and they really know how to *ROCK*. . ."

"Let's just try it," Jules continues backstage. "We'll see if someone out there can drum. If anyone can, we'll give them the throne and see if they can pull it off . . ."

The old Keith-Moon-collapses-and-so-the-Who-plucks-a-drummer-from-the-crowd thing.

Danny looks at Howie, who really does not want to drum tonight. Or ever again.

". . . and they've sold millions of millions of albums," Billy continues to the crowd, "and had hits with songs like 'Borderline' and . . ."

A few seconds later, Danny steps onto the stage and takes the mike.

"Hey," he says to the crowd. "First of all, I'd like to thank you guys for showing up tonight. We have a slight problem, though. Joey Mazz, our drummer, and without question one of *the* best drummers in the history of rock and roll, isn't feeling too well tonight. So what we'd like to do is . . . Hey, any of you cats out there know how to drum?!"

There's a buzz throughout the audience, half of whom are seated, half of whom are standing, all of whom are drinking. They don't know if this is a stunt or not.

"I'm being serious," Danny says. "We want to rock out for you. Is there anybody out there who drums and who has a faint idea of our tunes?"

It looks and sounds like a crowd scene in a biblical epic when Moses or someone else tells the non-believers they're all wretched sinners or are about to die. Finally some guy—a solidly built, ponytailed man in his early forties—raises his hand and comes forward.

"I'm in a band!" he says. "My name's Chad Brantley. I'm a serious fan. I'm in a local band called the Stinkin' Badges."—This gets a smattering of applause and one "Yay, Chad!"—"I've been drumming for thirty years."

"Well then, Chad Brantley, let's get it the fuck *on!*"

The place goes crazy. Chad tucks his Shins T-shirt into his jeans, takes Joey's seat at the drums, and Billy, as shocked as anyone in the house, says: "So let's give a warm New Mexico welcome to . . . the Furious Overfalls! Featuring Chad!"

The lights go down and the band, minus Joey, takes the stage. They plug in and Jules goes over to Chad, who looks as though he's questioning his having volunteered, and whispers: "Be cool, guy. It'll be a gas. You know 'Dog Water Girls'?" Chad nods confidently and adjusts the high hat and crash cymbal. "Okay," Jules says, "we're starting with that. Just keep watching me . . . you'll be fine, dude."

"Let's do it, Danny," Chad, twirling his drumsticks, says to Jules.

Almost two hours later the gig ends and the band, plus Chad, unplugs and files offstage. As soon as they make it into the hallway leading back to the dressing room, Joey, who sat in a chair and watched the whole thing near the sound manager, tosses a towel at Chad's head. "You were fuckin' terrific," he tells his substitute.

They go into the A/C-chilled dressing room and nearly collapse onto the couches and chairs . . . everyone but Chad, who remains

327

standing with the towel draped over him, looking like Peter O'Toole in *Lawrence of Arabia*.

Danny looks at him and tells him he wasn't bad. Chad got a little too enthusiastic in places, overdid it on some fills and sped up the tempo in the wrong places at times, but all in all the gig had gone down much better than it could have.

A few minutes later Danny says they should all be getting back to the hotel soon.

"So," Chad says, "are you guys gonna need me tomorrow? 'Cause I could do it."

Danny, Jules, and Howie all turn to Joey.

"I don't know right now," Joey says. He looks at Chad and says, "Maybe you should stick around, you know?"

A half hour later they're walking out into the mostly empty parking lot. It's after midnight and Danny looks up and doesn't think he's ever seen so many stars in one sky.

"So, uh," Chad says to Danny, apart from the others, "I'll be here tomorrow. And if you guys need me after—"

"Hey," Danny says, opening the door to the Suburban, "let me give you a small piece of advice. From someone who knows. You do not want this job. Okay?"

The next night Joey never made it out of the hotel room, and Chad, this time playing within himself, did better and knew not to get too showy or ask for full-time employment. There was no day off after Albuquerque, and right after the Duke City King gig, the band headed south by southwest to Tucson after picking Joey and their stuff up at the hotel. This time it was so dark out that they couldn't even see all the things outside that weren't there to see, and at one point Joey fell asleep in the U-Haul. He snored at first but then fell silent, and Danny looked at him. His face was wrinkleless but gaunt and ashy and the nostril hairs coming out of his dented potato of a nose were ghastly to behold . . . but the thing that stuck out was his elbows: the slack skin was as craggy as the desert around them. Danny worried for almost two hours that Joey might have died. But when they came to the exit for Silver City, just as the rising sun turned the desert from black to pink to brown, Joey started snoring again and Danny knew all was well.

The sonuvabitch, Danny thought, *is going to make it home. He's going to do it!*

He relaxed in his seat, shifted his body around, and, just as he felt something foreign poking his butt, heard "Mary Had a Little Lamb" begin to play. It was tinkly and very loud but it didn't wake Joey up. Danny twisted and reached around, found the little piano toy and turned it off, and dropped it down to the floor of the van.

Three nights in Tucson at the Rialto Theatre. Joey played the first night; the second night he couldn't make it and Danny tried to pluck someone from the crowd. They had too many volunteers, however, and it took three drummers and five songs before they settled on one (and he wasn't too good either), and afterward Danny was fuming but didn't want Joey to see it. Back at the hotel, Danny called Jessica and told her all about it; she told him that Emily was huge but in a good mood, and he let the subject of Joey drop. That night, he smashed another thermostat; it was number 980 and he wondered if his 1,000th would come on this tour or the next, but then he remembered there was no next tour. The third night, Joey was able to chug through, but they only eked out a two-song encore, and early the following morning they came to Phoenix.

It's two in the afternoon at the Hilton Garden Inn. Joey is asleep in the next bed and Jules hears a soft tapping on his door, which means it has to be Howie. Jules turns off *Days of our Lives* and goes to the door and opens it.

"He's asleep?" Howie whispers.

"Yeah. What's up?"

"Come to our room. It's important."

Jules, in torn and frayed floral-print lounge pants, follows Howie down the hallway and around a corner to Howie and Danny's room.

Howie closes the door behind Jules, who sees a solemn-looking Danny, in short plaid pants and an army green wifebeater, standing over the hotel's standard-issue round table. On the table is a rectangular silver object with about two-dozen buttons and switches and four jacks. It's slightly smaller than the typical inkjet printer and is connected to a cigarette-pack-size speaker.

"This, gentlemen," Howie says, "is a drum machine."

They look at it for a few seconds and say nothing.

"We're calling it Saul," Danny says. "After that schlemiel we auditioned at Moonrise."

"Hello . . . Saul," Jules says to it.

The drum machine doesn't answer.

"Does Joey know we—" Jules asks.

"Nope," Danny says. "No idea."

"So many fuckin' buttons. Can we even figure out how to—"

"Hit it, Saul."

Howie looks at Danny, who nods gravely, then hits a switch. Right away, the drumbeat intro to "Dog Water Girls" starts up. *Boom-boom-BOOM-boom, boom-boom-BOOM-boom.* Jules shakes his head, thinking it's going to stop, but then Saul jumps into the rest of the song.

"Okay," Jules says, "I get it, I get it."

Howie turns it off and says, "Thanks, Saul."

"Well?" Danny asks.

"It plays pretty good," Jules says. He asks Howie how long it took to program the thing, and Howie tells him it was easy.

"And he can play all our tunes if we want him to?" Jules asks.

"Yeah," Danny says. "Easily."

Howie says: "If we were to teach Joey how to program it—and I think he'd get it after a while—then maybe . . . maybe we wouldn't

330

feel so bad. He'd program all the songs, even the new ones we're doing like 'Crossroads' and 'When the Levee Breaks,' and then it would be like he was still drumming for us. After he's not."

"Hold on," Jules says. "I'll be back."

He leaves the room and Danny and Howie look at the machine and say nothing. A minute later Jules returns carrying a bag of Cheetos and a can of Mountain Dew.

He puts the Cheetos right beside the drum machine and sets the can of soda on top of it.

"There," he says. "That's more like it."

*

The first time Jules ever saw Keith Richards in the flesh was inside the Terminal Music store on Forty-eighth Street, when Jules was still working at Big Bertie's Stereo Outlet on Canal Street. The second time was at Vagrants when TFO was at their popular peak. Keith and Jules jammed for an hour before the plug was pulled.

The third time was fifteen years later at a Rock and Roll Hall of Fame event at the Waldorf Astoria in New York. Chunky Scrofa told Jules he could get him in, and Jules, knowing Keef would be there that night, tagged along. He sat through some pompous speechifying (rockers passing off the words of publicists— "otherworldly," "the seminal palimpsest," "ethereal ambiences"—as their own), nearly falling asleep at one point, and made it to the end of the festivities. (Keith was two tables away and at one point Jules was certain he had acknowledged him with a wink.) He leaned over to Chunky and said, "I'm going over to say hello" and stood up. Jules wove his way over and approached Keith from behind. He bent down so his eyes were just about even with Keith's skull ring.

"Hey," Jules whispered, "I'm about to split but I just wanted to say hello."

A big Jamaican guy with dreads and a big white guy with a platinum mullet sprang out of nowhere and put their hands inside their jacket pockets.

"And who are you, man?" Keith asked.

"Jules Rose, the Overfalls . . . You and I jammed at Vagrants like fifteen years ago? Ian Stewart, too. We did 'Carol' and—"

"Oh yeah . . ."

"Okay, buddy, that's it, you've had enough time," Platinum Mullet told Jules, grabbing his shoulders. The Jamaican had moved in, too, and Jules got the message and slunk away.

That's it, you've had enough time.

He's thinking about that night and cursing aloud as he glides the Suburban through the sunny streets of Scottsdale. He's on the outskirts, all the houses are adobe and flat-roofed and have about a half acre of lawn, and tall palm trees dot the sidewalks but provide little shade. He has a MapQuest printout on his lap and he's cruising around looking for Ellis Drive, which should be around the next corner.

"Fuck you, Keith," Jules mutters as he makes a right turn. He's at 5500 Ellis Drive right now and is looking for 10500. *How the hell,* he wants to know, *do they get numbers so high on a street that's only three blocks long?*

He thinks back to a few days ago, to San Antonio. He'd told the Shut Up Girl to go to the men's room, and she adjusted her halter top and headed back toward the restrooms. Jules looked into the Lucite eyes of the replica bull above the cash register, finished his Lone Star beer, and left the place. *How long,* Jules thinks as he comes to 9000 Ellis Drive, *did she wait there for me? Five minutes? Ten minutes? Maybe she's still in there.* He'd walked to the corner, pulled out his cell and erased TSUG from his directory, then went back to the hotel, whacked off, and took a nap.

The A/C is on low but his hands are freezing and his stomach is starting to simmer. *Am I really doing this? I should just turn around*

332

and head back to Phoenix. But he's come this far. Two thousand four hundred and twenty-five light-years from home.

On the corner of Barringer Hill Road and Ellis Drive, under two palm trees so tall their leaves disappear in the solar whiteout, Jules comes to a two-story cherry-blossom-pink home. This is it, 10500 Ellis Drive, which somehow is set right beside 10000 Ellis Drive. A gray mailbox with the *Scottsdale Times* logo stands in the little lawn, and there's an adjoining two-car garage, which is a darker shade of pink than the house.

He parks the car across the street and keeps the A/C on. By the time he gets back to Phoenix it'll be time to drive up to Flagstaff for a one-night stand at a place called The Elite Café. "Where are you off to," Danny had asked him when Jules hit him up for the car keys a half hour ago, and all Jules had said was "Somewhere."

The minutes pass, the sun gets brighter . . . Jules decides he'll give this no more than an hour. But an hour turns into an hour and a half and he decides he'll give it two hours max. Then the front door opens and a man in short khaki pants, an orange linen shirt, and yuppie moccasins comes out. He's on the short side of fifty, paunchy, almost completely bald, and about five-eight. Following him out is a smaller, tanned woman with short ash-blonde hair and slim shoulders. She's wearing oversize purple sunglasses and wedged purple sandals that add six inches to her height.

Jules's heart starts pounding and he can hear that he's losing his breath.

He looks at the couple and lowers the window but he cannot hear them.

What do I do? I gotta do something!

Rhonda Wentworth's husband heads toward the garage, which lifts its doors to reveal a lot of golfing equipment, a red Focus, and a blue Escape. Jules, whose old man sold Fords, has to laugh aloud.

The front door opens and a girl of about eighteen comes out, and the father of the girl makes a left turn out of the driveway in the

333

Focus and drives off. Without even thinking about it, Jules gets out of the SUV and walks across the street, getting closer and closer to Rhonda and the girl.

"No, you *know* what you have to do now," Rhonda says to her. "Come on."

"But do I *have* to?" the girl moans. She's in very short, faded cutoff jeans and has coltish legs. *Must wear a size two,* Jules thinks as he gets closer. *Not bad.*

The front door opens again and a boy with brown bangs, maybe a year younger than his sister, comes out holding a skateboard and shielding his eyes from the sun.

Rhonda looks toward Jules, doesn't recognize him . . . and then she does.

"Hi," he says, only a foot away from her.

"Oh my God," she says, muffling her words with her hand. Jules looks at the hand over her mouth and sees that it has aged. She has lines around her mouth, two or three creases on her forehead, and her neck is slightly wrinkled, but she still looks good.

"Is it okay?" he asks. "Is it okay I'm here? I was in Phoenix and . . ."

"Wow . . . who are *you?*" the girl asks, smiling and leaning on her mother's shoulder.

"Go back inside, Lucy," Rhonda says. "Please. *Now.*"

Lucy looks at Jules, at his long hair, zebra-print pants, and magenta ray-skin shoes, and doesn't want to leave, so Rhonda again orders her to go. The boy asks, "Hey, Mommy, can I—" and Rhonda says, "Yes, Jack! Whatever!" and the kid follows his older sister inside.

"Lucy, huh? Jack? Nice names."

Rhonda says: "I heard you guys were playing in Phoenix. I thought about maybe showing up but I didn't want to scare you or anything."

334

"That wouldn't have scared me. It probably would have scared you if you'd shown up and seen us. You look good."

"Oh, come on. I'm becoming an old hag."

"Uh-uh. I'm twice the old hag you are."

"You don't have one wrinkle, you lucky bastard."

"That's just the Botox and the Clinique talking—it's not luck."

"Is everything okay?"

Jules asks her how long her husband will be away; she tells him he's going to the store and will be back in about twenty minutes.

"Joey Mazz is dying." His voice cracking scares him when he says it, so he says it again, this time without the crack. "He's dying. He's on the road with us but it's like he's a ghost now. It's really been tough."

Rhonda looks up at him through her big purple sunglasses and right away the tears start to trickle down.

"Oh, I'm so sorry. What is it?" Jules points to his heart and she says, "He has kids, right?"

"Yeah, three. I don't think they have any idea. He doesn't even know."

"Will you tell him I said hello? Please?" Her voice sounds no different . . . she still sounds like the Syosset-raised daughter of a Brooklyn police detective and a Long Island school principal. "I always loved Joey."

She wipes the tears off her cheeks.

"The other thing," he says, "is that after he dies, the band is through. We're calling it quits. Can you believe it?"

"Is that *your* idea?"

"No. Danny's. I have no say in it. If it was up to me, we'd play together until I died, too."

She asks him what he's going to do, and he tells her he has no plans just yet.

"I don't know what else to say," he tells her after some awkward silence. "It's so good to— I didn't want to go my whole life without ever seeing you again."

"I'm glad you came. I just wish you would've told me."

"If I had warned you I was coming, you probably would have skipped town."

"Yeah, probably."

Five minutes later he's in the Suburban. *I'll tell Joey she said hello,* he thinks. *That'll make him happy. But nobody else finds out about this.*

He gets back on the road to Phoenix, catches a glimpse of himself for a second in the rearview mirror, and heads southwest as fast as he can go.

*

Dead End Road.

It took two weeks to get the house in Montauk wired properly. Eight guys, all of them mighty stoned, hauled all the equipment in and hooked it up. Howie moved in first and took a bedroom on the ground floor, near a bathroom. The day after he moved in, the mobile studio arrived; two days after that, Joey Mazz and Chunky Scrofa moved in. A week later Danny took a bedroom on the second floor. There was no view of the ocean, he discovered, not from any room in the house: his windows faced the butt end of a dune. Three days later, Jules moved in and took the room with the most mirrors in it.

The acoustics in the house were bad: the floorboards creaked, the ceilings were too low in some rooms, too high in others, the walls were flimsy, and the furniture shook. Joey had to play his drums in the basement. If they were going to bring in any horns, each player had to go up into one of the house's turrets to get the right clarity.

336

By the time everything was hooked up, there were twenty people in the house who shouldn't have been there. Jules had two girlfriends, Donna and Georgia, who were built and permed the same exact way. Georgia had a younger sister named Annie, and the first time he saw her Danny said to himself, "God, I hope I don't end up sleeping with her," and it took six days but he ended up sleeping with her. Donna and Georgia didn't get along with each other and sulked when they were together, and they were together a lot. Joey had a string of Bay City buddies and cousins, always bearing infants, toddlers, and Heineken, constantly going in and out. Chunky had three assistants who sometimes slept on the floor, sometimes slept in guest rooms, sometimes slept in the mobile, and were often too fucked up on blow to sleep at all.

They were there a month before it dawned on Danny that nothing was getting done. What had been meant to be a sanctuary was turning out to be a lunatic asylum.

When he'd called Owen J. Crowe months before to tell him that the Overfalls would no longer be availing themselves of his services, Owen had said to him, "I thought it best not to work with you anymore either, so I'd venture to say we're both cool." But now, as the atmosphere grew more frenetic and as Lew Aaronson and his minions at AaZ, finally answering their calls, kept pressing the band for material, Danny knew they needed him. He sucked it up and called Owen in L.A. but was told he was in Jamaica; in Jamaica they told him he was in Memphis; in Memphis nobody had any idea where he was. When Danny finally located him—in L.A.—Owen told him that he was tied up for the next six months. "Can you hold on that long, pardner?" Owen asked, and Danny slammed down the phone.

Danny wasn't doing coke anymore. Too many scares, too many people he knew damaged or gone. Now he contented himself only with FDA-approved pharmaceuticals: Nembutal, Seconal, Valium, Demerol, Tuinal, Librium. If it ended with an –al, an –ol, or an –um, the chances were Danny liked it. He'd wake up and take something and then, when the first effects were nestling in, he felt so relieved that he'd take two more. Rarely did anyone wake up before noon, and when they did wake up, there was mayhem: Joey and his buddies and their kids getting into fights with water guns and with real guns; Donna playing William Tell with Georgia one day and throwing a metal spatula at her forehead over and over again; Jules telling Donna and Georgia to take a hike, them smashing equipment, and him having to replace it.

Two months passed and they had nothing.

They had the bare bones, the outlines of songs; they had a vague idea of what to do with them, which was to add textures, arrangements, and atmosphere that they'd never dared use before. They listened to Louis Armstrong and his Hot Five and the MC5; to Count Basie and the Sir Douglas Quintet; to Jimmie Rodgers, Jimmy Reed, and Jim Reeves; to Blind Lemon Jefferson and Jefferson Airplane; to Robert Nighthawk and the Byrds; to Cole Porter, Nat King Cole, and "King Porter Stomp"; to Hank Williams and Cootie Williams.

But it wasn't working.

And the more it didn't work the more depressed Danny got, and the more depressed he got the more pills he took. One morning—it was October—he woke up and stared at the lowering ceiling, and the nightmarish thought struck him that he'd already written all the good songs he would ever write in his life. *Oh my God, what if it's true?* He heard leaves shifting outside and waves rolling in and out. *What if I'm done . . . what if it's all over?* He ran to the bathroom, gasping all the way, dry heaved, and took a Valium.

In the old days, it had been so easy. The sound of windshield wipers, gulls cawing. bees buzzing, glasses tinkling, tires going over a bridge's metal grating, an overheard conversation, someone laughing . . . it could all lead to a wonderful song.

But that wasn't happening anymore.

What was happening was bickering over small things, Jules and Danny spending days not acknowledging each other, Jules escaping to his Westhampton house for a week, and Danny further numbing himself. Now he was sure his nightmare had come true, that he was creatively spent and there were no good songs left in him. But he didn't tell a soul—he was afraid if he said it out loud, that would make it true.

It was late November and a good new song and Jules Rose were nowhere in sight.

"You know where he is?" Danny asked Joey, who was too mesmerized by what he was watching on TV and the onion dip he was digging his fingers into to answer.

Danny rubbed his chin . . . maybe Jules had moved temporarily to the Memory Motel, a dive hotel on Montauk Highway with a bar, right in the middle of town. A few days before, Danny, desperate to get out of the house and get his head clear, had spent the night there (and, never getting his head clear, already had zero memory of it).

"Try his joint in Manhattan," Joey said when Scooby-Doo broke to a commercial.

"No, you try it. Tell him to get his ass back here."

Danny thought of what Jules might be doing in the city, then wondered if he'd been going downtown to check out the music. He thought about Vagrants and suddenly it was as if someone had turned all the lights back on after they'd been off for months.

"No!" he said to Joey. "Tell him to stay there. Guess what? We're all going into the city. We're going to play Vagrants tonight as the Ventilators. How's that sound?!"

Six hours later the band went on—there were only thirty people in the crowd that night—and it was just like old times all over again.

*

Las Vegas, the end of the road now in sight.

339

Joey couldn't play in Flagstaff and stayed in his hotel room. Knowing he wasn't coming to the gig at The Elite Café, the band agreed it was cool to bring on Saul, which Howie had fully programed, without Joey ever learning of its existence. They drew over 200 people and pulled a drummer out of the crowd, but she lasted only three songs; they plugged in the drum machine and finished the gig. After the first set, Jules got scared and called Joey's room at the Holiday Inn Express. Joey answered and said he was feeling okay, but he didn't sound like it. At the end of the show, as he usually did, Danny introduced the band: "On the bass, violin, accordion, and alto glockenspiel, Howie 'Fifty Shades of' Grey! . . . On guitars, a legend in his own mind, Jules 'American Beauty' Rose! . . . And, sitting in on drums tonight, let's have a big hand for . . . Saul!"

On the way to Vegas, they stopped at a diner in Kingman, Arizona. Danny excused himself, got into the U-Haul, and found the business card Eddie Le Vine had given him at Moonrise. "Dave Litt . . . Vice President, Programming . . . Sirius." Hoping he'd reach voice mail, he dialed and, of course, Dave Litt picked up. Danny told him he'd love to do a show, Dave told him he'd love to have him do it.

"It's easy," he told Danny, "there's really nothing to be scared of."

"Did I say I was scared?" Danny asked him.

"Hey," Dave said, "I've even got the perfect name for your show: 'Ault Country.' Pretty cute, huh?" Grimacing, Danny said, yeah, it was pretty cute. Jules, Howie, and Joey came out of the diner, and Danny quickly made an appointment to meet Dave in New York and said good-bye.

They're staying at the Sahara Hotel tonight and performing at the 450-seat Stoney End Club, located a few yards away from one of the Sahara casino entrances. Once again, they have their own rooms and it's sweet, although there are much nicer hotels in Las Vegas.

They have three nights in Vegas and have already performed twice. The first two nights Joey was able to play, but when they left their rooms tonight, he told them he couldn't make it. "Do you need a doctor?" Howie asked him, and Joey said he was sick of doctors.

They waited until Joey went back to his room, and then Howie went into his and pulled out Saul from its hiding place under the bed.

"We're gonna leave you with one more song," Danny says from the stage. The crowd is your typical Las Vegas TFO audience: some long hair, some gray hair, and some baldies, men and women in their forties and fifties in Dockers, Ann Taylor, and Rockports. "Thanks for coming . . . you've been great!" (Danny hates Las Vegas so much it feels as if somebody else is dubbing in the words.) "We didn't write this song but, man, do I sure wish we had." They break into a smoking cover of Delaney & Bonnie's "Coming Home" and end the gig to a ten-second standing ovation and thirty vacated seats.

Danny, Jules, and Howie stick around the bar, shake some hands, sign an autograph or two, and sell twenty copies of *TFO 10*. Two hundred more bucks into the coffers. They get free drinks from the bartender and continue to hang around and unwind. A freckled blonde in her late forties with staggeringly white teeth, staggeringly fake tits, and a tangerine-color tan starts flirting with Jules . . . Popping out of a sheer pink baby-doll dress, she tells him she's originally from Green River and went to the same high school he did (but not at the same time). There's a circle of about ten people around the band; some of them are talking, some aren't. One of them is a very tall man with bad hair plugs and a long black beard; he's massively overweight and has on ungainly seventies eyeglasses. He hasn't said a word yet. Other fans ask questions and volunteer information ("So did you guys ever play the original Fillmore West [sic]?" "Did you ever meet any of the Beatles?" "I was sort of in kind of a rock trio, too, when I was a kid.") but Hair Plugs Guy just

341

takes it in. Ten minutes pass and Jules knows that all he would have to say to Freckled White Teeth, whose name is Lola, is "Hey, let's go upstairs to my room" and she'd go. Her hands are on his knees already and working their way up. Little by little, everyone but Lola and Hair Plugs departs.

"So where to again tomorrow?" Danny says. He's drinking seltzer with lime and wishing the seltzer were Jack Daniel's and the lime were a Seconal.

"Bakersfield here we come," Howie says, setting Saul down on the bar.

A few feet away Jules puts his arm around Lola's mottled shoulders and says something to her about connecting all the dots. The surgeon who worked her chest over, he knows, has to be one of the foremost experts in the field.

"I can't wait until this thing is over," Danny says. "I'm so beat."

"Oh yeah?" Hair Plugs says, nervously stroking his beard. "Too tough? Wow, you've really turned into a pussy, Danny."

Danny jumps off his stool and quickly Jules gets between him and the guy . . . then Jules looks back at him and says, "Holy shit! *Mickey*?"

Howie and Danny look into the guy's face, see past the clunky glasses, the lousy plugs, the beard, and the neck so fat it's a cylinder of lard segueing into his chin, and see that, yes, this time it really is Mickey Sanford.

"It's Mike now. Nobody's called me Mickey since you punks did."

"Don't call *me* a punk, loser!" Danny says. "I'm not the one who fuckin' bailed out like a pussy!"

By this time two bouncers have drifted over to the bar, but the bartender, Mickey, and Howie nod to them and tell them the situation is under control.

342

"Bailing on you guys was the best thing that ever happened to me," Mickey says. "And what were you gonna do, Ault, pound my head into the ground like you did that dude in San Francisco until it caved in?"

"Your head is too fat to cave in, scumbag," Jules says, feeling his face redden.

"Should I stick around, honey?" Lola says into Jules's ear, adding a quick flick of the tongue. "I've got something in my room I'd really like to share with you."

"Nah," Jules tells her. She stands there stunned for a few seconds.

"Wow," Mickey says, the flab in his jowls jiggling, "Jules Rose passing on a piece of pussy. Major news event. Film at eleven."

Lola huffs and then storms off, and Jules asks Mickey at which point in his life did he wake up in his bed transformed into a blue whale.

"Can I get a word in?" Howie says, looking up at his former drummer. "First of all, it's really not a pleasure to see you again. And the other thing is, why are you still alive? How did that happen?"

"Fuck you, Howie. You know what, you were just as expendable as I was if not more so—you just stuck around and I had the brains and balls not to."

Danny cannot believe that not only is he standing inches away from Mickey Sanford, but that he's standing inches away from Mickey Sanford and not strangling him.

Mickey tells the three of them that he skipped town only days after dropping out of sight. His life was never in jeopardy—he paid the Howard Beach crew the money he owed them and all was fine. ("Thirty years," Jules says, "of hoping you'd been hacked alive to pieces—all down the drain.") He moved to Akron, then Boston, never drummed again, and quit using and selling drugs. He eventually studied refrigeration and heating technology and joined

343

someone's business in Boxford. On some kind of junket in the eighties he saw Las Vegas for the first time and decided this was where he wanted to live; he moved there six months later and established his own business. He proudly names all the hotels, restaurants, and clubs he handles the air-conditioning for, as if that would impress his former bandmates. ("Nobody in this town," he says, "installs one single unit without seeing me first. Microwaves, too.")

Mickey orders a shot of tequila, slugs it down, and gets another. "Hey," he asks Jules, "remember that half-mulatto broad with the cockamamy red afro we fucked at the same time in the bathroom at Rumbottoms?" (Jules does remember but tells Mickey he doesn't.) "Jules gets the front and I'm stuck with the back door, of course. Gee, thanks a lot, asshole." Then he tells them he's on his third marriage ("Third time's a charm, knock on wood") and pulls out his phone and shows them pictures of his newest wife, a nasty-looking brute in her forties, and his kids. Danny gets a heaping tumbler of Jack Daniel's and ginger ale and tries to listen to Mickey, but he's thinking about a variation on the back cover of the Dead's *Europe '72*: all he wants to do is smash his glass into the guy's forehead.

"So what's up with the drum machine?" Mickey says after ordering another tequila and slamming it down (although some tipples over into his beard).

The Overfalls look at one another and don't answer.

"You know, I bought your records," Mickey says. "They weren't bad. Then they started to suck. So that moron you replaced me with—he's not in the band anymore?"

"He's in the band," Howie says. "He's just taking a break."

"You guys. You never should've let me escape. I'm telling you, had I stuck around you wouldn't be playing shitholes like this one. And you wouldn't have needed a machine to replace me with, ever."

"This from a guy who fixes refrigerators?" Jules says.

"I don't fix 'em, shitbag. I got fifteen niggers and spicks who do that. Look at you, Jules . . . you look like a wax-museum figure. Hey, they've got a Madame Tussauds here, right at The Venetian. You could get work over there posing as yourself."

Danny and Jules look at each other.

"Fuckin' drum machine," Mickey mumbles to himself. "Joey Mazz is so fuckin' dumb he can't even remember how to drum anymore? Brain-dead re-tards can play the drums but not him? What a serious moron you got."

Before Jules can do anything, Danny, with the swiftness of a featherweight, grabs onto to what little hair Mickey Sanford still has crowning his dome . . . With all his might he shoves Mickey's head down until it's level with his own gut, then kicks his leg up so his knee goes right into Mickey's jaw. It sounds like an axe being swung into a tree, and Danny, Jules, and Howie see three bloody teeth pop out onto the floor. Mickey stays on all fours for a few seconds and Howie and Jules, too shocked to move or say anything, stand there and look down at him while Danny signals to the bartender, tells him Mickey would like another tequila, and says that it's on him.

*

Across the scorched and silent Mojave to Bakersfield. The Skyline Club.

They planned their exit strategy a long time ago: either Jules will drive the Suburban to Long Island, and Danny, Howie, and Joey will fly, or they'll all fly home and Danny will unload the Suburban in Portland, the tour's final stop, where the gear will be shipped home. Jules has spent the last few days wishing he'd spent more time with Rhonda—he should have whisked her into his car and taken her along for the rest of his life.

Joey woke up this morning and said, over something purported to be scrambled eggs, that this was the best he'd felt in weeks. "I'm good to go tonight," he said. He still has no idea about the drum machine and thinks that they've picked drummers out from the crowd at every gig he's missed.

That final night in Vegas turned out to be quite an evening for Jules. He roamed around the Sahara casino and ran into Lola at a craps table and made good with her. "I'm sorry, darlin'," he whispered to her. "That's not me. Let me prove it to you." She waited until the dice came to her, crapped out quickly, and then the two of them left. She told him at a bank of elevators that she had to text a friend and he stood aside for a minute. Within three minutes she was in a crowded elevator toying with his dick and nobody, except perhaps the security people glued to their monitors, was aware of it. They went to her room and right away Jules could tell she was staying with a guy. Lola admitted she was vacationing in Vegas with Ray, her boyfriend, but that Ray was at a strip club downtown with friends and would not be back until two in the morning. Jules thought of bringing her back to his room, just to be safe, but decided he didn't want her lingering around afterward all smelly and leaky. She shimmied out of her baby-doll dress (and it was now that Jules saw that the surgeon had done no work at all on her tummy) and they got in the bed; he did all he could to her and then it was her turn to do it to him, but nothing she was doing could get him quite hard enough.

"Damn," he moaned. "Too much to drink."

"Don't worry, baby," she said to him as she weighed his balls in her palm. "Happens to the best of 'em." Her cell rang and she went to her dresser and answered it. It was Ray and he was on the other side of the door. Jules was able to discern this and leapt out of the bed . . . but Lola hung up and said: "Jules, don't worry . . . Ray and I, we have an agreement. Seriously, don't sweat it."

Lola, still naked, went to the door and let Ray in. He was small and bony and had a quiff of metallic brown hair—he looked like the slowest Italian greyhound in the history of the breed. The three of them talked for a while and it was obvious Ray had been drinking. "I just come from playing blackjack at Caesar's . . . I'm up a hundred and ten," he said. Lola shot a quick guilty glance at Jules— that was when it all clicked in: Lola had texted her boyfriend, Jules now knew, and told him to hurry up and come back to the room because she'd picked up a guy. Ray started massaging Lola's back from behind and then reached out and cupped her breasts.

"You like these, Jules, huh?" he said. "You like 'em, don't you?"

"Yeah," Jules said, "they're nice."

"Six grand for these tits. Ooh, look at 'em. Feels so good. Six fucking grand." He unzipped and started stroking himself. "You ever seen tits like before?" Ray asked.

Jules had, of course, many times, but told Ray he hadn't. Lola got on her hands and knees on the bed and Ray was doing her from behind (and slipping out a lot and cursing himself over it). He was yanking on her hair and asking Jules to jerk off. "Come on, rock star! Take it out and come in this bitch's face!" he implored. But Jules had neither the will nor the way and he got dressed and left. The last thing he heard, as he was closing the door, was Lola telling Ray to hurry up and get it over with.

"I can't tell," Jules said in the Holiday Inn Express breakfast room this morning, "if this is French toast or if it's the Teflon it was cooked on."

"You really feel good today?" Danny asked Joey.

"As good as new, bro, I'm tellin' ya."

"We go on at nine tonight. If you're still feeling great then, let me know."

Then, a few hours later, while Joey was napping in his hotel room, Danny gathered Jules, Howie, and Saul in his room with their guitars and told everyone he had an idea.

The Skyline Club is close to packed on a Thursday night and TFO is five songs into the show. Joey insisted to Danny before they went on that he was still feeling great.

"Waiting and Wilting" ends to a brief round of clapping. The band's most downbeat number, it never gets much applause; the lyrics are so dire and Danny's rendering of them so agonizing that it always comes as a relief when the song ends.

"Okay, we've got a huge surprise for you tonight," Danny says to the 200 shadows before him. He turns around and sees Joey looking more perplexed than usual. "We're gonna do a song that features our drummer, the King o' the Skins, the Lord of the Ludwigs, the Czar of the Zildjians, the Earl of the Pearls . . . Mister Joseph Gaetano Mazz. It's a Led Zeppelin song we retooled and it's called 'Moby Dick.'"

On the beat of four, all four of them, Joey grinning ear to ear, launch into "Moby Dick." They've slowed down the tempo to give Joey some rest before the upcoming deluge; they've made the song raunchier and more wicked. Danny disliked "Moby Dick" from the first time he heard it through all the times he's heard it since, but he knows Joey loves it.

They do the song's hook six times and then Danny, Jules, and Howie stop on a dime . . . Joey shrugs, not knowing what to do for a moment, not knowing if they are really going to let him take a solo, and then Howie yells at the top of his lungs, "Come on, Joey! Kick out the jams, motherfucker!" and then Joey rips right into it . . . He starts out softly on the floor toms but works his way into it, gathering speed and power. Danny and Jules step to one side of the stage, Howie to the other, and the woman in charge of the lights shines the spotlight on Joey, who, after three minutes of cascading stick-work, transitions into a relentless four-minute take on Gene Krupa's tom-tom solo on "Sing, Sing, Sing." After that, all hell breaks loose . . . He goes back to "Moby Dick" for two minutes, then breaks seamlessly into four minutes of Ginger Baker on

"Toad," jazzing it up and using the brushes on the ride cymbal and toms. From "Toad" he explodes into Michael Shrieve on Santana's "Soul Sacrifice." Then he goes back to Ginger Baker on "Do What You Like" for four minutes, and after that picks it up and slams down Cozy Powell's "Dance with the Devil." His cheeks are flushed, his hair is whipping all over the stage, and it looks as if his bones are rubber bands. After four minutes of "Dance with the Devil" he changes everything and slows things down to a jazzy hush with some Joe Morello "Take Five."

Over twenty-five minutes have gone by and Danny can see the crowd has given up (some people have even left); at one point, just when Joey starts pulling a John Bonham and banging the drums with his hands until they nearly bleed, someone cries out, "Oh, just end it already!" But Danny doesn't care: he knows Joey has waited decades for this. It's his first solo with TFO, and Danny, Jules, and Howie are well aware that it will be his last. After kicking into a stormy, revved-up version of Spencer Dryden on "She Has Funny Cars" for two minutes, Danny, Jules, and Howie take the stage again . . . Joey comes to a dead stop and Howie yells out to him, "Beck's Bolero!" and just as they'd planned and worked out in Danny's hotel room a few hours ago, the band kicks into "Beck's Bolero." Howie looks back at Joey and sees that the look on his face is ecstatic, transcendent, utterly euphoric. There's no piano, there's no Nicky Hopkins, there's no Jeff Beck, but the Overfalls climb up and up and soar toward the multi-orgasmic end, and these three minutes are the best time on Earth that Joey Mazz has ever had, ever, ever, ever, anytime, anywhere, ever.

*

In San Diego, Joey found out about the drum machine. He understood. "I know I haven't been pullin' my weight," he said. It was Jules's fault that Joey found out: it was his turn to hide Saul

349

under the bed but he'd set it on his night table instead, and Joey came into his room and saw it. "What the hell is that?" Joey said. But he knew what it was.

They did three nights in San Diego: Joey sat out the first and second nights and Saul filled in ("Hey, he's not bad," Joey, watching the show from the bar, said afterward), but he was able to make it halfway through the third show before an incompetent drummer in the audience and finally Saul spelled him. The next morning was bad: Jules discovered Joey staggering around in the hotel hallway, unaware of where he was and who was the kind, longhaired, butter-skinned man taking him back to his room. The band had to cancel their first night at the Disneyland House of Blues. ("You better show up for the second night!" the manager said over the phone to Danny. Danny told him: "And if you know what's good for you, you better not be around when we do!")

Joey refused to go to the hospital and wouldn't let them summon a doctor.

Anaheim. A Holiday Marriott Hampton Clarion DoubleTree Courtyard Express Garden Inn. Danny and Jules are at a radio station promoting the gig, and so it's just Howie and Joey at the hotel. Howie is on all fours laying down a terrycloth path from the bed to the bathroom when he hears a knock and sees Joey at the door.

"Hey," Howie says.

Joey looks down at the towels.

"Everything okay?" Howie says.

"Yeah. Just a little restless."

"You want to take a walk and get some fresh smog?"

Howie dreads that Joey will want to go to Disneyland and go on some rides.

"Is there any place to walk out here? I could use some sun, I guess."

A few minutes later they're walking around the parking lot. Joey shuffles slowly and at times Howie has to take his arm to keep him going.

"I don't know about tonight, bro," Joey says.

"Don't worry about it."

"I guess Sal might have to go on for me again."

"Yeah. Sal."

They walk around the hotel three times. Joey and Howie are wearing, respectively, black Frye boots and red Chuck Taylors, purple pajama pants and tan shorts, a red Hawaiian shirt and a green Frog Hollow Day Camp T-shirt—and it's a good thing, Howie knows, he slapped on two coats of sunscreen, SPF 500, before he left his room. The sun shines brilliantly and turns the hotel's dull brown facade a Nerf-ball orange.

"You want to make another circuit with me?" Howie asks.

"Nah. Let's go back up here."

They're at the back entrance to the hotel in the parking lot. In order to get back to the hotel from this spot they have to climb ten steps.

"Are you sure you don't want to walk to the front?" Howie asks Joey.

"I'm okay. Are you?"

Howie nods. In the building's shade now, he takes Joey's arm and they walk up the first step. Howie skips the second step but Joey doesn't and Howie has to wait for him.

"How long you been doing that for?" Joey asks.

"You know . . . for a long time."

"It's just a stair."

They walk up the next steps and when they come to the second-to-last step, Howie tries to let go of Joey's arm but Joey doesn't let him.

"Come on," Joey says.

He clings to Howie and won't let his arm go. Joey will not let Howie skip the second-to-last step.

"Come on," Joey urges.

"I can't."

"You have to. For me, bro."

Howie looks at Joey, who looks like he's aged ten years in the last few months. As sick as he is, though, there's no surrender in his eyes right now.

"Don't do this to me. Please."

"Watch this."

Using every ounce of his strength, Joey drags Howie where he doesn't want to go . . . to the penultimate step of the stairway. Both of Howie's sneakers are now on that stair and a breeze blows their hair around and Howie's breathing is loud and quick.

"See," Joey says. "This isn't so bad." He waits a few seconds, listens to Howie faintly whimper. "It's not so bad, is it? This is always the best one! And you've been missing it for years. Are you okay?"

"Yeah . . . I'm all right."

"Do you want to move up or you wanna stay here for a while?"

Howie thinks about it and says: "Let's stay here a while."

He looks down at his feet, at his red Chucks, at the step he's standing on. He looks up at the hotel and sees that it's not crumbling to pieces. He turns around and sees the sun blazing on all the parked cars and on all the cars crawling along the road.

"I'm tellin' ya," Joey says. "The next step before the top one and the one right after the first one—those are always the best two."

Howie's heart rate returns to normal. Two minutes ago he thought the wind would lift him up, carry him across the road, and smash him headfirst into Tomorrowland.

"You know what your problem is, bro? You think too much. That's everybody in the world's problem. Too much thinking goin' on. It can drive you crazy. I gave it up a long time ago. Best thing I ever did."

Howie laughs and looks up and down.

"Hey, how come," Joey says, "it's always Danny and Jules who go on the radio and talk to the newspapers? You ever notice that?"

Howie looks at Joey and says, "I guess they're more interesting than you and I are."

"Did you ever wonder why it's always them?"

Howie walks up to the top step, just to see if he can, then walks backward down to the penultimate one, just to see if he can. He says: "We used to go on the radio with them. Scott Muni, Vin Scelsa, John DeBella. We did lots of—"

"That was a hundred years ago, bro. Hey, do it again."

Howie walks up a step, then comes back down.

"If you ask me," Joey says, "they take us for granted. You and me . . . we're the backbone. The band never would've made it without us."

"They did write most of the songs. And they sing them."

"Yeah but come on. A band is nothing without a rhythm section. Can you imagine the Stones without Charlie Watts and whoever the other guy was?"

"Bill Wyman."

"Whoevuh. You take away those two, or you take away John Paul James and John Bonham from Led Zep, and nobody ever woulda heard of 'em."

"It's John Paul Jones," Howie says. "And, to tell the truth, I don't really want to do interviews anyway."

"Yeah, me neither. But they could ask us every once in a while, you know?"

Howie looks up. The hotel is still intact, the sky hasn't fallen, the world still turns.

Joey asks him if he wants to go back inside. He offers his bony arm and Howie takes it and together they head in.

353

Los Angeles.

Only five more shows, all one-nighters: straight up the coast to Santa Cruz, San Francisco, and Mendocino, then farther up to Eugene and Portland, then home.

They played the Greek Theatre last night, the second act of a four-act bill (REO Speedwagon and 38 Special were the big draws). Almost 3,000 fans, their biggest audience yet, showed up on a warm, clear evening, and the Brothers Cousins were the opening act.

"Where's Joey?" Skeeter Cousins asked backstage before the show began.

"He's under the weather," Danny explained.

Aiden Cousins asked who was drumming in his place, and Jules lifted up the drum machine and said, "Meet Saul."

"Unless," Danny said to J.P. Cousins, the drummer, "you wanna sit in for us tonight." J.P. asked his bandmates if that was cool and they said it was.

"Okay, then," J.P. drawled, "guess you got yourselves a drummer."

"On one condition though," Aiden said to Danny. "You got to sing 'It's All Gone' again with us."

Danny thought about it a second and said, "You got it, chief," and Aiden looked at Jules and Howie and said, "And I want all of y'alls else's asses up there, too."

The Brothers Cousins saved "It's All Gone" for last, and out came Howie with his accordion and Jules with his new cherry-burst Hummingbird. Danny reached down deep inside and sang the song with his eyes closed, and while he sang, the world vanished: it was just him, this song, and the cool evening breeze. He nailed it. When Howie's final chords died out in the Southern California night and

354

Danny opened his eyes, he was momentarily startled to see people in front of him in the crowd and people behind him on the stage.

"You *really* want to give this up?" Jules asked him as the applause died down. "I don't get it."

It's the following morning and the Overfalls are taking a break on Zuma Beach in Malibu. While Joey and Saul sit on a beach towel, Jules and Danny and Howie throw a football around in the surf. It's a weekday and they have the beach mostly to themselves. Soon they'll check out of their hotel, then hit the highway and go on at ten tonight.

"Go long!" Danny says, pumping the football and fading back in the sand.

Jules and Howie run toward the ocean . . . it's impossible to tell who's the receiver and who's the defender. Howie's shoulders and legs are white with sunscreen and Jules underwent a rigorous fake-bake on Hollywood Boulevard yesterday before the show.

"Come on . . . go real long!" Danny says.

Jules and Howie run into the surf—the water is cold and they yowl—and Danny hurls the ball as far as his achy back will allow. It sails over their heads and lands on the crest of a wave, and while Danny bends over and grits his teeth from the pain, the football tumbles back to the sand.

"You all right?" Joey asks, only a few yards away.

"I'll live."

Danny sees that Joey is tinkering with Saul, which is now on his lap.

"I think I got the hang of this doohickey," Joey says.

"Yo!" Jules calls out, throwing the ball back to Danny.

"Don't screw it up," Danny says to Joey. "We've got it programmed right."

Joey looks up at Danny and tells him not to worry, and Danny lets him be. Of the four band members, only Joey is in street clothes right now. He even has his boots on.

355

Danny hears his cell phone ring and limps over to his nylon bag and pulls it out.

It's Jessica calling from Long Island.

"Hey," he says. He looks out at the beach and sees Jules and Howie tossing the ball to each other and avoiding the frigid ocean water. "What's up?"

"Where are you right now?" his wife asks.

"We're on the beach in Malibu, just screwing around."

"You *are*?"

"Yeah, we've got a football and Joey's got Saul." Howie stretches out for a thrown football and falls headfirst into some wet sand, and Danny says, "Everything here is jake. Hunky-dory. Copacetic. A-OK."

"And you've got a *football*?"

"It's nice out here. I should've flown you, Em, and Lily out for last night's show. Hey, I even sang—"

"Well, speaking of Emily, the reason I'm calling is to remind you that your oldest daughter is still very pregnant and is due in a few weeks. So don't get any ideas about moving out there or booking a few extra dates."

"Don't worry. I will be home for the festivities."

"So do you want to tell me who Saul is?"

An hour later the four of them, having just checked out of a Clarion Hotel, are in the hotel parking lot, ready to roll up the PCH, when Jules gets out of the U-Haul and tells them to hold on.

"I should whiz again," he says. "One for the road."

He trots inside the hotel lobby, gets the keycard back from the hotel clerk, and goes back up into the room.

He has to make two phone calls and they won't be easy. Knowing he's doing the cowardly thing, he takes out his cell phone and makes the easier phone call first.

"Hey," a familiar voice on the other end says. "Jules?"

It's Ike Kates.

356

"Hey, Ikey, what's going on?"

"Where are you and what's up?"

Jules tells Ike he's calling from L.A. and only has a minute to talk. He asks Ike what's going on and Ike tells him he's at work now—he manages a RadioShack in Leonia, New Jersey—and cannot talk for too long either.

"Look, I'm back on the Island soon," Jules tells him. "This might sound like a strange question but . . . you remember my Raging Blue Balls, right?"

Ike tells him he sure does but that he has to go, and now Jules steels himself to make the second call.

Rhonda, it's me Jules, he will say to her. *Hope I didn't shock you the other day. It was great seeing you again. Look, I'm driving back cross-country. Do you want to maybe get lunch?* Or: *Would you want to maybe spend a few days together?*

Or something like that.

He dials her number. The phone rings once, twice . . . he walks to the window and sees Danny and Howie leaning against the U-Haul and Joey working on Saul in the Suburban's shotgun seat.

On the fourth ring Rhonda's husband picks up, says hello, and Jules hangs up.

He looks out the window, sees his bandmates growing impatient, and knows he has to get going.

*

They wound up staying in the house in Montauk six months longer than originally planned.

Every couple of weeks, the Overfalls would drive in to Manhattan and play Vagrants as the Ventilators. They kept their set list to songs from their first two albums or covers of songs they loved. One evening they did a honky-tonk cover of "Don't Let the Sun Catch You Crying" and it left some in the crowd in tears, and

357

others befuddled. In January, one night Jules went by himself to get a falafel on MacDougal Street. It was cold out and beginning to snow, all he had on was a thin leather jacket he'd bought at a flea market in Amsterdam (Contessa Vanessa van Vaseline had picked it out for him), and he was walking back toward Bleecker and the gig; when he made a left turn he bumped right into someone . . . it was a woman with blond hair, a faux-leopard coat, and high-heeled boots, and he almost knocked her over.

It was Rhonda.

"Whoa!" he said, holding her shoulders to keep her up.

She didn't know what to say. He let her shoulders go.

"Are you okay?" he asked her.

"Yeah. You?"

She buttoned the top button of her coat.

"So what are you doing around here?" he asked her

"I live on Thompson Street now," she said. "This is so weird . . . a friend of mine told me that some band called the Ventilators was playing tonight at Vagrants. I thought, well, that's kind of funny . . . so I thought I'd check them out. "

"It's us. The Ventilators. It's just this thing we're doing."

"It is?"

He nodded, and she shivered and stood up straighter.

"You'll still come and see us, right?" he asked. "We're on in like twenty minutes."

"Definitely. I'll be there."

The band was hemorrhaging money. The Montauk mansion, renting the mobile studio, the musicians they were bringing in, keeping all the hangers-on fed and fucked up . . . it was costing. One day Danny heard that the Tower of Power horns were in New York, so TFO had them helicoptered out to Montauk and brought them in to record tracks for four songs. A few weeks later Jules heard that the Brecker Brothers were staying at a house in East Hampton; he summoned them in and they recorded the very same tracks as the

Tower of Power horns. A month later the Memphis Horns were brought in. (In the final mix, exactly who did what, and on which songs and where, could never be fully agreed upon or accurately recalled.)

Jules would come up with a riff or a melody and play it for Danny. Danny kept trying to tell him, "No . . . that's old Overfalls. We're trying for something new." Then Jules would go off somewhere for a while, to his part of the mansion or to the beach or to Manhattan or L.A. He'd come back, play something else, and Danny would shake his head. Or Danny would have an idea, have no clue where Jules was, and then forget it. That February, during an ice storm, a girlfriend of one of Joey's Bay City buddies, drunk out of her skull, fell out of one of the turret windows and broke both her legs.

By March they had some songs, some segments of songs, some endings without middles, some choruses but no lyrics, some outros but no songs leading into them. In April, the weather warmed and the music began to come together in fits and starts. They would write a simple song that was three minutes long at most, then add horns, strings, reeds, atmospheric touches, and all sorts of flourishes of cosmic American music, and before they knew it the songs were eight minutes long and so dense they sounded like white noise. By the time they had ten songs finished it was early May, and neither Danny nor Jules was sure they even liked what they'd done. That month, one of Chunky's assistants overdosed on a speedball and had to be taken to the hospital in Southampton. The guy Chunky brought in to replace him brought an additional three people.

Every day Danny woke up thinking his well had run dry, and all day long he walked around panic-stricken.

When they listened to the songs, they knew that they had gone too far. "It's not *us*," Joey lamented. "I don't know who we are but this ain't it. And besides, it don't rock."

359

The owners of the house were coming back on Memorial Day weekend.

One night Danny went into his room and found two guys and a girl already asleep in his bed. They were barely out of their teens and he'd never seen them before. He packed up some clothes, grabbed two guitars and some pills, and drove to the Memory Motel. *I'll just stay here for a while,* he thought. An hour later he was lying in bed, terrified, when some headlights slowly swung across his window and a car ground to a stop on the gravel. Danny went to the window and watched Howie, carrying his duffel bag, Fender, and electric-violin cases, check in to the hotel and take a room four doors away. Twenty minutes later Joey checked in, and at 4 A.M. along came Jules.

At ten the next morning, buck naked, Danny went to Howie's room and pounded on his door.

"Wake up, Grey! Montauk police!" Danny said, disguising his voice. "We know you're in there, Jew Boy! You're surrounded!"

He turned around and looked at the drivers on the Montauk Highway checking him out and nearly crashing into one another.

Howie, scared out of his wits, opened the door . . . he saw his front man in the altogether before him and nearly fell over.

They ended up staying at the Memory Motel for two weeks, rarely going back to the mansion. Danny flushed all his drugs down the toilet and drank only an occasional beer, and the four of them, a band again, spent every second together in their rooms or at meals or on the beach. They re-recorded all the songs they'd composed, stripping them down to their skeletons, tossing out all the grandiose flourishes. The music crackled and sounded raw, angry, sexy, dangerous, and alive again. It was back to being the Furious Overfalls.

With three days left to go they came up with "It's All Gone," and Joey went to a drugstore and bought three rolls of Tri-X film, drove back to the mansion, and took pictures of the crooked yellow

360

sign that Danny and Howie had first happened upon a few months before. The contact sheets were to be the album cover.

By Memorial Day the mansion owners were back and everyone went home (the band, though, had incurred $25,000 in property damages), and AaZ Records had 802 hours of tape to deal with. But it was only hours 801 and 802 that mattered to the band—it was the material they'd recorded at the Memory Motel. *That* would be the album called *Dead End Road.*

Everything was ready to go.

Two years dragged by. Lew Aaronson, soon to do his minions and heirs the enormous favor of dropping dead at his regular table at the Four Seasons, refused to release the Memory Motel version, despite the vigorous protestations of the band and their excessively remunerated attorneys. AaZ Records didn't even want to release what eventually became known as "The Mansion version." The Mansion version was unlistenable, it was thought, and would not appeal to what was left of the TFO fan base, and the Memory Motel version was deemed to be crude, strident, abrasive, and, in some places, unfinished. ("But that's the whole point!" Danny insisted.) AaZ issued *Live in 'Lanta* and hoped they were rid of TFO once and for all, but that only engendered further legal conflict and more exorbitant bills—bills so high that their sums looked like typos but were not. A judge who proudly admitted to having listened to no music composed after 1899 reached the conclusion that AaZ had to release one version of *Dead End Road.* It was then discovered that the Lizard of AaZ, a week before he'd done a face-plant into his last slab of foie gras, had destroyed the master tapes. The Memory Motel version of *Dead End Road* no longer existed. It was gone.

The Mansion version was issued . . . and none other than Hal Clay, who'd screwed up the first TFO album, was brought in to polish it to oblivion. None of Joey's grainy black-and-white photos were used on the cover. For $200, the record company got a stock image of a healthy young man and woman in skimpy bathing suits walking hand in hand along a beach under a ketchuplike sunset. The photo could have been used for an ad to promote honeymooning in Aruba.

Six months after its release—and it was more like a vanishing act than a release—the band was in California playing to mostly empty houses. Six months after its release, Alan Wilbur Murdock in his ripped army jacket came at Danny Ault in the parking lot of a motel just outside San Francisco . . . He was cursing, spitting, scratching, threatening, poking his sharp fingernail into Danny's face. After Danny and the others got through with him, he never could do any of that again.

On Bleecker Street in the frosty air, Rhonda shivered and stood up straighter.

"You'll still come and see us, right?" Jules asked. "We're on in like twenty minutes."

"Definitely," she said. "I'll be there."

But she never showed up.

*

San Francisco.

Joey played for two songs in Santa Cruz but then had to sit, and Saul took over. Joey had figured Saul out, done some reprogramming, and the gizmo, as much as any machine could, now sounded like Joey at his very best.

"Anything you guys need," a young radio flunky, probably a college intern, offers now to Danny and Jules in the station's plush green room, "just let us know."

They nod at her and she leaves. The station feed is being piped into the room and, wouldn't you know it, "Help Me, Rhonda" is playing. It's just about ten in the morning and Danny and Jules are here to plug tonight's show. The DJ who's about to interview them

362

is named Joe Hay, and the station, which plays classic rock mixed in with the occasional snippet of new material, is called The Blast.

Danny stands up, sets down his red-and-black Blast coffee mug, and paces around the small dark room, his hands in his pockets. *I cannot wait to get home,* he thinks, *and become a grandfather.*

"Calm down," Jules says. "It's a radio show, not a murder trial."

"Yeah," Danny says. "You're right."

He sits down and stretches out in the chair but then starts fidgeting.

"You want me to go on alone?" Jules asks. Danny shakes his head and "Lola" by the Kinks comes on. Rhonda, then Lola—Jules listens, shakes his head, and smiles. He thinks of telling Danny why but doesn't.

"So," he says to Danny, gathering up his nerve, "any idea what you're going to do with your bad self, post-Overfalls?"

Danny leans forward in his chair and says, "I haven't really thought about it. I'll be a grandpa. But beyond that, I don't know." He leans back and says, "And you?"

"No plans," Jules says. "None."

A dumpy guy with thick glasses and all-over-the-place brown hair opens the door and comes in. He's forty years old, only five foot four, and is wearing baggy cords and a gray hoodie two sizes too big.

"Danny?" he says. "Jules?"

They stand up.

"Joe Hay," he says. "Thanks for coming. Huge fan, by the way."

"Joe Hay is your real name?" Danny asks, shaking his hand.

"Yep. Joseph Hay. That's me. Why?"

"You know . . . the Hendrix tune. 'Hey Joe'? Joe Hay?"

"Yeah, whatever. Okay, we're about to go to the news, sports, weather, and traffic, and then you'll be coming on in about ten minutes. Now, is there anything you *don't* want to talk about? That's what we always ask our guests. We'll plug the show tonight, play a few TFO cuts—we've got *TFO 10* already cued up—but, like, any skeletons in the closet or anything I should know about?"

"Which closet?" Jules says. "We got whole Taj Mahals full of 'em."

"Okay," Danny says, "we would really, really appreciate it if you didn't mention a certain incident that happened around here thirty years ago involving us."

"And what," Joe Hay asks, "would that be?"

"Well, if you don't know, maybe we shouldn't tell you."

"Fair enough. Don't worry. It'll be terrific."

He leaves the room and a few minutes later, as "Street Fighting Man" ends, Danny and Jules hear Joe Hay saying: "Wow . . . I just met Danny Ault and Jules Rose of the Furious Overfalls in the green room . . . They're going to be with us in just a couple of moments but first . . ." and then he segues into the news.

After the traffic report, TFO's "Hurt" plays, and the radio flunky ushers Danny and Jules into the studio, which is a lot larger than the ones they've visited so far on this tour. There are high-def TV screens, mannequins dressed as San Francisco 49ers and Giants; there are posters from The Fillmore and Avalon Ballroom from the mid- to late sixties.

"We're back on The Blast," Joe Hay tells his audience while Danny and Jules sit down and slip on their headphones. "That was, of course, 'Hurt' by the Furious Overfalls, also known as TFO, and the band, or at least two of them, have chosen to grace us with their presences today. Danny Ault and Jules Rose." Some guy with wraparound sunglasses on the other side of the soundproof glass presses a button and the sounds of applause peal throughout the studio. "Welcome, guys."

"Great to be here," Jules says.

"We'll see about that. So you're playing *where* and when tonight?"

"Uh, where are we again?" Jules asks Danny, who is squinting and trying to discern the band names on the psychedelic posters. He tilts his head and can make out Jefferson Airplane and Country Joe and the Fish, but everything else is indecipherable.

"Danny?" Joe Hay says. "Back to planet Earth?"

"Uh, what's the question?"

"Whoa! I'll have what *he's* having."

The sound-effects guy plays a noise of someone smoking a bong and coughing.

"Where are we performing tonight and when, he wants to know?" Jules says.

"We're at The Warfield," Danny says, snapping to. "Nine o'clock sharp. Be there."

"And this is," Joe Hay wants to know, "the *original* lineup of the band, right? No substitutes or kids sitting in or anything?"

"Nope, Joe, we're all here. Still alive and well," Danny says.

Danny and Jules shoot each other a glance.

"Now, the Overfalls have not played San Francisco in *decades.* I mean, it's been a long, long time. The last time you were around these parts there was some sort of major altercation, was there not? A serious brouhaha, it was. A kerfuffle?"

Danny feels all the heat in his body surge into his cheeks and eyes . . . he looks at Jules, who immediately straightens up in his seat.

"Didn't I tell you to not bring that up before?" Danny says.

"Yeah," Joe says with a smirk. "But guess what? I'm an a-hole."

The sound-effects guy smiles and presses a button, and the sounds of farting and toilets flushing rattle Danny's eardrums.

Danny clenches his fists, and Joe Hay says: "So what was it again? Some guy said something mean about your mom and so you banged him over the head with a shovel or something? You didn't kill him, did you?"

"No," Jules says, covering for Danny. "We never killed anyone. And you promised us you wouldn't—"

"Alan Murdock was the poor guy's name."

"That poor guy," Danny hisses, "got a lot of money from us."

"What would you do," Joe says, nodding to his engineer, "if I told you we had said Alan Murdock on the phone with us right now from Mill Valley. Alan, are you there?"

"Yeah, Joe," a croaking, warped male voice says out of the ether, "I'm here."

"Crazy Al's a regular caller to the show . . . how many years has it been, Craze?"

"Eight years, Joe. Eight years I been calling you."

"You're a real fucking piece of shit, you know that," Danny says to Joe Hay.

"Whoa!" Joe says. "I'm the only one allowed to curse on the air."

"Hey, Danny," Alan Wilbur Murdock says from his phone and wheelchair from whatever house he's confined to. "Long time, no see. Paralyze anyone recently?"

A new torrent of canned laughter plays, punctuated by the sound effects of fists hitting punching bags, men and women screaming in pain, and a bell ringing to indicate the end of a boxing round.

"You had it coming," Danny says. "You know, for years I felt guilty about it but now that I hear your voice again, it reminds me what an absolute piece of shit you were!"

"Danny," Jules says, grabbing Danny's arm. "Let's just go. We don't need this."

Danny shakes off Jules's hand, stands up, takes a few steps toward Joe Hay.

"Aww, c'mon, that's not very nice," Alan Wilbur Murdock croaks. You can tell, just from the sound of his voice over the phone, that he's been crippled for years.

"You lied to me!" Danny yells at Joe Hay, who looks up at him nonchalantly. "You're a douchebag just like he is!"

"So what are you gonna do?" Joe Hay says. "Turn me into a vegetable, too?"

More canned laughter, more boxing bells, sounds of gunshots and ricochets.

For decades, Danny has kept it all in. Sure, he'll yell at someone every now and then and once in a while he'll slam some moron up against a wall. And a week ago he knocked out a few of Mickey Sanford's teeth. But that was nothing. For thirty years he's kept it in, ever since his run-in with Alan Wilbur Murdock. For thirty years he's put up with idiots; with jerkoff waiters who don't write down his order and then get it all wrong; with dipshits and half-wits; with his daughters and his wife and his band; with dickheads who mistake two minutes on the Long Island Expressway for the 24 Hours of Le Mans; with faulty ATMs, reptilian club managers, express lanes in stores that never move and the dumbasses in them slowing them down; with turd-brained fans, uncreative schmucks in elevators saying, "This must be the local"; with asshat baristas who think their shit smells better than their coffee; and even with record executives—and still he kept it all in. A few weeks ago in New Orleans he was singing "Waiting and Wilting" when some zero in a cowboy hat shouted out, "Get a job!" Had they been alone, Danny would've clubbed him over the head again and again with his guitar until there was no cowboy hat or head to club anymore. But he kept it in. For decades he's seethed and walked it off or slept it off, and all the bottled-up fury ended up destroying his back, eating away at his stomach, and corroding his spirit. At times he thought his brain would fry itself.

But this guy has it coming.

The former tight end and middle linebacker of Pleasant Valley High rips off his headphones and grabs the collar of Joe Hay's hoodie.

"Anybody there?" Alan Murdock croaks. "Hullo?"

Danny lifts Joe Hay up off his seat and feels a hatchet plunge into his back and buttocks. "You scumbag!" he yells at the dumpy little DJ, whose headphones fall off his glib mussed-to-perfection head.

"Danny!" Jules, right behind him, says. "Let's split, okay?"

But Danny doesn't want to split . . . he only wants to split Joe Hay's head in two like a machete going through a coconut.

And then, in a flash so quick that Danny has no idea it's happening, Joe Hay grabs Danny by the arm and throws him to the floor. All 240 pounds of Danny Ault hit the thin carpet at once, somehow belly-first. He lets out a noise like *blwwwwrrgggh* and sees little Joe Hay assuming some sort of martial arts posture, hands and feet at the ready. *No, no,* Danny thinks, *this little West Coast twerp is just doing this to scare me . . . he's bluffing.* Danny shakes off the cobwebs and tries to stand, but in the act of doing so, Joe Hay comes at him—four radio staffers now run in and Alan Wilbur Murdock, not seeing any of this, tries to figure out what's going on—and drops Danny Ault as if he were a yo-yo. This time Danny lands on his back.

"Hey, is anyone there?" Alan Murdock asks the world. "Hul-*lo*? Hul-*lo*?"

Hullo, hullo, hullo is all that Danny hears—he hears it over and over again as though it were canyon echoes in a cartoon—and he sees Joe Hay standing over him, still in martial arts position, but now being pushed back by the four people who'd just rushed into the room.

Someone on the other side of the soundproof glass decides that now is as good a time as any to break away for a commercial or two.

"Are you okay?" Jules says. "Talk to me."

368

He's kneeling down and cradling Danny's head in his hands. Danny nods.

"Are you sure? How's your back?"

"It's fuckin' killing me. How's yours?"

Jules, with Danny's head still in his hands, shifts around so that Danny can sit up.

I can't do this anymore, Danny thinks. *Some little hipster twerp just kicked my ass.*

"Get them out of here!" someone orders. It might be Joe Hay, it might be the show's producer. Two minutes later, when "All You Need Is Love" comes on, Jules, his arm around Danny's shoulders, helps him out of the studio.

They walk past speechless radio station personnel, take the elevator, and exit the building, just the two of them. The street is empty and it's a gusty, cloudy day, and Danny cannot walk without Jules's help.

"Can you make it?" Jules asks.

"I don't know. I'll try."

"You ever wonder where the hell you would be without me?"

Before Danny can come up with an answer, Jules's cell phone rings. Danny buttons up his jacket, hears leaves rustling overhead, and leans against a squat redbrick building. He checks his back, hips, knees, and wrists to make sure nothing's broken or bleeding. *I seem to be intact,* he thinks. He's about to make a second sweep of his body but then decides not to press his luck.

"It's Howie," Jules tells Danny. "He's at the hospital. Joey's dying."

*

It's two in the morning and Joey lies in his hospital bed. Danny, the only other person in the room, sits in an actionably uncomfortable plastic chair near the door. Joey has his own room. Other than the

369

white lines pulsing on the vital-signs machine, the room is dark, and Danny can barely make out his own hands.

Howie brought Joey to the hospital and called Jules en route. Joey was rushed into the emergency room. An hour later a doctor told Danny that it was only a matter of time.

I'll have to call Angie when this is over, Danny thinks.

The door opens slowly. Howie walks in and closes the door and all is dark again.

"Here," he whispers to Danny. "A hamburger from across the street."

Danny takes a bite but isn't interested.

A few minutes later, the door opens again and it's Jules. There's only one chair in the room, and Jules leaves and soon returns with two more chairs.

"Where'd you get those?" Howie whispers.

"From two people," Jules says, "who, believe me, won't notice they're missing."

At dawn a few doctors and nurses shuffle in and out. The lights in the room are kept off but the sunlight coming in through the slits of the blinds brightens the room.

At around noon, Joey shifts in the bed and Jules walks over to him. Joey opens his eyes, can make out Jules and Danny and Howie, and then closes them. His mouth sounds dry so Danny goes into the bathroom, wets a towel, and moistens Joey's lips. His skin is almost blue. Half an hour later he mumbles something to Howie, and Howie nods.

"He wants music," Howie says.

Howie had brought some of Joey's personal effects in a backpack and reaches in and pulls out a yellow Sony Discman. Carefully, he wraps the headphones around Joey's ears. He presses the Play button and the music starts . . . it's *Machine Head* by Deep Purple. "Highway Star" plays, and Danny, Jules, and Howie look at one another and roll their eyes.

370

Midway through the song Joey shakes his head. He wants the music off for now.

He falls back asleep and the hours pass in silence. Nobody leaves the room.

At three in the afternoon Joey stirs, blinks his eyes, and asks for water. Howie brings him a paper cup and Joey takes a few sips and smiles.

"Danny?" he says.

Danny comes over to the bed.

"Somethin' I gotta tell you, bro," Joey rasps. "In private."

Jules and Howie stand up and walk out. The fluorescent light in the corridor dizzies them after so much time in the darkness of Joey's room.

"Any idea at all," Howie asks, "what that's about?"

Jules shakes his head.

Ten minutes later the door opens and Jules and Howie go back in.

The light coming through the blinds begins to dim. There are two more rounds of doctor and nurse visits and the room turns dark again. At nine Joey asks for the Discman. This time Danny puts the headphones on Joey. Joey, whose hands are ice-cold, squeezes Danny's wrist. Danny takes *Machine Head* out of the Sony, and Howie reaches into the backpack and pulls out something at random. It turns out to be Led Zeppelin's *Physical Graffiti*. Danny slips it in and presses Play. "Kashmir" comes on.

Danny asks if it's too loud and Joey rasps: "Not . . . loud . . . enough . . ."

Danny cranks it and Joey grins and closes his eyes.

Danny, Jules, and Howie back away from Joey's bed and, seconds after the song ends, their drummer's heart beats for the last time.

*

It's midnight and the remaining Overfalls gather around a table in Danny and Howie's hotel room. The room's one window looks onto a narrow shaftway and another section of the hotel, which probably has a much better view.

On the table in front of them is Saul.

"We have to remember to cancel Mendocino, Eugene, and Portland," Danny says.

"I can do that tomorrow," Howie volunteers while resisting the urge to sing "Mendocino," one of his favorite songs.

"Nah, I'm on it tomorrow, first thing. I'll dump the car here and ship the gear back. We'll fly home." Danny looks at Jules and says, "You don't want to drive back, do you?"

"No way," Jules says. "I'm flying."

He knows now he won't be seeing Rhonda on the way home.

Danny draws in a deep breath and says: "And now . . . we have to call Angie."

Danny knew—he's known for weeks—that it would fall upon him to make this call. It's three in the morning in Bay City and as soon as she hears the phone ring, Angie will know exactly what has happened.

Jules says the call can wait until tomorrow morning, and Howie agrees. Danny is not too upset that he's been outvoted.

"I can't believe this," Danny says. "He's gone."

They shake their heads in unison.

"So what do we do," Howie says, pointing to Saul, "about *him?*"

Danny gets up and goes over to the window and looks out.

"Help me open this goddamn thing," he says.

Straining with all their might, the three of them lift up the window and the cool, bracing air rushes in from outside.

Danny goes back over to the table, picks up the drum machine and the tiny speaker attached to it, and brings them to the window. He's just about to hurl them out when he accidentally hits a switch.

372

A red light flashes, then another red light flashes. A second later Danny, Jules, and Howie hear the drum intro to "Dog Water Girls" coming out of the dangling speaker.

It sounds just like Joey Mazz.

It *is* Joey Mazz.

Danny sets the machine back on the table, and Jules and Howie close the window.

They've come to the end of the road.

Part Four
Home, Home Again

Thirteen
Home, Sweet Home

Seventy-two people showed up for the funeral at Bay City Cemetery, and after Joey was laid into the ground, Danny, Jules, and Howie threw a pair of ProMark drumsticks, a bag of Cheetos, and a six-pack of Mountain Dew into the earth. On the flight back to New York, the three remaining Furious Overfalls—a band now officially defunct—had discussed what song they should play at the funeral: Some songs seemed too silly ("The Little Drummer Boy"), some too corny to even consider ("Candle in the Wind"), and some seemed apropos but they knew that Joey had never really liked them ("Salt of the Earth"). For five hours they tried to come up with a song Joey would have approved of, but you simply could not do "Smoke on the Water" or "(Don't Fear) The Reaper" at a funeral.

Or could you?

"How about," Howie suggested toward the end of the flight, "'Home Sweet Home' by Mötley Crüe? He loved that song."

Danny and Jules didn't like the song or the group but knew it made perfect sense.

The three of them, after having rehearsed it a cappella around a JFK baggage carousel, performed a sweetened, almost folkie rendition, and when they finished, a few people were in tears. Howie had found a piccolo trumpet in his garage and trilled softly in the background while Danny and Jules strummed and harmonized around the grave.

This is the final time, Howie thought as he played, *that we are ever going to make music together.*

The same seventy-two people now gather at the Mazz house in Bay City. There are hors d'oeuvres and gallon bottles of wine, and the house has been temporarily transformed into a shrine. Shockingly—or perhaps not so shockingly—Angie wears all white today. Her curly black hair is loose and she looks terrific . . . which

377

isn't settling so well with Jessica (but she can deal). Music plays faintly throughout the house, and scattered around the living room are Joey's drums and congas, Joey's drumsticks, photos of Joey from infancy to only a few months ago. Joey Junior slouches around in an ill-fitting black suit and a thin black satin tie; his sisters sit on the couch and gobble down tapenade and text their friends, some of whom are only a few feet away. While Howie, Melissa, and Michelle stand in a corner near the crooked staircase and keep to themselves, Jules, in black crushed velvet, works the room smoothly.

"Did you see this?" a cousin of Joey's says to Danny, shoving a copy of the *Bay City Star* in his face. "He made the paper!"

Danny remembers this cousin from the Montauk mansion. Decades ago he was a raging longhaired wild man who could drink a six-pack in five minutes and smoke two joints at the same time. Now he's just another bald, flabby grandpa with gimpy knees.

The obituary's headline reads: LOCAL ROCK DRUMMER DIES.

"It was in *Newsday,* too!" the cousin says.

While Danny scans the obituary, the cousin says: "It's too bad you guys are breaking up. But I guess that's the way it's gotta be with Joey gone."

Danny, wearing the only suit he owns (lucky for him, it's black), drifts over to a tray of caponata and crackers. He pours himself a seltzer on the rocks and looks up; a foot in front of him on the wall is a framed copy of *Come and Git It,* the vinyl edition.

Look at us, Danny thinks. *We were really something back in the day.*

"'Home Sweet Home,' Danny?" he hears Angie say. She's right next to him, facing the LP on the wall. "Look what it took to finally get you to do Mötley Crüe!"

He notices that beneath her half-open white silk blouse she has on a lacy white bra.

"It would've made his day to know we sang that for him."

378

"You didn't bring him back alive," she whispers to him.

"I'm very sorry about that. But he was having so much fun."

"I know. He was having a blast. You even let him take a solo, he told me." She looks up at the album cover, fans herself, and says, "Wow, you guys were smokin' hot. And skinny. And Jules with that hard-on. So guess what? Starting next week I have to start working full-time managing the salon. This is what I have to do now. Why couldn't the four of you have become investment bankers instead of rockers?"

"A day doesn't go by that I don't ask myself that same question."

"Well, you're retired now anyways," she says, not without a smidgen of venom.

Angie knows the band is breaking up, but the way it was relayed to her—by Danny—the Overfalls are breaking up because Joey died. Jules and Howie have agreed to go along with this version of the story. The kerfuffle with Joe Hay at The Blast brought in some publicity . . . the story made for amusing news from the West Coast to New York ("'Hurt' Singer Gets Hurt," one headline went), and classic-rock stations have been playing TFO's hits more often than they usually do.

Angie and Danny talk about other matters for a while, then she tenderly squeezes his arm and says, "So after this, am I ever going to see you again?"

He assures her that she will, and she tells him how strange and sad it will be without a man in the house and then goes into the kitchen.

Danny looks at Jules and Little Joey talking to each other near Joey's bass drum. Behind them, on a wobbly étagère, sits a vase filled with two-dozen roses sent from Rhonda Wentworth in Arizona. *How does* she, Danny wondered when Angie told him about it, *know about this memorial service?* That one, he just cannot figure out. Jules and Joey Junior hold huge goblets filled to the brim with red wine and, given the circumstances, are having an okay time. Emily, whose girth nearly eclipses the bass drum, walks over to them, and Jules bends over and puts his ear to her stomach while Joey Junior kicks the bass drum to simulate the heartbeat of the baby boy inside.

Danny slugs his seltzer and thinks: *Okay, so what the hell do I do about this?*

*

Moonrise Studios in Brentwood. Studio B.

Behind the glass, Chunky Scrofa, despite the three mocha Frappuccinos, struggles to stay awake at his board, and inside the studio Jules, Ike Kates, a young bass player named Kenny, and Saul wrap up a grueling four-hour session. This is the third occasion the four of them have gotten together, and it's not Saul the drum machine—it's the real, honest-to-God, walking-talking Saul Kaplan, the Hofstra dropout from Mineola who still lives with his parents. Jules remembered him and told Chunky to call him, and the kid couldn't believe his luck: he was joining a real rock-and-roll band! Before the first session, though, Jules pulled him aside and burst his bubble. "The Overfalls don't exist anymore," he informed Saul. "This is a different animal. Also, I tried to get four other drummers before you and they all turned me down."

Jules considered offering Howie the bass job but then thought it would be better, after all this time, to make a clean break. The *original* bassist from Jules Rose's Raging Blue Balls, Ike Kates had to tell Jules, had passed away three years ago; the original Blue Balls drummer's name was, unfortunately, Bob Smith, and he was impossible to locate; so the only two actual founding members of the band—which had never really been founded in the first place— are Jules and Ike. Knowing he couldn't get away with the name

380

Raging Blue Balls anymore, Jules came up with Jules Rose's Blue Magic.

"Should we do one more tune?" Kenny asks from a corner in the studio.

Jules looks and sees that Chunky has dozed off. Coffee foam is dribbling into his beard.

Ike Kates looks at his watch and says he has to get going to the RadioShack in Leonia.

Kenny and Saul put their coats on and leave, and Ike unplugs his electric piano and gets his stuff together. Jules stays in his chair with his Les Paul on his lap.

"So we're doing this again Sunday at noon?" Ike asks.

"I don't think so," Jules says.

"Huh?"

"It's not turning out the way I wanted it to."

Ike stares at Jules, waiting for him to say more.

The first time the four of them got together, the day after Joey's funeral, Jules discovered that Ike's pipes were shot. He wasn't a great singer thirty years ago and he hadn't gotten any better. Jules, it turns out, is the better singer now, even with his thin voice. Ike can certainly still play keyboards, but, musically, all four members of Blue Magic were on a different page in a different book in a different library: Jules wanted to do blues tinged with country; Kenny wanted to take Blue Magic into a jazzy-rock Jeff Beck Group *Rough and Ready*–type dimension; Ike wanted the band to be a retro acid-rock power quartet (*This is like being in Brittle Cringe all over again,* Jules kept thinking, recalling the second band he'd ever played in); and Saul . . . well, Saul was just Saul. He made the drum machine look like it had a soul.

"So that's it?" Ike says, just about to leave.

"I'm going to have to rethink the whole direction of this thing," Jules tells him.

For the second time in thirty years, then, Jules has to disband the same never-banded-together band.

Jules sits alone in the studio. He sets down the Gibson and picks up his old National—the very same gorgeous hunk of steel he'd once brought to Danny's house on an audition—and is playing and singing "No Expectations" when Eddie Le Vine, rotating his toupee clockwise, walks in without knocking. Eddie reminds Jules to clean up the studio and to wake up Chunky before he leaves.

"My nephew, Dave," Eddie tells Jules, "is having no end of trouble with that former boss of yours. That man isn't just difficult to work with, he's *impossible!*"

"First of all, he was never my boss," Jules says, "and the second thing is, yeah, you're right, he is."

"Dave gives him his own radio show, says he can play whatever he wants to play, and still the man isn't content. Always bickering. Always fussing. Bickering with Dave, with the engineer, with the producer. Even with his own studio guests! It never ends!"

Jules pops open a bottle of water and takes a long pull.

"And, Julius, the sponsors?" Eddie continues. "All Danny has to do is suck it up and be nice to these people and keep quiet . . . but can he do it? Can he maybe get along with Coca-Cola, Budweiser, or Wal-Mart? Hell no. The other day, Dave told me, he's telling the ad guy from McDonald's how to improve on their Big Macs!"

"Now you know what I put up with for almost forty years," Jules says.

He takes the National off his lap and carefully lays it down in its case.

"You're lucky to be rid of him. I hope you know that."

*

382

Eastbound traffic is as bad as it usually is on the Long Island Expressway on a weekday afternoon, and Danny weaves around cars and guns the motor of his new black Suburban when he can. He's fifteen miles away from the hospital. Forty minutes ago he was sitting in a radio studio near Lincoln Center playing records and interviewing none other than Owen J. Crowe, who somehow happens to still be alive. Danny and Owen were having a good time, relaxing and talking and laughing and playing the records that are presently sliding back and forth on Danny's shotgun seat, LPs by Matthews' Southern Comfort, Cat Mother & the All Night Newsboys, Lindisfarne, the Incredible String Band, Pentangle, McKendree Spring, McGuinness Flint. At one point during the conversation, Danny noticed, out of the corner of his eye, his producer and engineer making some maniacal hand gestures to him, but after having already recorded four shows already, Danny knew enough to ignore them. After they played a few more songs, though, Owen said, "You know, ol' buddy, I really would find out what those cats is tryin' to say to you. It looks kinda serious."

Danny stopped the show, and the producer came into the studio and told him that Jessica had called and that Emily was at the hospital. She was crowning.

Ten miles away from the hospital but still no break in the traffic. He swerves to his right, careens his way around a Town Car, then gets back in his lane. McKendree Spring falls to the floor of the new car.

"You fuckin' piece of shit!" the shit-heel driver to his right, rolling down his window, screams at him.

Danny glares at him and rolls down his shotgun window.

"Oh?!" Shit Heel—some suited middle manager in his forties with an MBA—yells. "You want a piece of me?!"

Danny thinks about it while Fairport Convention and Cat Mother & the All Night Newsboys tumble to the floor, too. Yes, he would like a piece of the guy. He'd like a few pieces of him . . . scattered from Valley Stream to Riverhead.

"Come on, douchebag!" Shit Heel barks out, flashing a smirk full of sparkling teeth.

They pass an exit and the traffic eases. Shit Heel's slickly coiffed head is mostly out of his window now and he yells at the top of his lungs. "I'LL FUCK YOU UP, ASSHOLE!" Danny thinks of playing bumper cars with him—the other guy's two-door would be no match for this tank—but then thinks better of it. The exit he needs is coming up soon. Then, he knows, he can get to the hospital via a different quagmire.

He looks over at Shit Heel, who again yells, "I'LL FUCK YOU UP, ASSHOLE!" Danny smiles and blows him a kiss, then rolls the shotgun window back up.

Fifteen minutes later he's at the admitting desk. There are four sick-looking people in front of him but he cuts the line and finds out that Emily and Jessica are on the second floor. Make a left out of the elevator, the receptionist tells him, then another left; go through three sets of doors and there you are.

Danny gets out of the elevator and makes a left. He misses the next left, goes back and takes it, and busts through the first two sets of doors. He made it in time for Emily's birth by a half hour, and Lily's by a matter of only minutes . . . he's not going to miss this one either. He's just about to go through the next set of doors when they swing toward him and floor him. A doctor asks him if he's okay . . . he's not but he keeps going.

He comes to a closed door and hears a birthing tumult from within. He opens the door and sees Jessica bending over one side of a bed, holding Emily's right hand. He cannot see Emily though. A nurse stands near Jessica; at the foot of the bed a doctor hunches over, and there's a man on Emily's left . . . maybe another doctor or nurse.

Push! . . . Push, Emily, push! Come on, push!

Everyone in the room is urging his daughter to push, and Danny takes a step in.

Exasperated but relieved to see him, Jessica turns to him and says: "You sure like cutting things close, don't you?!"

"Push, Emily!" the doctor yells. So does the man on the other side of Emily, who Danny cannot see.

"Em!" Jessica says to Emily. "Daddy's here!"

"Daddy?" he hears his daughter cry out pathetically.

"Come on, Emily," the doctor says. "I want a big push now."

Danny slowly walks toward the bed. One more push, he can tell from all the hoopla and gore, might do it. Emily reaches out to Danny, who takes his daughter's hand and draws in closer. Then he looks across the bed and sees Little Joey Mazz holding Emily's other hand and urging her to push, too. "Come on, baby!" the kid says, bending over so that he's right in Emily's pale, agonized, terrified, wrenched, blissful face. "Come on, push!"

Daddy's here all right.

*

"Howie?" a voice cackles out of the little round speaker in the wall.

"Yes, it's me."

"I'm on the third floor. Come on up."

The front door buzzes and Howie opens it. It's an old, gray three-story brownstone on the fringe of New Haven's Little Italy. A few nights ago Howie was hanging around the house with Melissa and Michelle when the phone rang: it was a Yale junior named Tyler calling. He had seen the card, he said, that Howie had posted on a bulletin board at a café and wanted to take lessons.

"What instrument do you want to learn?" Howie asked him.

"All of them," Tyler answered. "Make me a rock star, dude."

Howie starts walking up the two flights of stairs. Each floor has four apartments on it, and the hallways are dimly lit. When he

385

comes to the second and penultimate steps on the first flight of stairs, he hears Joey saying to him, "You have to. For me, bro." He makes it up the first flight, then goes up the second. The bottom of his left foot lands on and touches the second step; a few seconds later the bottom of his right foot lands on and touches the second-to-last step. *For me, bro.*

A door opens on the third floor and Tyler comes out and says hello. He looks to be about twenty, has a pint of gel in his platinum hair, and is only an inch taller than Howie. He has on a rose pink plaid shirt and baggy cargo pants that make it neither down to his ankles nor up to his waist: you can see the bottoms of his calves and the brand name of his underwear. His large titanium sunglasses are tinted an apricot color.

They shake hands and Howie resists the urge to wipe his hand off on his pants.

"Wait'll you see this," Tyler says as they enter the apartment.

Although he lives in a Yale dorm, Tyler also keeps this studio—his parents are paying for it—and in one corner near the window is one of the most expensive keyboard setups Howie has ever seen not on a stage or in a studio. There are four keyboards, each one looking as if it had never been touched, and one small swivel stool. Tyler tells Howie about himself—he doesn't study music, he says, but always wanted to be a musician, and he plans to go on *America's Got Talent* after he graduates—and Howie surveys all the equipment. There's a Yamaha synth that costs close to $5,000; there's a Nord dual keyboard combo organ ($4,000), and a sampler that goes for over $2,000; there's some Roland 88-key contraption that Howie has never seen before: he doesn't even know what it's supposed to do.

"So all this is yours?" Howie says, his heart fluttering as it sinks.

"Yes," Tyler says. "Seriously epic, huh?"

386

"And you're going to take this setup onto America's Got Talons?"

Tyler tells him that the name of the show is *America's Got Talent,* not Talons.

Howie asks Tyler if he's ever taken any lessons before, and Tyler says he took piano for two years when he was a kid but doesn't remember much. "Just the basics," he says. Howie asks him what sort of music he's into and finds that Tyler's taste is all over the place: he likes rap, emo, doom, trance, punk, metal, and pop, and "anything with a real phat groove to it that people will buy." He flicks on the Yamaha and the Nord and Howie looks out the window at the buildings across the street. On a crisp fall day not too far from here, he remembers, he'd once driven up to Drew Howell's apartment bearing the primitive synthesizer and mellotron he'd assembled from discarded parts. anaesthesia, he knows, would have sold their souls to have this kid's equipment.

(A few days ago Howie decided to throw out all his old practice discs, the discs—"Viola & Glockenspiel #4," "Bass & Flugelhorn #2" among them—he plays in his studio at home to cover up what he's really doing inside there. The only discs he's going to keep are "anaesthesia: Demo Tape 1," "anaesthesia: Demo Tape 2," and "anaesthesia: Roy G. Biv's Blues, Indigo Parts 1 and 2.")

Tyler tells him his new gear makes some incredible, sick, off-the-hook noises, and Howie says, "They're not noises, they're sounds."

"And you know how to work all this?" Tyler asks him. "I looked at the manuals but I'm having some trouble."

"I could work this."

He turns on the Roland leviathan and watches its lights flash and settle.

"My dad, by the way, was seriously into your band when he was young. I told him I saw your card and he said, Ty, *grab* it!"

Howie nods and Tyler begins playing the Yamaha . . . but not really playing it. He's playing *at* it, working it with more than one hand but not quite with two.

"Hey," Tyler says, "lay down a beat for me now."

"Where?" Howie says, looking around for drums or a drum machine.

"On yourself. Give me a beat, yo." Tyler takes his paws off the keyboard and mimics using his chest as a percussion instrument, then goes back to funking up "Chopsticks" and "Für Elise" on his brand-new $5,000 toy. A few seconds later he stops again and says, "Dude, you're not going to do the beat for me?"

"No, Tyler, I'm not going to do the beat for you."

"So tell me . . . could you make this thing sound like nature?"

"Like *nature*? That's what you want?"

"Yeah. Make noises like what's out there . . ."

He points to the window.

Howie looks at the gear, tells Tyler again that they are sounds and not noises, and sits down on the swivel stool. After selecting a couple of oscillators and tweaking some filters, he gets the hang of the Yamaha, Roland, Nord, and sampler. The Gates of Eden swing open now and out of the large speaker in the far corner of the room, as Howie glides his fingers across the keys, gushes the music of the spheres: waterfalls plummet and boom, swans trade trumpet calls; tiny turquoise, purple, crimson, emerald, and violet fishes run laughing through his fingers, and it sounds as though not one humpback whale but several pods of them are moaning, playing, and spawning in the hissing frigid waters at the bottom of the world. Thousands of birds warble while icebergs the size of skyscrapers float along the bubbling ocean, and Howie adds layers of cellos and violins and the ambiance of chimes, piccolos, stardust, moonlight in Vermont, autumn in New York, thirty seconds over Winterland, April in Paris, butterflies, summer in the city, zebras, cricket-song, dark stars crashing into the viaducts of dreams, fairy tales and polka dots and moonbeams, and the rhythm of rain pouring down into heaving waves. Whippoorwills whip, hummingbirds hum, willows weep. Streams burble over rocks and from their island in the sky a choir of Sirens coaxes men and women into throes of unending, unbearable rapture. Forests murmur, jungles sizzle, woodwinds wail, and every once in a while Howie, using the organ, provides a deep bellowing—something between thunder, foghorns, and lava surging down a mountain—that quakes the woodland floor, and he throws in the wind crooning through reeds and bagpipes whistling over a hillside. He's back in his house when he was a boy, when he played into his father's bulky Old World tape deck, except he doesn't have to resort to egg timers and the bathtub anymore; now he has all the sounds of the universe at his command, sounds that no human ear has ever heard before all at once. Not like this, at least.

After ten minutes he stops, takes in a long breath, and looks up at Tyler.

"You know," Tyler says to him, "maybe I need to look elsewhere."

*

Jules has returned from a rigorous microdermabrasion and Botox session in Commack and is doing what he usually does at home: the TV is on with the sound off, music is on the stereo, and he's picking up guitars, playing them, and putting them back down.

The second he sets his Hummingbird on his lap, the doorbell rings.

Who could this be? He'd flirted with the homely receptionist at the dermatologist's office and she knows his address. Hopefully this isn't her.

He gets up, looks through the window and sees Danny at his doorstep, and wonders if something is wrong. He opens the door and lets Danny in.

Danny sits on the couch, and Jules turns off the TV, then goes into a stereo cabinet drawer, rummages around for a minute, and comes out with a cigar.

"Yeah, genuine Cohiba," Jules says. "I was gonna send it to you but I haven't gotten around to it yet. Congrats, *gramps.*"

Danny sniffs the cigar, approves, and slips it into one of his many coat pockets.

"So everybody's healthy and doing fine?" Jules asks him.

"Eight pounds, five ounces, and perfectly healthy. I'd show you a picture but you're probably not that interested."

"Little Joey, huh? Wow. You must have been shocked . . ."

"Hey, I have to give Emily props for keeping it in the family."

He slaps the fabric of the couch and a cloud of black dust kicks up.

"Yeah, I haven't gotten around to cleaning for a while," Jules says. He sits down in a rumpled brown chair on the other side of the coffee table and says: "Is something wrong? What brings you to funky Kingstown?"

"How's Blue Magic working out for you?"

Jules doesn't want Danny to know the truth but tells him anyway.

"It's not working out. Back to the drawing board. By the way, I haven't listened to your radio show yet."

"You're not alone. Plenty of people haven't. Look, I'm here to tell you I need a drummer. Quickly."

"For *what*? And besides, there's always Saul."

Danny takes out the Cohiba and takes off the wrapper. "I don't have Saul anymore. Little Joey has Saul now. He's studying it."

Upstairs, someone sneezes a few times.

"Who is that?" Danny asks.

"Just some chick," Jules says.

"Don't you want to know why Little Joey has Saul?"

Jules says he figured that Angie wanted her son to have it.

"No," Danny says. "We wanted him to have it. Howie and I. You see, we're touring Europe in the fall. England, Germany, Holland, France, Poland, Hungary, the Wherever Republic . . ."

"Wait, wait," Jules says. "Who's *we*?"

"It's this sort of rock-and-roll combo I put together five hundred years ago on Long Island. Me, Howie, *you* . . . if you're interested. But there's our drummer problem."

Jules straightens out in his chair and grabs a pack of cigarettes off the coffee table. Just as he lights one, he remembers that Little Joey has Saul and is studying it.

"No!" Jules says. "Little *Joey*??? No way! Uh-uh. Just 'cause he's—"

"'Cause he's *what*?"

Jules stands up and picks up yesterday's cup of Dunkin' Donuts coffee.

"He's a *kid!* He's . . . what is he, twenty years old?"

"Actually, he's twenty-two."

"You really want to travel on the road with someone so young? I don't wanna be the one to have to keep track of him, feed him, and tuck him in at night. No thanks!"

"Do you even own a vacuum cleaner?"

"Yeah. Somewhere. But it's broken."

"Don't you think it would have made Joey happy to know his kid was succeeding him? And that *we* gave him a job? And don't forget . . . Joey programmed Saul. He got it just right. So we're going right back to the source. And besides, Angie needs the money that'd be coming in. You wouldn't hang an old flame out to dry like that, would you?"

Jules submerges back into the rumpled brown chair. He starts thinking about it. Sure, the kid can drum. He remembers Big Joey letting him play at Moonrise. Joey Junior could be a better drummer than each of the four drummers who refused to join Blue Magic.

"You know," Danny says, "if *my* kid ever wanted to play with our band and come on the road with us, I would be so proud of her. She's my daughter. I would love that."

"I don't get it. Okay, Little Joey is the father of your kid's kid but . . ."

Danny rolls his eyes and says: "You really don't get it, do you, bonehead?"

"Wait a second . . ." Jules says.

He stubs out the cigarette in an ashtray and flashes back to a few weeks earlier in Joey's hospital room in San Francisco; to Joey sending Howie and him out of the room so that he could talk to Danny alone.

"No way," Jules says. "No fuckin' way!"

"You really had no idea?" Danny says. "All this time? You never did the math?"

Jules feels as though someone is whacking him in his cosmetologically rejuvenated forehead with a baseball bat made of pure white light. He does the math. He fooled around with Angie . . . a few weeks later she marries Joey . . . a few months after that, Little Joey, who doesn't have Big Joey's hair, nose, skin color, or anything else, pops out.

"Jesus Christ," he blurts out. "Holy fuckin' shit!"

"Are you in with us or not, bro?" he asks Jules.

"Yeah, I'm in. Definitely. Always. Forever. What else can I do, right?"

Danny stand ups and Jules, stunned out of his wits, walks him to the door.

"Little Joey," Jules asks, "he doesn't know?"

392

"Joey knew, Angie knows, but Little Joey and the girls have no idea at all. Now, I told Howie and swore him to secrecy. But that's it. So we start breaking him in next Thursday at Moonrise. We better get our asses in shape. It's really fuckin' tough out there."

He hands the cigar to Jules and says: "And you can keep the cigar . . . *gramps!*"

*

In his wood-paneled sanctuary above the attached garage, Danny is on all fours on the floor, a huge, accurate, and completely unfoldable map of Europe splayed out in front of him. He's trying to figure out where to go, where to play, how to get there and when, and where to stay. On the walls around him hang guitars, photos of family and the band, and framed albums and records. The tour starts in September. It will be a monster.

He's trying to work but from inside the house he can hear Joey's jingly piano toy, which has been attached to his grandson's crib. It's playing "Twinkle, Twinkle, Little Star," and the boy is randomly kicking the nine plastic keys and playing along with it.

Melissa had sent him a list of every possible venue, of places the Overfalls have played before and have never played, from Belfast to Bordeaux to Bucharest, from Gothenburg to Golgotha. She attached photos, information about seating capacity, the names of who to contact and how, and the names of two- and three-star hotels in each city. He couldn't open the file she'd sent so he had to call her; she imparted instructions, he got off the phone as quickly as he could, and now he has over 400 pages to deal with.

He thinks he hears crying coming from the house and can't tell if it's the baby or the baby's mother. The piano toy has been turned up and now it's cranking "Mary Had a Little Lamb."

393

Danny stands up with a grunt; the old familiar pain tears into him from the base of his neck to the small of his back. He goes to the door, opens it, and the crying stops.

He closes the door. Back down to the floor and the map.

But the baby keeps bashing at the keys with his little feet. The piano is so loud now that Danny can no longer tell if it's Little Lamb or Twinkle, Twinkle or "Whole Lotta Love."

Stuttgart to Prague, he sees, is five hours on the road. Prague (Nový Express, capacity: 425) to Brno (The Sound Czech Club, capacity: 325) is two hours and change on the road. Brno to Budapest is three hours and ten minutes, but Brno to Vienna (Haus of Blaus, capacity: 550) would be only one hour and forty minutes. And on and on and on.

They have a few weeks at home in the spring. A few serene boring weeks without any wrangling, bitching, playing from dusk to dawn to dusk again; without any malice, grudges, manipulation, aching backs, wonky bladders, hair-trigger tempers, callused fingers, sore wrists, hurt feelings, loss of pride and loss of hearing, shattered egos, and farting in close quarters; without any backbiting, haggling, intrigues, sulking and storming out, and compromising; without snarky disc jockeys, scheming club managers, clueless interviewers, drunk hecklers tossing beer bottles; without shoebox hotel rooms, exploding toilets, crumbling moldy dressing rooms, creaky beds with freshly minted stains; without carbonated cat piss, french fries that smell like insoles, muffins that feel like drying Spackle, steak that tastes like old carpet. A few serene weeks to recharge the batteries, and then it will start all over again. The band will regroup, wage war with itself, flirt with perdition, fight one another tooth and nail over small things and big things, hammer out new music, put out *TFO 11: Come On, Push,* their next CD, and then take to the road again and try to make it through one more show.

The piano toy has been turned up even louder. The floor and the ceiling are shaking. Everything on the walls of his studio is rattling around. It feels like a minor earthquake.

Danny stands back up, limps over to the entrance of his studio, and opens the door. He sighs, smiles and with as much fury, scorn, passion, and grandfatherly love as he can summon forth yells: "TELL THAT KID TO TURN THAT GODDAMN THING *DOWN!*"

21840123R00223

Printed in Great Britain
by Amazon